Lynda Page was born and brought up in Leicester. The eldest of four daughters, she left home at seventeen and has had a wide variety of office jobs. She lives in a village near Leicester with her two teenage daughters. Her first novel, *Evie*, is also available from Headline.

Annie

Lynda Page

HEADLINE

First published in 1993
by HEADLINE BOOK PUBLISHING

First published in paperback in 1993
by HEADLINE BOOK PUBLISHING

20 19 18 17 16 15 14

ISBN 0 7472 4184 8

Printed and bound in Great Britain by
Clays Ltd, St Ives plc

HEADLINE BOOK PUBLISHING
A division of Hodder Headline
338 Euston Road
London NW1 3BH

For my grandma – Annie Pearson

How blessed I was when they dished out the grand-mothers and they gave me you. You epitomise the meaning of the word grandmother and I shall be eternally grateful for the endless love and guidance you have shown me throughout my life. I love you. Your granddaughter, Lynda.

ACKNOWLEDGEMENTS

To the people of Leicester, whose warmth and generosity were recorded in history long before I was born. I am proud to be one of you.

To Bill Knight for his help and friendship. I will never forget it.

To Keith Burbage, the likes of whom I will never meet again. You are unique. Thank you for your generosity.

And to Clare Going, whose enthusiasm for my efforts has spurred me on more than she'll ever know.

Chapter One

'Annie! Annie! A' you there, gel? You'll never guess what's happened!'

Annie's head jerked up, her face a picture of confusion as her cottage door burst open to reveal the massive body of her neighbour, Elsie Rowbottom, squeezing her way inside. Her voice boomed out so loud, the words seemed to vibrate off the walls.

Annie jumped up and clasped her hand to her mouth in fright. The scissors she was holding fell on to the stone floor with a clatter.

'What is it, Elsie? What's happened?' she shouted. 'Tell me, please tell me.' A feeling of impending doom shot through her and she uttered a small cry. 'Oh, my god, Elsie! It's our Georgie, ain't it? He's had an accident.'

Elsie's mouth dropped open as she stared at her neighbour. 'Eh!' she uttered, aghast. 'Oh, I'm sorry, Annie,' she said remorsefully. 'Is he badly hurt?'

'Who?'

'Your Georgie.'

'Well, isn't that what you've come to tell me?'

'No. I've got some gossip . . .'

'Gossip? Gossip!' Annie leapt forward, grabbed Elsie's fleshy shoulders and shook them hard. 'You mean to tell me you burst in here, bellowing at the top of your voice, nearly making me give birth – and all for a piece of gossip?'

Elsie lowered her head in shame. 'Well, yeah.' She looked up again. 'But it's good gossip, Annie, honest. Well, I think so anyway.'

1

'It probably is, knowing you, but I'm sure you can't have done me or the baby any good.' Annie placed her hand over her swollen stomach. 'The poor thing's kicking like mad now. God, Elsie, you didn't half give me a scare.'

'I'm sorry, Annie, I didn't mean to frighten yer, only I couldn't wait no longer,' Elsie said, wiping a trickle of saliva from the corner of her mouth with one fat, grubby hand.

Annie stared hard at her neighbour and then sighed in exasperation. She strode back into the room, bent down and awkwardly picked up the scissors, throwing them on the worn oak table along with all her other sewing impedimenta.

'It'll have to wait, Elsie. I've only just managed to get down to me work after getting our Georgie off to school, and you know how behind I am with this lot. I haven't even started me cleaning yet.'

Elsie blew out her fat cheeks. 'Cleaning?' she said in disgust. 'You're always bloody cleaning! Annie Higgins, they'll bury you with a brush and shovel in yer hand.'

'Well, it's a good job some of us do it. If it were left to you we'd all live in a pig sty!'

Elsie stood transfixed. A hurt expression appeared on her face and she stared for a moment at the tall young woman facing her. Annie's long, thick, near jet-black hair was scraped back into a becoming bun at the base of her neck and tiny tendrils framed a light-olive, heart-shaped face. Pregnancy suited her. It hadn't blown her out of recognition as it did most women and her once shapely figure would soon return after her confinement was over, as it had done when Georgie had been born six years previously.

The shabby second-hand grey linen skirt and loose white blouse she wore were spotlessly clean, as was the near derelict cottage she lived in with her beloved husband Charlie and son Georgie. Despite its peeling plaster, draughty doors and rotting windows, the cottage always shone and a faint odour of carbolic soap lingered inside it.

Elsie's eyes flickered downward over her own filthy appearance. Her wide shapeless black skirt and serge blouse were

2

stiff with grease and dirt and from a distance the tide mark encrusted around her squat neck could easily have been mistaken for a piece of brown leather tied for decoration.

In complete contrast to the room she now stood in, Elsie's cottage across the courtyard was cluttered with rubbish, and the broken pieces of furniture inside had never been properly cleaned since the day she had moved in with her husband nine years and twelve children ago. Bed bugs infested the straw mattresses and lice riddled the walls; the whole place stank of urine and stale food, and this smell now wafted silently up from Elsie herself, invading the sweet atmosphere of Annie's home.

Elsie's miserable existence was only made bearable by the friend she had found in her neighbour. Nobody who knew the two women could ever understand how their friendship had come about or had lasted. But lasted it had from the day Elsie and her brute of a husband Billy had arrived, their few meagre belongings stacked precariously on a hand-cart. He had tipped the contents off the cart and gone to find his mates in the local pub, leaving Elsie, eight months pregnant with her first child, to move in unaided.

She had thrown up her arms and laughed loudly, given the staring neighbours a mouthful of abuse and proceeded to hump the old bits of furniture into the empty cottage. Witnessing all this as she pumped water from the rusty standpipe into her iron bucket, Annie rushed over and welcomed her to the dilapidated courtyard. From that moment, despite the odds, their friendship had grown.

Elsie never thought too deeply about anything; never questioned why a woman whose character and standards were so far removed from her own should befriend her in such a way. She just accepted it, never thinking for a moment that anything she did or said would change the relationship. She behaved with Annie as she did with anyone else – loudly, brashly and at times uncouthly. Unbeknown to her, Annie respected her for this.

Elsie breathed deeply and took a step further into the

room. She raised her head defiantly and realised that Annie's usually laughing velvet blue eyes were glaring angrily at her as she rested her hands on the back of a chair by the table.

'Bit touchy this morning, ain't we?' Elsie muttered through clenched teeth. 'What's up? Ain't I good enough for the likes of you now you're making dresses for that posh lot up Uppingham Road?'

Annie slid down on to her chair, shut her eyes tightly and shook her head. 'That's not true and you know it.'

'I should bloody think not!' Elsie retorted as she lumbered into the room, grabbed a mug from the sink and proceeded to manoeuvre her heavy bulk down on to a chair at the table. She made a space and plonked the mug in front of Annie, waiting patiently while a measure of stewed liquid was poured. A button had sprung off her dirty blouse, revealing her overflowing bosom, and Annie silently shook her head, knowing for a fact that the greasy sacking apron Elsie wore over her black serge skirt hadn't seen soap and water for at least six months.

Despite her neighbour's slovenliness and ignorance, Annie could not help but like Elsie and had done so since the first moment they had met. Something inexplicable had made the pair click and Annie had felt herself drawn to this poor creature whose sense of humour and down-to-earth approach compensated for her other shortcomings. If Annie felt down or in need of a natter, it was to Elsie she turned. Like her own, Elsie's life was a continual round of battles against poverty and misfortune, but whereas Annie strove and fought to better herself, Elsie seemed content to accept her lot. As much as Annie tried to educate her within her own limited capacity, Elsie would not budge.

She eagerly accepted the mug of tea that was given her and gulped it down.

'Well?' Annie said.

'Well, what?'

4

'For goodness' sake, Elsie! What's this piece of gossip that couldn't wait?'

'Oh, right.' She plonked down her mug and an enormous smile of satisfaction spread across her face. 'You know that old slag across the way, Maggie Henshaw? Well, she's gone, owing half the courtyard one way or 'nother.'

'Gone!' Annie frowned disbelievingly. 'What, dead you mean?'

Elsie clicked her tongue. 'No, you silly ha'porth, she's done a moonlight. Her and the kids left in the middle of the night. Sneaked away like the thieving tart she is! And it were all over some man. That's what Aggie Atkins reckons, anyway.' Elsie folded her arms under her huge bosom. 'Well, it would be in her case: sex mad was Maggie Henshaw. Anything walking past in a pair a' trousers would make her eyes light up and she'd be in for the kill. She tried to make a play for our Billy, but I soon warned her off. Get a man of your own, I said. That was before I gave her a black eye and shoved her in the 'orse trough.'

'You never! When was all this?'

'Oh, just about the time of your Charlie's accident. I did try to tell you about it but you had other things on yer mind.'

Annie leant back in her chair. 'Well, I knew she was a rum 'un . . .'

'Rum 'un! That's putting it mildly,' Elsie spat. 'Well, I'm glad she's gone. All she did was flaunt herself in front of our men. Poking her enormous chest into their faces. Eyes begging 'em to come to bed.'

Annie sighed softly. 'I'm sure she wasn't as bad as that, Elsie.'

'Weren't she? You wouldn't be saying that if you'd known she'd made a play for your Charlie.'

Annie's face darkened. 'Did she?'

'No. See, I got you there, didn't I?' Elsie answered smugly. 'It's lucky for you your Charlie's got better taste and ain't so easily led – which is more than can be said for most of the

5

men round 'ere, my Billy included. He's only got to see a flash of leg and a bit of bosom and he's off, the dirty bugger!' She took a gulp of tea. 'Well, as I said, I'm glad she's gone. Maybe we'll get some peace for a while. That's until the next flighty bit moves in.'

Annie exhaled loudly. 'I must admit I never heard a thing last night. Mind you, I was really tired. I sat up sewing 'til late.' She shook her head slowly. 'I've just got to get these dresses finished by Thursday else I don't get me money or any further orders, and that wouldn't do.' She eyed Elsie thoughtfully. 'That Maggie Henshaw kept her move really quiet. I only saw her on Sunday. She never said a word to me about it.'

'Well, she wouldn't, would she? Kept herself to herself, that one,' Elsie answered sarcastically. 'Only found out by accident meself. Our young 'un started crying, that's what got me up, and I happened to look out of the window. When I saw what were going on I woke our Billy. The cart was well loaded by that time.' She sniffed loudly. 'I knew something was afoot 'cos I went across yesterday and she wouldn't let me in.' She unfolded her arms and wagged her finger at Annie. 'You know, she owes Straw's shop. Ain't paid her bill for weeks. I blame them,' she said mockingly. 'They shouldn't have let her have so much on tick.' She watched in alarm as she saw Annie's mouth drop open. 'Oh, Annie me duck, you ain't lent her money, have yer?'

'No, 'course not,' Annie answered quickly. 'How on earth can I lend her money? I've hardly enough to buy food as it is.' She lowered her voice. 'But I did lend her me cradle. You know, the one Charlie made for our Georgie, and the new baby's due soon.' Her eyes darted down to her swollen stomach. 'Oh, damn! I don't know what to do now. If you ask me she's got a damned cheek. I know it's not unusual, people doing a moonlight 'cos they can't pay the rent, but there's a limit, ain't there? It's one thing owing the landlord. Another owing the neighbours. Bloody hell!' She slammed the mug down on the table and let out a loud groan.

6

Elsie threw back her head and laughed. Her mouth gaped open, revealing rotting teeth. 'Annie Higgins! Well, I never,' she guffawed. 'It's not often I hear you swear.'

'It ain't funny, Elsie, and I can swear if I like,' she said angrily. 'Anyway, Charlie spent hours making that cradle for our Georgie before he were born, and she promised faithfully to look after it. I've a good mind to scour the streets 'til I find her and give her a piece of me mind. Cheeky devil! Who does she think she is, going off with my stuff? I've hardly anything left as it is.' She stopped abruptly and her shoulders sagged. 'Oh, I suppose it's my fault for being so trusting. I knew she had a reputation so I've only meself to blame.' She rested her elbows on the table and stared into space. 'I wouldn't mind that house meself. It's got another room and we could do with the extra space now that the baby's on the way.' She sighed loudly and brought her eyes to rest on Elsie. 'Oh, never mind. The rent will be too dear for us at the moment anyway.'

Elsie laughed. 'You're right there, me old cock. Ain't everything? I bet the landlord has the place filled before the week's out. You'll see, it'll be one of those families moving up from Northampton to work in the "Boot and Shoe". Bloody immigrants!'

'Immigrants have to live and work somewhere, Elsie. We'd do the same in their place. They've got to go where the work is. If you get the chance of a better life you have to grab it, and that's what all these folk are doing. I know I would. I get fed up scratting for a living day after day and nothing to show for it. You've only got to look at the poor people who do "out door" work, making socks and all sorts for a farthing a dozen. Slave labour, and we all know it. But what else can they do? If they don't work, they starve. Simple, ain't it?' She leant forward and narrowed her eyes. 'Life's hard, Elsie. You don't need me to tell yer.'

'All right, all right.' She raised her hand in capitulation. 'There's no need to get on yer high 'orse. But how you can say all that when your Charlie's been outta work for so long

7

beats me. Mind you, it's his own fault. He knew what would happen if he tried to get compensation for his leg. He's blacklisted now. Bin marked down as a troublemaker, I bet. I saw him going out again this morning, dragging his face along the floor. But he knows as well as I do that he won't get 'ote.' Elsie saw the look of despair cross Annie's face. 'I'm sorry, love,' she said apologetically. 'I was just saying me piece. You know what a big gob I've got.' She smiled wanly. 'Someone will take him on, you'll see, then you'll be able to get this house back to rights.'

The two young women looked around the room, remembering what it had looked like before Charlie's accident. The tiny all-purpose room housed a large stone sink by the entrance door and along the back a black iron fireplace where Annie did all her cooking and heated the water. At either side of the hearth sat two threadbare armchairs where she would sit with her husband of an evening when Georgie was asleep and talk over the day's happenings. An old oak dresser rested against the opposite wall. It was highly polished and covered by a runner, patiently embroidered by Annie as a child. The cupboard underneath held the few remaining dishes and cast iron pans that she possessed.

The recess at the back of the room was curtained off, hiding the put-you-up where Georgie slept. Charlie and Annie occupied the tiny bedroom reached through the door at the back of the room, the bed and a washstand the only furniture that could be fitted in. The room was lit by a single lamp standing on the dresser and as her eyes alighted on it, Annie remembered the oil to fuel it was just about finished.

She had lived in the two-roomed cottage all her life, she and her new husband Charlie having taken over the tenancy when her father had died unexpectedly. It broke her heart to think that all the best pieces of china and furniture that had been left to her, and some they had bought themselves, were now in the pawn shop or had been sold. The few bits that did remain she had placed skilfully to disguise the bareness, still managing somehow to keep the place homely.

Charlie's accident had come as a great shock. He had gone out to work early one frosty morning, whistling tunelessly and swinging his metal lunch box and the blue enamel billy can holding his morning tea. His hobnail boots clattered loudly over the cobbles as he strode to join his workmates entering the large iron gates that enclosed the six-storey early-Victorian redbrick factory, its two chimneys already spewing clouds of dense smoke into the early morning sky.

His foreman, a thick-set brute of a man, met him at his machine station where he grafted day in, day out clicking leather ready for the uppers of the thousands of shoes the factory produced.

'Give that a rest, Charlie lad,' he had bellowed over the drone of the machines. 'I want yer to give Nobby an 'and. The cutter's packed up again.'

And so an unsuspecting Charlie had as always obliged, and as he had struggled to lift the heavy metal cover protecting the sharp blades that cut through the thick layers of leather, with the foreman standing nonchalantly watching, it had slipped and crashed down on to his foot, smashing his ankle bone.

His recovery had been slow and painful, and because he had asked for money from his employers for his family to survive on while it healed, he had been sacked and marked down as a troublemaker.

Such an accident, whenever it happened, would have caused great hardship to a young couple like Charlie and Annie. As it was, it came just when they had thought they could afford to move out of the courtyard to a better area. They had pinned their hopes on securing one of the new style redbrick back-to-back houses the council were building to cope with the expanding population. That idea had been shelved for the time being until their financial position improved, if it ever did.

Managing on Annie's meagre income was proving extremely difficult. Luxuries such as butter, decent cuts of meat,

9

new clothes and shoes, had disappeared. But they kept smiling, praying that their hardship would soon end. 'Never mind, gel. You have to know what it's like to be poor to appreciate the better things in life,' Charlie would often say, and he was right of course. Annie smiled. Yes, she would certainly appreciate a few more coppers in her purse and her new house when they secured one.

The new houses were mansions compared to their tiny hovel with its old stone sink, rusty stand pipe in the courtyard outside and two middens shared between twelve families. Annie despaired of the state in which some of the neighbouring families left the middens and wash-house after using them; she would sigh and shrug her shoulders, wondering if they had ever heard of hygiene, and armed herself and her family with a bar of carbolic soap and a scrubbing brush whenever they had to visit. Georgie hid them under his jumper in case any of the other kids saw and called him a cissy.

Through all their hardships Annie had managed to stay cheerful and optimistic, but as the months dragged by she was finding it increasingly difficult to keep up her spirits. Elsie and Martha, her sister-in-law, were the only people she occasionally dropped her guard to. Poor old Elsie, thought Annie sadly now. How does she manage her ten grubby, snotty-nosed kids and that brute of a husband? The poor woman had lost two of her children to smallpox three or four years ago. At the time Annie had received the impression that her neighbour was relieved to have two fewer mouths to feed, but she always hoped that her impression had been wrong.

The elder members of her brood terrorised the residents of the adjoining streets and if any skulduggery was afoot you could be assured they were involved somehow. The younger children continually yelled and screamed and none of them looked healthy. Annie was not surprised. She had told her neighbour many times to make sure she boiled the drinking water, but Elsie, like others, either did not understand or did not care. Her husband, like most other men in the courtyard, enjoyed his drink – it was his release from the drudgery of life

– but with a few inside him Billy turned nasty, and it was not unusual to see Elsie sporting a black eye on a Saturday morning, or the children with bruises on their arms.

Annie often compared her life to that of Elsie and others like her. She knew only too well how lucky she was. Charlie lived for his family. Not once had she had to stand outside the pub to get his wages before he drank away his money. She had never had to take in other people's washing or go out in all weathers cleaning for the more affluent folk. If it hadn't been for the accident she would not have had to take in sewing. Charlie would have seen to that. They loved each other with a fierce passion and this episode in their lives was only making that love stronger.

Annie realised she had been day dreaming and looked towards Elsie who had grown uncharacteristically quiet and was absent-mindedly rubbing her arm, her face lined in pain.

'What's up, Elsie?' She frowned. 'And what's the matter with your arm?'

She stared at Annie for a moment. 'Eh? Oh, nothing. I was just thinking, that's all.'

Annie frowned. 'He's hit you again, ain't he?'

'So what if he has?'

'And I suppose he was drunk?' Annie said cautiously. She narrowed her eyes. 'You'll have to do something. He's always having a go at either you or the kids. If you don't watch out he'll end up killing yer one of these days.'

Elsie's face darkened. 'Oh, shut up, Annie. I know you mean well, but you do talk wet sometimes. You're lucky your Charlie's never took a swing at you. So just be thankful and leave Billy to me.'

Annie's temper rose. 'For God's sake, woman! Your husband's a bully. He treats you and the kids like slaves.' Her eyes softened and she lowered her voice. 'Look, gel, I'm only trying to help. We've been neighbours a long time and I hate to see you hurting.' She sighed deeply. 'There must be something you can do . . .'

'Do! Do what? Elsie erupted. 'He's entitled to his marital

11

rights, ain't he?' Her voice lowered. 'Don't matter if I don't feel like it.' She smiled wanly. 'Anyway, he didn't hit me 'cos I didn't want to do it, he hit me when I told him the glad tidings.'

Annie stared quizzically at her. 'Glad tidings? What glad tidings?'

Elsie leant back in her chair and waited as it slowly dawned on Annie just what she had meant.

'Oh! Oh my god, Elsie! You're not? No, you can't be. Why, your little 'un is only . . . what . . . six or seven months old?'

'Just keeping up the routine, Annie. One, sometimes two, each year. Can't say I'm over the moon, but . . . well, just have to get on with it. The trouble is I feel so bloody tired all the time. God knows where I'm going to put this one or what we'll call the little blighter.'

Annie looked at her neighbour and her heart went out to her. 'He weren't pleased then?'

'Pleased! He were that pleased he threatened to leave me.' She tutted nonchalantly. 'I told him to bugger off. Fat lot of good he is to me. Still, I married him so I've got to make the best of it.'

'It's still no excuse for knocking you about. If I told Charlie he'd . . .'

'Do what? Come over and punch Billy? Then he'd set about me again. Just leave things alone, Annie. Billy's my old man and I'll handle him. It ain't that bad. He only thumped me once this time before he passed out. It was my fault. I shouldn't have told him about the baby, I knew what kinda mood he were in. He'll come round, he always does. Anyway, you worry about your own baby and just be thankful it's only your second and not your thirteenth like me, eh?'

Annie shivered. 'All right, Elsie, but if you ever need any help, me and Charlie are always here.' She rose and supported herself on the table. 'Come on, gel, it's no good moping. What's to be will be. Let's see if we can squeeze any more tea out of the pot. Then I must get back to me work, else we won't eat next week,' she said firmly.

'Good idea. Come on, you put the leaves through the mangle and I'll stand the other side with the mugs.'

She laughed. Good old Elsie, she could always be relied upon to raise a laugh and that was just what Annie needed right now.

'Tell you what, Annie, if you don't get the cradle back, I'll lend you our best drawer. Seen our brood through, it has. When the baby cries you only have to shut it.'

Laughter filled the room and for a moment, at least, their problems were forgotten.

It was early spring in the year 1904 and Leicester was a thriving market town. Annie loved the town of her birth. The courtyard where she had lived all her life was a close community and the residents were always ready and willing to help each other and rally round in times of crisis – and there were plenty of those. The town was changing quickly, trying to keep pace with the ever increasing number of people arriving to look for work.

Leicester's boot and shoe industry was growing rapidly. Firms from other areas were moving in and bringing their workforce with them. New electric trams had been introduced into the town. Daily life had been severely disrupted when roads were dug up to lay miles of tracks to accommodate this new and much needed method of transport. The Grand Canal flowed with barges taking coal and goods as far as Manchester, ready to be transported all over the world.

When possible, in fine weather, women would find the time to sit on doorsteps for a chat or gossip, while the children who did not go down the pits or slave in the factories from six till eight played snobs, marbles and hopscotch.

Annie's favourite past-time was browsing around the shops on a Saturday night, planning how to spend her money, gazing longingly at the goods on display. She never dared venture into the larger department stores like Morgan Squires or Simpkin and James, she felt out of her depth in places like that, but she would stand outside and watch carters load large wicker hampers of fine food on to wagons for delivery to the more affluent members of society.

She herself was content to push and shove her way through the market, bargaining for goods the traders had been unable to sell during the week. She thrived on the good humour and banter there and felt satisfied if, after all her purchases had been made, she still had a few coppers left in her purse to put in the tin kept on the mantle. This, of course, had stopped when Charlie had been out of work and now the tin was nearly empty. She would walk miles for a bargain, never dreaming that the cost of shoe leather was more than the pennies she saved.

When Georgie came on these excursions, Annie would point out all the places of interest to him. The clock tower in the town centre with its four faces and figures of famous Leicester people carved into its column; the fine Victorian buildings with their arched windows; the old Tudor Guild Hall with its dungeons and torture chamber; and now there were plans to build a new concert hall on the London Road. It would be called the De Montfort Hall and would seat hundreds of people. Gardens were planned to add to the visitor's delight.

Annie filled Georgie's mind with tales of long ago, making him proud of his native town. To the little boy nothing could match the giant frying pan hanging from the ironmonger's premises near High Cross Street. He and his mother would laugh and banter, trying to guess how many rashers of bacon and eggs could be fried in it and what a feast could be made.

Life was hard for the working class at the turn of the century, but Annie and Charlie both knew that the only way out was to work. Many people's hopes and dreams never materialised, but theirs would, Annie felt positive. As soon as Charlie found work they could begin to build a better life. 'Let's just get over this bad patch,' he would often say, 'and the future is all ours.'

Chapter Two

Georgie Higgins pressed his back into the cold hard wall, absent-mindedly running his hand backwards and forwards against the red, knobbly bricks. He sighed deeply and frowned. He had been at school for four long days and he hated it. The older boys had taken a dislike to him. They called him names and taunted him because of his bright-red curly hair.

His thoughts ran rife as he waited impatiently for the school bell to ring. He could not wait to move to one of those posh houses his mother went on and on about. She had promised him his own room. It sounded wonderful: a whole room to himself. He shrugged his little shoulders. Anything was better that the put-you-up in the corner of the kitchen. He sighed deeply again. Talk of moving had stopped since his father's accident. If only it had not happened! It seemed to have changed everything. All his mother's nice things had disappeared. He was not supposed to know where to, but a big lad of six could not help noticing the increasing number of empty spaces. Maybe they would get all the things back when his dad finally got a job. But he would miss the courtyard. It would feel really strange living somewhere else.

What if he got lost and could not find his way home? He shivered with worry, then raised his head. He was a big boy now and big boys did not get lost. He sighed deeply. If only he were big enough to fight the school bullies! His eyes darted round the playground. He was relieved when he could not see any of them in sight. He dug his right hand down into his pocket and his mind wandered back to the courtyard. He loved it best in winter when the muddy puddles froze over and they could slide on the ice 'til it shone like glass. Oh, what fun they had. He supposed it was not funny when old Mrs Busby had fallen over and broken her leg. The other women had come out and clipped them all round the ear and put hot ashes over the yard. It had spoilt the fun for that winter.

But there was always the summer when they played outside all day, and sometimes well into the evening. Their mothers gave them bread and dripping to eat and shooed all the kids off so they could get on with their work. They played mostly on the railway embankment, using the shrubs and trees as hidey holes or dens. Some of the kids went to work now while he had been forced to come to this horrible place. I bet prison is like this, he thought ruefully. But I ain't done nothing wrong.

His eyes travelled around the playground again and envy rose up in him as he watched small groups of children playing together. A tear rolled down his cheek. I wish I had a friend, he thought longingly. Suddenly he took a deep breath as an idea flashed into his mind and his eyes sparkled. Why, that was it! Why hadn't he thought of it before? He'd tell his mother and father tonight, he wasn't coming back to school and that was that. Then his shoulders sagged as a terrible thought struck him. What if they sent him out to work instead? Elsie's kids went to work, even though the Board Man had threatened her with prison.

He shuddered. Work sounded a dreadful place judging by the horrific stories he had heard. You had to get up at five o'clock in the morning and were shut away all day in long, dark, dusty rooms, being beaten by the bosses, having your hands cut to ribbons, then coming home jiggered and looking so thin and ill all the time. That's if you were lucky and not sent down the pits. They were supposed to be worse. Georgie took a deep breath. Maybe this place wasn't so bad after all. Oh, but he hated it more than anything! He raised his head defiantly. He would have to face it like a man and stand up for his rights. He was not coming back after today, and if that meant going to work, so be it.

He rustled the brown paper bag he was holding, opened it up and peered inside. It was his favourite. Bread and dripping with plenty of salt. But he didn't feel like eating. His bladder was full and he felt most uncomfortable. He pulled a wry face. Would he chance going into the lavvys or would the big boys be in there? He decided to wait a little longer and his mind wandered again.

He hoped his dad was taking him fishing on Saturday. They usually went to the canal or, for a real treat, the river. He loved putting the hooks through the maggots and watching them wriggle about, and joy would surge through him when, after hours of waiting, they finally caught a fish and proudly took it home. If it was big enough his mother would cook it for tea. They had caught a pike once, a real monster that his father had been after for months, and what a feast they had had.

He loved his father so much and was very proud of him. At the moment they were making a cart out of old bits of wood they had collected together; they were going to put the wheels on tonight. They had been jubilant when old Mother Brown had given them a pair of old pram wheels, even if it was in exchange for his father cutting a pile of logs for her. Pram wheels were like gold and you could trek for miles for a good set. Reggie Rowbottom would be green with envy when he saw it and would plead with Georgie to have a go. Well, I won't let him, he thought spitefully. That'll teach him for pushing me on the railway lines when that train was coming. He hopped from foot to foot. He was really bursting now.

He wondered if things would change when the baby came along. He was quite content just to be by himself. That stork fella, whoever he was, had a lot to answer for, talking his parents into having another. Elsie had lots of babies, they screamed night and day, and you couldn't take a baby fishing

17

or let it help you make a cart. You'd think that stork had enough to do keeping Elsie supplied without bothering his mother and father. Babies were awful. They had runny noses and they smelt funny.

Georgie puckered up his nose, remembering the pungent smell that always filled Elsie's house. It was always full of kids, shouting and screaming. Wherever did they all come from? He could never work out where they all slept, and their dad was forever cuffing their ears and kicking them out of the door. He often found young Tommy sobbing on their doorstep and the poor lad never knew what he had done wrong.

Georgie's thoughts were suddenly interrupted as he spied two boys approaching him. He shuddered. They both looked ready for a fight and his body stiffened in fear. If only he could find a mate, maybe they wouldn't pick on him so much.

'Well, if it isn't George-Porgie. Kissed any gels today then?' The tallest and broadest of the two boys smirked sarcastically at him. Everyone was frightened of Ronald Morgan, and he was making sure that Georgie was too. He turned and addressed his friend. 'His dad's outta work. My dad says he's a troublemaker. He's bin blacklisted. He can't gerra job.' He turned back to Georgie. 'That's right, ain't it, Georgie-Porgie? He stole things and got caught.'

Georgie's face went red in anger and he puffed out his chest. 'You bugger off! My dad never stole anything. It's your dad that's the liar.' He gasped for breath, amazed at his own outburst. His bladder leaked and his underpants felt wet and uncomfortable as he watched Ronald clench his fists and take a stance ready to pounce on him. Suddenly, the smaller boy nudged Ronald in the ribs and for no apparent reason they sidled away.

George stared after them, confused. A hand touched his shoulder and he jumped. He quickly realised why the boys had slunk off. As he spun around, he came face to face with his teacher.

'Georgie, don't look so frightened, boy. I'm not going to

hurt you, I just need your help.' He pushed a small, timid, scruffy boy forward. The two eyed each other. 'Arthur has started school today and I need someone to show him the ropes. I believe there's a spare desk next to yours. Would you help me out?'

Georgie shuffled his feet, 'Well, yeah, if he wants.' Relief flooded through him. He was glad he wasn't in trouble. He'd heard of the cane and did not in the least fancy getting it. 'Come with me,' he said, grabbing the boy roughly by the arm. 'I'll show you where the lavvys are, first.'

Annie gazed out of the window at the other twelve dilapidated cottages that formed the horseshoe-shaped courtyard. The yard itself was not paved and in winter water would lie there in deep puddles while thick squelching mud would stick to boots and be trailed through all the houses. The cottages were situated close to the main Humberstone Road where, if you had the money, you could catch one of those newfangled trams into town. The people who lived in the courtyard usually walked; money was too tight for such luxuries. Most of the men worked for the railway yard on to which the cottages backed. The constant passage of heavy goods trains caused great problems. The cottages vibrated dangerously and the noise was deafening every time one rumbled past. But they all learned to live with it; housing for the poor was hard to come by.

How will I feel, she thought, biting her bottom lip, when we move and I have to get used to new people? But it looked as though that wouldn't be for a long time yet. She sighed deeply, wishing she could motivate herself to get on with her work.

Elsie had just left. Annie had stood and watched as her neighbour picked her way across the sodden yard. She had raised her skirts and Annie had a clear view of the bottom of her bloomers, her large fat legs wobbling dangerously as she carefully tried to avoid the muddy puddles. The sight of her ballerina act was too much and Annie could not help

19

laughing. She watched as Elsie squeezed through her door and kicked it shut behind her. The courtyard was once again silent and empty. Everyone was either out at work or inside trying to scrape a living together.

The view always managed to depress Annie. She often stood as she was now and imagined looking on to fields of green. She could almost smell the wild flowers scenting the air and see Georgie running barefoot through the grass, looking healthy and tanned. Charlie would be ploughing the fields. She smiled. He liked gardening but maybe she was pushing it too much to expect him to plough fields. Never mind, it was only a dream. It didn't hurt to dream, sometimes they were the only things that kept her going. She patted her swollen stomach and thought of the baby growing inside her and of how much better life could be.

Although the sun was shining, the room felt cold. She really should be busy sewing, she needed the money from her 'toffs' to buy food and pay the rent that was due. But she felt heavy with the baby and her mind was filled with worry.

She remembered the conversation she had had with her son that morning.

'Now come on, lad, you must go to school,' she'd told him, bending to straighten his shirt.

'Why? Elsie's kids don't, so why should I?'

Annie looked tenderly at him and kissed him gently. ''Cos me and your dad want you to get an education, that's why. Now come on, be a good boy.'

Georgie's face puckered and for a moment Annie thought he was going to cry. 'I don't want to go, Mam. No one likes me, they call me names.'

She ruffled his hair. 'I'm sure they don't mean it, we all get called names. Now come on, you're going to be late.' She playfully slapped him on the bottom and watched as he slouched out of the door.

She loved her son with a fierce protectiveness and if anyone should dare to do him harm, would not be responsible for her actions. After months of hardship, he now badly needed new clothes and shoes, a few pennies in his pocket for sweets or a cheap toy or book to read. None of those things could she give him at the moment, and although she knew that the other children were just as deprived as he was, and that Georgie, bless him, never moaned or wanted things he knew his parents couldn't give him, it hurt her dreadfully to think he was going without. Her heart reached out to him. She longed to run to the school and demand that all the other children be his friends, but she knew she could not do that. He had to learn to stand up for himself. It was a cruel world out there and he had to learn to survive in it.

She smiled to herself. Her son's red hair was often the cause of jokes as nobody seemed to know from whom he had inherited it. It certainly didn't come from her father's side. His hair had been black, the jet black of the Irish Celt who had sought refuge in England from the poverty of his homeland in the late 1860s. Maybe it had come from her mother's side? Annie would never know as the struggle to give new life to her had taken her mother's.

Annie's childhood had been secure and carefree, cocooned in the love of her father, a good, hard-working man who was well respected by his friends and neighbours. A man of few words, but one to whom people turned in times of trouble. A better, or more loving parent she could never have wished for, and she still missed him sorely.

Her hand found its way to her throat and she fingered the small silver locket given to her the night of her fourteenth birthday. Her eyes pricked with tears as she remembered how her father had hugged her tightly before parting with the only reminder he had of his beloved wife.

'Annie, you care for this.'

She had smiled up at him with tears in her eyes, sensing the struggle he was having to part with it. She kissed him gently on the cheek before she carefully unwrapped the precious parcel and gasped in delight at the delicate silver trinket. She fumbled clumsily with the clasp that held the two halves together. Inside were two photographs. Having

21

never seen one before, Annie was bemused and rushed over to the window to study them. She saw the dim impressions of two faces.

'That's your mother, the one with the dark hair and the lovely smile.' Her father looked lovingly at her. 'Just like yours.'

'Who's the other gel, Dad?' she asked softly.

Her father had shrugged his shoulders. 'All I know is that she was your mother's friend.' He stared into the distance and his eyes glazed over. 'How on earth they managed to get a photograph taken, I don't know. But that was your mother. Full of surprises.'

'I'll treasure it, Dad. To the day I die, promise.'

She held the chain up to the light and watched the locket spin slowly in the air. It was then that she noticed the rough engraving on the back. She lowered her hand and studied the clumsily written words.

'It says, "Mary Ann, Ratby, 1874".' Annie looked at her father. 'Is that me mam's name?'

The answer came slowly and reluctantly. 'Yes, and the village of her birth. But that's nothing to do with us. Your mother's gone and the past is best left.' He turned from her, the subject closed, never to be broached again, and Annie grew to accept that this knowledge was all she would ever have of the woman who had given birth to her.

The locket had been put safely away and only taken out when Annie was feeling low. On the eve of her wedding to Charlie she had taken the locket, placed it around her neck and never taken it off again.

Her father had died after a short illness just after her eighteenth birthday, and she had been desolate, aching badly for the man who had been both parents to her. The big loving man who had taught her all he knew, handed over a good amount of his wages in order that she ate good nourishing food and kept a warm fire going through the long winter months. In return she had kept his home, cooked and washed for him, filled his bath for his nightly scrub down after his long shift down the mine, sat patiently while he had awkwardly taught her to read and write, and listened enthralled as he sang beautiful soft ballads from the land of his birth.

She remembered the long walks through the fields with their sandwiches wrapped in brown paper and how they would sit on the riverbank silently watching the birds or the fish swimming through the weeds. Not once had he raised his voice or beaten her, not even when she had burnt his dinner or spent the housekeeping on some secondhand pots that a pedlar was selling. Many nights he had come home, cold and tired, to an empty cottage. He would find Annie collecting flowers in the fields or climbing trees with the boys from the courtyard. He would gather her up and sit her firmly on his broad shoulders, threatening a leathering which never materialised.

The fields had gone now to make way for the new buildings. The countryside in which she had spent so many happy hours was creeping further and further away.

Charlie had come into her life just before her father died and had helped her to recover from the traumatic ordeal of his loss. Neither had parents with whom to share daily life, but at least Charlie had an elder brother. Bert was five years older than Charlie but very like him in manner and appearance. He and his wife Martha were regular visitors to the courtyard. The two couples had spent many happy hours in each other's company, and through the years shared all the ups and downs that both families had encountered.

A factory hooter sounded in the distance and Annie blinked. Crikey! she thought, as the spell was broken. I've been standing idling for ages. Better get this dress finished at least or we definitely won't be eating next week.

Suddenly the door shot open and Charlie charged in, his face beaming and eyes shining. Annie swung round and knew as soon as she looked at her husband that something wonderful had happened.

'Annie! Oh, Annie, I've done it, gel. I've finally done it.' He

23

whipped off his cap and aimed it expertly towards the hook on the door opposite which led to their tiny bedroom.

She clasped her hands together in delight. 'You mean it, Charlie? You've really got a job? A real job this time?'

'Yep, and I start on Monday.'

He lunged forward, grabbed his wife round the waist and swung her round, just managing to get his arms round her swollen stomach. He let her go, stood back and gazed into her vivid blue eyes. His heart lurched as it always did when he was near her. How lucky he was that she had chosen him! He had been a tall, gangly eighteen-year-old apprentice clicker in the shoe factory when he had proposed marriage, with not much more in his pockets than his dreams, yet she had accepted. Now twenty-four years old, she had lost none of her appeal. If truth be told she was more attractive now than the day they married. She was a loving wife and a wonderful mother, and made their dismal little cottage light up with her infectious laughter, her good housekeeping and the appetising meals she cooked.

She still had two months left of her pregnancy and he grinned to himself at the thought that he would not be able to get his arms around her again for a while. He loved her so much and the thought of any harm coming to her or their son filled him with dread. She deserved the best did his Annie, and come hell or high water he was going to get the best for her. This new job was the beginning.

Annie in turn adored the husband she had been married to for the last seven years. The tall gangly youth had grown into a broad, handsome man, with a ready smile and an easy going nature. Not that he was a pushover, not her Charlie, he could stand his ground against any man. They were friends as well as lovers and she could never envisage life without him. He was a man whose name was renowned throughout their community and beyond. Her faith in him was total. She never thought for a minute that he would let her down. One day all his dreams and ideas would come to fruition and she would be there at his side. She would share

24

his triumphs and his failures. Whichever, her love for him would never diminish.

She looked up at him, eyes filled with love, and planted a kiss on his cheek.

'Come on, Charlie, come and sit down. You've obviously got a lot to tell me.' She grabbed her husband's arm and stepped back. 'Oh, Charlie, just look at your sleeve!'

He looked down and grinned. 'Sorry, me duck. I caught it on a nail. You can mend it though, I've done worse.'

Annie clicked her tongue. 'Yeah, but there ain't much left to sew, it's covered in patches as it is. I do wish you'd be more careful.' She slapped him playfully on the arm. 'Come on, tell me your news or I'll burst. Or shall I make some tea first?'

'Bugger the tea, I'll have one in a minute.' Charlie tried to pick his wife up again.

'Put me down, Charlie, Put me down.'

'My, gel, you're getting right heavy.'

'Well, that's your fault.' She grinned shyly at him, then added under her breath, 'Dirty devil.'

They both giggled.

'Charlie, I'm dying to hear the news. Is it asking too much to expect to be told today or do I find out from the neighbours? They always seem to know what's happening before I do!'

'Okay, you win. Sit down and make yourself comfy.'

They sat at the table facing each other. Annie placed her elbows on it, resting her chin in her hands. She fixed her eyes on her husband and waited.

'Well,' he started, 'I went along to Oliver's Factory this morning, but the queue were a mile long so I didn't bother to wait.' He sighed. 'I felt quite down, Annie, but I just couldn't come home today without anything. I couldn't bear the thought of letting you and Georgie down again, so I thought I'd go for a traipse by the canal and see if anything was going round there.'

'And?'

'Just a minute,' he said, irritated. 'I'm getting there if you'll stop interrupting.'

25

He rose from the table and walked over to the fireplace, resting his hand on the mantelpiece. Annie looked at her handsome husband and felt a warm glow of pride and love flow through her.

'Well, I saw this bloke trying to unload some boxes off a cart,' he continued. 'I couldn't very well stand there and watch him struggle alone, so I offered me help. I hadn't much else to do and I thought it might pass some time. He was really grateful, said it was lucky I'd come along or he'd have been there all morning. We took the boxes into a small rundown building and when we'd finished he offered me a cuppa and asked why I wasn't working. So I told him.'

'What, all of it?'

'Yes, how I tried to get compensation for me leg and think I must have been blacklisted because of it.' He paused for a moment. 'I got a shock, Annie, 'cos he agreed with me. He said I should get compensation for what I'd been through, and you for that matter. It seems his mother lost her thumb in an accident at work a few years ago. She worked as a clicker in the shoes, same as me, and got some glue in a cut on her thumb. It turned septic and eventually black.' He pulled a wry face and scratched his head. 'It was that bad she had to have it cut off. The stupid part is that she nearly lost her job because she had to take time off while she recovered.' He shook his head grimly. 'It's wrong, Annie, ain't it? You shouldn't be made to suffer 'cos of an accident at work that wasn't your fault.'

Her elbow slipped off the table as she fidgeted, silently urging her husband to get to the important part, but Charlie was not to be hurried. This was his good news and he was determined that she would hear the whole story.

'Annie, just be patient, I'm going as quick as I can,' he said. He raised his head. 'Anyway,' he continued as he walked back to the table and sat down, 'the bloke shook my hand and introduced himself. His name's Joe Saunt and he told me he's in the process of starting up his own business. A little factory producing exclusive shoes for the gentry. Not yer hobnail boots like we wear, but dainty little things all in different colours for wearing at grand balls and parties.'

'Oh,' she said in awe. 'Is he rich then, this Joe Saunt?'

'No. He's taking a big gamble. He's come into a bit of money. Not a lot, just enough to start up. But he saw this as his one chance to go it alone and he's prepared to take it.' He scratched his head thoughtfully. 'To be honest, Annie, I'm quite envious of him. To get a windfall like that out of the blue must be everyone's dream. Wouldn't it be great if something like that happened to us?'

'Yes, it would,' she agreed heartily. 'But as we've no rich relatives I think the chances are slim, so just get on with it.'

'Where was I? Oh, yes. He said it would only be a small business to start with but hoped to build it up, and as long as he made enough money to live on it would be better than working for someone else.' His face lit up with an infectious smile. 'That's when he asked me if I'd be interested in a job. Said he really could do with a bloke like me. Someone honest and reliable, who'd have a go at anything.' He paused and inhaled deeply. 'Annie, I can't tell you how I felt. After all these months of being turned down, here was a bloke offering me a job outta the blue. I nearly pounced on him and gave him a big kiss, I was that thrilled.'

'You never! Charlie, you never?'

He threw back his head and laughed loudly. 'No, I managed to contain meself, but how I don't know. I very quickly told him I knew everything about the shoe trade there was to know, and didn't mind what I did as long as it was good honest work. He asked me if I would be willing to attend one of those night schools to learn about repairing machines later on. I told him I'd be delighted.' He winked at his wife mischievously. 'Be another feather in me cap, eh! It'd prove I ain't just good at making babies.'

Annie giggled shyly.

'So there you have it. We shook on it and I start first thing Monday morning.' He paused for a moment and eyed her cautiously. 'I hope you don't mind but I said I'd go in tomorrow to help him sort things out? I could be all day.'

'Mind!' she said, opening her eyes wide in amusement. 'I don't mind in the least. It won't take me long to get used to not having you around so much. I can't wait to make your first pack up.'

'Ah, yer a grand little wife, Annie,' he said, smiling at her in appreciation. 'The wages ain't all that great, but better than I was earning, and Mr Saunt says if I prove all right and the business takes off, then he'll make sure I'm well rewarded. I don't doubt him. He seems a decent sort of chap, really got his head screwed on. He managed to get the building and some second-hand machinery real cheap, and there'll be just me, a couple of women and another bloke to start with.' Charlie clapped his hands in delight. 'Ain't you chuffed, Annie?' His beaming face dropped. 'What yer crying for?' He rushed round the table and put his arms around her shoulders, pulling her to him.

'Oh, Charlie, I don't know. I think its 'cos I'm so happy. It's been hell these past few months, watching your face get longer and longer and me not being able to do anything about it.'

'I know, love, and I'm so proud of you. You've never moaned or grumbled and we've always had some sort of meal on the table, though God knows how. Anyway, our luck has changed. It's straight ahead for us now. Our Georgie will be tickled to bits.' Charlie laughed then clasped his hand to his forehead and frowned. 'Damn! I promised to take him fishing tomorrow.'

'Don't worry about that, Charlie. Georgie will understand. He'll be happy that you're in work again. There'll be plenty of other times to go fishing.'

'Yeah, you're right. Tell yer what, I'll take him Sunday instead, then I won't be letting him down so badly. No, an even better idea. What about you packing up a picnic and us all going? Do us good to have a day out together. What d'you say, eh?'

'Charlie, that'd be grand, just grand.' Annie's shining eyes clouded over. 'Oh, but I can't. I've got to get this sewing done, else I'll lose me clients.'

Charlie stood up and put his hands on his hips. 'Listen, gel, you're the best little seamstress round here. They'll just have to wait. I'm putting me foot down. We're going on that picnic, and that's that. Where is our Georgie, by the way? Shouldn't he be home by now?'

'Give him a couple more minutes and I'll go look for him.'

'No, you won't, I will,' he said, tapping his finger against his chest. 'By the way, I got to thinking on the way home. If I work hard and Mr Saunt does see me right, we'll be able to move to one of them houses sooner than we hoped. We'll get all our stuff out of hock, get George some decent clobber to wear, and you might be able to give up this sewing lark.'

'Charlie, Charlie . . . not so fast! Let's walk first. See how this job works out. I don't want to put a damper on things, but anything could go wrong and we could end up in a worse state than we are now, if that's possible. Please, love. Don't build your hopes up too quick. You've got a job now and that's the main thing.'

'All right, all right.' He raised both his hands in the air in mock surrender. 'Good job you keep me down to earth, ain't it? Come here, give us a kiss, and then if you don't mind, I'm going to go and see our Bert and Martha.' He paused for a moment, deep in thought. 'You know, I just might be able to put something his way when I get my feet under the table.'

'Charlie,' Annie said tartly, 'Bert has a job, even if it doesn't pay much. So just leave things as they are for the moment.' She leant over and patted his arm. 'Go and see yer brother, he'll be so pleased for us. And don't be too long. I'm going to get the tea soon.' She laughed. 'Mind you, it'll only be a quick run round the table, but I'm sure I can manage to fill you both up with something.' She paused thoughtfully. 'Charlie, I won't tell our Georgie the news, I'll let you do that.'

'Yeah. I can't wait to see his face. Oh, bugger, I forgot. I promised to help him with his cart tonight.' He clicked his tongue. 'I seem to be breaking all me promises to him today, poor little mite. Never mind, I promise I'll make time when I come back. All right, love?'

'Don't know why you're making that cart, our Georgie will only end up breaking his neck on it.'

'Don't be soft. All the kids have got carts. Anyway, it'll come in handy for humping stuff, you'll see. I'm going to take it with me next time me and Bert go up the slag heaps. We can bring some more slack back with us that way. That's why I'm making it strong.'

'You and Bert are going to cop it one day. You know it's stealing.'

'No, it ain't, everyone does it. And they can't jail all of us, can they?' He grabbed hold of her gently by the shoulders. 'Even you have to admit that we'd all have frozen to death many nights if we hadn't had that slack to burn.' Annie nodded reluctantly in agreement and Charlie grinned. 'Right, enough of this talk. I'm too happy for it. If I go now, the quicker I can get back. And if I meet our Georgie on the way, I'll clip him round the ear for being late.'

'That'll be the day! Now be off with you. Just a minute, you're not going out like that. Let me sew that jacket first.'

'Oh, come on, Annie. It ain't that bad. I'm only going to see our Bert, not the King.' He tutted loudly. 'Anyway, there's blokes going round with their arses hanging out their trousers, they don't bother what they look like.'

'That may be so, but they ain't married to me. Now take that jacket off and let me sew it!'

'Stop fussing, Annie. You can do it when I come back, ready for me starting work.'

She smiled up at him and relented. Her husband was far too excited to worry about his torn sleeve. 'All right, see you later. And, Charlie . . .'

'What?'

'I love you.'

'I know you do, gel.' He stole back towards her and kissed

30

her full on the mouth. He put his fingers gently on her cheek and whispered hoarsely, 'I promise I won't be long.'

Annie hummed softly to herself. She had not seen Charlie so happy for such a long time. Soon, God willing, they'd be out of this hovel. The place had been falling about their ears for years. Charlie had done his best, but he was not what Annie would call a handy man.

She walked over to the sink and started to peel the potatoes, her mind full of the events of the day.

'Mam!' Her son's voice echoed round the room as he bounded through the door and Annie dropped the potato she was peeling.

'Oh, Georgie, yer frightened me to death! That's the second time today someone's done that.' She stared down at him. 'Where've yer been?' she demanded. 'Your dad's gone looking for yer.'

'Sorry I'm late, Mam,' he sang as he slammed down his old satchel. 'I've got a friend,' he announced. 'His name's Arfur. He asked me to go home with him and see his kittens. I'd love a kitten. Can I have one, Mam, can I? They don't eat much. Arfur's mam says if it's all right with you, I can have one for free. She don't want any money.' Georgie pulled at his mother's skirt in excitement. 'Arfur's sitting next to me at school, I really enjoyed it today. Teacher asked me to be in charge of him 'cos he's new. I shared my bread and dripping with him 'cos he said he forgot his dinner.' He ruefully shook his head. 'I don't think he had any really.' He grinned up at his mother. 'I like him ever such a lot, Mam. He's promised to be my bestest friend.'

'Georgie, slow down, son. You're as bad as your father. Let me get a word in.' Annie looked at her son for a moment. 'I don't know about the kitten, love, you'll have to see what your dad says. Now get your coat off and set the table for me, please, there's a love. You could maybe ask Arfur . . . Arthur for tea one night.' She faced him and wagged her finger. 'Only if you're good, mind. Now come on, get a move on. Your dad'll be back soon.'

Georgie pulled a face. 'Do I have to set the table?' he moaned. 'I've got things to do.'

Annie turned sharply and looked at him. 'Do as you're told else you'll get a clip round the ear and be sent to bed.'

Georgie opened his mouth to say something and quickly thought better of it. He slowly started to set the table. 'Is Dad still going to help me with me cart tonight, Mam?'

'You'll have to wait and see, won't you?'

While talking to her son, Annie had decided that Charlie deserved a treat. Carefully doing calculations in her head, and bearing in mind that her husband was now earning again, she lifted the battered tin from the mantle.

'I'm just going to nip down the shops to get something tasty for tea.'

'Oh, Mam, what we having then? Can I come with yer?'

'No, lad, I want you to stay here in case Dad comes back. And will you get a move on? I could have set six tables by now.'

'Well, you do it then.'

'What did you say?'

Georgie looked up quickly, his eyes wide with innocence. 'Nothing.'

Annie eyed her son. She picked up her straw shopping bag. 'I won't be a tick,' she said, pulling her shawl round her shoulders and hurrying out of the door.

The bell on the grocer's door clanged loudly as Annie entered. The different smells wafting through the shop tantalised her. Try as she might, she could not stop her mouth from watering. She could just taste the smoked bacon, freshly cooked ham, assortment of coffee beans and various cheeses which were all displayed along the dark wooden counter. A big housefly buzzed around, settling on the unwrapped food, but nobody, least of all the owner, Mr Straw, seemed to notice. As she waited her turn, Annie took a seat on one of the chairs placed by the counter. What to buy that was cheap and tasty?

Mr Straw finally looked in her direction. 'Right, Mrs Higgins, what can I tempt you with, me duck? Nice bit of bacon, got a nice Leicester cheese in just now, or fresh in this morning me wife's home-made faggots.'

'Yes, that'll do, Mr Straw.' She smiled, relieved to have her small problem solved. 'I'll have four faggots and two ounces of cheese, if you will, please.'

Mr Straw weighed the goods exactly. Generosity was not one of his strong points. People paid for what they got in his shop. Although he had been known once to give a small child an aniseed ball. It had been the talk of the street for a week. As he carefully wrapped her parcels, Annie's eyes travelled around the well-stocked shop.

'Oh, while you're at it, can I have a pair of black boot laces, please?'

Mr Straw's eyes widened. 'Is it good news then, Mrs Higgins?'

'It is, thank you, Mr Straw. Our Charlie's in work again.'

'That's good news, I must say. Will I put these on the slate?'

'No, thanks. I'll pay, same as always.'

'Wish all my customers did the same. Maggie Henshaw just up and left, owing me a small fortune. Nobody gives a damn about us shopkeepers. Glad enough to have our goods on tick but won't pay up when the time comes. Some of them walk miles sooner than pass my shop on pay night. I tell you, I'll go out of business soon.'

Annie frowned. 'I'm sorry to say this, Mr Straw, but you shouldn't have let Maggie Henshaw have so much tick. It's really your own fault.'

'That's what me wife says. Blazing mad she is. I'm going to put a sign up in here soon: No More Credit. See how they like that!'

Annie hid a smile. While there was a profit to be made, Mr Straw would not stop the credit or he would soon go out of business.

'I'll expect a big order next weekend then?' He looked at Annie expectantly.

'We'll see,' she answered him, knowing only too well that

33

bills had to be paid before luxuries came back on her shopping list.

As she left the shop she smiled to herself; the news of Charlie's good fortune would be all round the neighbourhood shortly, now that Mr Straw knew.

She turned the corner and collided with her sister-in-law. Although a plain, thin woman of thirty, Martha, like Annie, made the best of what she had. Her second-hand clothes, bought for a few shillings from the market, were kept spotlessly clean and, again like Annie, her neighbours thought her superior because she was forever washing and cleaning and made what little money they had spin out so as not to collect debts. Martha's eyes lit up and she slapped Annie gently on the arm.

'Oh, you didn't half give me a start!'

'I'm sorry, I wasn't looking.'

'Ain't it good news about your Charlie? Me and Bert are so chuffed. It's about time you two had some luck.'

'I knew you'd be happy. It's a weight off our shoulders all right. Look, are you and Bert going to come round later tonight? We can have a good chin wag. I'll do some sandwiches and we can make a night of it. And what about a game of cards? The lads'll love that. I'll send our Georgie over for a jug of beer.'

'Smashing. But we'll get the beer if you're making the sandwiches.'

'That's fine with me. Now I'll have to go, Martha, or Charlie'll think I've left home.'

'I don't think he'll be back yet, Annie. When I left, our Bert were trying to get him to go down the Tavern for a celebration drink.'

'Was he? Oh, well, it'll do him good. He never goes down the boozer. If I know Charlie, he'll only have one pint. Any more and he falls flat on his face. Never has been able to hold his drink. Oh, I hope they bump into Sonny Taylor. Apparently he knows where there's some wood going begging for the fire.'

34

Martha's face lit up. 'Good. We could do with some of that.'

'Yeah, well, don't go blabbing it about 'til we've got ours or there'll be none left.' Annie patted Martha's arm. 'See you later then.'

A light drizzle was starting to fall and Annie pulled her shawl tighter around her shoulders, treading carefully on the slippery cobbles. She quickened her pace, wanting to get home so she could make a start on the tea before Charlie arrived. On entering, the first thing she clapped eyes on was her son, happily carving away at a piece of wood.

'Georgie,' she snapped as she set down her shopping bag on the floor, 'you ain't finished setting the table yet. Well, you can just go straight to bed after yer tea.'

He sighed loudly as he put down the wood and pen knife. 'When's me dad coming home, Mam? I want to ask him about the kitten.'

'He won't be long,' she crossly. 'He's just nipped to see Uncle Bert about something. He's gonna tell you about it when he comes in. Now, are you going to move or not? This is your last chance.'

As time went by Annie began to feel troubled. Charlie knew only too well that she got cross if the meal was spoiled. She rubbed her wet hands over her coarse sacking apron. Ah, well, I suppose him and Bert must have met some friends down the pub, and they did have a lot to talk about. I'll be lenient, just this one time, she decided.

A loud knock sounded on the door and Georgie flew to open it before she had a chance to move.

'Mam,' he bellowed as though Annie was miles away, 'it's Uncle Bert and Auntie Martha.'

Annie looked up sharply. Bert and Martha were early. They hadn't even got dinner done with yet and she hadn't enough to go round them all. She quickly put a smile on her face and turned to greet them both. It took her a moment to register that Martha was crying and the look on Bert's face sent a shiver through her body. She looked from one to the other as she dried her hands on her apron.

'Whatever's wrong? And where's Charlie? He's supposed to be with you, ain't he?' She paused, staring at them in bewilderment as she waited for an answer. 'Bert, Martha, for goodness' sake, tell me. What's up? Is Charlie drunk or something and you daren't tell me, is that it?'

Her chest tightened. Fear and trepidation were building inside her. Quietly, Bert spoke the words that would live with her for the rest of her life.

'Annie. Oh, Annie love, I'm so sorry.' He stumbled forward, placed his arm around her shoulder and guided her to the nearest chair. 'There's been an accident. A terrible accident. It's Charlie. He's . . . he's . . . Oh, God, Annie, he's dead.'

Chapter Three

Martha gently closed Annie's bedroom door, walked over to the kitchen range and rested her hands heavily on the mantle. She raised tired eyes to the ceiling and inwardly groaned. The last three weeks had been a living hell, an eternity of grief and suffering on a scale she could never have imagined. There seemed no end to it in sight.

She lowered her arms, folded them under her bust and paced backwards and forwards. How much longer could she go on? How much longer could she carry her family through this trauma without breaking down herself? She pushed a strand of light brown hair behind her ear. Annie had to rally round soon. She couldn't keep herself locked away in her bedroom for ever, though as for Bert, she doubted whether he would ever come to terms with his beloved brother's death, especially as he blamed himself for what had happened.

The pair, jubilant at Charlie's success, had gone for a drink down the local pub. They were on their way home and, as they had done since childhood, were capering about.

Bert had slapped Charlie playfully on the shoulder. 'Yer lucky bugger. Fancy landing on yer feet like that,' he had said, laughing, before his face took on a serious expression for a moment. 'Can't say it's before time, little brother. Yer deserve some good luck, and me and Martha are as pleased as punch for yer both.'

Charlie grinned broadly as he mimicked the children's game of hopscotch over the cobbles in happiness. 'Ta. D'you think Annie'll like the flowers?' he asked as he waved a bunch of half dead daffodils in the air, wishing he had the money for red roses which was the least he felt she deserved.

'Like 'em! You soppy ha'porth, she'll call you a daft sod for spending yer last penny on 'em. And if buying them is what two halves a' bitter does for yer, I ain't taking yer down the pub again.'

'Ah, ged off. I ain't drunk. I know I ain't a drinker, but it'd take a lot more than two halves to see me crawl up the street. Anyway, Annie deserves something to cheer her up.'

'I could think of better things to spend me money on and I bet she could too. You mark my words, you'll get it in the neck when you get home.'

'Huh, I'd expect you to say that. I've never known you buy Martha a bunch of flowers,' Charlie scoffed, then wished he hadn't said anything as Bert's wage didn't run to such frivolities and he himself had only bought some for Annie on a whim.

'I wouldn't be seen dead with a bunch of flowers and I hope to God we don't bump into any of the lads, we'll both be joked about for weeks.' Bert scowled fiercely. 'Anyway,' he said, lowering his voice, 'what would Martha want with flowers?'

Charlie stopped his jigging for a moment and split the bunch of flowers in two. He held out half to Bert. ''Ere, give her these.'

'No, thanks,' his brother said scornfully. 'If I go home with them Martha'll think I had a turn or I'm after something. Anyway,' he muttered, 'if ever I buy me wife flowers, it'll be with me own money.'

'Suit yerself.' Charlie shrugged. He decided to change the subject, wanting nothing to spoil his feeling of well-being. 'Glad yer coming over tonight. It'll be like old times, having a game of cards.'

'Yeah, sure will,' Bert grinned. 'And I'll beat you at that, same as I will getting home, 'cos if we don't hurry we'll both get it in the neck!'

With those words, he spun on his heel and dashed across the road. Charlie paused for a split second, in his mind's eye seeing his elder brother reach home before him and himself the butt of his playful banter all evening. Without another thought he followed suit. Forgetting about the newly laid tramlines he caught his foot, tripped and fell forward. Bert's piercing screams were drowned out as around the corner lumbered a tram. Before Charlie could move it was upon him. He died instantaneously, his body crushed beneath its heavy iron wheels, the remains of the daffodils scattering in the wind.

It all happened in seconds. Tragic seconds that changed their lives forever.

Bert was inconsolable. The burden of guilt he carried over his brother's death was too great for him to bear. Try as he might, he could not push the horror of that night out of his mind. If only he hadn't persuaded Charlie to go for a celebration drink, he would still be alive!

The shock of Charlie's death had caused Annie to go into an early labour and on the morning of his funeral she had been gripped by searing pains. Martha had quickly taken charge of the situation.

'The baby's coming, Annie, and there ain't nothing you can do about it. Now get into bed while I send Georgie for Mrs Bates.'

Annie gripped the edge of the sink as severe pains shot through her. 'No, Martha. Leave me be. I'm going to Charlie's funeral, and I'll get there if I have to crawl.'

Martha ignored her and summoned Georgie.

'Go and get Mrs Bates. No, wait, she's at her son's wedding. Go fetch Doctor Hubbard, and ask him to hurry. Tell him the baby's coming.' She turned back to Annie. 'I think it'd be better if Georgie stayed at my house for the time being. This is no place for him at the moment. My mother will watch him. It'll do her good to have something to occupy her time.'

She turned back to Georgie. 'Go and collect some things, quickly now. Then after you've told the doctor, go and stay with Auntie Jean and tell her I'll explain what's happening as soon as I can. Have you got that?'

He slowly nodded. 'Good. Then hurry, like a good boy.' She bent down and kissed him on the cheek. She watched him run out of the door then she took hold of Annie's arm and led her firmly towards the bedroom.

'You're not going anywhere today, Annie, nature has seen to that.'

She was in too much pain now to protest. She knew, and so did Martha, that the baby was coming far too early. Her sister-in-law wiped the sweat from Annie's brow. Where was that damn doctor?

Annie grabbed her arm as another contraction swept over her.

'I'm losing the baby, Martha,' she wailed. 'I'm losing the baby we both wanted so much. Oh, God, I can't bear it!'

'Hush, Annie.'

'You don't understand.' Her voice rose hysterically. 'I've lost my Charlie, now I'm losing his baby. Isn't it enough that he's gone, without this too?'

Before Martha could answer the bedroom door opened and Doctor Hubbard entered. He was out of breath, his large kindly face flushed and grim. He looked at Martha and nodded in recognition.

'I'll boil the water and get the sheets ready, Doctor.'

He nodded again. 'Right. I'll just examine her.'

As Martha rested her head despairingly against the mantle, the minutes seemed like an eternity. She felt a hand on her arm and jumped. 'Oh, Bert, it's you.'

Her husband stood before her in his father's old suit, shaking his head. 'Georgie's told me what's happening.'

Martha looked at him a minute before she spoke.

'I can't go with you to the funeral, Bert. I can't leave Annie. You'll have to represent the family on your own.' He nodded slowly, looking at the floor. She patted his arm. 'While I'm here with Annie, keep an eye on Georgie. You know my mother can be a bit sharp sometimes and I don't want him any more upset than he is already.' Bert nodded again, turned slowly and walked out of the cottage.

Martha sadly watched him go, hating the thought that her husband had to face this ordeal without her by his side, and knowing that no amount of support from friends or neighbours would ease the pain.

Doctor Hubbard came back into the room, wiping his hands on a coarse white towel. The look on his face confirmed what Martha already knew.

'Why, Doctor? Why?'

He shrugged his shoulders and sighed. 'Just the shock, gel, just the shock of losing Charlie.' He placed his hand on her shoulder. 'It's not going to be an easy labour and I haven't told Annie yet that the baby's already dead.' He raised his head. 'When this is all over she'll need you like never before.'

'I know, Doctor, and I'll be here.'

Annie's labour was long and difficult, and the distress she felt at not being able to go to Charlie's funeral only added to her pain. It was two whole days before the baby was born. A little girl, the image of her father, and as she looked into the lifeless face of their much wanted daughter, Annie's heart froze. Before she was laid in her coffin she insisted that the baby be christened Charlotte in her father's memory.

Bert had carried the little coffin to the churchyard and it was placed beside her father's. No one ventured back to the house except Martha, Bert and Elsie. Annie wanted to be on her own, to lock herself away with her grief, but Martha refused to let her. Firmly she informed Annie that she was staying with her until she saw some colour in her cheeks again.

After Charlotte's funeral, Annie took to her bed and no amount of coaxing would move her. Nothing mattered to her now, not even her son. She neither washed nor ate nor talked. She showed not the slightest interest in anything.

Death was by no means a stranger in their walk of life. People died all the time, one way or another. For the others life went on. Money had to be earned, the kids had to be fed, and the pots still needed washing. But to Annie her life was over. The young woman that everyone loved and admired was gone. Left was an empty shell that had taken to its bed, and three weeks later was still there.

Elsie visited daily, trudging over the muddy yard, sometimes with a bowl of thin soup salvaged from the bottom of a cooking pot in the hope it might tempt Annie to eat, only to be turned away without seeing her friend. She missed her company badly and couldn't for the life of her understand why Annie was taking so long to come to terms with her grief.

Martha was finding the burden of her promise to Annie beginning to lay heavily upon her. Her sister-in-law showed not the slightest hint of recovery and this fact greatly worried her. What could she do about it? Just what would it take to jolt Annie back to normality? No instant solution or magic cure came to mind. All Martha felt she could do was to soldier on, giving comfort and support whenever possible, hoping and praying that something would happen soon before she herself cracked under the strain.

The creaking of the cottage door interrupted her thoughts and she turned abruptly to see young Georgie standing on the threshold. A sudden rush of love flowed through her as she looked down into the face of the boy she had always thought of as her own. She had never been blessed with children and to ease her pain had sought solace in Georgie. She suddenly noticed his ripped shirt hanging out of his short trousers and the cut on his lip, caked with dried blood.

'Oh, Georgie. What on earth has happened to you?'

'Nothing,' he answered sulkily.

Martha looked at him suspiciously. 'Well, don't stand there, son. Come on in.' She stood aside and watched, perplexed, as Georgie dragged his feet into the kitchen, letting his school bag fall off his shoulders on to the floor. 'Have you come straight from school? Does Auntie Jean know you're here?' she asked anxiously, knowing her mother would be standing at her door waiting for him. She saw his eyes fill with tears as he ran towards her.

'Oh, Auntie Martha,' he cried as he circled his small arms around her legs, hugging them tightly.

She knelt down, took his face in her hands and kissed his wet cheek.

'There, there, love. Come on, stop those tears. I know you've not seen much of us lately but you've had Auntie Jean. I bet she's spoiled you rotten.' A lump formed in her own throat as she watched tears well up in his eyes and cascade down his cheeks.

She wiped them on her apron, ran her hand through his hair and down the side of his face and pulled him gently towards her, resting his head on her shoulder.

'Auntie Martha, has me mam gone to Jesus as well as me dad? I miss them both so much and I don't know what to do,' he sobbed. 'I hurt, Auntie Martha, it hurts me here.' He drew back slightly from her and placed his hand on his stomach. 'Auntie Jean says me mam's ill, but I know she's dead. I just know she is. If she weren't I'd be able to see her, wouldn't I?' He looked up at her quizzically. 'What am I going to do?' The tears started to fall down his already tear-streaked face. 'I want to die, Auntie Martha, I want to be with me mam and dad.'

The horror of the situation hit her full force as it dawned on her that in their anxiety to help his mother overcome her losses, this poor little boy's feelings had been forgotten.

'Georgie! Oh, son, your mam ain't dead. She's here, love, I've been looking after her. No one's been telling fibs. She really hasn't been well and we thought it best you stay at my house.' Martha sighed deeply and swallowed hard to get rid of the lump that had formed in her throat. 'Come on now, let's see you smile. Your dad wouldn't want you to be sad. The pain will pass, believe me. It will take a little time, though.' She tried to smile and look cheerful. 'Just think of the happy times you all had together, and remember how much he loved you. He still does, you know.'

'Does he?' whispered Georgie.

'Oh, yes. Just because you can't see or feel your dad doesn't mean he's stopped loving you. He'll always be your dad, nothing can change that, and you must grow up big and strong. 'Cos, you see,' she leant forward and rested her cheek against his, 'he'll he watching over you in heaven and you want him to be proud of you, don't you?' Georgie nodded and managed a brief smile. 'That's better. Let's wipe these tears away. Now you're going to have to be brave for your mam's sake. Let her see she can rely on you to be the head of the house. Come on, I'll wash your face and then take you in to see her. She's lying down in the bedroom.'

Martha took Georgie by the hand and knocked gently on the door of the tiny bedroom. As she expected there was no response. Asking Georgie to wait outside, using the excuse she wanted to wake his mother before he went in, she hesitantly entered.

The room was dark and smelt stale. Martha wrinkled her nose. Going over to the bed, she bent down and gently shook Annie.

'Come on, love, you've a visitor. Come on. Wakey-wakey.'

Annie groaned and half turned over. 'Go away, Martha. I don't want to see anybody, not today. Maybe tomorrow.'

'You'll want to see this visitor, me duck,' she said tenderly. 'It's Georgie.'

Annie groaned again and looked at Martha pathetically. 'I can't see him, I haven't the strength.'

Martha ran her fingers through her hair in exasperation. 'Annie, will you please listen to me? That lad of yours needs to see you. He's being bullied at school and thinks . . .' She hesitated. 'He thinks you're dead like his dad. Now come on, you've got to see him. I don't think he can take much more.'

'And I said no!' Annie snapped as she turned and pulled the blanket over her head.

Martha's patience finally gave way as she whipped the blanket off her sister-in-law, grabbed her shoulders and shook her hard.

'Annie Higgins, will you sit up and listen to me? Your Charlie died three weeks ago, and so did your baby. For that

I'm sorry. So very, very sorry. But you're still alive, and so is Georgie. And in case you've forgotten, he's Charlie's and your son. Now wallow in self-pity if you must, but don't shut out Georgie. He needs you. Not me nor Bert nor my mother – you. Now sit up, will you!' She relaxed her grip and stood back.

Annie started to shake uncontrollably as tears ran down the sides of her face and on to the pillow.

'I can't, Martha. You don't understand, I haven't the strength to get up. I've no fight left in me. And what's the point anyway? The man I lived for lies buried in the churchyard with the daughter we both longed for. They might as well have buried me too for all I care now.' Her lifeless eyes turned and gazed at Martha. 'You take Georgie. You've always loved him and treated him as your own. You can give him what I can't. Charlie would have wanted that.'

Martha's mouth gaped open in horror. 'Charlie would want that?' she repeated. 'Well, I don't believe me own ears!' She clenched her fists so tightly her knuckles turned white. 'Annie Higgins, I've known and loved you a long time. I've envied you. Yes, I have. I envied the things you had that I didn't. But now I don't – I just pity you. I pity the way you've given up and are throwing your life away. Well, if that's what you want, that's fine with me. But as for Charlie . . .' She shook her head and set her mouth grimly. 'I knew my brother-in-law well and if he were here now, although he'd never laid a finger on you, he'd put you across his knee for what you're saying, and tell you to get off your arse and get on with living.' She raised her head and narrowed her eyes. 'Now I'm going to fetch Georgie and you can tell him yourself what you've decided, 'cos I ain't gonna do your dirty work for you. Then I'll take him home and you can get on with it yourself. I've had enough!' She turned on her heel and headed for the door. She had reached the door and started to open it when a whisper reached her ears.

'Martha, please wait.'

She turned to find Annie sitting with her legs over the side of the bed, her ashen face streaked with tears.

'I'm so sorry,' she sobbed. 'Please, please forgive me. Oh, God, Martha, I've been so selfish. I must have put you through hell.'

She walked slowly back towards the bed and sat down beside Annie.

'Yes, you have. But nothing like you've been through.'

'I loved him so much, you see, and without him life seems pointless. But you're right, Charlie would hate me for what I'm doing.'

'Not hate, Annie. Charlie would have been angry, but he loved you far too much ever to hate you.'

Annie smiled wanly. 'How do you carry on, Martha, knowing the person you want to see most will never walk through the door again? You'll never hear their laugh or feel their kisses.'

'I don't know, love.' She placed her hand tenderly on Annie's arm. 'But you'll learn. The strength will come from somewhere, you'll see. It's just you and Georgie now. That lad needs you more than ever. You'll be a comfort to each other, and me and Bert will always be there when you need us.'

'I know, Martha. I can't thank you enough for what you've done.' She sniffed and wiped her eyes on the bedclothes. 'Will you . . . will you let Georgie in, please?'

Martha nodded, stood up and walked towards the door. She turned and smiled warmly at her sister-in-law before she opened it.

Georgie's head peered hesitantly around the door then he ran beaming to his mother when he saw her sitting there, arms outstretched to welcome him.

Martha closed the door gently behind her and breathed a sigh of relief. She hoped with all her heart that this was what Annie needed to bring her round. She desperately yearned for a cup of tea and grimaced when she opened the caddy. There was not much left. She put it down, then picked it up again, trying not to feel guilty as she poured the boiling water over the leaves in the pot. Armed with the steaming mug she sat at the table and waited.

46

After what seemed like an eternity, the door opened and Annie and Georgie came hand in hand into the kitchen. Annie's face had changed. Gone was the sickly white pallor and the look of doom. Martha's shoulders sagged with relief. It was a step in the right direction. She was glad she had lost her temper, it had obviously made Annie see the light; being needed and loved by her son had given her a reason to live.

Annie walked over and placed her hand gently on her sister-in-law's arm. 'Georgie is going to go and fetch his things from your house. He's coming home.'

Two days later Martha popped her head around the door of the cottage and saw Annie sitting at the table.

'Sorry I never called in yesterday,' she said breezily. 'Only I had a mountain of things to do, and Mother . . . well, she was moaning as usual.' She sat down opposite Annie and smiled warily, noticing the look of anxiety in her sister-in-law's eyes.

'Martha,' Annie started hesitantly, 'I want to thank you . . .'

She raised her hand. 'There's no need to say anything, me old love. My thanks is seeing you on the mend.'

'Yes, well, it's all due to you. You have the patience of a saint. I feel so guilty keeping you here so long, but I just couldn't seem to rally myself round. I've no feelings left, Martha. They're all gone.' She shook her head sadly. 'I keep seeing little Charlotte. I can't help wondering what she'd have looked like in all the dresses I'd have made for her. But she never had a chance, did she?' She sniffed. 'I know it sounds daft, Martha, but do you know what hurts the most?'

'What, love?'

'My Charlie's jacket sleeve was ripped and he wouldn't let me sew it.' Annie's eyes filled with tears again.

'Don't,' whispered Martha, 'don't torture yourself. Things like that don't matter.'

'They do to me and I can't seem to get it out of my head.' Annie sighed deeply. 'But you're right, I know you are. I have to buck up, for our Georgie's sake.' Her eyes misted over. 'I love that little lad so much and couldn't bear to be without him. If you hadn't had a go at me, I dread to think how long I'd have gone on like that, pushing him further and further away. There's no telling what harm would've been done.' She raised her head. 'I've decided I've got to put on a brave face and keep my feelings to myself. I know it'll get easier as time goes by. People tell you that, don't they?'

'Yes, they do,' agreed Martha. 'But no one's asking you to forget Charlie or Charlotte. That'd be impossible. You're young, Annie, and the last thing Charlie would have wanted was for you to mourn them for the rest of your life. Anyway, I'm glad you're thinking this way, and as I've said before, me and Bert will always be there if you need us. You've never been one for bottling things up. So any time you want to talk, about Charlie or anything, I'll always listen.'

'Thanks, Martha.'

'No need for thanks. You'd do the same for me, I've no doubts on that score. What you have to do now is build your strength up and decide your future.'

'I know.' Annie shook her head forlornly. 'It's a terrible worry. But I've got to start managing by myself now and I think you should go home and see to your own family. I don't mean to sound ungrateful or anything, but your mother and Bert deserve your attention.'

'My mother can look after herself. But you're right about Bert. He took his brother's death badly and still blames himself.'

'Oh, he mustn't, Martha. Please tell him it was an accident. A stupid, senseless accident and no one's to blame, least of all Bert.'

Martha smiled. 'I'll tell him you said that, Annie. It'll be a comfort, I'm sure.'

She nodded. 'I'll tell him myself as well when I see him next.'

Martha looked at her thoughtfully. 'What are you gonna do for money?'

Annie shrugged her shoulders. 'Well, it's a worry, I must admit. But for a start, I could finish those dresses. The money I get should tide us over for a bit. Then I'll have to see about getting a job in a factory or something.' She looked around the room. 'Where are those dresses? Have you put them away?'

'Oh, Annie,' Martha answered apologetically. 'They were collected while you were ill. I tried to explain to them about your predicament, but it made no difference. They'd had instructions from their mistresses to collect the dresses whether they were finished or not. They were only doing as they were told, Annie. They just said they would get someone else to finish them off as they were needed. Quite shirty they were. I'm so sorry, gel.'

Annie looked aghast. 'It's not your fault,' she said, clasping her hand to her forehead. 'God, I put a lot of work into that lot and I only get paid on the finished article.' She sighed and held her head aloft. 'Never mind, I'm not going to let that get me down. I'll think of something.'

Martha nodded. 'Well, I'd better be going.' She rose from the table. 'Now don't forget, if you need anything send young Georgie round. Promise?'

'I promise.'

The two women hugged each other and Martha went on her way.

Annie stared around the room. How quiet and empty it seemed. It was going to take time getting used to Charlie's not being here. She felt the tears begin to well in her eyes again and took a deep breath. How long does it take for the pain to ease? she wondered sadly.

Squaring her shoulders, she walked over to the stone sink, poured in a measure of icy water and gave herself the first decent wash she had had in weeks. Then she brushed her long dark hair, racked the fire and sat down in her chair in readiness for Georgie's return from school. She jumped violently as a loud rat-a-tat-tat echoed round the room. She took several deep breaths to calm herself down and very hesitantly opened the door.

'Oh, hello, Sammy, it's you,' she said with relief at seeing a friendly face. 'Come in.'

'Afternoon, Mrs Higgins.'

'Why Sammy.' Annie looked at him quizzically. 'When have you ever called me Mrs Higgins? We grew up together, remember?'

Sammy took off his cap as he entered, a grim expression etched on his face. 'I'm sorry about your loss, Annie. Ada sends her best. If there's anything we can do, you've only to ask.'

'Yeah, thanks, Sammy, I'll bear that in mind. Want a cuppa?' She picked up the tea caddy and frowned when she saw it was nearly empty.

'No, thanks. Er . . . I, er . . .'

Annie snapped the lid of the caddy shut and looked at him thoughtfully. 'What's on yer mind? Come on, out with it.'

He bowed his head, eyes averted as he fiddled with his cap. 'This ain't easy for me, Annie.'

'What's not easy? Sammy, for goodness' sake, spit it out. And if you don't want a cuppa, you can at least sit down, I ain't going to bite you.'

'Sorry, Annie,' he said, pulling a chair out from the table. 'I've . . . I've come to collect the rent.'

'I thought as much.' She sighed deeply. 'Look, Sammy, I've never had to ask this before, but could you wait a bit longer? Only I ain't managed to sort things out yet.' She looked at him expectantly. 'D'you think you could give me another week? I'm sure I could come up with the money by then.'

'You owe four weeks already, Annie, and it's not up to me else I would, you know that, gel.' He looked away, avoiding her eyes. 'I've been told either to collect four weeks or give you notice.'

'What!' she said, her mouth dropping open. 'I don't believe it! This is his doing, ain't it, that damned landlord?'

Sammy nodded.

'Why, the swine!' she said icily. 'I've lived here all me life and never owed a penny. Me dad neither. Surely he'll wait another week, Sammy, surely?' Annie was pacing the room now and Sammy could not take his eyes off the floor.

'Ain't you got nothing you could give me?'

'Don't be daft, man. I've just buried two and you know Charlie'd been out of work for six months.' Her eyes narrowed. 'I can't believe this, I really can't. Has that man no heart?' She looked at Sammy apologetically. 'I know it ain't your fault, Sam. I know you're only doing your job.' She paused for a moment. 'Could you . . . could you say you never saw me this afternoon? If you did that it'd give me chance to think of something. Please, Sammy?'

'Oh, yeah, anything, Annie. I feel so awful, I've walked around the courtyard six times before I dare knock on the door. I think it's terrible, but he says he's got someone lined up for this place. I tried to talk to him, I really did.'

'Yes, I know. I know you'd do that.' She thought for a moment. 'What day is it?'

'Thursday.'

'Well, come back Tuesday then, that'll give me a bit of time, though God knows what I can do.' She hesitated. 'How long's me notice?'

Sammy cast his eyes down. 'Er . . . I'm sorry, Annie, but Mr Goldberg said you have to get out straight away. Said he'd lost enough money in this courtyard. You know Maggie Henshaw did a moonlight a few weeks back? I nearly lost me job through her. I'd let her off a couple of weeks. She promised to pay up but never did. He went mad when he found out, only kept me on 'cos he knows nobody else'd work for what he pays me. He's got me over a barrel and knows it. Since I done me lungs in down the pit there's nobody else that'd employ me and he really plays on it.' He stood up. 'Well, I'd better go. Tell you what, I'll tell Mr Goldberg that there was a note on your door saying you wouldn't be back until Tuesday morning. Then I won't get in trouble. Okay?'

'Thanks, Sammy, I'm really grateful.'

Annie opened the door to let him out and came face to face

with Elsie who was carrying a bowl of something steaming hot. She gave Sammy a dirty look and without waiting waddled her way past Annie and sat at the table. Annie followed her through.

'S'pose he's come for the bloody rent? Hope you told him where to get off?'

'Look, Elsie, I'm really not in the mood. What do you want?'

Annie could have bitten off her tongue as she saw her friend's face fall.

'Fine way to talk, I must say. You're still as high and mighty as ever. I only came to give you this.' She pushed the bowl forward. 'It's soup. Made it special I did, just for you. I saw Martha, she said you were feeling better. She never said you were in this mood.'

'I'm sorry. Thank you, Elsie. It's just . . . well, you know how it is. I've a lot on me mind at the moment.' Her eyes filled with tears.

'Yeah, I can imagine. But time don't stand still. It's not as though you can afford to sit on your laurels and wait for something to turn up. Your Georgie's gonna have to pay his way now. What you gonna do? Send him down the pit or something?'

'I'll never do that, Elsie! I'll never send him to work 'til he's got an education. Anyway, he's far too young, and it's against the law.'

'Against the law?' Elsie repeated sarcastically. 'What's the law got to do with anything? Needs must. You'll learn that quick enough, mark my words.' She looked at Annie and narrowed her eyes. 'You've been lucky up to now, ain't yer? You've never had to stoop to what some of us have to earn a crust?'

'What d'you mean?'

'Oh, Annie Higgins!' Elsie raised her eyes. 'The trouble with you is you've been mollycoddled all yer life, one way or 'nother. First by yer dad, then Charlie. Always envied you I did. You had the life of Riley. You're the type that'd fall down the lavvy and come up smelling of roses. You've no idea how some of us live even though you've been raised amongst us. You go round with your eyes shut half the time.'

'Elsie! I'm well aware of what goes on, and if you don't mind I'd like to be on my own for a while.'

She rose from the table and waited for Elsie to depart but her visitor was determined to have her say.

'No, you listen here.' Elsie's face clouded over. 'You've always looked down on me 'cos I send me young 'uns out to work. I know, you needn't look at me like that. D'you know how I've felt having to do that, do you? Seeing their little faces in the morning, pleading with me not to, and coming home at night jiggered and fit for nothing. And what for? So we can eat. 'Cos me old man only thinks of his booze and other women, nothing but himself.' She thumped the table with her fist. 'Bet you didn't know I was pretty when I was younger, slim an' all. Turned many heads I did, but I had to go and marry him. And d'you know why? Because I was desperate to leave home. Fourteen of us in one room, a dad that beat hell out of us and a mam that were drunk most of the time. I can't say as I blame her. I think my life's bad enough, but hers was a damned sight worse. When I met Billy, I thought the sun shone out of his backside. Now look at me. Twenty-eight and I look forty.' She paused for a moment and raised her head. 'I'll say one thing, though. At least I ain't sunk as low as Maggie Henshaw did.'

Annie stood and gawped at Elsie. She quickly worked her way to the other side of the table and sat down.

'What did she have to do then?' she asked, bewildered.

'Don't you know?'

Annie shook her head.

'She went on the game.'

'On the game?'

'She sold her body for money. Ain't you never wondered why her last two look nothing like the rest? She had to give it up though when she got pregnant again. It was the money she earned from prostitution that kept them going.' Elsie paused and pulled a face. 'Don't know what she's doing now. Probably in the workhouse.' She stopped and looked at Annie, playing with the spoon in the bowl. 'Oy, a' you gonna eat that ruddy soup or not?'

'Oh! Yes, thanks.'

Annie started to eat, her face still full of confusion.

'I never guessed. I mean, I know her husband left ages ago but I never thought where the money was coming from. But where did she go?'

'How the ruddy hell should I know? Up London Road, round the pubs, anywhere where the money's good, I suppose. It certainly kept them off the streets and her kids never had bread and scrape. It was always best mutton for them, and I seen her buy a cake once. A bought cake! Can you bloody credit it?'

'Oh, Elsie, I had no idea.'

'Well, that's what I mean. You go round with your bloody eyes shut, and if you don't watch out you'll end up in the workhouse.'

'That I won't, Elsie. My Charlie wouldn't rest if he knew we were in there. No, something will turn up, you'll see. I've a pair of hands and me health and I'm willing to have a go at anything.'

Elsie shrugged her shoulders as she looked at her, unconvinced.

Annie stood up. 'Thanks for the soup, Elsie, it was good of you to make it for me. Our Georgie will be back in a minute and I've to get me thoughts together and find something for him to eat.'

'Okay, gel. I wouldn't like to be in your shoes but I suppose there's plenty of other people worse off than you. At least you have a roof over your head. See you later.' She picked up the bowl and waddled out, leaving Annie staring after her, deep in thought.

Chapter Four

Next morning Annie rose with a firm resolve to get a job – any kind of job so long as it paid her a wage. She would have to work a week in hand but surely she could fob off the rent for another week and hopefully catch back the arrears, given time? Food would have to be scraps, begged or borrowed, but they would manage as long as she found work. Dressing carefully, and after seeing Georgie off to school, she made the rounds of the town, joining the long queues outside the various hosiery factory gates.

It was useless. Her determination slowly ebbed away as she was told time after time that there was nothing available for her. She was an expert at hand sewing but factories had machines. They would gladly have given her work if she had been a machinist – they were in great demand. As it was, they could offer her nothing.

Refusing to give in, she next tried the shops and stores, only to be turned away again for lack of experience. Shop workers were highly trained and had to serve an apprenticeship. She was too old for that.

Swallowing her pride, she resorted to visiting her old clients in the hope of obtaining a commission. But again she was turned away. They were happy with their new seamstresses but might call on her if anything changed in the future.

Later that night, weary and desolate, she knelt by the fireside, gently raking the last of the coal in the grate. She sat back in the chair with her hands cupped round a mug of tea. Georgie was tucked safely in bed, knowing nothing of her troubles. She had thought of every possibility, her mind going round and round in circles, but always came back to the same conclusion. She had no money and nothing to sell and there was no way she could raise the rent.

She could not impose herself on Bert and Martha. They owed money themselves and had already helped as much as they could. Her neighbours would help out with a bit of food but not money, that was out of the question. She tapped her fingers rhythmically on the edge of the chair and sighed deeply. There didn't seem to be any solution to her problem. There was nothing she could do to raise the money she needed at such short notice.

She took another sip of tea and her eyes widened. Or was there? Suddenly her conversation with Elsie came flooding back. She had said that Maggie Henshaw had sold her body for money. Could Annie do it? Well, could she? She took a deep breath. Why not? She was nothing special, no different from anybody else, as Elsie had kindly pointed out. She had nothing to lose, she was already at rock bottom, and it would certainly solve her problems short-term.

She poked the fire again, trying to salvage all the warmth she could as she went over and over in her mind the course she was about to contemplate. There was nothing left to do. She needed money now, and desperately. It was either sell her body or go to the workhouse, she had no other choice, and Georgie, her Charlie's son, was not going to land up in there, not while she was still living and breathing.

Standing up, she went over to the sink and washed herself down. Rummaging through her small supply of clothes she selected a clean skirt and blouse then brushed her hair. She tied it into a neat bun at the nape of her neck and placed a black woollen shawl round her shoulders. Having first checked to see that Georgie was tucked up and fast asleep, she went over and stood hesitantly by the door.

Oh, God, she thought wearily, her body sagging against the wall, what am I doing? Her legs began to tremble. She straightened her back and took several large deep breaths.

Stop this nonsense, she scolded herself. Stop it and get on with what's to be done. Don't lose your nerve, gel, or it's the workhouse for you and Georgie.

She raised her head and quietly let herself out of the cottage, checking to see that no one was about or looking out of windows. She slipped carefully round the corner and down the street. Elsie had said London Road was where Maggie had gone; it was quite a distance from where Annie lived so she quickened her pace. She supposed Maggie had gone there because of the railway station. People would be coming and going all the time. She hesitated as she passed the Grand Hotel, just as the smartly dressed commissionaire ran down the steps to help some new arrivals. His eyes rested on her for a brief second before he inclined his head, warning her to move on. Humiliation rose in her.

She lowered her head and scurried on, not stopping even to look at the finely dressed ladies and gentlemen alighting from hansom cabs in readiness for their evening out. She kept her head down and pulled her shawl tighter round her body, hoping to reach her destination before her nerve finally left her.

She had no idea what she would do when she got there. How would she act? What price to charge? If she should approach a possible client or would they seek her out? She would get there first, then she would tackle her problems.

Her legs shook violently as the station came into view. She slowed her pace. Her eyes took in the large, newly built redbrick building with its fine Victorian arches welcoming travellers. People were scurrying about. Normally she would have stood in amazement, soaking in the atmosphere, feeling envious. But not tonight. Tonight her mind was more than fully occupied with other thoughts.

A train had just arrived and the street was teeming with people. Porters were scurrying about with trolleys stacked high with luggage and weary travellers were milling around waiting for cabbies to take them to their destinations. The public house across the road was doing a roaring trade.

People were falling out of the door, laughing and pushing each other about. Her mind for a second pictured Charlie and Bert, but she quickly shook her head and took another deep breath.

Carefully she placed herself under a gas lamp and tried hard not to look anxious as she looked up and down. Ten minutes passed by. Nothing had happened. Annie's stomach was churning. She decided to walk slowly up and down: maybe that would attract attention.

'Oy!'

Annie swung round and stared straight into a pair of bright blue, heavily made up eyes.

'What's your game then?' The red lips spoke coarsely. 'I've bin watching you. You're new 'ere, ain't yer? Well, this is our patch, so 'op it.' Annie gasped and her eyes travelled down the woman's body. The shapely figure was dressed as gaudily as she had ever seen. Her clothes were like a chorus girl's.

'I'm sorry, I don't know what you mean,' Annie stuttered, looking bewildered and confused.

'Don't play games wi' me.' The woman stopped, looked Annie up and down and laughed. 'You ain't dressed for the part, are yer? Men like a bit of colour, me duck. They can get the likes of you at 'ome.'

Annie looked down at her attire and realised how drab she must look beside this woman, but her thoughts were quickly interrupted. 'Now I told yer, this is our patch. Scram 'fore I get the other gels together and make yer move.'

Annie's face reddened. 'I've as much right to be here as you,' she said.

'Oh, 'ave yer?' the woman exclaimed angrily as she lunged forward and pushed Annie forcefully on the shoulder.

She fell back and found herself gripped by a pair of strong arms.

'Well, well, what have we here?' a low, deep voice growled. 'Push off, Milly,' he addressed the woman.

Shaking with fear, Annie watched the woman hesitate.

'I said, push off.'

Annie saw her shuffle away and felt herself being turned around. She was greeted by a sneering face, teeth rotten and yellow. The man's breath stank of alcohol. He looked her up and down.

'Not bad. First time? Yeah, thought so.'

Annie struggled to release herself from his grip, suddenly realising that she had made a terrible mistake.

He misinterpreted her actions. 'Hey, not so fast. We could have a drink first. Fancy a gin? It'd loosen you up a bit. No? Oh, well. Have you got a place or is it round the back of the station?'

His free hand grabbed her breasts. Annie froze as a sickening fear rose in her stomach. She tried to draw back.

'Leave me alone, you've got it wrong! I'm not one of them, I'm not! Now let me go.' Her voice rose hysterically as she kicked the man and then bit his hand.

'Eh, you little bugger! What's your game?' He shook her hard. 'If you like it rough you should have told me.' He gripped her harder and grabbed her again.

Annie screamed as loud as she could, wriggling in desperation to free herself. She kicked his legs as hard as she could and lashed out with her fists. Stunned, the man pushed her away and she fell to the ground.

'I've met your kind before,' he hissed, rubbing his legs. 'Can't go through with it, can you, eh? Well, count yourself lucky. I ain't that desperate for the likes of you, you slut!' He brushed himself down and stalked off.

A crowd had gathered. Annie had never felt so ashamed or embarrassed as she did at this moment. All she could see was a sea of faces mockingly staring down at her. She felt the voices and faces drifting further and further away . . .

Through her haziness, she heard a woman's voice speaking from somewhere above her, but Annie couldn't make out the words. She felt a sharp stinging sensation across her face. The voice spoke again. 'Come on, wakey-wakey. You can't lie here all night. You'll catch yer death on these wet cobbles.'

Annie opened her eyes and tried to sit up. She ached from her fall. A hip flask was thrust at her and she was ordered to drink from it. The liquid felt hot and burned the back of her throat. Being unused to alcohol, she choked and spluttered. The voice spoke again and Annie looked up to see to whom it belonged. Though lined and heavily made up, the woman must have been pretty when she was younger but time had obviously taken its toll. Hers was a hard face, but kindly and full of concern.

'Feeling better?'

Annie nodded.

'Good. Let's get you out of here. Think you can walk?'

Annie nodded again and the woman helped her to her feet.

'Now, gel, I think you and I should have a talk. Come with me.'

Without waiting for an answer she led Annie across the road. She went like a lamb, glad to be away from the leering crowds. Through several side streets they walked in silence until they reached a tall, three-storeyed building. From the outside the house looked badly in need of attention but inside Annie could not believe her eyes. It was as though she had entered another world. It was beautifully furnished with settees and chairs placed strategically around the large reception room. Long curtains graced the windows, and the place had an air of lavish comfort the likes of which she had never witnessed before. Scantily dressed women were lounging about. They eyed her as she was led through into another room.

It was furnished like an office but with a touch of homely comfort nevertheless. Annie had to strain her eyes as the room was very dimly lit but her impression was of money, lots of money, and she felt very wary and out of her depth.

For the first time she looked properly at the woman. For her age, which Annie guessed to be about fifty, she still had a very good figure and carried the grand clothes she was wearing with grace. Her wrists and neck were covered in jewellery and Annie felt overawed and dull beside her.

60

The woman rang a bell push on the wall and sat down in a large leather-covered chair at the desk near the window. She motioned Annie to sit on a chair facing her.

The door opened and a maid came in. 'Gertie, bring some strong tea and sandwiches.'

'Yes, madam,' the maid replied, and closed the door behind her.

'Count this as your lucky night, my girl,' said the woman, leaning forward and looking Annie straight in the eyes. 'I don't often go out for a walk, but we ain't too busy here tonight and I needed some air. Now,' she said firmly, 'I want to know what yer playing at?'

Annie stared at her blankly.

'Come on. You've obviously never done this kinda thing before. So what's made you do it now?' She lowered her voice. 'My dear, I've been in this game longer than I care to remember and, believe me, I know you ain't the type. I can see it in your eyes and could tell by the way you were carrying on.' She paused. 'What's your name?'

At that point the door opened and the maid returned, carrying a laden tray.

'Ah, here's the tea. Thanks, Gertie. Put the tray down here.'

The maid did as she was told and as she turned gave Annie an almighty wink. She smiled back, just a little, and felt herself relax.

'Sorry, what did you say your name was? Mine's Gilda.' The woman pulled the tray forward and poured out the tea. She offered Annie a sandwich, then sat back and waited for her to speak.

Annie nibbled at the sandwich, which was quite delicious, and drank the tea, suddenly finding herself hungry and very relieved that this woman had saved her from such a terrible fate.

'Look, love, call me interfering, nosey, anything you like. It don't bother me, I've been called all sorts in me time. But believe me when I say I only have your interests at heart.

I've seen people come and go in this game. You have to be a special type of person. We don't all come crawling out of the gutter.' She leaned forward. 'I admit some gels think nothing of it, really enjoy what they do. To most it's the hardest profession in the world, but as there's nothing else for them to do, they shut their minds, think of the money they're earning and get on with it.' ˙

She paused and looked hard at Annie. 'I run a high-class establishment here and I look after my girls. I only entertain the kind of people who can afford to pay, and they pay well. I have none of the trash you encountered tonight.' She smiled. 'If this is the life you want, I can help you. I'll take you under my wing and show you all the tricks of the trade. You'd be safe and well looked after, and of course earn a packet with your looks.'

She eyed Annie thoroughly. 'You need sprucing up a bit, some good clothes, but with makeup you'll be a stunner. You carry yourself well. How old are you? Twenty-two, twenty-three?'

'Twenty-four,' she whispered.

'You can speak then? Good.' Gilda laughed and took a drink of her tea. 'As I was saying, I'll help you, but it's got to be what you want. And to be honest, love, I'm not sure about that. Is it?'

'I don't know what I want,' Annie said hoarsely. 'I just know I need money badly and this seemed an answer to my problems.' She put her head in her hands and sighed.

'Come on, me duck, let it all out. I'm a good listener.' Gilda poured Annie another cup of tea and pushed it before her. 'There's not much I ain't been through, nothing I ain't seen, so whatever you say won't shock me.'

Annie relented and the words came tumbling out. All the anguish, bitterness, her feeling of total devastation, poured from her. She told Gilda her life story and when she was finished felt exhausted at having to relive the nightmare again. But the relief she felt was great and she had the feeling that somehow Gilda understood.

Throughout, she had sat quietly, nodding here and there, but never once did she interrupt. Finally she stood up and walked over to a walnut cabinet. She poured them both a glass of sherry.

Annie smiled up at her. 'Thanks for letting me talk, I feel so much better.'

'Well, my girl, you've certainly got some decisions to make. But whether we like it or not, life still goes on.' Gilda paused and looked closely at her. 'It's only a thought, but why don't you go and find your mother's family?'

Annie gulped. 'Oh, I can't do that.'

'Why not! I bet they'd welcome you with open arms, especially your son.' Gilda smiled warmly. 'Come on, be adventurous, there's no harm in trying. Anyway, you ain't got much option, apart from joining me here.' She laughed and shook her head. 'I don't think this life's for you though.'

Annie quickly agreed. 'No, I don't think it is.' She looked thoughtfully into space. 'D'you think they would welcome us? I mean, I've no idea whether they know we exist or not. We might be a shock.'

'There's only one way to find out, and let's face it you've got to move fast because come Tuesday you and that lad of yours will be out on the street.' She bent down and opened her desk drawer, pulling out a tin money box which she opened. She selected three sovereigns and pushed them across the table towards Annie. 'Here, take these.' She laughed. 'I must be feeling good – I ain't usually this generous! It's just a loan, I want them back. Money's too hard earned to give away, but this'll help you while you make up your mind. Now come on, get out of here, I have a business to run.'

Annie looked down at the money. 'I don't know what to say.'

'Well, best not say anything then.'

She stood, went over and kissed Gilda on the cheek. 'Thanks. I'll repay this, I promise.'

Gilda reddened with embarrassment. 'You'd better!'

Annie walked quickly home, deep in thought. Never again would she judge people at first sight. Gilda had left a lasting impression on her and she felt so grateful that they had met. She fingered the three sovereigns in her skirt pocket. At this moment it was a fortune. But never, never would she tell anyone about tonight's experience. That episode would die with her.

She decided after a lot of thought not to pay the rent. Mr Goldberg had had enough money out of them over the years. Enough in fact to build several cottages. He was having no more. If Maggie Henshaw could do a moonlight, so could she. She would write a letter to Martha and Bert, explaining her plans, hoping that they would understand and asking them to speak to Elsie.

For the first time in weeks, she felt her heart lift. She had a purpose, a goal, and hopefully a new life for her and Georgie. She now desperately needed to meet her mother's family, to find out more about her origins. Her eyes lifted towards the sky.

Charlie, if you're there, please understand. What I'm going to do is for your son. I hope to God I'm doing the right thing.

She quickened her pace even more. She needed to be home now. There were things to do and time was short.

Chapter Five

The courtyard was in silence as she let herself into the cottage. After checking on Georgie she deftly went about her tasks.

A good two hours had passed when she finally sat down with a mug of weak tea, made with the last dregs in the caddy. The room had an air of desolation: one large bag was standing by the door. Annie turned and looked hard at it. It suddenly struck her that apart from the odd items of furniture, the contents of the bag were all she possessed in the world. Memories came flooding back. The cottage might be old and falling down, but her whole life had been spent here and it was going to be a terrible wrench to walk out of the door and leave its familiar, safe and comforting walls. But she had made her decision and there was no going back.

She reckoned it was about three-thirty. Time to make a move. She wanted to be away before the courtyard stirred. She stole quietly into the bedroom to wake Georgie and gently shook him. Her son was confused and still half asleep but did as he was firmly bid. Dressed, and with a piece of stale bread and warm tea in his stomach, Georgie was told of the adventure they were going to undertake.

She found it very difficult explaining to him. His questions came thick and fast now that he was fully awake and she was not prepared for them. He finally settled for the fact that they were going to seek out his longlost grandparents, and with its being a long journey they had to start out early.

'Mam, how are we going to carry that big bag?' Georgie asked.

'That's a good question, son,' she answered thoughtfully. 'Do you think we could carry it between us? I can't really leave anything that's in there behind. We've hardly got anything as it is.'

Georgie frowned, then his face lit up. 'We could take me cart.'

'You've no wheels on it, have you?'

'Yeah. Uncle Bert did it. I brought it home with me the night I collected me things from Auntie Martha's. It's round the back.'

'Oh, Georgie, it'll be a Godsend. Go fetch it, will you? Eh, and be quiet. Don't want to wake the neighbours.'

Georgie bought the cart round and they both struggled to load the bag on.

'See, Mam, it's got this piece of string. We can pull it along.'

'That's great, son, just what we need. Now put this bottle of water and these sandwiches down there.' She pointed to a corner of the cart where they could be wedged in without falling off. 'Then we can be on our way.'

Before she closed the door, Annie took a final look round. The letter to Martha and Bert was lying on the table. She walked over and picked it up, then placed it back down again, sighing softly. The rooms looked bare and uninviting and her heart was saddened. Memories came flooding back. Charlie throwing his cap on the hook as he came in from work; herself sitting sewing late at night; the joyous occasion of Georgie's birth in the tiny bedroom one bitterly cold night. She leant back against the doorframe and saw her father sitting in the tin bath trying to scrub his back.

So many memories of so many happy and sad times. She twisted her wedding ring absent-mindedly round her finger and remembered how Charlie had carried her over the threshold the day they had married. Her body sagged with the pain and weariness she felt. She jumped slightly as she felt a small hand touch her arm.

'Mam?' She looked down into Georgie's worried face. 'You all right, Mam? You look ever so sad.'

She took a deep breath. 'I'm fine, love. Just having a last look round. Come on, let's be going.'

She locked the door and put the key where it usually went, under a large stone by the door. With her head held high, she grabbed the cart string and Georgie's hand, and their journey began.

They were downhearted as they pulled the cart slowly through the town. Annie knew in which direction their destination lay from the conversations she had had with her father, but after Highcross Street, the territory was unknown to her. She had only hazy recollections of walks with her father many years before and felt a feeling of panic rise in her stomach. She had always been surrounded by familiar sights. Whenever she ventured out, she knew where she was going and how to get back home. Now she had no home and would have no familiar faces around her.

Georgie broke the long silence. It came as a relief to Annie to have to concentrate on something trivial.

'Mam, what about Arfur?'

'What about Arfur . . . Arthur, dear?'

'Well, me and him are bestest friends. He won't know where I am, will he? He'll be upset.' His little face puckered as he spoke. 'I'll miss him, I will.' Annie patted his head and Georgie looked up at her. 'Is there going to be any kids to play with when we get there? Will they have kittens? Will I have to go to school?'

'You'll have to wait and see, won't you? I expect there'll be plenty of animals though, it's a farm after all, and I'll write to Arthur – you can tell me what to say. As for school, you'll certainly be going, but let's see what happens when we get there first, eh?'

'All right.' Georgie started to skip beside her. 'Mam, you don't like animals, do you? I know you don't. You ran a mile when Elsie's Billy got that whippet.'

Annie laughed. 'You don't miss much, our Georgie, do you? Well, I'll just have to like them, won't I?'

'Me legs are killing me, Mam. Can I sit on the cart?'

'Don't be daft, it'll break. Tell you what. See up there?' She pointed in the direction they were going.

The houses that lined the Hinckley Road suddenly came to an abrupt end. Trees and fields, eerie in the early morning light, could be seen, stretching endlessly into the distance.

'We'll sit on the grass and have something to eat. All right?'

'Hmm.' Georgie sighed. He was all in favour of this adventure, but it certainly was taking its time happening.

They finally reached the top of the hill and Annie stopped and looked back towards the town. No wonder Georgie's legs hurt him. They had walked quite a distance. The sun was beginning to rise and was bathing the town with a pink and orange glow. It was going to be a lovely spring morning: the ideal morning for a walk in the country. It was just a pity about the circumstances. She surveyed the town stretched before her and a lump formed in her throat. How long would it be before she walked down those familiar streets again?

'Are we stopping here, Mam?' Georgie's voice rang out, breaking the spell.

'What! Oh, yes, here'll do nicely.'

They parked the cart securely and sat on the bank. Annie would have loved to take her boots off, but dared not in case her feet had swollen up and she could not get them on again. A sparrow flew down and pecked at the crumbs that Georgie scattered on the road. They both sat in silence and watched it, nudging each other when its friends came to join in the feast.

The sun was getting quite warm now. Georgie discarded his coat and idly picked a bunch of primroses that were scattered profusely around him. He handed the bunch to his mother who had closed her eyes and was beginning to doze.

Annie smiled warmly. 'They're lovely, thank you.' She yawned, 'Gosh, I was nearly asleep then. Come on, we'd better get going again.'

They both stood up and collected the uneaten sandwiches,

carefully wrapping them for later, and corked the bottle of precious water. Annie picked up the cart string and off they set again.

Their pace was slow and the cart grumbled and rumbled along the pitted dry dirt road. Annie was sure that any minute its wheels would come careering off, leaving them with the heavy load to carry. She looked up at the sky and judged the time to be about nine or ten o'clock from where the sun was situated in the sky. They had been walking for at least four hours and had only travelled about two or three miles. The cart and Georgie's little legs were holding them back.

The countryside was beginning to come alive. Colours shimmered in the sunlight, blossom was bursting open amongst the hedgerows and birdsong filled the air, mingling with the mooing of cows and bleats of the young spring lambs. Georgie was enchanted by the lambs and imitated their capering, to the amusement of his mother. Annie pointed out as much as she could to Georgie, answering his neverending stream of questions as best she could, filling him with interest and wonder. It also helped to take her mind off her own problems.

They were on the main Glenfield road now. Annie was praying that they were heading in the right direction when they came upon a signpost: 'Ratby 4 miles'.

'Mam, this place Ratby – is it full of rats? Why's it called that? Seems a funny name to me,' Georgie piped up suddenly.

Annie laughed. 'Yes, it does, doesn't it? But I don't think it's full of rats. Just the name of the village, that's all. Anyway, it's no good asking me about the place – I've never been before. We'll have to wait and see. It's bound to be different from what we're used to, living in a town.'

The road from Glenfield to Ratby was deserted. They hardly saw a soul except for the farm workers in the fields and the odd traveller and cart. Each time a dray passed, Annie had to pull their little cart into the roadside. On several occasions it got stuck and they had to unload the bag, pull it free and reload. They finally reached the edge of the village about four o'clock, just as the warm spring day was turning chilly. Annie decided not to risk pulling the loaded cart over the railway lines that edged the village. As she picked up the heavy bag once more, she knew there was no way she could have carried it all their journey and patted the cart affectionately.

A shout reached their ears.

'Help! HELP!'

Annie quickly pulled the cart aside and gave strict instructions to Georgie not to move. She ran in the direction from which the shouts were coming.

She made her way down the long garden at the back of a house and spied a middle-aged woman at the bottom of a ladder that was perched against a tree, her foot caught awkwardly in the bottom rung.

'Oh, thank God someone's heard me. I think me leg's broke,' cried the woman. 'I ain't never been so pleased to see anyone in all me life.' She looked at Annie sheepishly. 'Bloody cat from next-door got stuck up the tree and sooner than wait for one of my sons to come home . . .'

'You thought you'd do it yourself,' Annie said, smiling. 'You'd better tell me where the doctor lives? I think you're gonna need him.'

The doctor came and diagnosed a broken leg, and an hour later found Annie and Georgie settled in the woman's cluttered but spotlessly clean kitchen. Annie judged her to be in her mid-forties. She was plump and jolly and chattered away as Annie made her comfortable.

For the first time since they had met, the woman looked fully at Annie and a frown settled upon her face.

'Have we met before?' she asked.

Annie shook her head. 'No, I don't think so. Why?'

The woman shook her head. 'Oh, nothing. You look vaguely familiar, that's all.'

'Well, we'd best be on our way then,' said Annie. 'You did

say your sons would be home soon. Will you be all right now?'

'Oh, my dear, you'll stay and have a cuppa? My lad won't be home for an hour or so yet. His shift down the pit finishes at six o'clock. The other two will be in later. Will you stay with me 'til then? I'm not holding you up, am I? I'm so glad you came by. Don't know what I would have done otherwise. I still feel very shaky. Where are you headed, by the way? We see lots of travelling people come through here, you know. Some ain't got a clue where they're going.'

The woman looked at Annie and waited for a response. Her mouth had opened and closed rapidly as the questions came thick and fast.

'Well, to be honest, I don't rightly know where we're headed. Apparently, me mother's family come from round here somewhere and we're trying to find them.' She stopped abruptly and frowned down at her son, kicking his feet against a chair. 'Georgie, don't do that! If you're bored, go and have a walk down the garden. I won't be much longer.' She smiled at the woman in apology.

'Don't be so harsh on him, gel. I've had three sons meself. Now, what were we saying?'

'I was saying about me mother's family.'

'Oh, yes. Well, I might be able to help. I've lived round here all me life. What was her name?'

Annie sighed deeply. 'That's my problem. I only know her Christian name. It was Mary. My dad did tell me her surname, but that was years ago and I've forgotten it, unfortunately. I know her family did have a farm but I don't know anything else, I'm afraid.'

'Mmm,' said the woman, perplexed. 'You have got a problem. Let me think.' She paused thoughtfully for a moment. 'Do you know around how old she would have been?'

''Fraid I don't.' Annie thought for a moment. 'I've got her locket. It has a photograph in it. Maybe that might be of some help.' She fumbled with the clasp round her neck and handed the locket to the woman.

She turned the locket over in her hand, frowning slightly. 'It's very pretty. How d'you open it?'

Annie took the locket and gently opened it to reveal the photographs. She handed it back to the woman. 'They're faded but you can just make out the faces.'

The woman's mouth gaped as she stared at the photographs.

'Goodness gracious!' she exclaimed. 'Why, that's me and Mary Ann Burbage. Them photographs cost her mother a small fortune, but she wanted Mary Ann to have something to treasure all her life. And Mary, bless her, insisted I was taken as well. A man from Leicester came out special to do it. We had to sit for ages without moving. We were the only ones in the village ever to have our photographs taken.' She looked at Annie in surprise. 'You say this was your mother's locket?'

'Yes. Me dad gave it to me when I was fourteen.'

The woman's face clouded over in confusion. 'What was your dad's name?'

'Patrick O'Flynn. Why?'

'Oh! Oh, nothing.' She looked at Annie keenly. 'So, you're Mary Ann's daughter? Well, I never. No wonder you look familiar.'

She lapsed into silence as she stared at the young woman before her. Annie fidgeted under her scrutiny until she could contain herself no longer.

'You knew my mother then?' she asked hesitantly.

The woman looked up sharply. 'I'm sorry, my dear, I was miles away. You'll have to forgive me, this has come as a bit of a shock.' She ran her fingers through her grey hair. 'Yes, I did, very well as a matter of fact. We were best friends until she left the village.' She paused for a moment. 'Do you know what?' The woman laughed. 'We ain't introduced ourselves. My name's Matilda Cobbett. But to me friends I'm known as Matty.'

Annie rose and took her outstretched hand.

'I'm Annie, and I'm very pleased to meet yer.' She proudly

placed her arm round her son's shoulders. 'And this is Georgie.'

'Annie. Mmm . . . Mary Ann's mother's named Annie.'

She watched as tears came to Matty's eyes.

'You'll excuse me, I'm sure,' Matty said softly. 'Only you've brought back a lot of memories for me.' She smiled and took a deep breath. 'Now where was I?' She sniffed loudly. 'The farm you want is about a couple of miles from here. The old man's passed over now, but the son and his wife still farm it. The old lady is still alive. Only just, mind, or so I've heard.' She paused. 'There was only Mary Ann and her brother, Archie.' She looked hesitantly at Annie, as though she was choosing her words carefully. 'I went into service at sixteen. Mary Ann came to visit me a few times, then we lost touch.' She looked worried and then hurriedly continued, 'I was up at the big house, the one at Kirkby Mallory, 'til I got married and Mary Ann went away. It's funny us meeting like this. Fate I'd call it.'

'Yes, it is,' Annie answered. 'A bit of luck really.'

Matty grinned. 'I'll say. I'd still be under that tree, yelling in pain, if you hadn't come by.'

Annie sat upright in her chair. 'Do you think we would be welcome at the farm, Matty?'

She looked down at her leg and gently rubbed her hand along it, wincing slightly in pain. 'Can't see why not. But folks can be funny.' She raised her head sharply. 'No, I'm sure you'll be fine, gel.'

'Whereabouts is this farm? Is it far?'

'Oh, let me see. You go up Station Road and just as it joins Main Street, there's a track to the right. Turn up there and go about a mile or so along. You come across a signpost saying "Meadowfield Farm", you can't miss it. It's about a quarter mile up the track after that.' She stopped abruptly. 'You're not going now, are you? It's getting late. You could easy stay the night here. We'll squeeze you in somewhere. I'd be glad of the company. I don't get many visitors, you know, and it would be like paying you back for your help.'

73

'I appreciate the thought, Matty. But I'd like to get this over with before my courage leaves me.'

'All right, if that's what you want. Only, remember, if things don't work out, you can always come back here for the night.'

'Thanks, but I'm sure we'll be fine,' Annie said with more conviction than she actually felt. 'We'll come and visit you, though.'

'Do that, me duck. Please do that. I'll look forward to it.'

She watched them leave, stroking her chin thoughtfully. There's going to be fun and games up there all right. I wouldn't like to be in that young girl's shoes. She grimaced as she tried to make herself more comfortable. So, Mary Ann, me dear friend, you had a daughter and I'd have known her anywhere. Well, well, well.

Box Tree Farm, situated on the edge of Desford Lane, loomed up eerily in the dark night. Candlelight flickered in the window and Annie could see, as they passed by, a large roaring fire burning in the grate. It looked so inviting. Annie felt alone and suddenly frightened. She had no warm fire to welcome her.

The road forked to the left and they stood for a second peering along it into the darkness. She prayed that they would not meet anyone before they reached their destination. Trees whistled in the rising wind and the occasional rustle of an animal could be heard in the undergrowth. They both walked as close together as possible. On and on they seemed to go, until at last they came to the sign that said 'Meadowfield Farm'.

74

Chapter Six

'It can't be far now, son,' Annie whispered, sliding her arm protectively around his shoulders and giving him a reassuring hug. She looked down at him and smiled. 'Georgie,' she said hesitantly, 'when we get to this farm, I want you to be really good. Just speak when you're spoken to and don't forget your manners. You see, they ain't exactly expecting us and, well, we might be a bit of a shock.'

'What do you mean, not 'specting us?' He looked at his mother quizzically. 'And I'm always good, ain't I?'

'Look, Georgie, just do as I ask,' she said sharply.

They both lapsed into silence, exhaustion taking its toll as they plodded on and on up the long, winding, rutted track. High hedges of hawthorn lined the way, giving the impression of a long dark tunnel. This effect only heightened Annie's fear of the approaching encounter.

Suddenly the cart gave a loud groan and disintegrated in a heap, two of its wheels rolling backwards down the hill, disappearing into the darkness.

'Oh, no!' Annie cried in despair, staring in disbelief at the pile of wood surrounding the brown bag and the remains of their food.

Georgie started to cry. She knelt before him and hugged him tightly. 'Don't be upset, son. That cart lasted far longer than I thought it would. We'll manage without it.'

Georgie sniffed loudly. 'Me dad made it . . .'

'I know, son,' she said quickly, swallowing hard to get rid of the lump in her throat. 'And he'd have been proud of his handiwork. But he didn't make it to stand up to the kind of journey we've had.' She kissed his cheek. 'Come on. Let's pick up the pieces and put them out of harm's way. I bet some travellers spotting this lot will think it's their lucky day. It'll make a grand fire.'

'D'you think so?'

'I know so.'

Their task completed and with heavy hearts they continued up the hill, pulling the brown bag as best they could between them. An owl hooted in the distance and they huddled closer together, trying to quicken their pace. Rounding a bend, the dark, eerie shapes of buildings loomed before them and Annie stopped abruptly and let go of the heavy bag. She took several deep breaths, raised her head, and pushed open the gate.

They both stood now in the rutted yard, flanked on both sides by outbuildings and a large barn. At the far end stood a two-storeyed farm house. Candlelight flickered in a downstairs room and Annie could make out the shape of a woman moving around inside. She stifled a scream as, suddenly emerging from the barn, loomed a large figure carrying a lantern.

'Who's there?' a deep voice demanded.

Georgie cowered in terror behind his mother's skirt as the figure lumbered towards them.

'I said, who's there?'

Annie froze as a tall man approached, holding his lantern high. Its light reached her and the man let out a loud sigh.

'For God's sake, gel, you didn't half give me a fright! What on earth you doing out here this time of night?' He lowered the lantern to get a closer view of the intruder. He gasped for breath, uttered a loud cry and dropped the lantern which smashed into smithereens. The yard was in darkness.

The man's cry and the breaking of the lantern jolted Annie. 'Are you all right?' she asked in concern. 'I'm so sorry I startled you.'

The man grunted and took a deep breath. 'It's all right, gel. Weren't your fault. I thought you were someone else.

But you can't be her, you're too young.' He bent down and groped around for the broken lantern. 'S'pose you're a traveller wanting a bed for the night? Well, I'm sorry, gel, I can't oblige. It's not me, you understand, it's my wife. She don't like strangers hanging about. And I don't suppose a pretty girl like you is on yer own.' He straightened up, holding several pieces of glass and mangled metal in his hands. 'Head towards the village. I'm sure Box Tree Farm will let you use their barn for the night.'

'Oh, I'm not a traveller . . .'

'You're not?'

'No. My name's Annie Higgins and I'm looking for my mother's family. They have a farm hereabouts and a woman in the village pointed me in this direction. I've come from Leicester,' she blurted, 'walked all the way with my son.' She reached behind her back and pulled the quaking Georgie forward. 'I was kinda hoping this was the place I was looking for.'

The man took off his cap and scratched his head. 'Oh, were you?'

'Yes.'

'Well, I don't think this is it, me duck. You must have took a wrong turning somewhere.'

Annie looked up at him in dismay and to her shame burst into tears.

'I'm sorry. I'm just so cold and tired and I was so hoping that this was the place.'

The man grunted with embarrassment. 'Come on, gel. No need for this. Er . . .' he looked about him. 'Come into the barn, it's warmer in there, and I've another lantern.' He turned on his heel and strode across the yard. Annie grabbed Georgie's hand and trotted after him.

She reached the barn and felt sudden relief at being sheltered from the cold wind. The man struck a match and reached up to light another lantern hanging from a hook on a support beam.

77

His task completed, he turned to face her. He stared, his whole body taut in shock as his vivid blue eyes opened wide in astonishment. He fought to regain his composure as his face registered bewilderment.

'Just who are you?'

Annie looked back at him quizzically. 'I've told you, Annie Higgins. Why? What's the matter?'

He exhaled loudly and narrowed his eyes. 'Forgive me, me duck. It's me eyes playing tricks. You remind me so much of someone, that's all.' He held out his hand. 'Come, sit down and tell me your tale and I'll see if there's 'ote I can do.' He smiled down at Georgie. 'That little feller is fair worn out. It's a good journey from Leicester, especially on foot.'

Annie lowered herself on to the welcoming straw and Georgie huddled beside her. She sighed softly, raised her eyes and studied the man before her. He was in his mid-fifties. His lined, weatherbeaten, bearded face was kindly and his eyes twinkled as he looked fondly at Georgie cuddling into her side. He was over six foot tall and his thin frame looked in need of nourishment. His trousers bagged at the knees, the bottoms were tucked inside heavy black hobnailed boots. He had an unkempt, uncared for air and Annie's maternal instinct screamed to take him in hand and mother him. She managed a brief smile.

'Yes, it's been a long day,' she agreed, feeling her body relax against the inviting straw. 'And as for my tale . . . Well, I don't know where to begin really. I've not much to go on. But I do know my mother came from around here. A farm just outside Ratby.'

'There's a few farms round here,' he said, picking up a piece of straw. He placed it between his teeth and leant back again against the post. 'Have you nothing else to go on?'

'Only this.' She fumbled through her clothing until she found her locket. She undid the clasp and handed it to the man. 'It were me mother's. My father gave it to me on my fourteenth birthday.'

The man accepted the locket and looked hard at it.

'It's got her name scratched on the back and a picture inside. Look, I'll show you how to open it.'

She reclaimed the locket, opened the clasp and handed it back.

The man held it up to the light. He stared at it. Looked at Annie, then back at the picture. He snapped it shut and inspected the crude engraving on the back. His face turned ashen and his breath came in short bursts as he clutched the locket to his chest.

'Where did you say you got this?' he whispered.

Annie flinched. 'From my father.'

'And Mary Ann. What about her?' he asked hesitantly.

Annie lowered her head. 'My mother's dead. She died the night I was born.'

The man let out a cry of anguish and sat down heavily. His arms encircled his legs and he buried his head against his knees.

'No! No!' he wailed. 'Not Mary. Not my Mary Ann. She's not dead, she can't be!'

Annie stared at the man. 'You knew my mother then?' she cried.

He raised his head and looked at her through watery eyes.

'Yes, I knew her,' he answered hoarsely. 'She was my little sister. And I'd no idea she was dead.'

Annie clasped her hand to her mouth. 'I'm sorry,' she said, 'but I don't understand . . . ?'

'No, neither do I,' he cut in quickly. 'All this is a hell of a shock to me, I can tell you. I never expected her to be dead. I always hoped to see her come skipping up the track, like she used to.' He stopped abruptly, wiped his nose with the back of his hand and sniffed loudly. 'I loved my sister. She was like a spring lamb, so full of life. Always laughing she was, and never sat still for two minutes. People loved her. Something died in me when she left.'

'Why did she leave?' Annie asked quietly.

'I don't know. Nobody knew. But leave she did, early one

79

morning twenty-five years ago, and nobody has seen hide nor hair of her since.' He sighed deeply. 'I made lots of enquiries but nothing came to much.' He reached in his pocket and with shaking hands filled a pipe with tobacco taken from a cloth pouch. He lit it and took several deep puffs. He eyed Annie thoughtfully.

'I thought you were her. You're her image, and your fair made my heart turn. I thought for a moment she'd come back 'til it dawned on me you were far too young. She'd have been middle-aged by now.'

Annie saw a tear trickle down his cheek.

'I'm sorry. Grown men shouldn't cry, should they?'

Annie looked at him sympathetically. She felt a weight resting on her hip and looked down to find Georgie had fallen asleep. She gently moved him to a more comfortable position and looked back at the man whose despair at her news still showed upon his face. She felt her heart reach out to him. Easing her aching body off the straw, she went over and knelt before him, placing her hand gently on his arm.

'I'm sorry I had to bring you such bad news.'

'Oh, it's not your fault, gel. You weren't to know,' he said sincerely. 'You'd think the loss of someone you hadn't seen for twenty-five years wouldn't affect you. But it does. It hurts like mad.'

'Well, she was your sister,' she said softly.

'Yes,' he said. 'And you're her daughter. Well, I never.' He smiled. 'Meeting you kinda makes up for her loss.'

Annie felt warmth flood through her. 'Thank you.'

'Well, I suppose I ought to introduce meself?' He held out his hand. 'Archibald Burbage. Or Uncle Archie to you.'

'Oh!' she exclaimed. 'Yes, you are, aren't you?'

'Are what?' he asked, perplexed.

'My uncle.'

Archie laughed and his eyes twinkled.

'Come on.' He stood up and helped Annie to her feet. 'Can't have my newfound family sitting in the barn. Come up to the house and I'll introduce you to my wife, Kath . . .' He stopped abruptly and stared into space.

'What's the matter,' she asked.

'Eh! Oh, nothing.' He looked over at Georgie. 'Best get that little mite to bed. We can make our introductions to him in the morning.'

Annie watched as he picked up her son, put the sleeping boy over his shoulder and marched out of the barn. He also picked up the heavy brown bag they had dragged all the way from Leicester, turned and headed for the house. She followed a few yards behind him, heeding his warnings to be careful of the thick, churned-up mud. They entered the back of the farmhouse. As he opened the door a dog came up and greeted him.

'Down, Scrap,' he commanded, putting down the bag and affectionately patting the dog on his head. 'You can meet your new family later.' He placed Georgie on the peg rug in front of the enormous black-leaded kitchen range and trotted over to a thick oak-panelled door which led through to the rest of the house. He yanked it open and called loudly: 'Kath! Kath! Come and see what's turned up in our yard.'

As he waited for a response Annie looked around the large stone-flagged kitchen. Copper pans hung from wooden beams crossing the ceiling. A large well-scrubbed wooden table stood in the centre of the room and by the range were two wooden chairs, one a well-worn rocker which had been padded with thick cushions.

Archie shouted again, walked back into the room and motioned Annie to sit down.

'While we're waiting, I'll make you a cuppa.'

He took the big black kettle off the range and filled a brown teapot.

'It's a lovely house you have,' she said, awed.

Archie's eyes quickly scanned the room. 'Is it?' he said in surprise. 'It's been in the family for donkey's years. It was only a small house to begin with and has been added to over the years. It's got four bedrooms, you know. Several

81

generations of Burbages have farmed this land,' he said proudly. 'I'm the last of the line, though.' He sighed deeply. 'I can't see our Lucy, that's my daughter, taking to farming.' He looked over at Annie and his face lit up. 'But we have you here now, and the little lad. Eh, that puts a different light on matters.' He poured three pint mugs full of tea and placed one before her. 'Drink this while it's hot, there's sugar in the bowl there, and I'll get you something to eat in a minute.' His voice lowered. 'After you've met Kath.'

Suddenly the door at the far end of the room burst open and a small, shapely, very pretty woman of around forty barged through.

'What's all this shouting?' she demanded, wiping her hands on her apron. 'I've just got your mother down . . .' Her eyes settled upon Annie and for a split second they opened wide in recognition. She quickly turned to face her husband, a deep frown furrowing her brow.

'What have I told you about letting strangers into my kitchen? All thieves and vagabonds, the lot of 'em. Now get her out and that . . . that child off my rug.'

At her remark Annie's back stiffened, but she restrained herself from passing comment.

'That's just it, Kath,' Archie said cheerily. 'They ain't strangers. Take a good look at her. Go on. Who does she remind you of?'

'Nobody,' Kath snapped. 'And she doesn't remind you of anyone either, you soft ha'porth.' She lowered her voice menacingly. 'Now get 'em out. I have work to do before I go to bed, even if you ain't.'

She made to leave the kitchen but Archie stopped her by racing over and grabbing her arm, pulling her across the room to face Annie.

'Now look at her, Kath. Can't you see the likeness? She's our Mary Ann's daughter, and the little chap on the rug is her son.'

Kath wrenched her arm free. 'Balderdash! You ain't got the brains you were born with, Archie Burbage.' She wagged a finger at him. 'A young chit of a lass turns up here in the dead of night saying she's your niece and you believe her? Huh, you'll be telling me next that Queen Victoria's still alive and living in our barn.'

Annie made to rise. 'I'd better go . . .'

Archie turned abruptly. 'Stay where you are,' he ordered. He turned back to Kath. 'I'm telling you, this is our Mary Ann's daughter. She has proof. So you'd better get used to the idea.'

'Okay, so she's your Mary Ann's daughter? Fine. Now tell her to go. We ain't got room for her here.' She turned on her heel and stormed out of the room, slamming the heavy wooden door behind her.

Archie looked at Annie and shrugged his shoulders apologetically.

'Sorry about that. Kath works very hard and she gets tired. She'll be fine in the morning, you'll see.'

Annie sighed deeply. 'I don't want to cause any trouble, Uncle Archie. I think it's best we go.'

'No,' he said, raising his voice. 'You're not going anywhere. I've told yer, she'll be fine in the morning. You've been a shock to her, that's all.'

Annie smiled wanly. 'Okay, I'll stay.' She yawned loudly. 'Oh, I'm sorry.'

'That's all right, gel. You must be fair worn out. Tell you what, let's get you something to eat, then we'll get you both settled for the night.' He rubbed his hands together. 'Oh, I can't tell you what your coming here means to me, and there's so much I want you to tell me. My mother will be thrilled . . .'

'When can I see my grandmother?' she interrupted.

'As soon as possible. Tomorrow. Oh, I can't wait to see her face.'

Annie sank down into her chair, feeling a new warmth creep through her. As Archie busied himself cutting huge slabs of bread, cheese and a piece of home-made pork pie, she began her tale and through mouthfuls of food told her newfound uncle all. Archie sat and listened, a look of sadness crossing his face.

When she finally finished, he scratched his head and looked at her fondly.

'Well, you've certainly been through it, gel. I can only say I'm glad you found us. 'Cos this is where you belong, with your family.' He leant back in his chair and clasped his hands together. 'I wish you'd have known your mother. She was a lovely girl and she'd have been so proud of you. It gladdens my heart to know she was happy with your father, even if it was for such a short time. He sounded a fine man, it's a pity I never met him. Still, that's all in the past. We have to think of the future. I'm sure there's plenty for you to do round here. Kath's just lost one woman . . . well, we won't go into that just now. But she'll be glad of your help, I know that, and as for the lad . . .' A smile spread across his face. 'Oh, there's lots I can show him.'

'What about his schooling?' Annie asked.

'Oh!' He thought for a moment. 'See our Kath about that. I suppose he'll go to the village school with our Lucy. She's seven. How old is Georgie?'

'Six and a half.'

'Fine, they'll make good playmates.'

The relaxed mood was abruptly interrupted as the door shot open and Kath stood on the threshold wearing her night wear, her long honey blonde hair piled under a linen cap.

'Is she still here? I thought I told you to get rid of her,' she addressed Archie savagely.

'Kath, they'll be sleeping in the small bedroom at the back . . .'

'They will not!' she exploded, folding her arms under her shapely bust. 'If they have to stay, it's in the barn.'

'Kath . . .'

'In the barn.' She turned, and once again the door was slammed so hard it shook, rattling the copper pans together on the beams.

Archie's mouth opened and closed in embarrassment.

Annie, seeing this, leant forward and placed her hand on his arm.

'The barn will be fine, honest,' she said softly, managing to cover her distress at Kath's reaction.

'Are you sure?' he answered meekly.

'I'm sure. I could sleep on a clothes line, I'm that tired.'

He bowed his head, scraped back his chair and went over towards the range. He gently scooped up Georgie, nestled him in his arms and turned to face Annie.

'I'll get you settled then,' he said, forcing a smile.

Archie let himself quietly into the bedroom and looked over at his wife, feigning sleep in the large oak bed they shared.

'Kath,' he said softly. He waited for a response but none came. 'Kath,' he said, louder this time.

'Oh, for God's sake!' she exploded, raising her head and staring at her husband with large brown eyes. 'What d'you want? I'm trying to sleep.'

'About those two . . .' he began.

'Oh, I might have guessed. What about those two?'

'I want them to stay, Kath.'

'Oh, do you? She sat bolt upright and folded her arms. 'And what next? Do we get the rest of them camping on our doorstep, claiming to be longlost relatives?'

'Kath, our Mary Ann's dead . . .'

'Is she?' she interrupted nonchalantly. 'Well, I'm sorry to hear that, but you've only that gel's word for it and I personally don't believe a word she says.'

Archie walked over to the bed and wearily sat down.

'This young girl is my niece, she's had a rotten deal and I want to help her. We're her family, Kath, all she's got in the world. She's no one else to turn to and by rights this farm will be half hers when me mother finally goes.'

Kath's eyes blazed. 'No, it will not! This is our farm, she's no claim to it.'

'Oh, but she has. Me mother always said before her mind went that it was to be shared equally between me and Mary

85

Ann. Mary Ann is no longer with us. So her share should automatically pass to Annie.'

'We'll see about that,' she retorted angrily. 'There's me and Lucy to consider. She needn't think that she's gonna waltz in here and take over. Your mother's never liked me, the old cow!' she hissed under her breath as she turned and stared fixedly across the room. She thought deeply for a moment before turning back to face her husband. 'It's not my fault, what's happened to her. I don't see why I should have to put up with her staying here.'

'No one's saying it is your fault,' Archie said in surprise. 'Where's your compassion, Kath? If it was one of your lot you'd soon be giving them hand-outs.'

'I would not. What I've got, I've worked for. No one's gonna take what's mine.'

'No one's trying to, Kath. That girl only wants a roof over her head and some food. She's willing to work, she's not expecting charity.'

'And she'll get none.'

'Come on, be reasonable,' he begged. 'You need help around the place, what with Lily just leaving like that. Annie turning up here is a Godsend, one way or another.'

'A'you saying I can't keep me staff?'

'No,' Archie said quickly, before adding, 'Well, you are sharp with 'em, Kath.'

'Well, someone's got to keep on their backs. You're no good. You wouldn't say boo to a goose, you're that soft. Anyway, how's a townie like her gonna be any good to me? She probably don't know the meaning of hard work. I can't be running after her all day or that lad just 'cos they claim to be family. Why not give her a few bob and send her packing?'

'Kath, no. She's staying. I lost Mary Ann and I ain't gonna lose these two, not if I can help it.' He raised himself up and stared at his wife. 'I'm sorry, Kath, but I can't send her back to face the workhouse. She's staying and that's that.'

Her mouth dropped open in surprise. Archie had never crossed her like this before. He hadn't the guts. This girl had certainly got under his skin. She'd better be careful. Thoughts flashed through her mind. Her carefully laid plans were in danger. They had taken years to come to fruition, and if she wasn't clever she could put everything in jeopardy. What if she seemed to accept this girl yet somehow forced her to leave? Yes, that was the answer. She would work her so hard that the workhouse would seem a haven. She would flee back to town, hopefully never to return. Kath put a sweet smile on her face and looked up into her husband's eyes.

'All right, Archie, I'll give her a trial. But if I find out she's not who she says she is, or if she doesn't pull her weight, then they go. I can't say fairer than that.'

His shoulders sagged in relief. 'Oh, Kath, thanks. You won't regret it. They'll bring a bit of life to the place, you'll see.'

She opened her mouth to speak, then thought better of it.

'Yes, I'm sure they will,' she said pleasantly. 'Er . . . just one thing, Archie.'

'Oh?'

'Let's keep this from your mother. She's not in any fit state to take this in at the moment. A shock like this could be the death of her.'

'Kath, me mother's as tough as old boots. This is just the tonic she needs.'

'Balderdash. I tell you it'll kill her, and I ain't taking that responsibility.'

Archie thought for a moment. 'I suppose you're right, only Annie won't understand.'

'Don't matter what she thinks. I just want her kept away from your mother 'til I think she's strong enough.'

Archie nodded. 'Okay, Kath. I'll leave it to you.'

She hid a smile. 'Yeah, you do that. You leave things to me.'

Chapter Seven

Annie woke with a start and it was several seconds before she realised just where she was. She had slept surprisingly well, exhaustion overtaking her troubles, and felt refreshed and better than she had done for weeks. The morning air was chilly and she quickly rose and dressed, brushing down the caked mud on her skirt, trying to make herself as presentable as possible. Georgie was still fast asleep, his hair all tousled and his face the picture of innocence. He looked so peaceful lying there, unaware of the struggle that lay ahead for them both. She smiled and ran her fingers gently over his head. She would protect him to the best of her ability from the harsh realities of the outside world until he was old enough to face them on his own.

She wondered if Archie had managed to reason with her Aunt Kath. Panic rose up in her. What if he hadn't and they were going to be turfed out? What would they do then? Don't be silly, she scolded herself, families stick together. And they were family, she had proved that.

Her uncle seemed such a nice man, but he was obviously ruled by his tiny wife and that could present problems. She hadn't liked the look of Kath and knew the woman was not going to accept them easily. So it was up to her to prove their worth, by hard work and humility. The humility part would not be easy, but she would have to try, not for herself but for her son. He needed stability now and that's what this new life would give him.

She left Georgie to sleep and found her way out of the barn. She raised her skirts and walked slowly down towards the big gate. The morning was still dark and apart from the candlelight coming from the house, the rest of the world still seemed to be asleep. She wanted a few moments to herself to gather her thoughts before she faced her future. Supporting herself against the gate, she surveyed the yard.

Apart from a few flagstones near the kitchen entrance the yard consisted of churned up, rutted mud. A water pump and stone drinking trough stood in the middle and several large wooden buildings edged the sides. Stone walls and the occasional bush and tree lined the rest of the area. The large wooden gate she was resting on completed the enclosure. She wondered what all the buildings were used for, her knowledge of farming being practically non-existent. It was certainly a large farm, going by the house and number of buildings, and she wondered how many fields they owned and what animals they had.

She turned around and gazed towards the open fields, fixing her eyes on the rising sun. The mist was beginning to clear and the whole world smelt clean and crisp. She breathed deeply, savouring the sweet air.

Sounds in the distance jolted her thoughts. She strained her eyes to see a herd of cows meandering round the bend in the track that led up to the farm. Expertly guiding them was a bent old man, wielding a large stick.

As he approached the gate he caught sight of Annie and glared at her. He eyed her suspiciously for a moment before his toothless mouth broke into a leering smile.

She cringed at the sight of him and felt her skin crawl.

'So you're the young thing that's causing havoc up at the 'ouse?' He gave a loud chuckle. 'She's got it in for you, she has. She's flying round the kitchen like a bat out of hell. You've sure caused some trouble.'

Annie stared at him questioningly. 'What d'you mean?'

'You'll see, gel, Now a'you gonna open the bloody gate or stand there gawping like an idiot all morning? I can see you know n'ote about farming. Oh, this is gonna be fun.'

Annie indignantly stepped back and watched as the old

man pushed open the gate and herded the cows through.

'Come on, Jessie, Mabel. Come on, gels, through you go,' he shouted, slapping their rears with his stick.

The cows advanced towards Annie. A terrible stench filled her nostrils and she recoiled in horror. The black and white beasts filled her with terror and she ran with all her might towards the wall, pressing her back against it for safety.

She sighed with relief, then suddenly gasped, realising that they were heading for the barn where Georgie was sleeping. Pulling up her skirts she ran as fast as she could and grabbed her son in her arms just before the cows trampled over the straw where he had been lying.

Georgie woke abruptly and screamed aloud in shock.

'It's all right. It's all right,' she soothed. 'It's just the cows come for their breakfast.'

The old man turned towards her. 'Breakfast?' he repeated sarcastically. 'You really are a townie.' He chuckled uncontrollably and Annie stared at him in indignation.

'Okay, so I come from the town. I'd like to see how you'd cope in a factory or down a pit! I'd soon be laughing at you, I bet.'

The old man stopped his laughing and stared at her. He opened his mouth to speak, but snapped it quickly shut as he spotted his master enter the barn.

'You're both up then,' Archie said warmly. 'Good, I hope you slept well?'

'Yes, thank you,' Annie said, forcing a smile.

'Right, come on up to the house and get your breakfast.' He looked over at the old man and nodded. 'Everything okay, Reggie?'

He turned and flicked his finger against his cap.

'Yes, boss,' he said before turning his attention back to the cows.

'Good.' Archie looked at Annie. 'I see you've met our Reggie. He was born on this farm and his father before him. He's my right hand. That's right, ain't it, Reggie?'

He turned and gave a nod of his head.

'Yes, there's not much Reggie doesn't know about farming.'

Annie put Georgie down and looked hesitantly at her uncle.

'Uncle Archie,' she said slowly, 'what about Auntie Kath? Is she all right now about us staying?'

'Oh, yes, yes,' he said a little too quickly. 'She was just tired last night and you were a bit of a shock. No, she's fine now. She has your breakfast ready and afterwards she's gonna show you what to do. She's a good woman is Kath, though she can be a bit sharp sometimes. Once you get to know her you'll be good friends.' He smiled down at her and placed his arm around her shoulders. 'Stop worrying, Annie. You're with your family now. We'll take care of you.'

Her shoulders sagged in relief. 'Oh, thanks, Uncle Archie. It's a load off my mind. I'll repay you by working as hard as I can, all hours God sends if necessary.'

He placed both his hands on her shoulders and held her at arm's length. 'Listen to me, Annie Higgins. We all pull our weight around here. You'll not be expected to do any more than anyone else.' He let go of her and leaned against a wooden post. 'I'll not deny that farming's hard and there's always plenty to be done. But we do relax sometimes.' He rubbed his hands together. 'Come on, get Georgie sorted out. You must be starving and I've to get to the bottom field. I need to finish the planting today.'

Archie opened the kitchen door, poked his head around and addressed his wife.

'Er . . . Kath. They're here.' He turned back to Annie and stood aside, allowing her and Georgie to enter. He smiled at her as she passed him. 'I won't come in, I have me muddy boots on.' He lowered his voice to a whisper. 'Kath gets in a right state if I make a mess on her clean floor. Anyway, in yer go. I'll see yer tonight.' With that he turned and made his way down the yard, whistling tunelessly.

'For God's sake, come in and shut the door. Were you born in a barn?'

Annie turned abruptly to see Kath, hands on her hips, face like thunder, staring at her.

'Well, am I talking to meself or what?'

Annie took a deep breath and walked over the threshold, closing the door behind her. She went straight over to Kath and held out her hand.

'I'm so pleased to meet you, Auntie Kath.'

'Don't "Auntie Kath" me! I ain't no idiot, Annie Higgins, so don't think for a minute you've fooled me with yer tale. Even if that soft lump of a husband of mine has been taken in.'

She paused for a moment and looked Annie up and down, then turned her attention to Georgie. Annie felt uneasy, her palms clammy with sweat under the scrutiny.

Kath pursed her lips together and folded her arms. She continued: 'If you think you're in for an easy time of it, you're mistaken. I've promised Mr Burbage to give you a try. But let me assure you, I'm the boss around here and what I say goes.' She unfolded her arms, walked over to the table and rested her hands on the back of a chair. 'It's lucky for you that I am in need of some help. So we'll forget this relation business. It was a good ploy, I have to admit that. You'll get board and lodgings plus a shilling a week. And if yer don't work, and I mean both of yer, yer go. Is that clear?'

Just then the door opened and a young girl of about fifteen scuttled through. She was carrying a large black coal bucket. She eyed Annie for a second, then lowered her head. Kath turned on her.

'You!' She addressed the girl sharply. 'Get the water in. Stop dithering, gel. Get on with it.'

Annie held her breath as the girl, shaking with fright, hurried past her and made for the back door. She turned back to face Kath, feeling the hairs on the back of her neck stand on end. An uncontrollable surge of anger rose in her and she clenched her fists tightly. The woman facing her was one of the nastiest she had ever encountered, and she had known some in her life. After what she had been through she was not going to be treated by anyone in this manner. She raised her head and took a deep breath.

'I can assure you my story is true,' she said coldly. 'And

93

whether you believe it or not is up to you. But your attitude towards me and my son I don't need.' She grabbed Georgie's hand and held it tightly. 'I wouldn't work for you if my life depended on it.'

Kath let out a bellow of laughter. 'Ah, but it does, doesn't it, or why else are you here? Let's face it. It was here or the workhouse, and this was obviously the best bet.' She let a slow smile spread across her face. 'Well, go. Don't let me stop you.'

Annie's eyes narrowed. A picture of the workhouse flashed through her mind. She saw the poverty and disease, the sheer desperation of the folk residing there. 'Oh, no,' she blurted. 'You don't get rid of me that easy. This was my mother's home. I've as much right to be here as you.'

Kath opened her mouth, then snapped it shut. This girl was stronger willed than she had first thought. Not like her mother who had been easily dealt with. This was going to be harder than she had imagined. She would have to be careful how she acted or Archie just might get suspicious. She quickly changed her tactics.

'Okay, I've maybe been a bit harsh. But we get all sorts turning up asking for work and some ain't easy to get rid of. Archie's a soft touch, he believes what anyone tells him.' She scratched her chin. 'I'll make no bones about it, I don't want you here. Townies don't make good farm workers and I can't afford to be running around clearing up after you. But we'll give it a try on both sides. I can't say fairer than that. If you don't come up to scratch, you go. And if you don't like it here, you can leave of yer own accord. Is it a deal?'

Annie breathed deeply. 'It's a deal.'

Kath nodded. 'Good. Now there's porridge in the pot on the range. Help yourself,' she said abruptly. She picked up the big black kettle and filled it with water from a bucket by the enormous stone sink. 'In future we rise at five o'clock. There's work to be done before we have breakfast and I'll expect you to be here to help, not lazing in bed 'til all hours. The lad . . .'

'His name's Georgie.'

Kath froze. 'The lad can feed the chickens and help muck out the barn.'

'What about his schooling?' Annie interrupted.

'Oh, there's no point in sending him to school 'til we're sure you're stopping.'

'We'll be stopping long enough to send him to school,' Annie said sharply.

Kath clenched her fists. 'I'll make enquiries as to a place. In the meantime he can make himself useful.'

'Thank you,' Annie said slowly. 'I'm sure Georgie'll do a good job. Eh, Georgie?' She smiled down at her son who was pressing himself into her side. 'You like the animals, don't you?'

He raised his eyes towards her and nodded.

Kath picked up a tray and placed it on the table, proceeding to set it. 'There's a room over the barn,' she said, avoiding Annie's eyes. 'Needs cleaning up a bit. I'll get you some blankets. Be better for you than living in here and us all being on top of one another. You'll have your privacy.'

'Thank you,' said Annie, lowering her gaze.

So they weren't going to be allowed in the house. I wonder why? she thought.

'Okay, enough chat. Get your food. There's work to be done and I've to see to the old lady.' Kath stopped abruptly and stared over at Annie. 'She's very ill, her mind's gone, and the slightest upset could mean the end.'

'I could sit and hold her hand . . .'

'Oh, no,' Kath cut in quickly. 'Strangers upset her. She's allowed no visitors. Doctor's orders. It'd be on your head if anything happened to her.' She picked up the tray and headed out of the kitchen door.

Annie stared after her then looked down at Georgie and managed a smile. 'Well, son,' she said lightly, 'let's get something to eat. I bet your little tummy is rumbling like mad.' She knelt down and hugged him to her. 'Don't worry. Everything will be fine, you'll see. You're going to have a lot of fun looking after the chickens.'

She stood up, walked over to the range and slapped large spoonfuls of thick porridge into two bowls. She placed them on the table and they both sat down and ate hungrily. The porridge was delicious. Kath could certainly cook.

Annie became conscious of another presence in the room and turned her head to see the servant girl had returned and was hovering hesitantly by the doorway, staring at them both through dark blonde lashes. She was fairly tall and slender, her ash blonde hair looking as though it had been hurriedly scraped up and bundled beneath the white cap that was slipping off the back of her head. Despite the petrified expression on her face, Annie could see that in a short space of time the girl would blossom into a very attractive woman.

'Hello,' Annie ventured.

The girl lowered her eyes, staring intently at the floor.

'Hello,' she said again. When she still got no response, she rose and walked over to the range. She picked up another bowl and filled it with porridge. 'Breakfast?'

Without lifting her head, the girl nodded. Annie placed it on the table and sat down again. She smiled over at Georgie and motioned him to finish his food. The girl sat hesitantly down.

'My name's Annie and this is Georgie, my son. What's yours?'

The girl stopped eating and stared at her. Her large brown eyes blinked in astonishment.

'Molly,' she muttered under her breath, nervously fingering a tendril of hair that had escaped from her calico cap.

'Pardon?'

Molly inhaled deeply. 'Molly,' she repeated with great difficulty.

'Oh, pleased to meet you, Molly. Georgie and me are going to be working here. I hope we can be friends. You'll maybe help me out.' Annie laughed. 'I know nothing about farming.'

Molly raised her head, a slow smile forming on her lips, her intelligent eyes lighting up in pleasure. She opened her mouth to speak, but quickly snapped it shut as the door burst open and Kath charged in.

'Oh, I see you've met Molly.' She threw down the tray, the crockery rattling dangerously. 'That woman is impossible. If she wasn't Mr Burbage's mother, I'd have her committed.' She looked over at Molly and her eyes narrowed. 'Ain't you finished yet? Come on, hurry up. I want all the grates black leaded today, the rugs taking out and beating and the furniture dusting. But first I want you to show the ... Georgie how to feed the chickens.' She clapped her hands together. 'Now get to it, gel.'

Molly jumped up, raced around the table, grabbed Georgie's hand, yanking him up from his chair, and headed for the door.

Kath turned back to face Annie.

'Right. The first job of the day for you is the butter making. What we don't eat of our dairy produce, we sell at the Saturday market. I have very high standards and I expect them to be maintained. Ready?'

Annie nodded, rose from the table and followed Kath across the yard and into the small dairy. The stone floor, sinks and wooden utensils were spotless. Her aunt walked towards several milk churns.

Annie listened intently, her eyes darting backwards and forwards as Kath blabbed out instructions at a furious pace. Fifteen minutes later she was on her own. She stared around the dairy, her eyes wide in horror. Now just what was it that Kath had told her?

An hour later, Archie popped his head around the door.

'How's it going, Annie?' he asked hesitantly.

She raised her eyes wearily and managed a smile. 'Fine. I think I've got the hang of it now.'

'Good,' he said with a mixture of relief and delight. 'Now, don't worry about young Georgie. He's coming with me down the end field.' He winked over at her. 'Don't tell Kath, but I'm hoping to get in a spot of bird watching.' He gave Annie a boyish grin and vanished.

She turned back to her work. Her arms and back ached,

but there was a fierce determination within her to prove her worth to Kath. She picked up the wooden handle of the butter maker and began once again to turn.

Annie stared up at the ceiling, watching the shadows from the flickering candle stub dance across the wooden beams. The straw-filled mattress and warm woollen blankets comforted her numb body. She was so exhausted it had been an effort to get washed and undressed. Georgie lay nestled beside her, deep in sleep. She was used to work but not on this scale and had reservations as to whether Archie had any idea of how hard Kath pushed her.

She managed a smile. She had showed Kath. Oh, how she had showed her! All the tasks set had been done quickly and well. Annie had retired to bed with pride intact and her aunt quite speechless. What did the morning hold? she wondered. Archie had mentioned showing her how to milk the cows and that thought filled her with dread.

To Georgie, his time on the farm had been like a holiday. Archie had taken him for the day and filled his mind with the beauty of the countryside. He had returned exhausted, eaten his dinner and gone straight to bed.

Not even a brief introduction to surly, spoilt seven-year-old Lucy had blotted his day. The girl had sat silently at the table, eyeing him maliciously from under her lashes. Annie had watched her and known Georgie was in for a rough time ahead. But he would handle her. He would have to, like she would Kath, if they were to stay.

Still at least they had a roof over their heads, and at the moment they had to be thankful for that. She had been pleasantly surprised by the room over the barn. Her imagination had conjured up all sorts of monstrosities, but to her delight it was in a far better condition now that it had been cleaned up than her own cottage. The approach to the room was dicy; the ladder badly needed mending and she must speak to Archie about getting it fixed, but apart from that the room was very habitable. There were even a few old pieces of furniture, all covered with dust and cobwebs, but once she had set about cleaning them, along with the floor and tiny window, the place had quite a homely feel to it. Somehow she felt at peace here, it had no alien feeling to it, and this most of all surprised her.

She felt her eyelids droop. Raising herself slightly, she blew out the candle, settled down and was soon fast asleep.

They had been at the farm for nearly three weeks when one morning Georgie trotted across the yard towards the kitchen door in order to get his breakfast. He had finished feeding the chickens, making sure his favourite, a little brown hen called Jenny, had got more than her share. Now he was feeling very hungry. As he approached the back door it burst open to reveal Lucy. She folded her arms, eyed him haughtily and let a slow smile spread across her face.

'Me mother says I ain't to talk to the likes of you and that woman. She said you've both come here scrounging.' She paused for a second and looked at him in utter disgust. 'Have you?'

Georgie looked at her blankly, not understanding her question. He made to push past her and she stopped him.

'I asked you a question and I want an answer. Have you come scrounging?'

'I don't know what you mean,' he answered slowly.

'Oh, a halfwit. My mother said you were thick and she's right,' Lucy laughed mockingly. 'Good job you ain't gonna be allowed to go to school. You'd be the laughing stock.'

'I would not,' he snapped. 'I bet I know more than you, and I *will* be going to school . . .'

'You won't,' Lucy cut in. 'Me mam says you won't be here long enough.'

'What d'you mean?'

'I mean, you'll be off soon. Won't be able to stand the work.' She leant back against the doorframe and crossed her ankles. 'I think you should go back to where you came from, and good riddance.'

Georgie stared hard at her, a look of utter distaste crossing his face. She certainly was a nasty piece of work. His stomach rumbled. Breakfast called, and if he didn't get a move on his Auntie Kath would clear everything away and he wouldn't get any. Lucy could wait until later. That would give him more time to think up some equally nasty replies.

He made to push past her again. Lucy stuck out her leg and tripped him over; he fell hard on the concrete step, badly catching his right knee, and let out a yell. Tears of pain and anger sprang to his eyes. Before he could rise the door was yanked wide open and Kath stood glaring at him, sprawled upon the floor, her eyes ablaze in fury.

'What the hell's going on? Get up, you stupid boy,' she hissed.

'It were him, Mam, he tried to push me over but I fought him and he went over instead. He said I looked like a tart. He's jealous, Mam, 'cos I've got nice clothes and he looks like a tramp. Honest, Mam.'

Kath turned purple with rage. 'He said what? Right, you little devil.' She grabbed hold of Georgie by the scruff of his neck and hauled him into the kitchen. 'Get yourself off to school, our Lucy. I'll deal with this little ruffian.'

Lucy picked up her school bag and skipped down the yard, a broad smile etched across her face.

Kath grabbed Georgie by the shoulders and shook him hard.

'Don't you go near my daughter again. You're not fit to be in her presence,' she spat. 'If I ever catch you as much as in shouting distance of her, I'll have yer legs from under yer. Am I making myself clear?'

She swung back her arm and whacked him straight across his head.

Georgie let out a shrill scream.

'Now get out. And for that you'll have no breakfast. Go and get your work done, and woe betide you if it ain't done properly.'

He bolted out of the door, running as fast as his little legs would carry him. He burst into the barn and flung himself down on the straw. Several minutes later he sat up and rubbed the side of his smarting face and examined his bleeding knee. As well as the cuts a big lump had come up and a bruise which was turning black. Worried in case his mother would hear him, he stifled his sobs as best he could, burying his head in the newly laid straw. He was too late. His mother had heard the commotion and came flying into the barn to find out what had happened.

Kath in the meantime was singing as she went about her tasks. She turned in surprise as the kitchen door flew open and Annie charged in.

'What have you done to my son?' she demanded, shaking with anger. She laid her hands flat on the table and glared over at Kath. 'I said, what have you done?'

Kath banged down the saucepan she was holding. 'What have I done to your son?' she queried, raising her head defiantly. 'It's what your son did to my daughter. He got what he deserved!'

'That's not what he says.'

'I don't care *what* he says. He's a little liar. I'm telling you, he attacked my daughter so I punished him.'

'My son is no liar,' Annie shouted. 'He did not attack your daughter.' She lowered her voice to a menacing whisper. 'And if you ever lay a finger on him again, you'll have *me* to deal with.'

Kath stifled a laugh. 'You! Don't make me laugh. I ain't scared a' you.'

'Well, you should be. Where my son is concerned, I'd kill if necessary.'

'Are you threatening me?'

'Take it any way you like, Kath. But if you ever lay another finger on my son . . . Well, just be warned.'

Kath's mouth dropped open. She snapped it shut and set it grimly. 'I think you'd both better leave.'

Annie's back stiffened. 'Oh, no. I ain't leaving, Kath. This is my uncle's farm and he says we're welcome to stop as long as we like. You've no complaints about my work, I've made sure on that score. I do the work of three people and you know it.' Annie eyed her up and down. 'Just what is it you're afraid of?'

'Afraid of?' Kath's eyes opened wide. 'I ain't afraid of nothing. It just ain't working out between us, that's all.'

'And whose fault's that? Certainly not mine. I've bent over backwards to accommodate you, and in return you've been nasty and spiteful. Well, carry on,' Annie said nonchalantly. 'Your attitude doesn't bother me in the slightest. But leave my son alone. And while we're at it, tell that daughter of yours too. 'Cos my patience has been pushed to the limit.'

Kath turned red with anger. 'Now you listen here, I'm the mistress in this house. How dare you speak to me like this?'

'Nobody's questioning your position. Just your attitude. I know what work I have to do, so I'll keep out of your way as much as possible. In future Georgie and me will take our meals in our room. I'm sure that'll make things easier for you. And another thing, while we're at it—'

'Oh!' Kath uttered.

'I ain't cleaning out the pigs.'

'Oh, ain't yer?'

'No, I ain't. I'm willing to milk the cows when Archie shows me, make the butter and everything else, but I ain't cleaning out the pigs.'

'You'll do what I say . . .'

'Not everything, Kath. Reggie's looked after the pigs since he was a nipper. He enjoys it, loves those pigs, and you know it. It quite upset him when you handed the job over to me.' She narrowed her eyes. 'For whatever reason.'

'And what d'you mean by that remark?'

'Exactly what I said. You're no fool, Kath. Everything you do has a reason behind it.' Annie took a deep breath. 'Don't underestimate me. Just 'cos I come from the town don't mean to say I ain't got a brain. It didn't take me long to work you out. You've been against me from the minute we arrived and have done your damndest to get us to leave. Well, it won't

102

work, Kath. I like it here, despite everything. The air's good for my son and I'm with my family.'

'Family! I've only your word on that.'

'And I've already told you, it's the truth.' Annie sighed deeply. 'Look, Kath. This is getting us nowhere. I'm willing to start again if you are. We could be good friends . . .'

'Friends?' She stared icily at Annie and narrowed her eyes. 'Listen, gel, I know what your game is. You want to take over and push me out. Well, it won't work. My hard work and pushing Archie built up this farm. It was losing money when I married him and I ain't having no upstart coming here and taking over.'

'Taking over?' Annie stared questioningly at Kath. 'What makes you say that? I don't know the first thing about farming so how the hell can I take over? I'm only here to work, for a roof over our heads and food. Nothing more. I've been through a very bad time and at the moment this place seems like paradise.' She placed her hands on the back of a chair. 'I hate to say this, but in a way I admire you and what you've achieved. Archie's a lovely man, kind and considerate, and he thinks the world of you. But he's hard work, I can see that. I also know you need staff. The women in the village refuse to work for you. To be honest, I'm surprised Molly is still here, the way you treat her.'

She let go of the chair and walked around the table to stand inches away. 'Let's face it, you need me, Kath, and you'd better get used to the idea that I'm staying until I decide what's best for me and my son. Now, I'm willing to forget all about this and start again. If you're not, then that's up to you. But in the meantime, I'd be obliged if you would give my son his breakfast. And, please remember, he's a little boy and doesn't deserve your treatment of him.' She turned on her heel and headed for the door. 'I'll send him over, and collect our dinners when it's time.'

She walked out of the door, closed it behind her and headed for the barn where she instructed Georgie to go and get his breakfast. She then walked into the dairy, let out a long sigh and rested her back against the whitewashed wall. She placed her head in her hands and rubbed her eyes. Had she really just confronted Kath? She felt elated. It had taken more nerve than her bullying aunt would ever know. Oh, I hope things are easier from now on, she thought longingly. She rubbed her hands together and proceeded with her work.

Kath stared for an age at the closed back door. She pulled a chair out from under the table and sat down. She smiled. Despite herself she found that she was beginning to like Annie. In other circumstances they could have been friends. Between them they could have scaled new heights. But that was not to be. She could not forget who Annie was, and despite warming towards her, could not let that get in the way of her plans. She narrowed her eyes, stood up and took several deep breaths. She grabbed the large blackened pan and started to slap large spoonfuls of porridge into a bowl for Georgie's breakfast.

The days stretched into weeks, each one filled with work and little sleep. It seemed that Kath could not bear to see anyone idle and Annie now had a rota of tasks that had to be completed daily, and done perfectly, or she would suffer her wrath. It saddened Annie to think that their long talk had made little impression. Kath was still surly and off hand and would snap and snarl at the least little thing.

Annie had managed to get herself into a routine: each job had its set time and if she managed to get it done quicker, she would find a hidden spot and have a few quiet minutes to herself.

Archie had taught her to milk the cows. It had been a long painful process and she had hated every minute of it. Touching the cows' udders had disgusted her and she had recoiled in horror. Daisy had retaliated when she had pulled too hard on her teats and the bucket of milk that had taken so long for her to acquire went flying, along with Annie who had both a bruised backside and hurt pride. They had managed to clear up the mess double quick. How Archie managed to cover up the loss of milk Annie never did find out and she never asked.

Georgie had been taken under Archie's wing. Annie was grateful for this and her son seemed to be adjusting to the life very well. Surprisingly enough he was also getting on well with Reggie and the old man had taken to letting him round up the cows with him for their evening milking.

Georgie had come bounding into the barn one morning, proudly bragging of his new friend Frederick.

'Who's Frederick?' Annie asked.

'Oh, Frederick's a cow,' he answered proudly. 'I've been talking to him. He's a boy cow, Mam. He's in the field at the back.'

'Oh,' laughed Annie. 'he's a bullock then.' She felt pleased that with her limited knowledge she at least knew the difference between the sexes of the beasts.

'A what?' Georgie said, perplexed. 'Oh, no, he's a cow, only he ain't got rudders, like the ones you get milk from, and he's got little horns growing out of his head. I'm going to let Molly meet him.' He flung his arms around his mother and hugged her tightly. 'Got to go, Mam, got to get some water for Auntie Kath.' He looked at his mother and pulled a face. 'She's in a tizzy again. Molly dropped the porridge pan all over the floor this morning, and you should have heard her.'

He bounded out and Annie continued her work, her shoulders shaking with laughter.

Apart from Frederick, Georgie had made two other friends. Scrap the Collie dog followed him everywhere when he was not out herding the cows and Georgie loved it. The other friend was Molly the kitchen help. Annie felt sorry for the young girl. Kath kept her on the go continuously. Whenever they bumped into each other Molly's pretty face would light up and she would give Annie a broad smile. Apart from those times, she would scurry about her work with her head low.

The farm was much bigger than Annie had at first thought. As well as the dairy herd, they kept pigs, chickens,

105

ducks and geese, and also grew potatoes and other vegetables which they sold at the stalls in Market Bosworth. Travellers were taken on during harvest time and also helped to mend fences and with general repairs before the onset of winter. At the back of the house was a small orchard that was filled with apple, plum, greengage and pear trees. Tiny fruits were beginning to form and Georgie's eager eyes monitored their progress in readiness to get his share before the fruit was harvested and bottled for the winter.

Their nearest neighbouring farm was run by a bachelor. It was just a smallholding and he had come home from sea after his parents had died to take over the reins. According to Reggie he was a charmer, rather fond of the ladies and very friendly with Kath. Reggie loved to scandalmonger and Annie decided to take no notice of his gossip, remembering from old days in the courtyard that gossip caused nothing but trouble. She preferred to find out matters for herself.

The farm was sandwiched between the two villages of Desford and Ratby, the latter being closest. Nearby was a large estate, and the squire and his family could sometimes be seen out riding or driving in their carriages. Annie bombarded Archie with questions on life in the country. The information she gathered was then passed on to Georgie who was fascinated by it all.

She was en route to Archie one fine morning when the sounds of horns blowing, dogs barking and horses thundering past frightened her rigid. When Archie explained, she was horrified. How on earth could grown men hunt and kill poor defenceless foxes in such a way? He laughed and patted her affectionately on the arm. It was sport, he had told her, and if she was to become countryfied she had better get used to sights like that.

She had a lot to get used to, she knew that, and if they were to stay, it was her that would have to conform to country life, not the other way around. The countryside was doing them both good, helping to heal the open wound of Charlie's death. She thought of him often and hoped he would be pleased at the way she had managed without him. Her longing for him had not lessened, but by throwing herself into her work she found she was able to cope better with her loss. She knew without a doubt that he would have been proud of her and his son, and felt comforted by this.

One fine Sunday afternoon Annie decided that it would be good to pay a visit to Matty. Previous Sundays had gone past and she had made do with just a walk around the surrounding countryside but now she felt able to venture further. She had often thought of the older woman and it would be good to see her and tell her how they were faring.

She washed and brushed their hair, made them both as presentable as possible and set off. As she closed the farm gate behind them she felt a sense of freedom envelop her. Six free hours that were all hers and Georgie's! She wanted to celebrate by taking off her boots and running barefoot through the grass, screaming and yelling in delight.

As they entered the village of Ratby, they stopped and gazed around. Several factory chimneys rose high above the old terraced houses from factories that produced socks and knitwear and kept many of the village residents in work. The slaughter house situated further along Main Street was alive with the sound of beasts awaiting their grisly end. Annie shuddered and turned her attention to the several shops that lined the street, which included a blacksmith's. Annie knew from what Archie had told her that the village dated back to before Roman times and was steeped in history. There were also five local pubs and several other farms located in the vicinity. The people of Ratby were noted for their friendliness. She could tell this by the number of people passing who acknowledged her presence with a smile and a good afternoon.

They walked slowly across the road to look in the grocer's window. She was amazed at how well stocked it was, comparing very favourably with Leicester's shops. As they scrutinised the goods on sale the grocer came out of the door with a bucket and cloth in his hands and greeted her with a friendly smile.

'No rest even on a Sunday.' He started to wash the large shop window. Then stopped what he was doing and turned to face her and Georgie. 'You're new round these parts, ain't yer?'

'Yes,' Annie answered warmly. 'From Meadowfield Farm.'

'Ah.' The grocer nodded his head. 'I had heard there was a young woman and a boy there now. I also heard you're the longlost grand-daughter. That right?'

'Yes, that's right. Well, nice to speak to you.' Annie grabbed Georgie's hand and prepared to leave.

'Besta luck, gel. You'll need it with Kath. Know her well, I do. You'll need yer wits about yer to handle her.'

'Thanks for the advice. Well, we must be on our way.'

'Tarra, me duck.' The grocer stared after them shaking his head as he watched them walk down the street. He tutted loudly as he turned and continued his task.

Matty was delighted to see them. She was still having great difficulty getting out and about and welcomed the company. She apologised for the state of the little house, complaining laughingly that her lads would never make skivvies, although her future daughter-in-law had been helping whenever possible. Georgie was shooed outside to play with the children next-door and on Matty's instructions, Annie made a large pot of tea, cut several slices from a large home-made fruit cake, and both women settled down for a good chin wag.

Annie told Matty all the happenings at the farm and also about her disappointment at not yet having met her grand-mother.

Matty tutted. 'I know the old lady's ill, but even if she is at death's door, it wouldn't do her any harm to see you and the lad. My, some folks are funny. Pour us another cuppa, gel.' She inclined her head towards the enormous brown teapot. 'You know, it makes you wonder . . . Oh, eh, it makes you wonder,' she said, ruefully shaking her head.

'What makes you wonder, Matty?'

She was silent for a moment then took a deep breath. 'I'm going to tell you something, Annie. Rightly or wrongly, I think you should know.' She pulled herself further up on the chair and took a gulp of tea. 'Years ago,' she began, 'Archie and me were engaged.' She paused and watched the look of astonishment pass over Annie's face. 'Life's full of surprises, ain't it? Anyway, I'd grown up with the family and I'd always had a soft spot for him.' Her eyes softened. 'He were a lovely man, Annie. Kind, considerate . . . needed a good push now and then, but we were very happy. We'd been engaged for years and I'd just about talked him into walking up the aisle when *she* – Kath – comes on the scene. He met her at the local fair. I was sick that day and told him to go on his own. Seemed a shame for him to miss it just because of me.'

'That was bad luck,' Annie said ruefully.

'You needn't tell me!' Matty shrugged her shoulders. 'If I'd been a fortune teller I'd have gone to the fair, ill or not. Still, it was too late, she'd got her claws into him and he were smitten. Mind you, if I say it meself, she was young and pretty – and me like the back end of a cow.'

'Oh, Matty, that's not true.'

'Yes, it is, Annie. Come on now. I'm nothing special and I've never pretended to be. Anyway, I could see what she was after. She wanted to be mistress of the farm and she went hell for leather for him. He was like a lamb to the slaughter and never stood a chance.' She paused, looked at Annie and sighed. 'I still feel for him, you know,' she said sadly. 'I suppose you could say I married me husband on the rebound, but I think that would be a slur to his memory 'cos we had a good life, although I never did quite get Archie out me system.'

'Oh, Matty, I'm sorry,' Annie said with feeling. 'I'm sure you'd have made a lovely farmer's wife.'

'Yeah, I know. Still, never mind, that's all in the past. I used to see your grandmother quite often. She'd come down here of an afternoon and give me all the gossip about the goings on at the farm. But since she got housebound I ain't been able to see her. For obvious reason I can't go to the farm meself.'

Annie nodded.

'She never got over your mother's disappearance and kept saying that Kath knew something about it.'

'Did she?'

'Yeah. Quite definite about it, she was. I'm sure it was all instinct, mind. I don't think for a minute she had any proof or she'd have done something about it.' She paused thoughtfully for a moment. 'Well, actually, come to think on it, she *did* do something.'

'She did? What?'

'She made her will. Though God knows what's in it. But she was certainly pleased with herself. She made the journey into Leicester and dropped in on her way home. "I've made me will," she said. "That'll put paid to her little schemes."'

'Did she say anything else?' Annie asked keenly.

'No. Just that. And I didn't feel it was my place to pry. After all, a will is kinda personal, ain't it?'

Annie nodded in agreement.

Matty drained her mug and slapped it down on the table. 'Still, as I said before, all this is in the past. But I just had to tell you why I'm so interested in what happens up there.'

'Yes,' Annie said slowly. 'You must feel cheated somehow.'

'Cheated?'

'Yes, you should be up at the farm, not Kath.'

'Ah, well. Maybe I should be. But it's all fate, Annie. It's all written in the cards, and there ain't much I can do about it now.'

They chatted on. Matty was beside herself when she found out that Annie and her son were not allowed to sleep in the house.

'Why?' she exclaimed. 'There's plenty of room in that house. What on earth is she playing at? And I don't think much of Archie for letting her get away with it.'

'Oh, it's no bother to me,' Annie cut in. 'We have the room

110

over the barn and I feel very safe and happy there. I've made it really homely, Matty. It's a pity you can't come and visit us.'

She laughed. 'Well, I never. The room over the barn, you say? Me and your mother used that room as our den.'

'Did you?' Annie exclaimed. 'Then that's why I feel so comfortable in it.'

Matty smiled. 'Mary Ann had it all furnished, you know. Your grandmother was left some furniture by an old auntie that'd died and your mother wangled it out of her. Some good stuff, I'll tell yer. Mind you, we were too young to appreciate that. Fancy you having to sleep up there.' She scratched her chin thoughtfully. 'Mary Ann had a hidey-hole up there somewhere. She used to hide her precious things so no one would see them. 'Specially Kath.' She narrowed her eyes. 'Your mother never liked her either. They never saw eye to eye.'

'Do you know where the hidey-hole is, Matty?' Annie asked excitedly.

'No. Sorry, me duck,' she answered, shaking her head. 'She never showed even me and I was her closest friend. Bet you could find it though,' she said, clasping her hands together. 'Your mother was quite clever. It will be somewhere simple but clever like, if you see what I mean. Oh, do try and find it. There might be something still hidden.'

'I'll look, and if I find anything, you'll be the first to know.'

They chatted for a while longer until it was time for Annie to leave. Matty made her promise to come back soon and after summoning Georgie, they made their way back.

Georgie was excited after playing with the children next door.

'I showed 'em how to make a cart and we're going to play on it the next time I come down.'

They had just turned into Desford Lane when a horse and rider came into view. Annie pulled Georgie into the side. The rider was middle-aged and very smartly dressed. She bowed her head as he passed but could not help noticing the shock of red hair that protruded beneath his hat: the same colour as Georgie's.

'That's the "squeer" from the big house at Kirkby Mallory. He's got two sons and a daughter and lots and lots of servants,' Georgie piped up unexpectedly.

'How do you know that?' she asked.

'Uncle Archie told me. The "squeer" rode by on his big grey horse one day when we were in the fields. He stopped and asked Uncle Archie how the farm was doing, and said hello to me.'

Annie stared after the man as he rode away into the distance. She grabbed Georgie's hand and they continued their journey. As they entered the farm gates a weight settled itself once more on her shoulders. The carefree mood had passed.

Chapter Eight

Archie tiptoed into the bedroom and peered hesitantly at his wife. He stood for a moment and wiped his hand backwards and forwards across his forehead. She was pretending to be asleep yet again. He saw her eyelids flickering in the candlelight. Kath was a bonny woman. He felt a great need rush over him but knew it was no good feeling like that. He breathed deeply. Kath had never enjoyed the physical side of their marriage. Their lovemaking had always been very infrequent and as the years had gone by it had grown less and less.

It still amazed him how their Lucy had come about. It was a miracle. He shook his head. Yes, miracle was the word. He would have given anything to feel Kath's arms encircle his tired body and warm towards his touch. He started to get undressed. Kath really did seem to suffer every month. He felt sorry for women, the torture and pain they went through. She seemed to have a lot of monthlies. In fact, it seemed like every week to him. I'm just too soft, he thought, 'specially where she's concerned.

He folded his clothes on the back of the chair. I just wish she looked at me the way she does at John Matthews, he thought longingly. Then shrugged his shoulders. Kath and John were around the same age and had things in common. It did no harm. After all, John had no wife to flap over him and Kath was always in a good mood after one of his visits which meant that life was easier for them all for a while. He half smiled as an idea came to mind. Annie and John would make a lovely couple. He'd speak to Kath about introducing them. He stood for a moment in thought. Maybe it was a bit too soon after Charlie's death? He nodded. Better let nature take its own course. If the pair were meant to get together they would, without him playing Cupid.

He pulled the cover back on his side of the bed and climbed inside. He accidentally touched Kath's leg and humiliation washed through him as he sensed her flinch and move further over her side. Her nearness caused the hot feeling to run through his body again. He desperately tried to stem it but his heart was heavy with longing for her. He turned over, and surprisingly, fell into a deep sleep.

In the room over the barn Annie tossed and turned in her bed. The night was hot and airless, and although she was extremely tired, sleep's magic relief from the real world would not come. Her own restlessness worried her. She didn't want to wake Georgie, snoring peacefully beside her. Finally, in desperation, she decided to go for a walk. Maybe that would do the trick.

She made her way down to the farm gate, opened a gap wide enough to inch herself through and ambled slowly along the thick hedging boundary that separated the farmyard from the fields. Several yards on she came to a small hole in the hedging, in the middle of which sat a large flat stone on a small raised mound of earth. Without thinking, she stepped into the hole and tested the stone. It wobbled slightly but seemed safe enough to accommodate her light weight. She sat down and made herself comfortable. She felt safe here, hidden from view, surrounded by peace and tranquillity, with the soft warm night air enveloping her body.

Suddenly, she stiffened in fright as the sound of whispered voices startled her. Who on earth can that be at this time of night? she wondered worriedly. Was it travellers or even thieves or vagabonds on the prowl? She pulled her shawl closer round her nightdress and peeped hesitantly through the leaves. She frowned as she made out the shapes of two people walking towards her. They were about ten yards away and one was definitely a man. The other she could not see clearly enough to identify. They suddenly stopped and leaned against the gate, turning towards each other to embrace. Annie inwardly groaned. These two were definitely lovers and she felt embarrassment steal over her at being a witness to their courtship. She slunk as far back into the bushes as she could and hoped they wouldn't discover her.

She stiffened as she heard their footsteps very slowly advance towards her. Her heart thumped noisily against her chest.

The footsteps stopped several feet away.

'No, I couldn't get up before now,' she heard the man say abruptly. 'I don't sit around waiting for your summons.' The voice faltered for a moment and Annie heard the scrape of shoe leather against a stone. 'You shouldn't listen to gossip.' There was another pause. 'Don't look at me like that, my gel, you could kill a bloke with one of your looks. Anyway, I'm free, ain't I? And if I don't put up a show for the locals they'd begin to think I was a nancy boy.

'Look, gel, you know how I feel about yer. The other women . . . well, they're just for appearances. How many times do I have to tell yer?'

Annie frowned, curiosity getting the better of her. Just who were these two people? And, for that matter, what right did they have to come and do their courting up at the farm? She grimaced thoughtfully. One of them must be married or the conversation didn't make sense.

The rest of it was to be denied her as they walked away, heading once more for the gate. Annie felt annoyed, she wanted to hear more.

She shivered. She was desperately tired now . . .

She woke with a sudden start and it took her several moments to realise where she was. The farmyard was deathly quiet. Carefully she stuck her nose out of her hiding place and sighed with relief. The couple, whoever they were, had gone. She eased herself up, stretched, and quietly made her way back to the loft where she fell into a deep sleep.

115

Archie felt that it was about time Annie and Georgie were allowed to come to market. They had been at the farm for over three months and a treat was well overdue. Despite being his niece, Annie was a hard worker, worth two of any of the other women they had had to help at the farm. He had grown very fond of her and Georgie and couldn't imagine life without them. He found he could relax with his niece. She would listen attentively, adding a comment here or there, but never belittling him like – he hated to admit – his wife did.

He hesitantly approached Kath with the idea and as expected she was not at all keen on the outing. She threw several excuses at him and only very reluctantly relented when she saw Archie was not to be moved. She declined to go herself. She had things to do, even if other folks hadn't.

Georgie jumped about in glee and screamed in delight when his uncle gave him a silver threepenny bit to spend. Oh, if only Molly could come! What fun they would have, running in and out of the stalls and choosing what to spend his money on. But he knew better than to mention the fact in case his Auntie Kath put a stop to the treat after all.

So, early on a fine Saturday morning, perched on top of the dray cart with the dairy produce secured firmly in the back, the three started their journey to Market Bosworth, a quaint market town several miles away.

It was bursting at the seams. Carts arrived one after the other, loaded with wares, and the air was filled with the traders' shouts and banter for customers. Georgie's eyes opened wider and wider as he clutched his mother's skirt in excitement. He couldn't wait to explore the stalls. They helped Archie unload the cart and he proudly introduced Annie to Tommy, a portly, jolly little man in his late-fifties. He and Archie had been dealing together for years and were firm friends.

'Morning, Tommy. How's things?'

'Can't grumble, Archie.' He looked towards Annie and

grinned. 'So this is the young lady who's put a smile on me old friend's face?' He held out his hand to her. 'Pleased to meet yer, I'm sure. I'm Tommy. If we wait for your uncle to introduce us the butter will have turned to cheese.'

Annie smiled warmly and accepted his proffered hand.

'I'm not surprised he's kept you hidden away. My, but you're a bonny gel, all right.'

Archie laughed. 'Don't mind him, Annie. He's like this with all the women. That's why his stall's so popular.'

Tommy ignored his friend's quip. 'If you get fed up at the farm, Annie, you can come and help me. We'd make a good team. I'd have the men as well as the women flocking round . . .'

'Leave her be, Tommy. Look, you've made her blush now.' Archie slapped him on the shoulder. 'These two are going shopping, and I'll meet you as usual in the pub around twelve. Okay, Tom?'

'Fine by me. See you again, Annie.' He turned and proceeded to serve his customers as the other three picked their way past the stalls.

Archie stopped. 'I'll see you in a couple of hours then, love. I've a few errands to do before my appointment with Tommy.'

'Yes, Uncle Archie. I'm looking forward to this.'

They parted company and she made her way after Georgie. She stopped for a moment and breathed deeply, savouring the atmosphere. Oh, this was like being back home in Leicester on a smaller scale. The surroundings conjured up memories of her home town and the many happy hours she had spent browsing around the market stalls there. She raised her head as a surge of pleasure shot through her. She was going to enjoy this morning.

She found Georgie gazing longingly at a colourful display of haberdashery laid out on a stall. She laughed as he gaily skipped off between the people, stopping here and there to examine something that had caught his eye. His money was burning a hole in his pocket and he wanted to spend it. He finally chose two pieces of brightly coloured ribbon which he carefully put away for safekeeping. They were for Molly and he could not wait to see her face when he gave them to her.

Annie, meanwhile, scoured the second-hand stalls and triumphantly found a good coat for herself and several items for Georgie that she could alter for the winter. She handed over two shillings of her hard earned wages and gladly accepted her brown paper parcels.

Georgie stood perplexed. He still had a penny left and didn't know what to buy. Suddenly his little face lit up in pleasure and he made a dash, returning with a hot pie for each of them. Annie was thrilled at his thoughtfulness. Her son had been given money and not one penny had he spent on himself. Feeling honoured, she sat with him on a wooden bench as they revelled in the good humour of the people and the tastiness of the pies.

All too soon it was time to return to the cart for the journey home and they both walked jauntily back, laughing and joking together at the day's happenings. She spotted her uncle's head through the crowds and Georgie ran to meet him.

Archie bent down and ruffled his hair. 'Well, lad, show me what you bought.' He smiled warmly as Georgie showed him his gift for Molly. 'That's a nice thought, lad, a very nice thought.' He acknowledged Annie as she arrived. 'Enjoy yourself then?'

'Oh, yes, thanks,' she breathed ecstatically. 'I had a wonderful time.'

'Good.' He placed his arm around her shoulder and pulled her forward. 'This is our neighbour, John Matthews, Annie. He owns the farm next to ours.'

She raised her head and found herself looking into the piercing blue eyes of one of the most handsome men she had ever met.

'I was just telling John about yer. He was hoping you'd come back before he left so he could say hello.'

Annie managed a smile and shuddered as his blue eyes stared penetratingly into hers. She accepted John's hand. He shook hers firmly.

118

'Glad we've met at last,' he said huskily. 'I've been hearing about you.'

'Oh!' she gasped at his touch.

'Nothing bad,' he said, laughing. 'Seems most of the village men are talking of the pretty woman who's moved into the farm, and I can see for myself that it wasn't idle chatter for once.'

'Now, John,' Archie said sternly, 'less of that. We don't want her embarrassed.'

John turned his attention to him. 'Only speaking the truth, Archie. I'm sure Annie's used to compliments.'

She dropped her head and studied the cobbles beneath her feet. There was something about this man she couldn't fathom ... She felt uneasy, alarmed even, and there was something behind those intense blue eyes that she didn't like. She could feel him staring at her and against her wishes felt her gaze being magnetically drawn back to his. To her immense relief she heard her uncle speak.

'Well, we must be going. We'll see you soon, I trust?'

'Definitely,' John replied, giving Annie a smouldering glance. 'I'll be up to the farm shortly and hope to see you there.'

Annie smiled briefly, hitched up her parcels, grabbed Georgie's hand and walked away. Archie quickly caught up with her.

'You all right?' he asked in concern.

She stopped abruptly and stared at him. 'Yes, fine, Why?'

He stared quizzically at her and shrugged his shoulders. 'Oh, nothing, but you seem in an awful hurry to get away.'

She sat in silence, unaware of Georgie's constant chatter as the cart pulled off and headed out of the town, desperately fighting to steer her thoughts away from John Matthews. Her first alarming thoughts had been dispelled. All she could see was his handsome face, the way his dark hair curled round his ears, the strong jawline, and those eyes ... Oh, those magnetic blue eyes! A wave of disgust flowed over her. Disgust for the way she was feeling for a man she hardly

119

knew, and so soon after her beloved husband's death. Had she no morals, no shame? She was pulled back to reality by a dig in the ribs from Archie.

'What's the matter with you, gel? That's the third time I've spoken.'

'What? Oh, I'm sorry, Uncle Archie. I . . . I was just thinking what a wonderful day it's been, and I must thank you for taking us.'

'Been my pleasure,' he said warmly. 'It's been grand having your company. What did you think of our neighbour then? He's a decent sort of bloke, but needs looking after. Not married, you see.' He turned his head and grinned at her.

'Mmm,' she agreed softly. 'He did seem like a nice man.'

'Don't understand why he's not married meself. Whoa, Neddy!' Archie shouted. 'Bloody holes in this road get bigger.' He regained control of the horse. 'Got a string of women after him, you know, but he's never taken the plunge. Gets on well with our Kath. They're about the same age and I suppose have things in common, whereas I . . .' He paused, turned and saw that Annie's mouth had dropped open.

'You mean he's in his forties?' she asked.

'Must be,' Archie replied matter-of-factly. 'Let me think. Our Kath's forty-two and our Mary Ann would have been . . .' he paused, 'forty-one or two. Yes, that's right. He's about forty-three. It must have been all the sea air.'

'It must have been,' she said. 'I'd never have put him as old as that.'

'Hey, watch it,' laughed her uncle. 'I'm nearly sixty.'

'I didn't mean . . .'

'I know,' he said, giving her a friendly wink. He turned his attention back to the road. 'Our Kath's quite motherly towards him. She sends young Molly down with pies and bread.' He laughed and shook his head. 'She doesn't think I know about it. But I don't suppose it does any harm being neighbourly, do you?'

'No.'

'He comes up to visit now and again, and is always willing to give a hand if we need him.'

'Archie,' she said, bemused, 'you're not trying to match-make, are you?'

'Was I?' he said innocently. 'Well, you could do a lot worse.' He nudged her arm and lowered his voice. 'That lad of yours will need a man's hand now and again as he gets older. Not that anybody could take the place of Charlie,' he added hastily, 'but I'd just like to see you happy, gel, that's all.' He smiled at her. 'And you'd still be close by. I couldn't bear to lose sight of yer now.'

'I know, Uncle Archie. I feel the same. But I'm not ready for any romance yet.'

Life at the farm had settled into a routine and both Annie and Georgie felt they had been there for years. Annie was surprised at how much she was enjoying the life and Georgie was certainly blossoming. He had a healthy tan and appetite, and loved nothing more than getting in amongst the animals.

About once a month they would both accompany Archie to market. They looked forward to these trips and Georgie would always bring Molly back a present. Her delight in receiving the ribbons was something that he never tired of and the pair were becoming close friends. Annie had managed to find a few odds and ends from the second-hand stalls to enhance their room. It felt like home now and her one place of sanctuary, where she could sew or read without the watchful eyes of Kath boring into her.

Lucy became the bane of Georgie's life. The girl would plan and scheme countless ways of getting him into trouble with her mother. She was very clever, though, always waiting until no one was around before carrying out her dirty deeds. The things he was blamed for were endless and to him it seemed he was always in trouble, with not a clue as to what he was supposed to have done. Lucy would giggle herself to sleep, and Annie worried herself sick in case Georgie really was responsible. But she had noted, and with anger, that whenever anything happened, nobody else was around to witness it. Annie had no choice other than to appear to punish him. But unbeknown to Kath, she neither spanked nor starved him. Had her aunt known, all hell would have let loose.

The atmosphere between the two women was still strained but tolerable, and Kath, much to her own annoyance, was getting used to having Annie around. The interloper was more than proving her worth and she found it extremely difficult to pick fault with her work. She knew that Annie was becoming very settled and content and this unnerved her, as did her niece's singing and laughing. She desperately wanted to get rid of her but no appropriate excuse would come to mind. So, for the time being at least, life at the farm was pleasant and rewarding for at least some of its occupants.

About three weeks after the first trip to market, John Matthews paid an unexpected call on the farm and surprised Annie in the dairy. He stood on the threshold and watched as she, unaware of his presence, went about her work.

'Hello, Annie,' he said after a while.

She swung around, gave a sharp intake of breath and reddened.

'Hello, Mr Matthews,' she answered, swallowing hard.

He advanced further into the dairy. 'Oh, surely you can call me John? After all, we are neighbours.'

'John,' she said slowly.

He gave a crooked smile. 'That's better.' He ran his hand through his thick black hair. 'I came here today hoping to see you.'

'Oh!'

'I wondered if you'd care to take a walk with me one night?'

'Oh!' she uttered again in alarm. 'A walk?'

'Yes. You could tell me about life in the town.'

A feeling of apprehension raced through her as she stared for a moment up into his handsome features. He made a striking figure leaning against the doorframe. He was a man many women would be proud to walk alongside of. So why was it she felt uneasy in his presence? As though sensing her fears, he smiled warmly at her.

'You'll be safe with me, Annie. I don't bite, you know. A walk through Martinshaw Woods will do you good.'

'Yes, maybe it would. Only I'm far too busy at the moment. But thanks for the offer.'

'Come on, Annie. Kath surely doesn't work you that hard? She must give you some time off?'

'Well, yes, she does,' Annie answered sharply, feeling pressurised to agree to his offer. 'But I like to spend my spare time with my son.'

'Oh, I see.' His face dropped. 'You could bring him if you wanted to. Or is this a way of saying you have someone else?'

'No,' she said quickly. 'I'm just not used to being asked to go for a walk, that's all. At the moment I don't feel ready for it.' She lowered her gaze and her voice. 'Not so soon after Charlie's death.'

He sighed deeply. 'I apologise, Annie. My offer was thoughtless. Maybe some other time?'

'Yes.' She managed a smile. 'Another time.'

'Fine.' He turned to leave her. 'Any time you're passing by my farm, feel free to drop in.'

'I will, thank you.'

She watched, legs trembling, as John left the dairy. Then she lowered herself down on to a stool and breathed deeply. He certainly was a handsome man, and, as Reggie had said, very charming. Why hadn't anyone snapped him up before now? She absent-mindedly picked up a wooden butter pat and passed it from one hand to the other. Why did she feel so uneasy in his presence? Was it because she found him attractive and didn't like to admit the fact? He was getting to her. He was creeping under her skin and she felt helpless, knowing no way in which to stop it. The thought of spending time with him was pleasant, very pleasant indeed.

Surely though she shouldn't feel like this about another man, not so soon after Charlie's death? What was happening to her? Was she becoming a harlot? She mentally shook herself and gave herself a good scolding. The man was old enough to be her father, even though his stature and looks defied his age. He was just being friendly. There was no future for her with him so there was no point in even thinking there was. Work for you, gel. Hard work, that's the cure for ailments and fancy thinking, she chided herself.

She struggled to lift a heavy metal milk churn, tipping the contents into the large stone sink ready to begin the cheese making.

A warm sunny morning found Kath scattering the corn to the hens and she watched intently as they pushed and jostled each other to get their share of the corn mixture. Me bloody life would have been like them chickens, she thought ruefully, if I hadn't got that silly sod to marry me. She smiled to herself. Getting Archie to marry her had been the easy part. One of the easiest things she'd ever done. She shook her apron to be rid of the last of the corn, and sighed. Wish me other plan was as easy.

'Oh, God,' she groaned aloud. 'Why doesn't the old bugger just die, so this mess can be cleared up?' She quickly looked around, frightened in case someone had heard her, then breathed a sigh of relief. Watch it, gel, you're getting sloppy.

She grimaced. Things were getting messy, especially since Annie's arrival. Archie had taken a real shine to the girl and her son. It made things a lot more complicated. She wiped her hand across her brow. Annie was a nice kid. She'd got guts too. Couldn't have been easy for her to leave Leicester and dump herself on a family she didn't know.

And the way she stands up to me! Yes, it's a shame, I like her, but I can't let her see that . . .

Kath looked around her, taking in the farm buildings and the house, its windows glinting in the hot sun. She held her arms out wide. 'This is mine, mine! It's my work and ideas that's made it what it is, and I ain't giving it up.' She shook her head. The old lady was becoming really difficult, wanting to know why she wasn't allowed out of her bedroom, and then there was Annie, desperate to meet her grandmother. The excuses Kath made were getting thin on the ground and she knew the girl did not believe her.

I can't risk Annie meeting her, I just can't. That would really ruin things.

Kath scratched her ear and her eyes hardened. It would all be worth·it in the end. She had to control her patience, something she was running out of. All she had to do was hold on just a little longer. She walked towards the gate and banged it shut behind her, turning to watch the chickens flying over the pen.

Just like my life with my mother – scratting for a living. Well, I ain't going back to that again! No, never.

Kath looked round the farmyard. Annie had made a difference since she had been here. It was a pity she would have to go.

She decided to go for a walk and made her way down towards the farm gate. She leant on the top bar and looked across the fields. She spotted her husband in the distance and a feeling of revulsion swept through her. What a weakling he was! She had always hated weak men. She hated everything Archie stood for. His tall, thin frame, his feeble nature, his eagerness to please . . . he did everything she told him. Oh, what it would be like to have a good row now and again. She grinned maliciously. Archie didn't like harsh words, he'd go out of his way to keep the peace. She had never seen him get angry. He hadn't got it in him.

But that was Archie before Annie had arrived. Now he was different. He was beginning to stand his ground. She didn't like this, and his changing character worried her greatly.

His mother, now, she was different. She had me weighed up right from the start, thought Kath. But Archie was so in love with me there was nothing she could do. She frowned. The feeling of power she had felt before Annie's coming was ebbing quickly away. She felt panic rise in her stomach. Would she lose the grip she had on Archie as he got more fond of the girl? Annie was bright, there was no doubt about that.

She might start putting two and two together. Archie might even start listening to her. I'll have to be careful. I've planned long and hard and I'm not giving up now, Kath fulminated. She shook herself. Pull yourself together, gel, and stop being stupid. Nobody and nothing's going to get in the way. She smiled wryly. No, nobody and nothing. Not even Annie.

Harvest was soon upon them. Everyone was kept busy gathering the crops. Annie's afternoons were now spent entirely in the kitchen, helping to make pies, bread, and huge saucepans of stew for the tired workers. Fruit picking and preserving was yet to come and the days sped by in a continual round of work and sleep. Because Annie was now there, Kath did not bother to hire any more help for the kitchen. But to give Kath her due, she worked as hard as Annie herself did.

After a particularly hard morning, Annie left the spotless dairy to get a drink of water from the pump and was greeted by an agitated Kath.

'Ah, there you are. Listen, I have to go into the village, me mother's taken bad. There's plenty for you to do and I should be back before supper.' She spoke hurriedly whilst pulling on her cotton gloves.

Annie listened intently. This was the first she had heard of Kath's family.

'Mind you,' her aunt continued, 'why they can't manage themselves is beyond me. I've enough to do. Still, you only get one mother, don't you? And I don't want no one saying I don't do my bit.'

Annie flinched at this cutting remark, but managed a warm smile.

'I'm sorry to hear your news but I'll manage. Is there anything special I should know about my grandmother?'

'In what way?' Kath said icily.

'Well,' Annie shrugged her shoulders, 'her lunch and . . .'

'No need to bother yourself about that. Molly has her instructions.'

'Oh!'

126

'You just concentrate on yer own work. There's no need for you to go up to the house at all. I've put all the lunches in baskets and Molly will take them to the fields. So you get on out here, all right?'

'Okay,' Annie said slowly. 'I do hope your mother gets better soon.'

'So do I. I can't be doing with two invalids on me hands. One's enough.'

With that she flounced off. Annie stared after her, clenching her fists in anger. Kath was taking every precaution to make sure she never came in contact with her grandmother. She sank down on an upturned box outside the barn and put her head in her hands. So engrossed in her thoughts was she that she did not hear Molly approach.

'Annie, I'm just off up the fields.'

She raised her head. 'Sorry, love. What did you say?'

'I said, I'm just off up the fields with the lunches.'

'Oh, right. D'you need a hand?'

'No, I can manage, thanks. It'll make a nice change for me will this.' Molly smiled, lifted the heavy baskets and went on her way.

Annie watched her go, thinking what a nice girl she was. Given the chance and the right guidance she could have had a bright future. She sighed. Fate certainly had it in for some people. Molly would probably never know there was a life outside the village. She would more than likely marry a local lad, have a dozen kids and grow old before her time. A bit like Elsie. I wonder how she is? Annie thought. Pictures of the courtyard came to mind and she smiled wanly. It seemed such a long time ago that she had belonged to that life.

She rose and stretched, trying to motivate herself towards her work. Suddenly a movement from the house caught her eye and she froze. The kitchen door was slowly opening. Her thoughts raced. No one was in the house except her grandmother, and she was bedridden.

After a moment a figure appeared. Annie stiffened in alarm and strained her eyes. The figure was an old woman's, dressed from head to toe in a white linen nightdress. Long, straggling, iron grey hair fell in wisps to her shoulders. Her bare feet stepped noiselessly over the threshold. Suddenly she stopped, glanced around, then started to dance. Round and round she went, her arms uplifted, nightdress billowing in the hot air.

If this had been at night, Annie would have thought she was looking at a ghost. But this was no ghost. Ghosts didn't appear in broad daylight. She clasped her hand to her mouth in horror. Oh, God, this must be her grandmother. The shock of the realisation made her sink back on to the box.

She watched, her mind a blank, not knowing what to think or do. The old woman suddenly stopped, spotting Annie for the first time. She gave a wide toothless grin and slowly made her way over.

'Oh,' she said excitedly, in a high, cracked voice, 'you're new here, ain't yer? Well, you won't last long.' She giggled and made Annie move up on the box so she could sit down. Annie thought she resembled a small child trapped inside an old body. She moved up, unaware of doing so, unable to take her eyes off her grandmother.

The old lady turned and stared at her for a moment and her eyes narrowed in bewilderment. 'Do I know you?' she cackled.

Annie felt her face redden and shifted nervously on her seat. Did she take this opportunity to announce herself? What if she did? What would the consequences be?

'Well, do I know yer?' the old woman asked in agitation.

'Er ... no. I've only just started working here,' Annie answered, feeling her opportunity had slipped away.

'Ah! You'll be skiving then,' she said, nudging Annie in the ribs. 'Can't say as I blame yer. Works 'em all to death, she does, then moans they don't do 'ote.' She grinned broadly. 'See, I ain't that stupid. I knows what goes on. They've all gone out, ain't they? I love it when they all go out. That silly gel Molly left me door unlocked. She does that sometimes. Anyway, they think I can't walk, so leaving the door unlocked doesn't matter.' She put her hand over her mouth and giggled. 'I come out at night sometimes. She thinks I'm off me head. Can't wait

128

for me to die.' She turned to face Annie. 'Thinks she's getting the bloody farm when I go.' She puffed out her chest. 'Well, I've got news for her.' She got up, faced Annie and wagged a bony finger. 'Me son – he's a wet blanket. Don't marry her, I told him. You'll make a rod for your own back. But he did. Wouldn't listen to me. Now he's paying for it.' She chuckled again. 'You don't say much, do you? Well, I got to go.' She bent down and whispered in Annie's ear, ''Case they come back. Wouldn't do for 'em to catch me here, and me bedridden.' She gave a giggle and waved her hand. 'Tarra.'

'Just a minute . . .' Annie started. But the old lady had gone.

She sat in shock, wondering if she had imagined it all. She did not notice Molly come back and jumped when the girl gently touched her shoulder.

'Annie, a'you all right?' she asked, her voice full of concern.

'Yes, Molly. Yes.' Annie started to laugh, and laughed so much that the tears started to roll down her cheeks. Molly was dumbfounded.

She wiped her eyes. 'I'm sorry, Molly, I've just had a terrible experience.'

'Well, it must have been something funny to make you laugh like that.'

'It wasn't funny, Molly. It was awful.' Annie took a deep breath and clasped her hands together, desperately trying to compose herself. 'Molly, I've just met me grandmother. I've been desperate to meet her for so long and she behaved just like a child. I can't get over it. I can't describe how I feel.' A tear rolled down her cheek. She wiped it away. 'Sit down a minute, Molly. It's all right, Kath won't be back for a while yet.' She patted the space beside her and the girl sat down hesitantly.

'Molly, how long has me grandmother been like that?'

'Oh, Annie, I can't say nothing. Kath . . .'

'Don't worry about her. Look.' She placed her hands on the young girl's shoulders. 'I know she's warned you not to say anything. I won't mention we've been talking. Honest, I won't. I just need to know about her. Please, Molly?' she pleaded.

'Well . . .' She hesitated. 'I ain't been here that long, but she has good days and bad days. She rambles a lot, then another time she speaks more sense than anyone. You have to learn to be able to tell the difference. Kath keeps her locked in her room since you came.' She bit her bottom lip and bent her head. 'Before, they used to have her in the kitchen. But since you came, well, Kath's made the excuse that your grandmother has got worse so she has to be kept in her room.' Molly's face grew sad. 'It's locking her in her bedroom that's made her worse. She was all right when she was with company. I think it's a shame keeping her cooped up like that, but who am I to say what goes on?'

'It's all right, Molly,' Annie whispered sincerely, patting the girl's knee. 'It's not your fault, you do your best.' She pondered for a minute. 'Molly, if I tell you something, will you promise not to say anything?'

''Course I won't.'

Annie took a breath. 'I was sitting here having a breather when me grandmother came out, danced around the yard, then came over to talk to me. 'Course, she didn't know who I was. Stop laughing, Molly, it's true.' She playfully punched her on the shoulder. 'Afterwards I didn't know whether I had dreamt it or not.'

Molly was flabbergasted. 'You mean, she can walk? Honestly! The old devil.' She clasped her hand to her mouth. 'Whoops! Sorry, Annie.'

'It's all right. I got a shock as well.'

'I must have forgotten to lock the door. Kath will skin me alive if she finds out,' Molly said in alarm.

'Well, we'd better not say anything. But I can assure you that I intend to speak to Archie about my grandmother as soon as I get the opportunity.' Annie smiled wryly. 'We'd better get back to work.' She rose and made to walk away, stopped and turned back. 'Molly, I didn't know Kath had any family.'

'Oh, yes. She's a mother and two sisters, I think.' She's ashamed of them and dreads the thought of them coming up here.'

'Why?'

'Well, she's above them now, ain't she? Her married to a farmer. She forgets she was born in a shack at the bottom of the Skittings and would still be there if she hadn't met Archie.' Her hand flew to her mouth again. 'I'm sorry, Annie,' she said, aghast. 'There I go again, letting me big mouth run away with me. I shouldn't speak like that, her being your auntie 'un all.'

Annie laughed. 'Don't worry, Molly. I understand perfectly.'

The girl grinned broadly. 'Her sisters work with my mam in the hosiery factory in Church Lane. They make fishermen's socks. Me mother, bless her heart, didn't want me to end up like her, slaving away from dawn 'til dusk for a pittance.' She laughed. 'She thinks I've the soft life here. I daren't tell her what it's really like, she'd go mad.' She stood up to face Annie. 'I'm only biding me time here, you know. 'Til I'm older. I want to work in Leicester, one of them posh shops. So in the meantime, I just puts me head down, holds me tongue and gets on with it.'

Annie laid her hand on Molly's arm. 'You speak a lot of sense for a girl your age.'

'It was our Vicar that taught me that, Annie. In fact, he taught me a lot. He wanted to be a teacher, but his family were all clergy and he was forced to follow. Me dad was his gravedigger and when I was little I used to go over every afternoon for lessons from the Vicar.' She sighed deeply. 'Me dad had an accident and got killed, so Mam had to send me off to work. Mr Grimble, that's the Vicar, tried all sorts of things to keep us together, but it didn't work out.'

'Oh, Molly, I am sorry.'

'Oh, that's all right. I'm over it now and things could have been worse. My mam manages all right. She has her wages from the factory, such as they are, and the bit me and me brother give her. He's down the pit so he earns more than me. She always protests when we hand it over, but we both know that without it she'd be on the streets. I love my mother, Annie,' she said emotionally. 'I'd like to take you to meet her sometime.'

'Molly, I'd like that.'

'Would you? I'll make arrangements then.' She grabbed Annie's arm. 'Oh, I'm so glad you and Georgie came to the farm. You've made my life bearable now. At least someone speaks to me proper and not like I'm a lump of muck.' She leant over and kissed Annie on the cheek. 'Thanks for that, Annie.'

She turned and ran back towards the house. The unexpected show of affection made Annie feel very humble and glad that their coming had pleased the girl.

She walked slowly towards the barn, confused thoughts running through her mind. What if Kath's actions had caused her grandmother's mind to deteriorate? And why was she willing to let that happen? It was cruel to keep a dog locked up, let alone a human being.

She entered the barn and threw herself down on the straw. But what if Molly was wrong? Young girls were known to exaggerate. What if her grandmother's mind had started going before Annie herself arrived, and locking her in her bedroom was just a coincidence? Oh, God. If Molly was right, then Kath was really out of order. But if Molly was wrong, then Annie would be poking her nose in on an already sensitive subject, and Kath would be justified in any recriminations she decided to make.

Annie leant back and rested her arms behind her head. Her grandmother's state of mind didn't appear so bad. In fact she seemed quite lucid and certainly knew what was going on. Annie tutted. Molly had said she had good days and bad. Maybe this had been a good day? Anyway, Archie would surely intervene if anything untoward was happening to his mother? Yes, of course he would. The answer must be that Molly was exaggerating. But one question still remained unanswered. Just why was it that Kath didn't want them to meet? Will I ever find out? Annie wondered.

The walk back to the farm seemed to get longer and longer. They had been in the fields for three whole weeks, picking a record crop of potatoes, and Annie's back and arms ached dreadfully. Everyone's spirits were running high though at the thought of the forthcoming barn dance. The dance was held in the large barn each year after harvest. Most of the people from the surrounding area came. Now good humour and banter was rife as they all trudged back, singing and laughing.

Annie did not see the rider until after she had landed on her backside in the ditch. He dismounted and rushed to her aid. With nothing hurt but her pride, she brushed herself down and blushingly accepted the apologies of the gentleman standing before her. Archie rushed forward, doffed his cap and stuttered a greeting.

'Sir James, this is Annie, my niece. She's fine, sir. I'm sorry, we weren't looking where we were going.'

'Don't apologise, man. It was entirely my fault. I shouldn't really have been riding down here. I just took a short cut.' He looked at Annie with concern. 'Are you sure you're all right?'

'Yes, thank you, sir.'

'Good. I can only apologise again.' Sir James Richmond smiled warmly at her and turned to face Archie. 'So, this is the longlost niece you mentioned a while back?' He turned back to Annie. 'I've met your son, my dear. He's a fine lad. Bring him up to the house sometime so he can see the horses.'

Her eyes opened wide in astonishment. 'Why, thank you, sir. He'd be delighted.' She gave a small curtsey.

'My pleasure.' He made to walk away towards his horse, stopped and turned back. 'I remember your mother, my dear. Pretty little thing she was, used to come to the house. Had a friend working there if I remember rightly. For some reason, on one visit she ended up in a pile of manure. It was the talk of the servants' quarters for weeks.' He laughed loudly. 'Right, I must be off. Nice to have met you.' He mounted his horse and rode away.

Annie looked at her uncle agog. 'Is that true, Archie? Did me mother fall in the manure?'

He laughingly shook his head as they made their way up the track. 'I can't remember, gel. But your mother was always up to something or other. Anything she did came as no surprise. She probably never mentioned it in case me dad gave her hell. Eh, fancy the squire remembering that. Mind you, she was always off up the big house on one excuse or another.' He looked coyly at Annie. 'She had a friend working there, I believe.'

'D'you mean Matty?'

'Matty? Er, yes.'

'I know Matty, Uncle Archie. She was the woman who pointed me in your direction the night I arrived.'

Archie lengthened his stride. 'Was she?' he said slowly.

Annie quickened her pace to keep up with him. 'Yes. And I visit her. She's a very nice woman.'

He sighed deeply. 'Yes, she is.' He took off his cap and ran the back of his hand across his brow. 'Phew, it's too hot. Looks like another sleepless night,' he said, changing the subject.

Annie took the hint. 'He seemed a nice man, for gentry like.'

'Yeah, he is,' Archie answered, slowing his gait. 'One of a few, I'd say. Other folks in his position wouldn't give the likes of us the time of day.' He nodded. 'Yes, he's a good bloke. Knows all his servants by name and treats them really well. Gives them all huge food hampers and a big party at Christmas. Do you know, he even came to me dad's funeral? Now that says something, doesn't it?'

'Do you think he means it, about Georgie going up to the big house? He'd love to go, I know he would.'

'Oh, yes, he means it all right. We'll all go one Sunday afternoon. I know the young stable lad, he'll take great care of Georgie.' He hooked his arm through Annie's. 'Come on, we'd better hurry. The others will be back by now and Kath will be in a right tizzy.'

As they entered the farm gate, Archie stopped for a moment.

'Have you ever seen anything of John Matthews? he asked hesitantly. 'Only I wondered if there was any developments?'

'What do you mean, developments?' she asked sharply, eyeing her uncle suspiciously.

'Well, he seemed quite taken with you when I introduced you at the market. I just wondered if he had come a-courting at all?'

'Archie Burbage, I thought I told you no matchmaking.' She elbowed him in the ribs and he gave a playful yelp.

'I know what you said,' he laughed. 'But I also noticed the way you blushed when he spoke to you.'

'Blush? No, I never. I was hot. And to answer your question, no, he ain't come a-courting,' she lied. 'Even if he did, there'd be nothing doing.'

Archie raised his eyebrows and his eyes twinkled. 'Well, we'll see. The barn dance is coming up, ain't it? And he's sure to be there.'

Annie threw him a black look and marched away from him towards the house. The talk of John Matthews had sent little thrills through her body. As much as she tried not to let it happen, the man was getting under her skin and without realising she started to plan what she would wear for the dance. She settled on her forget-me-not blue dress. It was fairly old but the colour suited her dark hair and bought out the colour of her eyes.

She entered the kitchen to see Kath's frozen expression. Archie saw the look and quickly slipped back out of the door before his wife spotted him.

'Where have you been?' she bellowed. 'The others got back ages ago.' She banged down a plate of stew on the table and scowled. 'You're your mother all over,' she spat as she scurried around the kitchen. 'She'd disappear for hours on end, with never a thought for anyone else. You were supposed to come straight back from the fields and give me a hand here.' She wagged a finger menacingly in Annie's direction. 'I've had to dish up the dinners all by myself. Ungrateful little bitch, you are, and where's Archie? Slunk off somewhere, I suppose. Well, his dinner can go to the pigs.'

Molly, who had been washing a pile of dirty dishes, picked up a bucket and slipped outside.

Annie took a deep breath. 'If you'll let me explain . . .'

'Explain! There's nothing to explain. You're just a chip off the old block, Annie Higgins. Your mother was a dab hand at getting out of the chores. She was the laziest liar I've ever met . . .'

'Just a minute!' Annie snapped, her face clouding over. 'I've never shirked my work. How dare you say that I have? And as for my mother, you leave her out of this. She ain't here to defend herself.'

'No, she ain't, thank God. I dread to think what having two of you around would be like.'

At this remark, Annie shot around the table and grabbed Kath's arm, gripping it tightly. 'How dare you blacken my mother's name? If this is how you treated her, then I'm glad she had the sense to leave and make a life for herself away from you.'

'Life for herself? You don't know what you're talking about, gel.' Kath shook her arm free, picked up the broom and started to brush furiously.

'What d'you mean? She did make a life for herself,' Annie said icily. 'She got away from here and met me father, and if she'd have lived I know she'd have been happy. My father was a good man,' she said, jumping out of the way as the broom headed towards her.

'Your father?' Kath stopped brushing and laughed savagely. 'That man wasn't your father! Your mother tricked him into marrying her because she was pregnant.' She stopped abruptly and gasped for breath. 'There, now you know,' she announced triumphantly.

Annie froze, her face full of bewilderment. 'He *was* my father! How dare you say otherwise?' she shouted. 'You're lying.'

'Lying, am I?' Kath stared at Annie, her face full of malice and spite. 'I'll tell you this, my girl. Your mother . . . that wonderful creature that could do no wrong around here, the woman that everyone idolised . . . was pregnant when she ran away. Messing about she was. Brought shame on the family, and I damn' well told her so.' She folded her arms under her bosom. 'So you ain't got nothing to be proud of, have yer? Going round here like butter wouldn't melt in yer mouth! If the truth be known, you were nearly a bastard. Now how do you feel about yer mother? She ain't the wonderful woman you thought she was, is she?'

Annie grasped the back of a chair, desperately trying to contain the rage and confusion that were building inside her.

'So that's why she went?' she said coldly. 'It was you . . . You made her leave.'

'She left of her own accord,' Kath answered haughtily. 'Anyway, it were best.'

'Best for who? You or me mother? Let's face it, Kath, with her out of the way you could queen it here.' Annie banged the table with her fist.

'Shut yer mouth!' Kath spat, and narrowed her eyes. 'You don't know the half, and if you want to stay here you'll keep quiet about this. Nobody else knows. It would kill Archie and the old lady if they heard that their precious little girl was a slut.'

The two women glared at each other for what seemed like an age. Finally, Annie fled from the kitchen and up to her room where she threw herself on the bed and sobbed.

After a while she sat up, wiped her face on her skirt and stared unblinkingly around. This room, the one she had made so homely, felt alien and cold. She trembled uncontrollably. The bombshell Kath had so evilly delivered had shaken her to the core. The thought of her mother leaving the farm so desolate and alone hurt her more than she could bear. That and the knowledge that the man who had so lovingly brought her up, and taught her nearly all she knew, was not even related to her.

137

Tears cascaded down her cheeks. Christ, her mind screamed, how much hurt can a body take? She stood up and walked slowly around the room, touching the walls as though for comfort but receiving none. The walls remained cold and aloof. Her mind reached the one question she had not dared to ask yet. Who was my father?

A picture rose before her, bold and clear. The rider with the red hair. Oh, no! She gasped in horror. Surely not? Surely her mother had not been taken in by a handsome man? But if she had, did this mean Annie was related to the folks in the big house? It would certainly answer several questions. The reason for her mother's frequent visits to the house, and Georgie's hair colour.

She sighed deeply and paced up and down as a thought struck her. If only she could find her mother's hidey-hole. Maybe she had left something that would reveal her secret? She stole round, looking in every conceivable place. She poked behind the bed, in the old chest, banged the walls, but found nothing, not even a hint of a crevice or space that could have held a piece of her past. She sighed, a deep lingering sigh, and held her head in her hands. Then her heart suddenly lifted. Matty . . . Surely she would know something? Annie would have to wait 'til Sunday and in the meantime would go about her business, not letting Kath know how upset she was. At least she could keep her pride.

Chapter Nine

Lucy brushed away a fly and ran her hand across her brow, wiping away the sweat. She was bored and needed something to do. What she really wanted was to plan something. She splashed her feet in the water and watched the ripples curling over the surface of the stream. If I had a stick, she thought cruelly, I could hit that fish over the head. She watched it swim away, thinking how lucky it had been.

Oh, these hot days are boring. At least this water is cool. She laughed to herself. She had been clever managing to get out of going to the fields yet again. Anyway, why should she go? The daughter of the house shouldn't be made to do menial tasks, that was for poor folk. She certainly was becoming a mistress of excuses. She had heard her mother calling, the agitation in her voice apparent. Lucy had shrugged her shoulders and pressed her body flatter against the wall, waiting for a chance to escape. It had come, as she'd known it would, and here she was, dabbling her feet in the cool inviting stream.

She thought of her father. He was all right, she supposed, as fathers went. But he was soft, and Lucy knew he let her get away with murder. He would just give her one of his smiles and pat her on the head, whatever she did. Her mother never seemed to have much time for him. Not like she did for John Matthews. Whenever he came over or they visited him, her mother seemed different, even silly sometimes. Lucy liked John. He was always nice to her and gave her little presents.

She conjured up a picture of Georgie. If she was honest with herself, she quite liked him. But for some reason her mother did not, so Lucy wouldn't allow herself to either. She found it better to keep on the right side of her mother: it made life easier. She splashed the water with her feet again, reflecting her savage mood. She picked up a stone, turned her head and threw it over her shoulder. It landed against a tree, causing the birds to disperse into the air. Suddenly an idea came to her and she yelped in delight. She clasped her hands together, threw back her head and laughed. It was just the right kind of idea to get rid of Georgie and Annie once and for all, and really please her mother.

Her plan would have to take place on a Sunday, she thought, because on Saturday it was the Crowpie Festival and she didn't want anything to interrupt that occasion. It was the one outing to which her father always took her. Her mother would not lower herself to mix with the 'riff-raff', as she put it. Lucy always dressed in her finery and had ribbons put in her hair, and would strut around the stalls knowing that all the village girls were jealous of her fine clothes.

She rubbed her hands together. Thinking of the Crowpie was hindering her plans. She thought long and hard. Putting her plan into action would take real cunning, but if anyone could make it work, she could. She jumped up and shook herself. Time to get back to the farm and get things in motion.

Back at the farm she found Georgie sitting in the barn stroking Scrap who was lying at his feet. She sauntered in and stood before him, resting her back against a post.

'What you doing then?' she asked offhandedly.

'Nothing,' Georgie answered, not even bothering to look up. Lucy was bad news and he did not want to get involved.

'Where's your mother?' she asked hesitantly, not wanting to be overheard.

'She's in the dairy making the butter. Why?'

'Oh, nothing. I just think she ain't looked very happy since she had that row with me mother.'

'What row?' asked Georgie, looking up at her.

He had been worried about his mother for a couple of days. She had not been herself somehow, but he had not been able to

140

put his finger on the reason why. He had been concerned that it had been something he had done.

'Oh, they had a right ding-dong. Old Reggie was chuntering on about it. Don't know what it was about though.' Lucy looked nonchalantly at Scrap. 'Don't know why you take on that stupid dog, he's got fleas.'

'No, he ain't. Anyway, he's my friend,' Georgie said, placing his arms lovingly around the dog's neck.

Lucy pouted. 'I could be your friend. If you want me to.'

'Why should you be? You ain't bothered up to now.' Georgie looked questioningly at her. 'What you up to?'

'Nothing, just thought we might as well.' She picked up the hay fork and started to prod the straw.

'Don't do that.' He jumped up and grabbed her arm. 'There might be some chickens nesting. Don't! Lucy, don't.'

'Well, they shouldn't be in here, should they?'

'Chickens don't know that.'

'You're a baby, you are. You should come in here sometimes. I hide and watch the hired workers courting with the girls from the village.' She stroked her hair and looked at him boldly.

'What's courting?'

'Don't you know anything?' She smirked and slid her back down the post 'til her knees were touching her ears. 'It's when a man puts his hand up a woman's skirt and she lets him touch her "nellies".'

'Nellies?' queried George.

'Shut up when I'm speaking!' Lucy snapped. 'Then he pulls down his trousers and they go at it.' She looked knowingly at him. 'You know, like the dogs when they're on heat. The woman giggles and says, "Be careful. Don't make me have a baby." They moan and groan and there's lots of kissing.' She laughed at Georgie's face. 'Sounds horrible, don't it? Anyway, then they look round to see no one is looking and run out.' She looked triumphantly at Georgie who was totally bewildered. 'You can put your hand up my dress if you like.' She slanted her eyes and looked provocatively at him.

'What!' he said, his mouth gaping open. 'That's rude.' He

grabbed hold of Scrap and stroked him so hard the dog gave a yelp.

'No, it ain't,' Lucy said sharply. 'You're just a ninny.' She stopped herself from having a go at Georgie, remembering her plan. She took a deep breath and continued.

'Would you like to go down the stream on Sunday?' She watched the surprised look form on the lad's face. 'We can catch some fish. I'll get a jam jar from Molly. And there's some birds nesting – I'll show you. Only if you want to. I ain't bothered like.'

Before he had time to think, Georgie clapped his hands in delight. 'Oh, yeah. That'd be great.' He frowned. 'I can't come 'til the afternoon though, I have me jobs to do in the morning.'

'That's what I was thinking. We'll wait 'til they're all having a rest after dinner.'

'My mother doesn't rest. We usually go for a walk.'

'Well, you'll have to get out of it somehow,' Lucy said abruptly, then smiled sweetly. 'You'll think of something. I have to go to Sunday School in the morning so I'll meet you about two o'clock. I'll wait for you over in the top meadow.' She eyed him thoughtfully. 'Don't tell anybody, though. You know what me mother's like. If she gets an inkling, she'll put a stop to it.' She wagged her finger at him and went towards the door.

'I'll have to tell me mam 'cos she worries,' Georgie shouted after her.

Lucy turned on her heel. 'No. I said don't tell anyone!' She walked back and stood before him. 'Don't worry, she won't find out. Trust me.'

Georgie shrugged his shoulders. 'Okay.'

'Good.' Lucy turned and headed out of the door, a secretive smile playing around her lips.

Georgie placed his arms around Scrap and hugged him tightly. This was a turn up, Lucy being friendly. He smiled. He was really looking forward to their trip. It would be like an adventure. In return he would take her to meet Frederick. He jumped up and ran to find his mother. He was suddenly very hungry and could not wait for Sunday to arrive.

Outside in the yard Annie was carrying two heavy buckets of water towards the kitchen when Archie caught up with her.

'Are you all right, gel? Only you ain't been your usual self these past couple of days.'

'I'm fine, Uncle Archie, thank you. Just a bit tired, that's all. It's good of you to ask, though.' She paused thoughtfully and put down the buckets. 'Uncle Archie, did . . . did me mother have a boyfriend at all?'

'A boyfriend?' He looked perplexed. 'I don't rightly know. Why?'

'Oh, just interested, that's all.'

'Well, she was a good-looking gel, all right. It wouldn't have surprised me. But me mother and father kept her on a tight rein.' He laughed. 'She was smitten by the squire's son – the squire now as is. The one we met the other day. She used to romance about him. I told her not to be so daft. I'm sure that's why she used to visit the house so often. I used to tease her about it. But I'm sure it was only a young girl's fancy. You girls get fancies, don't yer?'

'Yes, we do.'

'Well, let's face it, the likes of the squire's son weren't going to take up with a poor farmer's daughter. And to be honest, I can't think of anyone else, although there was lots of young men in the village that hung around.'

Annie lowered her head. Had her mother been taken in by the handsome squire, then dumped when he knew she was pregnant? Things like that did happen. She just wished Sunday would arrive so she could see Matty. She bent over and made to pick up the buckets.

'Here, let me do that,' her uncle said, grabbing them.

'Thanks, Uncle Archie,' she said gratefully. She looked at him out of the corner of her eye. 'I'm going to visit Matty on Sunday. Will I tell her you were asking after her?'

Archie stopped and looked at her. 'You could do,' he said. He started to walk again. 'I'm glad you're going. A visit to Matty will do you good. You need a break.' He changed the subject, conscious that he was getting hot under the collar. 'Are you going to take young Georgie to the fair on Saturday? It'll do you both good.'

'Well, I'd love to, only me work . . .'

'You'll have finished by then. You'll enjoy the fair, Annie, and I know Georgie will.'

'Mmm,' she said thoughtfully. 'I suppose I could take him for an hour at night-time. It won't upset Kath if we go then. I love fairs, Archie. Are you going?'

'Well, I usually take our Lucy in the afternoon, after all the hirelings have finished. You know,' he said, shaking his head, 'she dolls herself up and prances round, showing off to all the other kids. They all take the mickey, only she doesn't realise.'

'Well, that's kids for you. Lucy should realise how lucky she is.' She looked at him for a second then spoke again. 'Archie, do you love Lucy?'

''Course I do. What a silly question,' he said, giving her a quizzical look. He stroked his chin thoughtfully. 'I do worry about her, though. She's so like her mother . . .' He shrugged his shoulders. 'Come on, our Kath will wonder what's keeping us. Oh, hello, here's young Georgie. How's it going, young fella me lad? You look like the cat who's got the cream.'

'What's that mean?' Georgie asked, skipping towards them.

'Oh, just happy, lad,' Archie explained. 'Are you hungry?'

Georgie nodded.

'Come on then, let's help your mother with these buckets and then we'll see what your Auntie Kath has for our tea.'

It was a clear, warm night that saw Annie and Georgie setting off across the back fields towards the village. The upset of the scene with Kath lay heavily upon Annie, but she was determined, for the sake of her son, to put on a brave face and appear to be enjoying herself. The hum of the fair could be heard in the distance and as they drew nearer the shouts and laughter sounded louder and louder. Georgie was having difficulty controlling his excitement and was pulling his mother along, silently urging her to hurry even more.

Annie suddenly stopped, raised her skirts and challenged her son.

'Come on then. I'll race yer. Last one there's a cissy!'

Georgie gave a loud 'Whoopee'.

He tore across the field as quick as his little legs would carry him and both reached the outskirts of the fair, panting heavily and ready to collapse.

'Hold on there, son,' Annie pleaded. 'Give us a minute to get me breath back.' She straightened her straw hat and rearranged her shawl round her shoulders. 'Come here.' She pulled him towards her and wiped a smudge off his cheek. 'Let's at least try to look dignified.'

The fair was held each year in a big field at the back of the Plough Inn, and the pair were soon caught up in the pleasant, jovial atmosphere. They ambled around the stalls, mingling with the crowds, and stopped now and again to watch performances by acrobats and strolling players.

Georgie was delighted when he triumphantly pulled out a stick of barley sugar from the bran tub. He broke it in half, some for himself, the other half to save for Molly. They went on the swing boats and the merry-go-round and finally, too tired to stand any more, sat on the grass tucking into small pork pies and mushy peas. Replenished, Georgie stood up ready to join the thronging crowd once more.

'Oh, no,' Annie groaned as she jumped up and grabbed him by the arm. 'We've had enough for one night. We'd better be making tracks.'

'Oh, Mam! Not yet. Can't we stay just a bit longer? Please.' Georgie's bottom lip quivered. Annie frowned. She had been up since five o'clock and was desperate for her bed, but the look on Georgie's face changed her mind. Before she could answer him a voice from behind made her jump.

'Not going so soon, are you?' The words made her colour rise and she swung round.

'Er, yes, I'm afraid so. We have to be up early in the morning.'

John Matthews stood before her, his tall lean body outlined

against the moonlit sky. She felt herself starting to tremble as his eyes bored into hers, mouth curling in a smile. Her heart quickened. He really was a handsome man. There was nothing she would like more than to stay and spend some time with him. Her spirits soared when she heard his next words.

'Stay a bit longer, Annie. I'd be glad of the company. It won't hurt for once to be late. The fair only comes once a year.'

'Please, Mam. Please let's stay a bit longer,' Georgie pleaded, pulling at her skirt.

She looked down at him and then back again to John. She was about to relent when she saw him stumble. She quickly realised that he'd had more than his fair share of drink, frowned and grabbed Georgie's hand.

'No, I'm sorry, we have to go.'

'Well, in that case, I'll walk back with you,' said John, hiccuping loudly.

'No, no. We'll be fine, thank you.' She made to walk away with a dismayed Georgie dragging his feet alongside her, his face the picture of misery.

John caught hold of her arm. 'I won't take no for an answer. Besides,' he gave her a crooked smile, 'it's a grand evening for a walk with a pretty lady.'

He fell into step beside her, and Georgie, realising that he was defeated, jumped and skipped ahead of them, disappearing from view round a bend in the track. Annie nervously clutched the ends of her shawl and folded her arms, pulling the shawl tightly across her.

'You never did come to visit me,' he said, breaking the awkward silence. 'I've looked out for yer. I did mean the invitation, you know.'

'Well, we've been busy. I just haven't found the time.'

'Well, what about tomorrow? That's your afternoon off, ain't it?'

Annie sensed she was being pressurised into making an arrangement and felt suddenly threatened. 'It is,' she answered firmly. 'But not tomorrow. I've other arrangements.'

John came to an abrupt halt and grabbed hold of her arm.

'What's the matter, Annie? A'you afraid of me or something? Or is it that I ain't good enough for you?'

She shook her arm free and looked questioningly at him. 'I told you I'd been busy, and I meant it,' she snapped. 'Anyway, I think you've had too much to drink.'

'Oh, do you?' He smirked. 'Let me tell you, Annie Higgins, I can drink anyone under the table and still keep me faculties about me.'

'Oh, can you? Well, I've seen what drink can do to people. Anyway, why are you wasting your time with me? I'm sure there's plenty of women at the fair willing to go for a walk with you.'

John threw back his head and laughed. 'Oh, you bet there is. I can pick and choose from any number. But there's something about you that fascinates me. So come on. What about it?'

Annie pulled her shawl tighter and started to walk. 'What about what?' she asked.

John ran forward and stepped in front of her, blocking her way. 'Oh, I didn't realise you'd be such hard work.'

'Eh?' she uttered in bewilderment.

She tried to walk past him but he moved with her, still blocking her path.

'Oh, come on,' he growled. 'Don't play the wide-eyed young innocent with me. You can save that for others.'

Suddenly his mood changed. His features turned ugly and Annie felt afraid. Her eyes darted around desperately searching for Georgie, but he was nowhere to be seen. The path they were walking along was deserted and she felt panic rise up in her.

'Please move,' she said, trying to keep her voice even. 'I have to find my son.'

'Georgie'll be fine,' he said, running his eyes over her body. 'He's old enough to find his own way home.' He licked his lips and gave her a sly smile. 'It's just you and me, Annie. There's no one around to spoil our fun.'

'Fun! What d'you mean?'

John gave a low laugh. 'I love the act. You could fool anyone.'

'I can assure you, John Matthews, I ain't trying to fool you or anyone. Now if you don't let me pass, I'll . . . I'll . . .'

Annie suddenly turned on her heel and tried to make a dash for it. But John was too quick for her and grabbed her arm, pulling her close towards him. His face was inches away from hers and she recoiled at the smell of his whisky-soaked breath.

'You bitch,' he said icily. 'You've given me the come on since the first day we met and now you're trying to back out. Well, you picked the wrong man, lady. You've maybe got away with it before, but you ain't this time.'

Annie's heart banged loudly in her chest. 'You lay one finger on me . . .'

'And you'll what?'

He gripped her arm tightly and dragged her across the field into the long grass. He threw her down and stood looming over her. She fell, banging her arm on the hard soil, and stared horrified into his distorted face.

'Don't pretend you don't want this, Annie. A widow like you must have missed a man?'

'No! No! I haven't,' she screamed, inching herself back. Her skirt caught on a piece of wood, exposing her shapely legs. 'You've got it wrong.'

'I ain't got anything wrong,' he said, leering down at her. 'You're desperate for me and have been since the first day we met.'

He fell down on top of her, pinning her arms to the ground with his knees. Annie struggled against him and let out a piercing scream.

'You can make as much noise as you like,' he said harshly. 'No one will hear you.'

She squeezed her eyes tightly shut, her body taut in fright. He wrenched open her shawl and tore her dress and camisole to reveal her breasts. He pawed at them savagely. Then he leaned back to unbutton his trousers and as he did so, she tried once more to escape. To no avail.

It was over in minutes – minutes that to Annie seemed like hours. His lust spent, John rolled off her, stood up, re-buttoned his trousers, and without a glance in her direction, stumbled back towards the fair.

She lay there, clutching the torn dress against her exposed chest, tears of anger and humiliation cascading down the sides of her face. She felt dirty, used, and a great hatred of this man enveloped her. She inched herself up and felt the bruises on her buttocks where his hands had grabbed and squeezed her hard. She winced and pulled her skirt down, covering her bare legs.

The distant sound of Georgie calling her name shook her rigid. He must not find her like this. She wiped her face on her skirt and pulled her shawl tightly round her shoulders in an effort to cover her nakedness where her dress had been savagely ripped. She awkwardly rose, took several deep breaths and waded slowly through the long grass towards the track.

'Mam! There you are.' Georgie skipped towards her. 'I've been looking everywhere. What were you doing in the grass?' He glanced up at her and his face puckered in bewilderment. 'What's up, Mam? Have you been crying?'

'No, no. I've got something in my eye.'

'Well, how come yer dress is ripped?'

'Oh, is it?' Annie quickly looked down to see her shawl had slipped. 'I must have caught it,' she said, clutching at the shawl and pulling both sides together. She grabbed his hand and started to walk up the track. Her legs trembled and she found difficulty in putting one foot in front of the other. Georgie skipped happily beside her, unaware of his mother's trauma.

'Where's Mr Matthews gone, Mam?'

Annie looked anxiously down at her son. 'He's . . . he's gone home,' she said, her voice trembling.

'Oh, has he? I like him, Mam. He gave me a penny.'

Annie stopped abruptly. 'When?' she gasped.

'When he came to the farm yesterday. That's when he asked if we were going to the fair, and he gave me a penny to spend and said he might see us.'

'You never told me!'

'He told me not to. Said he wanted to surprise you.'

149

Annie inhaled deeply. The bastard! she thought angrily. He had planned the whole thing.

She tightened her grip on her son's hand. 'If anything like that happens again, you tell me. Is that clear? You tell me, Georgie.'

'You're hurting me, Mam,' he wailed. 'Anyway, it was supposed to be a secret. You were supposed to be pleased.'

'Oh, Georgie.' Annie sighed deeply and loosened her grip. 'Come on, let's get home.'

They managed to arrive back at their room unobserved. Georgie had wanted to run and find his uncle and tell him about the wonderful time he had had. Annie flew into a panic. She couldn't let him go into the house alone, and if she went with him there would be questions asked about her appearance. She finally managed to convince him it was too late. His tale would wait until the morning. It was a relieved Annie who finally climbed the ladder after him.

Georgie was exhausted from his night of revelry and was soon sound asleep. She carefully tipped cold water into the tin basin and gently washed her sore body. She dabbed wychhazel on to her bruises and abrasions, donned her calico nightdress and climbed carefully into bed, clutching the bedclothes tightly underneath her chin.

Loneliness and desolation stole over her. The ice cold wash had done nothing to relieve the pain and defilement she felt. Tears of helplessness rolled down her face. How could she have misjudged a man so badly? How stupid she had been!

'Oh, Charlie, Charlie,' she sobbed. 'If ever I needed you, it's now.'

Chapter Ten

'Stop gulping your dinner, Georgie. You're eating like there's no tomorrow and if you don't watch out you'll get indigestion.'

'In-didi-gestion! What's that?'

Annie frowned. 'Just eat your dinner and slow down, else you'll be sick,' she said, pushing her food around her plate.

Georgie tried to slow his pace. He had to be out soon if he was to keep his appointment with Lucy and as he had no way of telling the time, thought he would get there early so as not to miss her. Excitement filled him. He couldn't wait to discover the delights of the stream. His mother interrupted his thoughts.

'What's all the rush for? We ain't going out for about another half hour.'

'Eh?' Georgie's eyes opened wide in alarm. He had forgotten to plan his escape. 'Oh,' he uttered, his mind racing as he tried to think of an excuse. 'Er . . . I ain't coming with yer today.'

'What d'you mean, you ain't coming with me?' she repeated sharply. 'Why not?'

'I thought I'd stay here with Scrap.'

'But we're going to Matty's and you were looking forward to playing with the kids next-door. Something to do with a cart, wasn't it?'

Yes, it was. Micky and Willy were expecting him. What did he do now? He raised his eyes heavenwards. He had never been in a situation like this before and wasn't sure what to do. He wanted to see Micky and Willy. Playing on the cart was going to be such fun. But his promise to Lucy was more urgent. She wouldn't take his non-appearance as kindly as the two boys and he would suffer from her annoyance.

He quickly made a decision and lowered his eyes, putting a pathetic look on his face.

'I really want to come, Mam. But I don't feel well.'

Annie jumped up and ran round the table, placing her hand gently across his forehead.

'Well, you feel all right to me,' she said. She stood back and eyed him. 'What's going on, our Georgie?'

'Eh? I don't know what yer mean.'

'Yes, you do. There's nothing wrong with you. So why are you saying there is?'

Georgie was cornered and he knew it.

'I ... er ... I promised Lucy I'd go down the stream with her.' He raised his eyes hesitantly to meet his mother's. 'We're going to fish and she's gonna show me the birds nesting. Honest, Mam. She wants to be me friend.'

'Friend!' Annie snapped. 'Lucy doesn't know the meaning of the word. Now you listen here, my lad. You ain't going on no fishing trip with Lucy. I've told you before, she's bad news. If she's offered to be your friend, believe me, there's something behind it. If you want to go fishing that badly, I'll take yer some other time. Now get yourself washed.'

'Ah, Mam.'

'Ah, Mam, nothing!' she snapped. 'Get yourself washed and quick. Come on, do as I say.'

Georgie scowled and stamped his foot underneath the table.

Annie placed her hands on her hips and glared at him. 'Georgie Higgins, you do as you're told else you'll get a thick ear. Now move or you'll regret it.'

He sniffed loudly, pushed back his chair and stood up. He was defeated and knew it. He went over to the washstand and sullenly started to wash his face.

'That's better, son. Now hurry up so we can be on our way.'

The walk to Matty's seemed to take for ever. The late August sun beat down relentlessly and there was not a breath of wind. The gardens in the village were full of summer flowers and children played barefoot in the streets as their parents had their Sunday afternoon rest. Annie noticed none of this. She was too anxious to arrive at her destination.

She found Matty bustling around the kitchen and the older woman showed delight on seeing them. Normally, Annie would have laughed at the sight that greeted her. Matty, a home-made crutch under one arm and a broom in her other hand, was trying her hardest to sweep the floor.

'Give me the broom,' Annie ordered. 'You make the tea.'

'Oh, ta, me duck,' came the relieved reply. 'We've the house to ourselves this afternoon. The lads are down the pub, their usual Sunday ritual. And then they go visiting.' She winked at Annie. 'You know, girlfriends and such like. So we'll have peace to chat. And by the look on your face, we need to.'

Ten minutes later the women sat facing each other across the well-scrubbed pine table. Matty poured two huge mugs of scalding tea and passed one to Annie.

'Right, come on then. What catastrophe has befallen you? You look as though you have the weight of the world on yer shoulders.'

Annie took a deep breath. The lump in her chest rose to her throat and tears welled up in her eyes.

'Oh, Matty!' She shuddered. 'I don't know where to begin.'

'At the beginning. That's the best place,' her friend said softly.

Annie poured out her story. Starting with the revelation Kath had so spitefully delivered and finishing with the happening at the fair.

Matty listened in silence, her anger mounting. Had this girl not suffered enough? Over the past few months Annie had had more than her fair share of trouble. It wasn't fair. But then life in general wasn't, she thought ruefully. She shifted uncomfortably in her chair as Annie finished her story.

'What am I to do?' she sobbed. 'John forced me, Matty. I feel dirty and horrible. I feel he's taken all me dignity away. And what if I'm pregnant?' she wailed. 'I never encouraged him, honest I never!'

'Hush, hush, child. I know that. But who'll believe yer?' Matty sighed. 'Matthews will deny it, and as you've no witnesses, you have no proof that he ever did force yer.'

'Oh, God, Matty! So a man can do what he likes and get away with it?'

'Yes, that's always been the case. It'll be your word against his, and if it comes out, you'll never live it down. And as for being pregnant . . . Well, let's just hope that you ain't, eh?'

Annie gulped hard. 'You're right, Matty. But how am I ever gonna face him again?'

'Oh, I'm sure he won't dare show his face for a long time.'

'I hope not, Matty. I just hope not.' Annie groaned loudly and clenched her fists. 'I wouldn't be responsible for me actions if he did,' she said icily.

'Ah, come on, gel. No man's worth spending time in prison for.'

'I would for him, Matty. I'd swing for him, you see if I wouldn't.'

'I believe yer,' she answered gravely. 'But who'd look after Georgie? Poor lad'd be without a mother or a father.'

Annie sighed deeply. 'Okay, you've made your point.'

'Thank God for that,' Matty said with relief. 'Now pour us another cuppa, gel. I'm parched.'

Annie did as she was bid, then placed her elbow on the table, rested her cheek in her hand and eyed Matty.

'What d'you make of what Kath said?' she asked softly. 'D'you think she was telling the truth about my father? Oh, I hope not, Matty. I really don't think I can take much more.'

'Drink your tea,' the older woman ordered. She rubbed her

leg. Christ, it was sore today. She must try and rest it more or it would never heal. She looked across at Annie and took a deep breath.

'Kath is telling the truth, my dear.'

'She is?'

'Yes, I'm afraid so.' Matty paused. 'I think there's a story you should hear. You need to know some facts about the past, Annie, and I'm the only one who'll tell you anything like the truth. You'll have to bear with me, 'cos twenty-odd years have passed and yer mind tends to play tricks. Obviously I don't know it all. Your mother's the only one who knew all the details, and she's gone, bless her. Anyway, just listen and I'll do me best.'

Annie leant back in her chair, her stomach churning as a sickening fear rose in her.

Matty inhaled deeply.

'As you know, your mother and I were very close friends. I was a couple of years older than her, but that didn't make any difference to us. My mother used to help your grandmother up at the farm. That's how we got to know each other. When I was thirteen I went to work up in the big house at Kirby Mallory and Mary Ann often came to visit me. She used to bring me baskets of food. Not that I needed it. They looked after me well, which is more than I can say for some poor souls in service.' She smiled. 'Your mother must have thought I was daft, 'cos the main purpose of her visits were obviously to get a glimpse of the squire's son. She had a right fancy for the lad. Actually, it was quite funny, 'cos Mary Ann would pretend to be the mistress of the house. She'd prance about and try to talk posh. There was no harm in it, it were just a giggle.'

'Did he like her, Matty?'

'Oh, I don't think for a moment Master James had any idea of her feelings. If he had, he was too much of a gentleman to take advantage. And don't forget, they were only young at the time and he was away at school, except for holidays and such like.'

155

'Oh!' Annie exclaimed.

Matty shook her head. 'That's one idea you'll have to drop, Annie. I can assure you, you ain't related to the Richmonds and that's a fact.' She picked up her mug and drained the dregs, ignoring Annie's dismayed expression. 'One harvest . . .' she continued, then paused thoughtfully for a moment. 'Your mother would have been about fifteen, it was well after me and Archie started courting, a young man turns up at the farm looking for work. He said he'd walked all the way from . . . oh, I can't remember, somewhere up north. Kind of handsome in a funny sort of way, and I'll never forget his name – Thomas McIntyre.' She lowered her voice. 'And his hair was as red as the sun. Your grandfather took a liking to him and set him on. Your mother and him hit if off straight away and from what I gathered at the time, it seemed she had fallen pretty badly for him.' She shook her head. 'Though to be honest, I could never see what she saw in him. He weren't the usual type she usually took a fancy to.'

'What d'you mean?'

'Well, I suppose I shouldn't air me views to you about him but I always thought on him as being gutless. Always sucking up to yer uncle and grandfather, following them about and doing everything anyone told him. No, not the kind of man I thought yer mother would have set her heart on.'

'But she did love him?' Annie interrupted.

'Yes, I'd say so. The way she talked about "her man" you would have thought he was a god. However poor and uncouth Thomas McIntyre was, he certainly must have had something to capture yer mother the way he did. She was besotted by him, I've no doubts on that.'

Annie sighed deeply. 'Well, at least they loved each other. I suppose that's something.' She shifted awkwardly in her seat. 'So what happened?'

'Happened? I don't really know. The next thing I knew was your mother telling me she was pregnant and had to go away.'

'But why? If they loved each other, why didn't they just get married and settle at the farm?'

'Oh, my dear.' Matty looked aghast. 'That would have been out of the question. Your grandfather was a farmer and Thomas McIntyre a poor traveller. No, that wouldn't have gone down well at all. All hell would have been let loose had it come to light.'

'Oh, I see.' Annie frowned, biting her bottom lip. 'So my mother left the farm then and went away with Thomas McIntyre?'

'No, she didn't. If you'd just be patient, I'll explain what happened.' Matty paused for breath and took a sip of her tea from her replenished mug. 'During this time,' she continued, 'we had a spate of robberies in the area. The big house suffered, lots of silver was took, but the biggest theft was the payroll from the Bardon Quarry.'

'Bardon Quarry?' Annie queried. 'Where's that?'

'About five miles from here. Around five hundred pounds went missing from the safe. They never caught whoever was involved, but there was a lot of talk about a gang from up north being the culprits, and for all anyone knew they'd done what jobs they wanted and gone back. One had been spotted though.' She hesitated. 'It seemed he had flaming red hair.'

Annie's head jerked up sharply.

'It was only hearsay,' Matty hurriedly continued. 'As I said, no one was ever caught.' She paused and stared into space. 'To be honest, I can't see McIntyre being the leader of the gang – that's if he ever belonged to it. More like a look out or something. He hadn't the brains to plan anything on that scale.' She turned her attention back to Annie. 'You must understand that during this time Archie had met Kath, dumped me and married her. I was going through a bad spell myself and was in no mood to listen to gossip. I didn't see much of Mary Ann during this time. She obviously felt bad about Kath and Archie and also had her own problems to sort out. But I do know that Thomas McIntyre disappeared and your mother never saw him again.' She paused and frowned deeply. 'But I did,' she announced quietly.

'Did you?'

'Yes. But I'll come to that in a minute. The morning she left the farm, yer mother came up to the big house. She told me she thought she was pregnant and that the only thing she could do was to go away and save shame being brought on the family.'

'Oh, Matty!' Annie groaned.

'She loved her family, Annie, and would not have wanted them to suffer for something she'd done. You have to understand – living in a village, scandal gets round before you know it and folks never let you forget things like that. I tried to talk her out of it. Said her family'd help her. But she was adamant. The man she loved didn't want her and the only course left was to go away. She left as quickly as she arrived, caught the cart into Leicester, and that was that.' She drew in her breath, folded her arms under her bosom and leant on the table. 'I've no proof but I feel sure Kath knew about her condition and got at her.'

'That woman has a lot to answer for,' Annie said icily.

'Doesn't she just? But we've no proof, Annie.'

'Oh, but we have, Matty,' she said fiercely. 'Kath told me herself that she'd had a go at my mother about her predicament.'

'Ah, well. It's too late for all that now, gel. Your mother's dead and twenty-five years have gone past. Anyway, what good would it do to tell Archie now? It won't bring yer mother back. And, besides, he'd take a lot of convincing. He worships the ground Kath walks on.'

Annie nodded. 'Yes, you're right.'

'I never heard a word from your mother after that. We all worried for months. Archie and your grandfather had people looking for her, but no luck. You're the only news we've ever had.'

'And not good news, eh? Telling you she was dead.'

'Better than nothing, gel. At least we know now.'

Annie smiled wanly. 'You said you saw Thomas McIntyre again?'

'Oh, yes. It must have been a couple of months after your mother left the farm. I'd slipped up quietly to see your granny. She had caught pneumonia and was really poorly. By then Kath had got her feet firmly under the table and she tried to order me out, but I stood me ground. I wouldn't leave without seeing Annie. That woman had been a good friend to me and I wasn't about to let an upstart like Kath get in my way.'

'So she was nasty even then?'

Matty nodded. 'She was barely sixteen and as hard as nails. After me visit, she let rip. Said I was trying to come between her and Archie. We had harsh words and I stormed out. I was that mad. That little madam had accused me of all sorts. I stood with me back against the wall by the kitchen door to get meself together when I saw a figure slinking out of the barn. God, it frightened me to death. I couldn't move for fear. I knew old Reggie would be down the pub with his cronies and that Archie and his father weren't back from the market. I had to strain me eyes but I suddenly recognised who it was.'

'Thomas McIntyre!' Annie exclaimed.

'The very man. I shouted over to him: "What the hell a'you up to?" He got such a shock when he seen me, I can tell yer. He rushed over, grabbed me by me arm and told me to shut up, case anyone heard. He pulled me over to the barn. I was too scared by his manner to struggle. I could tell, though, that he was really nervous. He kept looking round to see if anyone else was about. Inside the barn he shook me hard and demanded I tell him where Mary Ann was. I can remember being confused because I thought of all people he should know where she was.'

'Didn't you say that?'

'Yes,' Matty said thoughtfully. 'I think I did. I said, "What you asking me for? You know damn' well where she is, being's you got her into trouble in the first place."'

159

'And what did he say to that?'

'Er . . .' Matty suddenly sat back and gazed into space. 'He said he didn't know what I was talking about, and at the time I thought he was just saying that to cover things up.' She leant forward and eyed Annie. 'I'm beginning to wonder now if your mother ever told him she was pregnant.'

'Oh!'

'Well, it would explain his reaction. Which I never thought much about at the time. But he was annoyed, Annie, really annoyed. He wanted to speak to your mother about something important and demanded that the next time I saw her she was to leave word saying what she'd done.'

'Done! Done about what?'

Matty shrugged her shoulders. 'I dunno.'

'This is all very strange.' Annie grimaced. 'Didn't he seem concerned about her at all?'

Matty frowned. 'No. Not concerned. Just mad.'

'Mad? Why? Because she had run away and he loved her and was worried?'

'No. That's not the impression I got.'

'What impression did you get then?'

'Oh, it's difficult to put into words. But he didn't seem bothered by the fact that she had disappeared. More interested in what she'd done, whatever that might have meant. What I'm trying to say is that he seemed to have something more important on his mind than her disappearance. Anyway, before he ran off, he told me once more that when I saw her again I was to ask her what she'd done. Really stressed the point he did.'

Matty shrugged her shoulders. 'I suppose we'll never find out. Unless . . .' Her eyes opened wide. 'There's only one explanation for that remark, Annie,' she said gravely. 'And that's that he'd been involved in the robberies and your mother knew where he'd hidden the money.' She quickly shook her head. 'That doesn't bear thinking about. Your mother was honest and wouldn't be involved with anything like that. And as far as I know, Thomas McIntyre never did

160

return. Where he went or what happened to him remains a mystery.'

She leant back in her chair and looked fondly at Annie. 'Well, that's me story. I'm just sorry I had to tell you. I was hoping that things would work out at the farm and that you would never need to know about the past. And surely you realise now, Annie, Thomas McIntyre must have been your father? There was no one else that I knew of around at the time.' She smiled tenderly at the young woman. 'Why, my dear, you only have to look at Georgie for proof.'

'Oh, Matty,' she sighed, her voice thick with emotion. 'What a mess.' She wiped a tear away with the back of her hand. 'Here's me thinking I might be related to the gentry, when all the time my father was no more than a common criminal!'

'Ah, we don't know that for sure, me duck. I must admit, it looks that way, but we've no evidence.'

'No. But it doesn't make me feel any better.' Annie stood up and paced backwards and forwards in front of the fireplace. 'But what about me dad, Matty? I don't mean Thomas McIntyre, I mean the man who brought me up. He was such a good man. I couldn't have wished for a better father. How could he have done all he did for me, knowing about this?'

Matty shrugged her shoulders. 'He maybe never knew. If your mother died the night you were born, they didn't have that much time together. I'll say this though, love. He must have been something special to marry a girl who was already pregnant.' She smiled up at Annie and her eyes softened. 'You just be thankful he did, else your life could have been very different.'

'Yes, it could have.'

'Your mother was a good gel, Annie. Never forget that,' Matty said softly. 'What happened to her has happened to many others just as good.' She raised her voice slightly, unable to prevent the anger she felt from showing. 'Kath had no business making her feel bad and forcing her to leave the

161

farm. Your granny would have stood by her, I know she would.' She lowered her voice again. 'But that's all in the past and you've got to forget.' She saw Annie's anguished look. 'I know, me duck. I know it's easy for me to say, but you've got to forget all this business and build a life for you and Georgie now. That's all that matters, you and him.'

Annie walked back to the table and sat down. 'You're right, Matty. I should be grateful that I had such a good man to bring me up. And I had Charlie,' she added emotionally. She paused for a moment, a hard look crossing her face. 'I wish I could leave the farm and go back home. But there's nothing left for me to return to. If I was on my own it wouldn't be so bad, but there's Georgie to consider. I can't turn to Martha and Bert, they've their own problems and have already helped me more than they could afford.'

'You could always come here,' Matty offered. 'We'll find a space for you somewhere and you might be able to get a job in one of the factories.'

'Oh, thanks, Matty.' She leant over and patted the older woman's arm. 'I do appreciate your offer but you've hardly any room as it is.' She sighed deeply. 'No, I have to stick it out at the farm for the time being. Actually it's not as bad as it sounds. I'm beginning to get really fond of Uncle Archie, and he treats Georgie like his son.' She smiled. 'Georgie's fairly blossomed since we arrived and it wouldn't do him any good to be dragged away now. And to what? The workhouse?'

Matty nodded in agreement.

'I keep out of Kath's way as much as possible, that way life's fairly bearable, and of course there's young Molly.'

'Molly?'

'Yes, Molly Machin.'

'Oh, Freda's young gel. 'Course, I forgot she was there.'

'She's a nice kid. Georgie loves her too. So you see it ain't so bad, Matty. Not compared to the workhouse at any rate.'

'Hmm,' Matty agreed. 'If you put it like that, no, it ain't. But don't forget my offer. If anything else happens, you and Georgie come straight here, understand?'

'Yes, Matty, and thank you.' Annie smiled warmly. 'Where would I be if I hadn't you to turn to?'

Matty smiled broadly. 'I don't know, gel, but I'm glad you do. I'm here any time you need me. Now,' she said, making a grab for her walking aid, 'do you want something to eat?'

'Oh, no, thanks all the same. My stomach's turning somersaults at the moment. But I bet Georgie'll be starving.'

'I've never known a young 'un yet that ain't,' Matty jovially answered. 'I'll get him a sandwich. I got some nice potted meat from the butcher's yesterday and he can have a thick slice of me fruit cake.'

Annie felt slightly better from her talk with her friend, but her emotions were still in such a turmoil that she was only half listening to her son's constant chatter as they made their way back to the farm. He'd had a wonderful afternoon playing with the boys next-door.

'I couldn't have made a better cart meself,' he chuckled. 'It was big enough to carry the three of us.'

'Was it? Oh, that's nice.'

'I didn't half scrape me knee, though. Look.'

Georgie stopped, bent down and eased up his knicker-bockers. Annie absently surveyed his leg.

'My God, Georgie!' she gasped. 'How on earth did you do that? And you've ripped yer best trousers.'

'On the cart – I told yer. We all fell off when we crashed into the railway lines. Anyway it doesn't hurt.'

'It's a wonder!' Annie snapped as she pulled out her handkerchief from the sleeve of her blouse, spat on it and tried to wipe away the caked in grit and dirt. 'If this goes septic, you'll have to have your leg off,' she said sternly. 'Why didn't you say something at Matty's?'

'I forgot,' Georgie said sullenly, the happiness he felt suddenly draining away at the thought of the impending amputation. 'I won't really have to have me leg off, will I?'

Annie straightened up. 'I shouldn't think so. But we'll have to clean you up properly when we get home. In future, stay away from those railway lines. What if a train had been

163

coming? You wouldn't be around to have your leg off, you'd have all been splattered to bits, with nothing left to bury. Have you thought on that?'

'No, Mam,' he said, choking back a sob.

'Well, in future be more careful,' she snapped. She suddenly realised she was taking her mood out on her son and knelt down in front of him, hugging him to her. 'I'm sorry, son. I didn't mean to snap. Only I couldn't bear anything to happen to you.' She stood up and grabbed his hand. 'Come on, let's get back. We have some chores to do before bedtime, and I don't know about you but I'm dog tired.'

As they rounded the bend in the track that led towards the farm gate, Annie frowned in bewilderment as she spotted Archie running towards them.

'She's not with you then?' he asked breathlessly.

'Archie, calm down. Who's not with us?'

'Oh, Christ. It's our Lucy. She's gone missing. We ain't seen her all afternoon. Kath's frantic. We've looked everywhere, Annie, I was hoping she was with you.'

She looked down at Georgie. 'Tell your uncle where you were going this afternoon.'

'Eh?' he gulped, and stared up apprehensively at his uncle. 'We were going to the brook. The one past the village. We were going to fish and have a picnic, only Mam said I couldn't go 'cos we were going visiting.'

'The brook!' Archie exclaimed loudly. 'She knows she's not allowed down there. For one thing it's dangerous. It's quite deep in places, and for another it's too far away. What were you both playing at, making arrangements to go down there? My God, Annie!' He looked at her, his eyes wide in alarm. 'She could have fell in and drowned. I'd better hurry.'

'Hold on, Archie, I'll come with you. Georgie, run and tell your Auntie Kath where we're going and get Molly to see to your knee. Run now.'

Georgie fled towards the farm whilst Annie and Archie ran in the opposite direction. Through the village they went, past Matty's house and on towards Kirby Muxloe. Between the two villages ran a broad brook, edged by small clumps of trees and bushes. Annie, who was already exhausted, found the journey very hard going. Archie was well ahead of her and she kept having to stop and catch her breath. Her thoughts were for Lucy; as much as she disliked the child she hoped with all her heart that nothing had happened to her.

Archie reached the area that Georgie had described and began to search frantically along the edge of the brook. The water level was quite low as there had been no rain for several weeks and his hopes lifted slightly. She could not possibly have drowned in that depth, unless of course she had been paddling, slipped on a stone and banged her head.

Annie arrived. 'Any luck?

Archie shook his head. 'No. I've been right up to that clump of trees there.' He pointed over to his right. 'And there's no sign.'

'D'you think we've got the right place?'

Archie shrugged his shoulders. 'From what Georgie told us, yes. But who's to say she didn't change her mind and go off somewhere else? Oh, Annie . . .'

'Uncle Archie, don't!' She quickly placed her hand on his arm. 'Look, let's try down the other way.'

'Okay.'

The trees and bushes were quite thick and they practically had to hack their way through. Annie was covered in scratches and bruises by the time they finally found Lucy in a small clearing. She was lying under a tree, soaking wet, and had a large, egg-shaped lump on the top of her head. Much to their relief, she was still breathing. Archie knelt down and gently placed her head on his lap.

Annie also knelt down and checked her over. 'Apart from the bump, I can't find anything else wrong.' She felt the girl's forehead. 'She's burning up.' She gazed around in bewilderment. 'Looks to me like she's been attacked. Oh, look,' she exclaimed as she quickly walked over to a clump of bushes. Behind were the remains of a picnic. Half eaten sandwiches and a bottle of home-made lemonade lay scattered over an old piece of cloth. 'Look, here's the picnic basket. D'you think it could have been travellers, Archie, after her food?'

'Oh, I don't know, Annie. I'm just thankful she's still alive.'

Lucy's eyes flickered open. 'Oh, Daddy, Daddy!' she cried.

'Hush, child,' he soothed. 'You're safe now. Don't try to speak. We're gonna get you back home. You can tell us what happened later.'

Lucy closed her eyes and her body sagged. Archie gathered her up into his arms and began the trek home. Annie collected the basket, quickly packed it up and followed her uncle back to the farm.

They were met at the gate by a distraught Kath. She quickly examined the state of her daughter and shouted to Molly to find old Reggie and send him for the doctor. Lucy was put to bed while they awaited his arrival.

Reggie was not amused. 'I can't go, I'm busy,' he wheezed.

Molly placed her hands on her hips. 'Kath said you were to go. I've got to boil the water for the doctor's arrival.'

'She ain't having a bloody baby!' he snapped.

'Reggie, the doctor will need to scrub his hands and Lucy needs a wash, she's filthy.'

'Serves her bloody right. She knows she ain't allowed up the brook. If she's gone and got herself brained, then that ain't my fault. She's just a nuisance anyway. If you ask me, we'd all be better off if she wa' out of the way.'

'Reggie, no one's asking you. Now, are you going or not?'

'Oh, I suppose I'll 'ave to.' He grabbed his cap, slapped it on his head and, mumbling and grumbling to himself, headed out of the barn door.

Molly shook her head and headed back towards the kitchen.

Annie, Archie and Georgie were sitting silently. Molly had plied them all with cups of hot, strong tea. The doctor came and assured them that all Lucy had was a concussion. Nothing was broken, she had been very lucky. It looked as if a large stone had either fallen on or been thrown at her. All she needed was rest and quiet for at least a week. They were

166

all at a loss to work out what had happened and were waiting for Lucy to inform them.

Kath sat by her daughter's bedside, wiping her forehead with a cold wet flannel.

Lucy groaned and flickered open her eyes. 'Where am I?' she asked as she gazed up into her mother's ashen face.

'Hush, darling. Mummy's here.' Kath dipped the cloth in ice cold water and applied it again to her forehead. 'How d'you feel?'

'Awful,' came the pathetic reply. 'Where am I?'

'Oh, darling, you're at home, safe in bed, and Mummy is here to take care of you.' Tears of relief gushed down Kath's face. She bent over and kissed her daughter gently on the cheek. 'You've had a nasty accident, dear. Can you remember what happened?'

Lucy's face filled with pain. She eased her arm out of the bedclothes and took her mother's hand.

'Oh, Mam. It were awful.' She closed her eyes and sighed deeply. 'Don't ask me to tell you. I don't want to get him into trouble.' She opened her eyes and stared up at her mother. 'I don't really think he meant to do it.'

'Who? Meant to do what?' Kath asked, trying to keep her voice under control. 'You must tell me, Lucy.'

She swallowed and took a breath. 'It was Georgie. He . . . he tried to put his hand up me skirt and I wouldn't let him, Mam. I wouldn't, honest. I told him it was rude. But he kept asking. Then he flew into a temper and pushed me in the water. He threw a big stone at me, Mam. It hit me on the head. Oh,' she groaned loudly, 'it don't half hurt. He ran off and left me, and I had to drag myself out of the water.' She squeezed her mother's hand. 'I only suggested the picnic to try and make friends. I was trying to be nice.' She lowered her eyelids. 'I know you said not to play with him, but I felt sorry for him, you see.' She tried to raise herself from the bed and flopped back, wincing in pain. 'I don't want him to get into trouble, Mam. Really I don't.'

'Trouble! I'll give him trouble. Now you rest, my angel. I'll

167

be back soon.' Kath stormed out of the bedroom, unaware of the smug smile spreading across Lucy's face.

The kitchen door bounced off the back wall as Kath burst through it.

'You!' she screamed, pointing to Georgie. 'It were you. You nearly killed my baby, you dirty little bugger.' She ran forward and made to grab him by the hair. Archie and Annie both leapt up. Archie grabbed Kath and held her back while Annie pulled Georgie off his seat and protected him behind her back. Molly ran out in terror and up to her room in the attic.

'What are you talking about, Kath?' Archie demanded, struggling with her as she tried to break free from his grasp.

'He wanted to put his hand up our Lucy's skirt and when she wouldn't let him, he tried to brain her, that's what. Now let me get at him,' she screamed.

'Just a minute, Kath,' Annie said coldly. 'When was this supposed to have happened?'

'This afternoon, you silly cow! When d'you think? Our Lucy was trying to be kind and be friends, and he does this to her!' She pulled away from Archie and shot forward. She faced Annie, body shaking in temper as she tried to make another grab for Georgie.

'Kath, there's no way he could have been involved. He's been with me all afternoon, and all morning he was helping Archie.'

'What?' Kath stepped back, a stunned expression on her face. 'That's a lie. Our Lucy says . . .'

'I would check with her again if I were you. I have witnesses to prove he was with me.'

'Witnesses! Who?' Kath spat. 'I don't believe yer. I think you're lying to shield him.'

Annie narrowed her eyes and turned her head towards Archie. 'Uncle Archie, was Georgie with you this morning?'

'Er . . . yes, he was. Right up 'til dinnertime.'

'Thank you.' She turned back to Kath. 'He had his dinner with me and then we went out.'

'You went out. Where?'

'I don't think that is any of your business. But if you must know, we went down to the village to visit an old friend.'

'Old friend. What old friend?'

Annie raised her head and looked Kath straight in the eyes. 'Matilda Cobbett.'

'Matilda Cobbett! How come you know her? What's going on?'

'Nothing's going on. I've known Matty a while. She and I talked all afternoon. Georgie was playing with the boys next-door.'

'Ah, there you go,' Kath said triumphantly, wagging a finger in the air. 'Matilda Cobbett lives not far from the brook. How d'you know that Georgie . . .'

'I do,' Annie cut in sharply. 'He was playing with the boys next-door all afternoon and has the bruises to prove it. If you don't believe me, I'll take you down to see the boys.'

Kath shrank back.

'I think you should go and speak to Lucy and get the truth, Kath.'

'She's right,' Archie said, clearing his throat. 'I'll come with you.' He walked over to Kath and took her arm.

'You'll not.' She pushed him out of the way. 'I can sort out me own daughter, thank you very much.' She turned on her heel and stormed out of the room towards Lucy's bedroom.

Archie looked at Annie, unable to find any words.

'We'd better go to our room, out of the way.' She pushed Georgie towards the back door, then stopped. 'Maybe Georgie won't be so readily blamed now when things happen round here.'

Kath walked into the bedroom and closed the door behind her. She stood for a minute, her back pressed against the hard wood. She stared over at her daughter, lying against the snow white pillows, her eyes tightly closed. She walked across the room, sat down on the bed and poked her in the shoulder. 'Right, madam,' she said coldly. 'What really happened?'

Lucy's eyes opened in alarm. 'I told yer,' she said hesitantly.

'Told me! Oh, yes, you told me all right. But it was a pack of lies.'

'No, Mam!'

'Lucy, Georgie was with his mother all afternoon.'

'Eh?' Lucy pressed herself into the mattress and pulled the bedclothes further up. She was suddenly very anxious that her plan had gone badly wrong. She was so frightened of the potential consequences that she could not speak.

'Well,' said Kath, 'I'm waiting.'

Tears welled up in Lucy's eyes and she started to shake. 'I'm going to be sick,' she wailed.

'Sick? I'll make you bloody sick! You've made a right fool outta me. Now you tell me, girl, what really happened?'

'I . . . I was going to get Georgie good and proper, Mam. I thought if my plan worked it would get rid of them both and you'd be really pleased with me.' She pulled nervously at the covers. 'I know you don't like 'em being here and I hate to see you so upset.'

'Lucy . . .'

'Oh, me head hurts, Mam. I need to sleep.'

'Out with it!' Kath snarled.

Lucy gulped. 'I arranged for us to have a picnic down by the brook, and I was going to fall in and tell you that he'd tried to drown me. Only, he never turned up. I thought he'd got lost so I thought of a better plan.' She bit her bottom lip and lowered her lashes.

'And?' Kath demanded.

'Well . . .' Lucy stuttered and started to cry. 'I rolled about in the water for a bit then I balanced a big stone on a branch of a tree and jumped underneath. Oh, it really whacked me one. I must have fainted with the pain 'cos next thing I knew, Father was bending over me.' She wept louder. 'I only wanted to please you, Mam. I wanted to get rid of them and make you proud of me.'

'You fool!' Kath snapped angrily. 'Don't you realise you

could have killed yourself? Now all you've done is made me look stupid. You've really done it this time. Nobody is ever going to believe a word we say against them in future.' She stood up and paced the room.

'I'm really sorry, Mam.'

'I should damned well think so,' fumed Kath. 'Planning takes lots of work, Lucy. You need to be a hundred per cent sure it'll work before you carry it out. Let this be a lesson to yer.'

'Oh, it will, Mam. It will.'

'Now you'll stay in bed for a week.' She walked towards the door and turned to face her daughter. 'You're not going to the barn dance.'

'Oh, Mam. Not that, please. You know how I love the barn dance.'

'I know,' Kath said sharply. 'You think what it means to you missing the barn dance, while I try and put this mess right.'

'Mam, I said I was sorry. Please let me go to the dance? I'll be good, honest. I won't do anything ever again,' pleaded Lucy.

'No,' came the sharp reply.

Kath pulled open the door, stormed through and slammed it shut behind her.

She stood facing her husband in the kitchen.

'She fell into the water and banged her head. The poor thing dragged herself out and then fainted. She made up the story about Georgie because she knew she shouldn't have been down there.'

'Codswollop!' Archie said. 'She planned the whole thing to get Georgie into trouble. Only it backfired, and you know it.'

'Don't you dare say that about my daughter,' Kath raised her voice defiantly.

'Our daughter, Kath, ain't she?' he looked at her and narrowed his eyes.

'Of course,' she answered hurriedly. 'But you'd sooner believe that little liar up in the loft than your own kin. I think that's dreadful.'

'That's not true and you know it. But I've no other choice, Kath. The lad was with his mother all afternoon, there's no way he could have done what Lucy said. Anyway, you know she's always telling lies.'

'She does not!' Kath exclaimed angrily. 'For God's sake, Archie, the child is only seven and you're trying to make out she's a conniving liar.'

'No, I wasn't,' he replied wearily. He sat down in the fireside chair. 'I think she should apologise to Annie and the lad.'

'Oh, do you?'

'Yes. It's the least she can do.'

'Well, we'll see about that. She's too ill at the moment to do anything. She's to stay in bed for at least a week and I've told her she's not going to the barn dance.'

Archie looked up at his wife in surprise. Kath turned away from him and busied herself at the table.

'I think that's punishment enough,' she said. 'Now, I'll get your tea and maybe we can forget all about this.'

Meanwhile, up in the safe confines of their room above the barn, Annie helped Georgie out of his clothes.

'Thank God I found out what you were up to this morning. I dread to think of the consequences had I left you here and gone to see Matty on my own.'

Georgie lowered his head.

'I told you, didn't I? I just knew it. I knew she was up to something. Thank goodness I made you come with me.' Annie sighed loudly. 'Let's just hope things are a bit more peaceful round here for a while, eh?'

She kissed the top of his head. Georgie wrapped his arms round her waist and gave her a squeeze.

'I don't think we shall see Lucy for a while, but if you should . . .' She pulled away and held Georgie at arm's length by the shoulders. 'Just keep out of her way. Okay, son?'

He nodded and climbed gratefully into bed.

Annie sat in the chair by the wood stove watching the

light from the candle casting its shadows around the room. It had certainly been an eventful couple of days. Events that she could well have done without. She sighed deeply and laid down her sewing. She knew that she could not stand any more upheaval. During the last year she had lost her husband and baby, found her longlost family, discovered her origins, and been raped.

Surely that was more than any woman should suffer in a lifetime, and here she was not quite twenty-five. What did the next twenty-five years hold in store? she wondered, and managed a brief smile. Whatever it was, it couldn't be anything worse than the last few months.

She grimaced as a severe pain shot through her stomach. A pain she knew well. For the first time in years she was relieved to feel it. At least that was one thing she didn't have to worry about. She put her sewing away, attended to herself and retired gratefully to bed.

It was late-September and autumn was evident. The countryside glowed with deep shades of red, gold and brown and the early mornings saw the fields covered with mists and dew. Georgie had been busy collecting conkers, acorns and cones. Annie had stored them ready for the winter fires after Georgie had selected the biggest conkers and threaded them with string ready to challenge anyone who would play with him.

All the fruit from the orchard and meat from the slaughtered animals had been preserved for the winter; the fields had been ploughed ready for the spring.

Everyone was in good spirits, even Kath. Lucy had been confined to the house for the last few weeks but whenever they met she was very polite and amiable. Annie was unsure how long this truce would last, but while it was in operation did her utmost to keep it going.

The school term was to start a couple of weeks after the barn dance and she had made up her mind to speak to Archie on the subject of Georgie's schooling. Obviously Kath had no intention of doing anything and it worried her greatly to think that Georgie had gone nearly six months without any education.

Much to her relief she had not seen John Matthews since the night of the fair. If he had paid a visit to the farm then he must have been very discreet as Annie had not seen him. She had been so busy anyway that all thoughts of him had been pushed to the back of her mind. These chilly mornings saw her attack her work with a spring in her step and a light heart.

The day of the barn dance arrived and the whole farm became a hive of activity. Barrels of beer and bottles of cider and ginger beer had been brought up by cart from the local public house. Long trestle tables were put up in the large barn and bales of straw stacked round the sides for people to sit on. Molly was getting in more and more of a tizzy as Kath gave her contradictory orders. She ran by Annie, who was collecting water from the pump, groaning loudly.

'Reggie's disappeared. I can't find him anywhere and Kath wants him.' She grabbed the ladle out of the bucket of water and took a long drink. 'I bet he's up the pub with his cronies, and us run off our feet.'

Annie laughed and straightened up to relieve her aching back. 'Shows he's got sense. I wish I could do the same. He'll be back, you'll see, in time to join in the fun.'

Molly nodded in agreement and ran towards the barn where she was helping to clear a space ready for the dancing. Annie picked up the buckets and headed towards the house, wondering what task Kath had in store for her next.

Later that evening Molly climbed up the ladder into Annie's room and did a twirl in front of her.

'Well? What do you think?'

Annie, who had been dressing her hair, turned from the broken piece of mirror propped up on the tallboy and surveyed the girl. 'I think you look lovely. That shade of green suits you perfectly.'

'Oh, Annie, I feel like a princess. This dress is wonderful. I can't thank you enough for helping me alter it.' The young girl's face was full of delight and she ran to Annie and hugged her.

'It was my pleasure. You're certainly going to get the lads queuing up tonight.'

Molly's face turned the colour of beetroot. 'What are you wearing?' she asked, frowning slightly at the grey flannel dress lying on top of the bed. 'You ain't wearing that, are you? What about your blue dress?'

'Oh, no. I'm not wearing that. My grey flannel will do nicely.' Annie turned from Molly and continued to do her hair as the girl looked at her in confusion.

'But you look lovely in that dress. You go to market in the grey flannel.'

Annie smiled. 'I know. But I've found out that Kath is wearing blue and you know what will happen if she thinks I've dressed in the same colour on purpose. She'll think I'm trying to outdo her.'

Molly's face fell. 'Haven't you got anything else?'

'No.'

'Oh, well.' The girl's face suddenly lit up as she smiled. 'You'll still look prettier than Kath, grey flannel or not.'

Annie laughed. 'Thanks, Molly. But I'm sure I won't get as many dances as you.' She finished her hair and swung round to face the girl. 'Have you seen Georgie? It took me ages to get him spruced up and I bet he's playing with Scrap.'

'No, he ain't. Kath's got him wiping all the glasses. He doesn't look very happy about it either.'

Annie tutted. 'I shouldn't think he is. We already did that this afternoon. Oh, that woman! I wonder how her mind works sometimes. Anyway, at least I know he's out of trouble.' She went over to the bed and slipped on her dress. 'Now, how do I look?'

Molly looked her up and down and paused, trying to find the right words. 'Well, you look nice, Annie.'

She smiled and took Molly's arm. 'Come on. Let's go and see how many hearts you can break tonight.'

'D'you really think I look that nice? Do you really?'

'I do. Now stop going on about it, else you'll get too big headed.'

The barn dance was in full swing by the time they climbed down the ladder ready to join in. Annie was immediately commandeered to help dish up the food. Kath took her aside.

'Don't pile up the plates too high. Some of them are greedy buggers. Probably ain't eaten for weeks, knowing how much of a spread I put on. So keep your eyes on them and make sure they don't come back for seconds.' Annie nodded and sighed, determined that whenever Kath was out of sight she would let them have as much food as they wanted.

Molly was having a wonderful time. All the local lads were milling round her, much to the annoyance of the other local girls. She weaved through the throng of people towards Annie, arriving out of breath, the beads of sweat clinging to her brow.

'This is great, Annie. I ain't stopped dancing since we arrived. I'm nearly worn out. I'll have to sit the next dance out.'

Annie laughed as she handed a guest a huge slice of cold meat pie.

'Molly, for goodness' sake, you're only fifteen. You can't be worn out yet. Go and get stuck in there.' She pulled the girl aside. 'Have you seen that tall lad over there? He can't take his eyes off you.'

Molly fingered the bun at the nape of her neck and caught a tendril of hair that had escaped.

'Oh, Annie, that's Timmy White. His mother and father own the stocking factory on Main Street. Is he really looking?'

'Yes. Now go and dance with him.'

'When are you going to come and dance? I've seen several men asking.'

'I'm quite happy, Molly, thank you. Now be off. I've got to find Georgie and see what he's up to.'

'Oh, he's under a table at the back of the barn. He got a plate of food and him and Scrap are sharing it.'

Annie smiled as she watched Molly make her way through the crowd of people. She stifled a yawn. She had been up since five o'clock and it was starting to tell on her. She had turned and begun to load a tray with glasses when she felt a slight tap on her shoulder.

'Not dancing, Annie?'

She dropped the glass she was holding and swung round in disbelief, her mouth gaping in horror as she took in the figure of John Matthews, standing before her. His eyes twinkled with amusement as he noticed her reaction to his presence. The hatred she felt for him filled her and she clenched her fists tightly.

'What are you doing here? You've got a nerve showing your face after what you did to me!'

His eyes opened wide in surprise. 'What do you mean?' he said, raising his voice over the noise of the dance.

Annie's body started to shake. She desperately tried to control the emotion she felt. 'You know damned well what I mean!'

He paused for a moment. 'Oh, that,' he said nonchalantly, and shrugged his shoulders. 'Come on, Annie. You wanted it as much as I did. Anyway, why make a fuss? We both enjoyed it.' He took a gulp of beer from the glass he was holding. 'D'you know, I can never make you women out. You've always got to make a big deal out of everything.'

Annie nearly choked on his words. She gasped for breath, her eyes glaring in distaste.

'You forced me against my will, and now you try to make out it was nothing! How dare you?' Without thinking, she swung back her arm and smacked him hard across the face.

John staggered back, spilling his beer. Annie's eyes darted as she realised many people had stopped dancing and were staring across at them.

John regained his poise. 'It's okay,' he shouted. 'Just a little misunderstanding.'

To Annie's relief everyone turned and continued with their enjoyment of the evening. John turned back to her and grinned sarcastically.

'I take it you don't fancy a dance, then?'

'I wouldn't dance with you if my life depended upon it.'

'Oh, well,' he said, shrugging his shoulders. 'If you won't, there's plenty of others who will.' He made to leave then stopped and faced her once more. 'If you fancy a repeat performance of the other night any time, I won't say no.' He narrowed his eyes and gave her a wicked smile before he turned and was swallowed up in the crowd.

She stood frozen to the spot. The arrogance of the man. How dare he treat her like this?

'What's going on between you and John?'

Annie swung around and came face to face with her Uncle Archie, a mug of beer in one hand and a sandwich in the other.

'Your face looks like thunder, gel,' he said, taking a bite of the sandwich. 'You two had a row or something?'

Annie fought for words. 'No, no. He just wanted to dance and I don't feel like it, that's all.'

'Come on, gel. You should have said yes. You're not here to work all night. You've got to have some fun.'

'I'm fine, Uncle Archie. Please let me get on with collecting the glasses or there won't be any clean ones to drink from.'

He took a gulp of his beer. 'Get Molly to give you a hand.'

'No, no. Let her have some enjoyment for a change. Anyway,' she added, managing a false smile, 'I don't think she'd thank me for interrupting her just now.' She inclined her head towards the barn door where Molly was deep in conversation with a tall, spotty youth.

'Oh, yes. See what you mean.' Archie slapped her on the arm. 'I'm off to get another beer and find our Kath. I ain't seen her all night. I must say, though, I'm really enjoying myself.'

'You deserve to, after all the work you've done on the farm. Now go on before the beer runs out.'

'Oh, we've plenty of that, Annie. If we run out, the fellas would fetch some more up from the Plough.'

Annie watched as her uncle left her and made his way towards the beer table.

She breathed deeply. She was badly in need of some fresh air. She quickly filled a tray, picked it up and headed for the door. On her way out she spied Kath and John dancing together. She shivered as she took in Kath's happy, smiling face, her arms encircling John's lithe body as they attempted a square dance. Her head started to pound and bile rose in her throat. She turned and rushed out of the barn.

It came as a relief when the evening finally drew to a close and the revellers gradually departed, their singing and bantering still to be heard as they trudged down the track towards their homes.

She surveyed the debris left behind and turned to Molly.

'Get yourself off to bed. I'll tackle this lot.'

'I wouldn't dream of such a thing,' the girl said firmly. 'You can't do all this lot by yourself. Besides, I'm far too excited to go to sleep.'

'Well, I can't say I wouldn't welcome the help,' Annie said wearily as she picked up a stack of plates.

'Where's Archie and Kath?' Molly asked.

'Archie's in bed. He had too much to drink and could hardly stand. As for Kath,' she shrugged her shoulders, 'I haven't seen her for ages.'

'Oh!' Molly uttered. 'What about Georgie?'

Annie laughed. 'After he'd been sick I put him to bed. Scrap's up there with him.'

Molly tutted. 'It's just you and me then. 'Cos you can bet yer life, Reggie's nowhere around.'

'Well, the sooner we start, the sooner we finish,' Annie said, yawning loudly.

It was settled. Georgie started at the village school the following term. Annie had visited the headmaster herself and explained the situation. Her son had been welcomed with open arms and set off on the first morning with his books strapped together by an old leather belt; his lunch bag, consisting of a piece of bread, a chunk of cheese and an apple, clutched firmly in his hand.

It came as no surprise to him to find Lucy had very few friends whereas he, aided and abetted by Micky and Willy, was soon in the thick of school life and settled down to it with relish. He returned in the late afternoon, full of the day's happenings.

Annie was pleased by the way he had settled in so quickly, unlike his last school which she knew he had hated.

As she became more familiar with their surroundings, Annie would take him further afield on their days off. On the odd occasion that Molly did not visit her mother she would accompany them on their walks through the countryside. The two women were becoming firm friends. Molly would speak of her hopes for the future, reminding Annie so much of herself when she had been that age. Georgie always insisted they took along Scrap for protection and it warmed her heart to see the pair of them running together through the tall grass, stopping now and again when they found something of interest.

She would often stand on the top of the hill at the back of the farm and marvel at the beautiful Leicestershire landscape. On a really clear day she could see straight across to Old John, a monument sited on top of a hill in Bradgate Park. Archie had told them that this park was once owned by the Grey family and that their daughter Jane had been the nine day Queen. The young girl had met her end on the scaffold. Annie had felt very sad for the poor creature who had lived so long ago and died so tragically.

One Sunday they had ventured to the next village of Kirby Muxloe and walked round the ruins of the medieval castle. Georgie had loved this excursion and while Annie sat on the grass, he played knights of old, pretending to be Sir Lancelot on his white charger, saving the fair maiden. Annie's peace had been shattered when he had roped her in to be the fair maiden and they had spent a happy afternoon charging in and out of the ruins.

Georgie was growing fast. The country air was doing him the world of good and he was filling out nicely. She had already had to let out his trousers twice. Although she was getting acclimatised to the country ways herself, Annie still missed her beloved city and her friends there. She knew in her heart though that one day she would return. How or when eluded her, but she knew that she could not live with her relatives for ever. One day she and Georgie would have to leave and make their own way in the world.

In readiness for the winter she had knitted herself a thick warm shawl, and as the mornings grew colder was thankful she had taken the trouble to do so. The old folk in the village forecast a bad winter and preparations were being made by Archie just in case their prophecies came true. He had set about repairing the barn and Annie had none too gently reminded him about the ladder to the loft. She had nearly fallen off one morning as it had swayed and creaked under her light weight. Now she was growing really concerned about its safety.

She still saw Matty as much as possible. The older woman's leg had healed and she was getting about without the aid of crutches. Her son Arnold's wedding had been the talk of the village for weeks. Everyone was invited and most of them turned up to see the happy couple tie the knot and then to celebrate afterwards. Annie had managed to slip along at the night-time and had joined in the revelry with relish.

She and her uncle were becoming very close. Occasionally he would come up to her room after his work was finished for the night. While Annie sat and sewed, Archie would sit opposite her and reminisce. She enjoyed these visits immensely and would make strong, hot tea to sip whilst they talked.

Days at the farm had settled into a peaceful routine. She began to feel she belonged and that life was worth living.

The odd skirmish with Kath did nothing to dampen her spirits and she began to hope that her aunt was now beginning to accept her. She still thought often of Charlie, but the pain had now lessened and instead of the tears his memories used to bring, she would smile and remember all the happy times they had shared.

She began to start her day with a smile, thinking how good it was to be alive.

Chapter Eleven

One freezing cold November morning, Annie woke to find her washing water frozen in the blue-patterned china jug. She washed as best she could, hurriedly dressed and scurried out to milk the cows. She left Georgie asleep. There was no point in their both suffering the cold. The chickens could wait for their food for a while.

It was a very dark morning and as she picked her way gingerly across the slippery, sodden yard, Annie's mind was filled with thoughts of Christmas. This would be the first she would spend away from Leicester and without Charlie. Would Kath invite them to eat the festive dinner in the house? If not, she would have to try to make a special effort for herself and Georgie. She presumed Molly would go to her mother's for Christmas dinner. If not, she would ask her to join them. The few coppers she had managed to put by for little presents wouldn't go far and she would have to plan very carefully how she was going to spend them.

It had taken her two hours to milk the cows. For some reason they were being uncooperative which didn't please Annie as she still found she detested this job more than any other. Reggie had collected the herd now and was on his way back with them to the fields. She finished clearing up and was making her way out of the milking shed in order to wake Georgie when she heard a muffled thud. She looked back into the empty shed and frowned, unable to understand what had caused the noise. She shrugged as she surveyed the empty shed. The noise, whatever it was, had obviously not come from there. She decided she must have been fancying things and made her way out into the yard. She was just about to enter the barn when Molly came flying out of the kitchen door.

'Annie! Annie!' she shouted, running over.

'What's up, Molly? You look panic-stricken.' She caught the girl by the arm.

'It's yer grandmother, Annie. I've just been in with her breakfast and she ain't there. I've looked all over the house and she's nowhere to be seen. Oh, God, Annie. Where could she have got to?'

'I don't know,' she answered, perplexed. 'A'you sure she ain't hiding somewhere?'

'No. I've even looked in the cellar.' Molly gave a gasp. 'I'm supposed to be keeping an eye on her. Kath'll kill me.'

'Calm down,' Annie said firmly. 'I'll help you look for her. She can't have got far, can she? Not in this weather. You go down the yard and look in the old cow sheds, I'll start up here. She's definitely not in the milking sheds. I've just come from there.

'Righto, Annie. Thanks.'

They both sped off in different directions. Annie scoured all the old out-buildings that were used for storing materials and farming implements, taking great care to check behind and inside anything that could hide an old lady. After a thorough search she gave up and went to try the large barn. She pulled open one of the heavy wooden doors and her eyes went immediately to the ladder, the one they used to climb up to the room above. She gave a loud gasp. At the bottom, lying on her back in the straw, was her grandmother.

One of her legs was caught in the second rung. The third had snapped in two. Annie gave another cry as she ran over and knelt down before the old woman. She knew instantly that she was dead. She eased the old lady's leg from the ladder and laid it gently on the straw, pulling down her nightdress. Annie looked sorrowfully down at the old lined face. Picking up her gnarled hand, she held it carefully in hers, gently caressing the fingers.

A noise behind startled her and she turned her head quickly to see Molly approaching.

'Oh, Molly, Molly!' she sobbed. 'She's dead. My grandmother is dead. Oh, I don't think I can bear it.'

Molly swiftly joined her and knelt down, placing an arm around her shoulders. 'Oh, Annie.' She looked at the old lady and sighed deeply. 'What d'you think happened?'

'Well, it looks to me like she was trying to get into the loft and the ladder broke.' She shook her head and looked at Molly. 'Have you any idea what she would want to go up there for?'

Molly shook her head. 'No, I ain't, sorry.'

Both women lapsed into silence.

'Annie,' Molly whispered, 'we can't stay here. We'll have to get her back into the house.'

'Yes,' she answered slowly. 'And we'd better tell Archie. Is he still in the kitchen having his breakfast?'

'Oh, no, Annie. They've both gone to market. That's why I were keeping an eye on her. There's no one else here but me and you.'

'Yes, I forgot they were both going out.' Annie gasped for breath, her eyes opening wide in astonishment. 'The old lady must have known!' she exclaimed. 'She must have waited 'til they'd gone and taken her chance to slip out. But why?'

Molly raised her eyebrows and shrugged her shoulders. 'We might never find out.' She saw tears run down Annie's cheeks. 'Come on, Annie. Don't upset yourself.' She grimaced. 'I'm sorry, that was a silly thing to say in the circumstances.'

Annie sniffed. 'We all say daft things when we least want to.' She put down her grandmother's hand and awkwardly rose. 'Let's get her into the house. D'you think we can carry her between us? She doesn't look as though she weighs more than a breath of wind. Oh, Molly. This is awful. Fancy the poor thing meeting her end like this!'

Molly froze at the sight of her distraught friend. She had

never been in a situation like this before and didn't know quite how to handle it.

'Look, er . . .' she began softly. 'Why don't you go and make some tea and I'll er . . . get the handcart.'

'The handcart!' Annie exclaimed.

'Yes. I'll put her in it and wheel her over the yard, and then we can both carry her through into her bedroom.'

'Oh, Molly!' Annie started to laugh. She laughed so hard that tears spurted from her eyes. She grabbed hold of the girl and hugged her tightly. 'Oh, Molly. You are a blessing. Who else would have thought of an idea like that?' She pulled away and looked at her friend fondly. 'We'll surely manage to carry her between us? It would be unseemly to put her on the handcart. Come on, let's get this over with. Then we'll have that tea.'

They were just about to begin to lift her when a little head popped through the trap-door above. Annie and Molly both looked up simultaneously in surprise to see Georgie's disgruntled face.

'What's going on, Mam? I've been lying waiting for ages for you to wake me up.' He looked down at the two women questioningly.

Annie quickly stepped in front of the body in order to hide it.

'Nothing's going on, son. Now get dressed and come into the kitchen for something to eat.'

'Who's that on the floor?'

'What! Oh, that.' Annie's thoughts raced, not wanting to explain to her son what had happened. 'Oh, it's a scarecrow. His arms fell off and me and Molly are fixing him.'

Georgie's eyes opened wide in delight. 'A scarecrow? Oh, goody. I'll come down and help yer.' He made to climb down the ladder, lost his balance and grabbed hold of the supporting beam that ran directly under the room. A piece of wood dislodged and tumbled down, landing at Annie's feet.

Georgie quickly regained his composure and grinned mischievously. She stared up at him.

'Georgie, you could have done yerself a mischief then.

186

Here,' she said, climbing several rungs of the ladder and handing him the piece of wood. 'Put this back before the whole barn falls down, and get dressed like I asked yer. And be careful – the ladder's broken.'

Without further ado, Georgie did as he was told and disappeared back inside the loft.

Annie descended the ladder and faced Molly. 'Quick, let's get her into the house. He might have forgotten all about the scarecrow by the time he comes over for his breakfast.'

The two women set about their task. They managed to get the old lady back in her bed and after placing two pennies over her eyes, went into the kitchen and mashed a much needed pot of tea. Georgie had joined them and was tucking into bread and dripping. The two women sat at the other end of the table so that he could not hear them talking.

'Don't know what Kath is going to say about this,' Molly said forlornly, cradling her mug in her hands. 'She'll blame me. Say I killed her.'

'Molly, stop that! No, she won't. Anyway, for all anyone will know, she died in her bed and you found her.'

They both jumped and grimaced, preparing themselves for the worst as they heard the sound of horses' hooves and the cart rolling into the yard.

Kath came through the door and stopped abruptly as she spied the three of them around the table.

'Oh, yes?' she said, raising her head in the air. 'So this is what happens when I go out. Lucky for me we came back sharpish, ain't it? Really caught you all this time.' She whipped off her gloves and threw them on the table. Archie, who had been scraping his boots on the step outside, entered the kitchen and immediately saw that something was up.

'Come in. Come in,' Kath addressed him sarcastically. 'See for yourself what the staff get up to when I'm away. Loafing around when they should be working. But I've caught them red handed this time.' She looked at him in triumph. 'Well, what are you going to do about it? Or, as usual, I suppose you'll leave it up to me?'

He scratched his head. 'The girls are entitled to a cup of tea, Kath.'

'Oh, entitled are they?'

Annie stood up. 'Kath . . .'

She swung round. 'Don't interrupt me when I'm talking!'

'Kath, will you please listen?'

Annie's tone made her stop in her tracks. She glared at Annie, her face distorted in anger.

'Well, spit it out.'

Annie swallowed hard. 'I'm sorry to have to tell you this.' She turned to Archie. ''Specially you, Uncle Archie, but you see, well . . . we found the old lady this morning.'

'Found the old lady! What the hell are you going on about?'

'For goodness' sake, Kath. Let her finish.'

Her head jerked at the tone of Archie's voice. Her mouth snapped shut as she turned and glared at Annie.

'We found your mother, Uncle Archie. I'm afraid she's dead.'

'Dead?' He stared in disbelief at his niece, then took off his cap and sank slowly down on to the fireside chair. 'Dead?'

Annie quickly looked over at Molly before turning back to her uncle. In the meantime no one noticed Kath slip out of the room.

'She died in her sleep, Uncle Archie. Molly found her when she went in to take her breakfast. I'm so sorry.'

She turned to Molly. 'Get him a mug of tea and put plenty of sugar in it.' The girl nodded and quickly did as she was asked. Annie knelt before her uncle and took his hands.

'She'd had a good life. You told me that yourself.'

'Yes, she did,' Archie sniffed. 'But you expect them to live forever, don't yer?'

Annie gave him a wan smile.

Just then Kath returned.

'She's dead all right,' she announced as she took off her coat and placed it on the back of the chair. 'There's no will. I've looked all over and can't find one. Anyway, it doesn't matter, the farm comes to us.' She stopped her speech abruptly and glared at Annie kneeling before her uncle. 'Get up, girl. There's work to be done. And you,' she faced Archie and wagged her finger, 'have a funeral to arrange. Good job our Lucy is out for the day. Wouldn't have wanted the little love to have been part of all this weeping and wailing.'

Annie's mouth dropped open in amazement at her non-chalant attitude. She glanced over at Molly and raised her eyebrows. Swiftly collecting Georgie, she walked out into the yard.

He tugged at her skirt. 'Who's dead, Mam?'

She stopped and looked thoughtfully at her son. 'Just a very old lady, me love. Just a very old lady. No one we knew.' She sighed and patted his head affectionately then sent him off to feed the chickens.

Later that day she encountered Molly.

'I've just slipped out,' she whispered, her face the picture of misery. 'Oh, Annie, it's pitiful, it really is. He's sitting in the bedroom with his mother. I popped me head round the door and he's stroking her hand and sobbing. Kath ain't said one word of comfort. Not one word. It's bloody disgraceful. She ain't got no heart, Annie. No heart at all.'

Annie placed her arm around Molly's shoulders. 'Come on. Upsetting yourself won't make the slightest bit of difference. We'll have to comfort Archie as best we can between us.'

'Yeah. I'll do me best, but I'm only the kitchen help.'

'You're more than that, Molly. Well, to me at any rate.'

Molly managed a smile. She paused thoughtfully. 'Do you know, Annie, I could swear Kath's delighted the old lady has gone. I'm sure there's a smile on her face. I've caught her unaware and I'm sure she's laughing.'

'Yes,' Annie agreed. 'I got that impression as well.' She shrugged her shoulders. 'But there ain't much we can do about it. I'm only here on sufferance, and now the old lady's dead, I'm sure Kath will do her level best to get rid of us.'

'She won't do that, Annie, I'm sure,' Molly gasped. 'Why, you do the work of three women. No,' she said, shaking her head. 'She won't do that.'

'She will, you know. I'm positive she thinks I'm after my share of the farm. The share that would have been my mother's had she lived. That's why she tried to keep me out of me grandmother's way.'

'Oh!' Molly looked at her in disbelief. 'Do you really think so? If it's true, then she's a wicked woman!'

'Not really, Molly. She's only looking after her own interests. In a way, I can't say as I blame her. After all, we did turn up out of the blue.'

'Huh. She was still quick enough to try and find the will. Blimey, the old lady had only just died. You'd think she could have waited.'

'Yes, I agree, Molly. I don't understand that at all.' Annie sighed deeply. 'I'm just relieved the doctor didn't mention the bruises on her body. If he had made a rigmarole out of that, we'd have had to tell them about finding her in the barn.'

'Oh, but he did, Annie.'

'Eh! And what happened?'

'Kath told the doctor she was always falling out of bed.'

'Oh, I see.' Annie frowned and set her mouth grimly. 'Well, if the doctor's satisfied with that explanation, there's no point in us saying otherwise. I doubt we'd be believed anyway.'

'But what about the ladder to the loft, Annie? How are you gonna explain how it got broke?'

'Yeah. You've a point there, Molly.' She paused thoughtfully. 'I'll fix it myself.'

'You will?'

'Yes, I know where there's some nails, a hammer and some old wood. By the time I've finished no one will be able to tell it's been mended.' She patted Molly's arm affectionately. 'Come on. There's maybe been a death in the family but the animals still need looking after, and I'm only halfway through the butter making.'

'Work, work, that's all we ever do,' Molly moaned.

Annie tilted her head to the side and gave a wry smile.

'Well, you'd better find yourself a rich husband, then you won't have to lift a finger.'

'Phew!' Molly laughed. 'Fat chance. I'll end me days skivvying, I will.' She paused thoughtfully. 'I wonder if she'll put a big spread on after the funeral?'

'I would think so,' Annie said gravely. 'My grandmother must have known a lot of people. Matty was telling me that she was a grand old lady and very well liked. Archie'll want a proper do, and if I know Kath she won't stint when she's entertaining other folks. She likes to make a good impression.'

'Yeah, you're right, Annie. I'll give you one guess though who'll be doing all the work.'

Annie laughed. 'There's no need even to guess. We'll manage between us, Molly. We didn't do too badly with the barn dance.'

'No, we didn't,' she agreed. She gave Annie an unexpected hug, turned, and ran back towards the house.

Chapter Twelve

Preparations for the funeral were well underway. Because it was certain that the squire would attend, Kath insisted the house be cleaned from top to bottom, and the majority of the work fell upon Annie and Molly.

Annie didn't mind the prospect of all the extra work. It would give her a chance to examine the rest of the house which before now had been denied her. It was far bigger than it appeared from the outside. It had four large bedrooms, a parlour, breakfast room, large hall, two small servants' quarters in the attic, and an enormous cellar filled with all sorts of bits and pieces left over by previous generations of Burbages. All the rooms were adequately furnished, the parlour being the most elaborate. Even Molly's room in the attic held a bed, single oak wardrobe and tallboy, and Annie momentarily fumed at the thought that she and Georgie could easily have been accommodated without any disruption whatsoever to the rest of the family.

The parlour floor was covered by a large red Axminster Chinese-patterned rug which had been purchased by Archie many years before in a house sale. Annie had had to kneel and hand brush every square inch, making sure not a speck of dust remained. The surrounding floorboards were waxed and buffed and all the furniture polished until reflections could clearly be seen in them. Every window in the house was washed inside and out and the outside toilet white washed and fixed with a new wooden toilet seat made by a disgruntled Reggie.

'I'm a bloody cowman norra carpenter,' he grumbled as he put the final touches to his handiwork. 'You'd bloody think it wa' royalty not just the squire coming. I bet he won't visit the lavvy anyway, just wait 'til he gets home.'

As she scrubbed and polished, Annie conjured up pictures of her mother as a child living within these walls. She sensed that times had been happy for her, cocooned within the love of her mother, father, and doting elder brother. What a pity fate had dealt such a terrible hand to this family, with the marriage of Archie to Kath instead of Matty, and her own mother's misguided feelings towards a man who was no more than a common thief. One wrong turning on the path of life and it was ruined forever, she thought ruefully.

With the house clean and sparkling and fires ready to be lit, both women returned to the kitchen to help Kath with the making of huge meat pies, bread, savouries, a large roast ham, slices of succulent beef and cakes for the funeral lunch. These were to be set out on the large mahogany table in the breakfast room, once the coffin had been removed, and Annie and Molly had been given strict instructions on how to lay the table and serve the food.

'Ain't you going to the funeral then, Annie?' Molly asked as the two women snatched a breather in between tasks.

Annie set her mouth grimly and eyed the younger girl thoughtfully. 'I haven't been asked.'

'You ain't? But she was yer granny. Surely you'll go to pay your last respects?'

'I'd like nothing more, Molly. But I think it would cause too much trouble between me and Kath. Besides, someone has to be here to see to the meal and attend to the mourners when they return, and by the looks of it we're expecting quite a few.'

'I could do that.'

'You'd never manage on yer own. As soon as the funeral party leaves for the church, we have to lay the table, mash loads of tea and change our clothes. It's too much, Molly, even for you.' She shook her head. 'If the church was nearer, I could have changed quickly and nipped down for the service and been back to help you finish off, but it's too risky – I'm bound to be spotted. Kath's got eyes in the back of her head.' She sighed deeply. 'Anyway, I sat with the old lady last night, when Archie and Kath had gone to bed.'

'Oh, Annie.' Molly's mouth dropped open. 'You never sat with a dead body? It gives me the creeps just knowing there's one in the house. I'll be glad when she's gone.'

Annie smiled. 'She's not just a body to me, Molly. You have to appreciate that she was the grandmother I never knew, and by sitting with her I felt she would somehow know I existed. It's not morbid, Molly. I sat and prayed that wherever she's gone she'll be with my mother, Charlie, and Charlotte, and the four of them will be up there now watching over us.'

'Oh, I never thought on it like that before.'

'Well, it gives me comfort, Molly. I know it'll sound daft to you, but when I sat with her, I told her all about Charlie and Georgie and about our lives together.'

'D'you think she heard you then?' Molly asked questioningly.

'Who's to know? But I hope so, 'cos it was damn' cold in that room and I'd hate to think I was talking to meself all that time.'

Annie smiled at Molly's expression.

'Come on,' she said. 'Let's get these dishes done. Kath'll be back soon and she'll accuse us of idling.'

The day of the funeral dawned. A thick frost clung to the trees and bushes and the freezing air chilled Annie to the bone as she picked her way across the frozen yard and headed towards the kitchen. Georgie had been told to stay clear of the house until the funeral was over. His meals would be brought to him and he was to keep himself busy feeding the chickens and clearing up the barn.

Annie's thoughts were for Archie. Her uncle was beside himself with grief and had sat motionless by his mother's coffin for hours, his unblinking eyes staring transfixed upon her waxen features. Annie had tried on several occasions to coax him into eating or to rest, but to no avail. It grieved her terribly to see him suffering so much. She would be glad when her grandmother was finally laid to rest. Hopefully her uncle would then begin to mend and pick up the pieces of his life.

She felt that Kath was partly to blame for his state of mind. The woman had shown no kindness towards her husband and had gone about the funeral arrangements without a thought for Archie's well-being or consulting his wishes. I think we shall all be relieved when this day is over, Annie thought ruefully as she entered the back door and mentally prepared herself for the long day ahead.

The mourners started to arrive. They filed in through the front door and Annie, peeping through a crack in the kitchen door, watched in awe as they walked through the hall and into the parlour.

She turned to Molly who was putting the finishing touches to a plate of sandwiches.

'I never realised my grandmother was so well respected. You should see the kind of people coming in.'

Molly raised her head. 'I shouldn't get too excited, Annie. Most of 'em are only here for the food afterwards.'

'Molly!'

'It's true. My mother says folks round here love a funeral. Gives 'em the excuse to dress up and have a good feed. It also gives 'em chance to have a good look round and catch up with the latest gossip.'

Annie shut the door and walked towards the girl. 'I suppose you could be right. I ain't seen any of this lot visiting in all the time I've been here.'

'And you won't see 'em again either. Not 'til the next funeral, that is. Any sign of the squire?'

Annie shook her head. 'No. Not yet.'

Molly smiled. 'I tell yer now, he won't be here.'

'Won't he?'

'No. Mrs Boldicott, the woman who came to lay out the body, told me. He's been called away to London on business.'

'Oh, Molly.' Annie hid a smile. 'Kath won't be pleased.'

'I know.' Molly giggled. 'Serves her right. She's been telling everybody how well connected she is. They all know that if he'd have come it would only have been to pay his last respects to yer granny, nothing to do with her.'

'Molly, we really should say something.'

'Why?' she said, aghast. 'Annie, by rights you should be in there with that lot, not here slaving. You're part of the family, whether she likes it or not, and I think what's she's doing is awful. All right, I know I'm only fifteen, but that don't mean I ain't got eyes in me head.' She paused for breath and narrowed her eyes. 'Mr Burbage is that grieved he don't know what time of day it is, so we can't blame him. But her . . . well, I can't find words strong enough to say what I think about her.'

'Oh, Molly!' Annie said, shocked at the young girl's outburst. 'I never knew you felt like this.'

Molly lowered her eyes. 'I'm sorry. I know I shouldn't speak in this way, it ain't my place to. But I like you, Annie. You've been a good friend to me, and if this pays her back a little for what she's doing . . . Well, it'll certainly make me feel a bit better.'

Annie rushed forward and hugged her tight. 'If I'm honest, it will me too,' she said, quickly pulling away. 'But mark my words, she'll get her comeuppance one day.'

'Huh!' Molly exhaled loudly. 'But will she? It seems to me she gets away with murder. She swans round the village as though she owns the place. The traders hate her. You should hear what they say behind her back. Why, even Lady Richmond doesn't behave the way she does.'

'Don't worry, Molly. One day you'll leave this place to go on to better things. And if working here has taught you how to treat people, then that can't be bad, can it? Just believe me when I say she'll get her comeuppance. In the end people like her always do.'

'I hope so, Annie. I really do.'

She smiled warmly. 'It's just a matter of time.'

Just then a loud knock sounded on the back door. Annie rushed to open it and was confronted by a footman from the Richmond household. He handed Annie a letter.

'It's from Sir James,' the man said. 'His apologies for not being able to attend the funeral. Please give it to your mistress.'

'Thank you,' said Annie politely. 'I'll see she gets it straight away.'

She closed the door just as Lucy barged into the room.

'Mother wants another decanter filling with sherry,' she ordered. 'We're only waiting for the squire, then we'll be off. What's that?' she asked, pointing to the letter in Annie's hand.

'It's for your mother . . .'

'I'll take it.' she commanded, snatching the letter out of Annie's hand. 'You'd better hurry with that decanter. Mother won't be pleased if she can't offer the squire sherry when he arrives.' She turned on her heel and glided out of the room.

Molly turned to Annie, a smile of satisfaction on her face.

'Told yer, didn't I?'

'Yes, and I told you. This is what's called comeuppance, Molly.'

'Is it?'

'Yes, of course. She's gone to all this trouble to impress the squire and now he ain't coming.'

'Oh, yes.' Molly laughed. 'Serves her right. I like this comeuppance business, Annie. I really do.'

They didn't witness Kath's reaction to the letter, but about ten minutes later everyone started to file out. The dark oak coffin, carried by six pall bearers, was placed inside the black coach drawn by two black horses adorned in funeral plumage. And with the procession behind, the funeral march began.

Both women then began the second phase of their preparations and by the time the mourners returned were exhausted.

'This dress has seen better days,' Annie said, wiping her hands over her black serge and patting her hair. 'But it'll have to do.' She picked up a tray of glasses and proceeded through to the breakfast room where most of the mourners had gathered and were already piling their plates high with food and tucking in.

As she approached the doorway an extremely fat old woman sidled up to her. She was dressed in a dirty dark brown coat, big hobnail boots and a felt hat from which the remains of a feather protruded. The woman eyed Annie thoroughly as she bit greedily into a piece of pie. Annie recoiled at the extremely unpleasant smell that reached her nostrils.

'Ah; so you're the wench that's causing our Kath so much trouble?' she said, chewing noisily. She smacked greasy lips together, swallowed hard and took another bite of pie. 'I'm her mother. And when me and her sisters move up here,' she stabbed Annie in the shoulder with a short, dirty finger, 'you and the nipper move out.'

Before Annie could speak a sharp voice from behind made them both jump.

'What a'you doing here?' Kath hissed. 'I told you never to come up here uninvited.'

'Just paying me last respects.' The woman sniffed loudly and wiped the back of her hand under her nose.

'Paying yer last respects?' Kath snarled, trying to keep her voice low. 'You hardly knew Annie Burbage.'

'I did so. Anyway, we're related by marriage. I've a right to be here.'

'Right! You've no rights at all. And look at yer. Don't you ever wash?'

Kath grabbed her mother's arm and dragged her towards

the kitchen. Annie unwittingly followed. Inside the kitchen, Kath slammed the door shut and glared at her mother, who was still tucking into her plate of food.

'How dare you show me up in front of all my friends?'

'Friends! Don't make me laugh. None of these people a'your friends. They've only come for a good feed and a nosey round.'

Kath's face turned purple with rage. 'How dare you?'

'Oh, I dare, Kathleen Burbage. I'm yer mother and I know the dirty little tricks you used to get up to before you married poor Archie. Me and yer sisters ain't good enough for yer now, are we? You think we're beneath you. You forget, our Kath. Most of the people here know your beginnings, you ain't fooling anyone with all yer airs and graces. If you had any conscience, you'd let me and your sisters come up here to live, instead of leaving us to fester in that hovel.'

'Never!'

The old woman sniffed loudly again and threw her empty plate on to the table. 'You might regret turning yer back on us one day. You might need us.'

Kath gave a loud laugh. 'Me, need you? That'll be the day. What have you or my sisters ever done to better yourselves? I'll tell yer – nothing. You just accept the food baskets and the money I send down, and sit on yer fat arses and moan about what awful lives you've got.'

'Huh!' the old lady grunted. 'That stuff you send down is only to clear yer conscience.'

'Oh, is it?' Kath narrowed her eyes. 'Well, just watch out. I might stop doing it and then where would you be?'

'Oh, you wouldn't do that, our Kath? I didn't mean it.'

'Look, you've had some food, now get out. I've guests to see to.' She turned and for the first time saw Annie standing agog behind them. 'What a'you doing here?' she demanded. 'Get out! Get out!' She watched in fury as Annie left the room. She turned back to face her mother, eyes ablaze with anger. 'Now, a'you leaving or do I have to get Reggie to throw you out?'

'I'm going, I'm going.' The old woman sniffed. 'But I could do with a few coppers for a jug of Ma Bradley's sloe gin . . .'

Kath exhaled loudly. 'Stay there,' she said coldly. She left the room and a moment later returned with two pennies which she placed in her mother's outstretched hand. 'That should keep you going.'

'Ta, me duck. You're all heart and let no one say otherwise.' She turned and headed for the kitchen door. 'I'll expect me basket as usual on Friday, and I wouldn't say no to a few extra eggs this time.'

She departed, leaving Kath staring icily after her. She raised her head, took a deep breath and headed back to her guests.

Annie weaved her way in between them, clearing plates and handing out drinks as required. Snatches of whispered conversation reached her ears and she felt humiliation steal over her.

'It's such a shame . . . she's the grand-daughter . . . you wouldn't treat a dog the way Kath's treating her.'

Oh, please, let this day be over, she prayed longingly.

All through the proceedings Archie had functioned in a daze. Annie looked across the room to see him standing by the fireplace, a fixed smile upon his face as he tried to converse with the Vicar. Without a word of warning, he moved away, walking right past her and into the kitchen. The Vicar stared after him in surprise. Annie turned and hurriedly followed him. Finding the kitchen empty, she headed across the yard and into the barn where she found him slouched in a corner, sobbing uncontrollably into the crook of his arm.

She quietly approached, knelt before him and laid her hand on his arm.

'Uncle Archie,' she said softly.

He raised his head and looked at her through red-rimmed eyes.

'Oh, Annie, me duck. What am I to do? I've lost me mother and she meant everything to me, she did. She was a

201

wonderful lady, Annie. I wish you could have got to know her.'

'I know, I know, Uncle Archie. But she was old and well past her time, and you told me yourself she'd had a good life,' she said soothingly.

He sniffed loudly. 'Yes, she did. But I miss her.'

'That'll get easier, as time goes by. Believe me, I know.'

'Oh, Annie.' Archie looked apologetically at her. 'I'm sorry. Here's me pouring out all my troubles and you've got yer own.'

She smiled wanly. 'That's all right, Uncle Archie. I understand only too well what you're going through. But I'm sure my grandmother wouldn't want you to be mourning her like this. From what people have told me about her, she'd have given you hell!'

'Yes, she would.' He managed a brief smile. 'Never one for nonsense, was my mother. When you're gone, you're gone. Life's for living, she used to say. But that don't help the folks that's left behind, does it?'

'No, I agree, it doesn't,' Annie said, raising herself up and sitting down on a stool a couple of feet from Archie. 'But you've a lot to be thankful for, Uncle Archie.'

'Have I?' he asked.

'Why, yes. You've Kath, Lucy and the farm.'

'Oh, Kath.' He exhaled loudly. 'Yes, I have Kath and Lucy,' he said forlornly.

Annie frowned. 'What's worrying you, Uncle Archie?'

He raised his eyes to meet hers. 'Worrying me? What d'you mean?'

She lowered her gaze. 'Something's on yer mind.'

He clasped his hands together. 'You don't miss much, do yer?'

'It's not hard to see,' she said softly.

He ran his fingers through his beard. 'It's Kath, Annie. I often wonder why she stays with me.' He paused and eyed her wearily. 'I know what they say in the village. They say I've no backbone and let her walk all over me. That's true,

202

Annie, I do. But it's only 'cos I love her and want her to be happy. She ain't got it easy here. Farming's hard work and there's not much time for socialising. A woman like her must miss that.'

Annie's eyes flashed angrily. 'Uncle Archie, Kath has a good life here. It's far better than the one she came from.'

'Oh, I grant yer that, Annie. But I often wonder if she should have married someone younger, someone who could have offered her more.'

'In what way?' she asked sternly. 'You're a good man, Uncle Archie. You're kind and caring and you provide a good living. Kath wants for nothing. And Uncle Archie . . . She tilted her head and looked straight at him. 'Kath married you. It was her choice, you didn't force her.'

'No, I didn't,' he said slowly. He paused thoughtfully for a moment. 'Yes, things might be better now Mam's gone. Kath always felt she wasn't completely the mistress. Well, now she will be, won't she?'

Annie nodded slowly.

He wiped his eyes on his handkerchief. 'I know she's got bad points. She bullies and grumbles, but in a way that's been good for me. When Dad died and our Mary Ann went, I sorta let things slide. It were Kath that bullied me into doing things. This farm wouldn't be so profitable if it weren't for her.'

Annie slowly nodded again.

'Yes, it's just us three now – and you and Georgie, of course. At least Kath won't have the burden of me mother now, so maybe she can have more time to herself.' He smiled wanly. 'Yes, maybe it was a blessing she went. She hated being bedridden and dependent on everyone, and there was also her mind. She rambled a lot towards the end and didn't know one day from the next. She complained bitterly that Kath ill treated her when I know that's not true. That must have got her down, 'cos she did all she could for my mother.'

Annie listened to Archie in silence, keeping her own counsel.

'We'll have to see about you and the lad moving into the house. There's no reason for you to stay over the barn now, is there?'

'No,' Annie agreed. 'But I think it'd be wise to leave things as they are for the time being, Uncle Archie. Let things settle down. Then we'll see about it. We're quite cosy in the loft.'

'Yes, you have made it homely, I'll say that for you, gel. And if I'm honest, I love sitting up there with you both.'

'Well, you're still welcome. Nothing's changed.'

'Ta, gel. Oh, I do feel better for our chat.'

'I'm glad.' Annie stood up and brushed her hand over her skirt. 'I'd better get back before I'm missed. What about you?'

'I'll be over in a minute. Just give me a few moments to get meself together.'

She walked over and gave him a kiss on the cheek, then she turned and made her way towards the kitchen.

Their talk had unnerved her. She had always known that Archie was completely under his wife's domination. Her grandmother's death didn't look as if it would change anything. Kath could do or say whatever she liked and Archie would let her, for fear of losing her.

Before she opened the kitchen door she brushed a piece of straw off her blouse. What had Kath in store for them now? Maybe the next move was to get rid of her and Georgie? She smiled ruefully. Probably the only time her uncle had ever stood up to his wife was when he'd insisted on their staying at the farm. Not that she despised him for his lack of manliness. She knew it was his nature to be kind and considerate and to turn his back on unpleasant things in order to have an easy life, as it was Kath's nature to be hard and conniving. If that's what had made their marriage successful then who was she to question it? What the future held for her now was in the hands of Kath, and whatever it was she would have to face it.

She turned the handle on the door and silently prayed.

Chapter Thirteen

To Annie's great surprise life at the farm settled into a happy routine. The whole spirit of the place seemed to have lifted and everyone went about their daily tasks with a light heart.

'I can't believe it,' Molly said to Annie one morning as both women filled water buckets by the trough. 'She's a changed woman. Even Reggie says so.'

'Yes,' Annie answered thoughtfully.

'You don't seem sure?'

'Oh, I am,' she answered quickly. 'It's just taking a bit of getting used to, that's all. It's good to see my uncle so happy. He's even whistling.' She sighed deeply. 'I'm sorry, Molly. It just seems too good to be true.'

'What d'you mean?'

'Well, I've never seen such a dramatic change in anyone. It's as though the old Kath we knew never existed. She's even being nice to Georgie. Gave him a penny this week for collecting all the eggs without any breakages.'

'Did she? Ah . . . that was nice of her.'

'Yes, it was.' Annie picked up the two buckets of water. 'Forgive me, Molly, but I can't help feeling she's up to something. I must go and see Matty, find out what she's making of all this.' She turned and headed towards the dairy.

She emptied the water into the large stone sink and scrubbed it round. Why can't I get rid of this feeling of impending doom? she thought wearily. Just then her uncle appeared and smiled at her warmly.

'Ah, Annie. Just the girl I wanted to see.'

'Oh!'

'Don't look so terrified, I only want you to do something for me.'

He walked towards her carrying a sheaf of papers.

'You can write, can't yer?'

'Er . . . yes. Not very well though.'

Archie laughed. 'It's all right, I only want your signature. I need you to witness these documents.'

'Documents! Oh, I don't know anything about documents, Uncle Archie.'

'You don't need to, Annie. I just want you to sign here, here and here.' He indicated several places on the various forms. 'It's for the solicitors, legal stuff to transfer the farm into my name. I need two witnesses so I have to search for Reggie next. He can't write so his cross will have to do.'

'Oh, I see,' she said, biting her bottom lip in bewilderment. 'Shouldn't I read them first?'

'Oh, no. That's all been taken care of. I just need you to witness that I've signed them, that's all. Anyway, you'd never understand all this legal jargon. I don't. I've left it all in professional hands. Farming's my business, that's all I know about.'

Annie accepted the quill pen and dipped it in the bottle of ink that Archie had brought with him.

'There,' she said, after she had painstakingly written her name as legibly as possible. 'Is that all I have to do?'

Archie collected the papers together. 'Yes. Thanks, Annie. Now once Reggie has done the same, everything will be all above board and legal fashion.' He leant back against the sink and eyed her thoroughly. 'Things are better now, aren't they?' he said softly.

Annie looked at him for a moment. 'You mean with Kath?'

'Yes. Since me mother died, she's changed, hasn't she?'

'Yes, she has,' Annie agreed in an easier way than she felt.

'She's being really good to me, Annie. Taken care of all the paperwork to do with Mam's death. She even went to the

206

solicitor's to save me the bother. She knows I'm no good at this legal business, so she took over for me. All I've had to do was sign a few papers. Don't you think that was good of her?'

Annie managed a smile. 'Yes, I do,' she lied. She patted Archie's arm affectionately and smiled at the wet mark that was left from her hand. 'Things are a lot better, Uncle Archie. I feel so much more settled,' she said convincingly.

'Good,' he said happily. 'I'm gonna speak to Kath about giving you some money.'

'Money?'

'Yes, you and the lad need some decent clothes and other bits and pieces. If me mother had left a will there would have been provision left for Mary Ann and that would have come to you under the circumstances.'

'Oh, Uncle Archie, there's no need. You've done enough already.'

'You've worked for what you've got from us, Annie. It's about time we did something for you both as members of the family.'

'Okay.' She smiled warmly. 'But let's see what Kath says first.'

'I will. It's only fair to consult her. But she'll agree, I know she will.' He straightened himself up and smiled at her affectionately. 'Right, I'll go and find Georgie. He's coming down the fields with me once I've finished getting these papers signed.' He paused thoughtfully. 'I wonder if Lucy'd like to come?'

'Why don't you ask her?'

'I will.'

With that he left. Annie stared after him, deep in thought. She finished her tasks and made her way towards the kitchen. Daylight was short now and the sun hadn't put in an appearance for ages. She shivered at the thought that there was still at least another four months of winter left ahead of them. She scraped her muddy boots on the iron bar outside the door and entered. Kath looked at her sharply before putting a smile on her face and beckoning her to sit down.

'There you are, Annie. I was beginning to wonder where you'd got to.' She placed a mug on the table and poured her a cup of tea. 'Here, that'll warm you up. It's a cold 'un today, ain't it?' she said, passing her the sugar basin. She turned to Molly who was busy washing dishes in the sink. 'What about you, Molly? It's about time you had a break. Come and have a cuppa.'

'Oh, thanks, Mistress Burbage,' Molly said, her pretty face lighting up in pleasure. 'I could murder one.'

Annie stirred her tea and took a sip. The hot liquid burnt her throat and she gave a small cough. 'I'll take this in the dairy with me. It'll help keep me warm while I make a start on the cheese.' She started to rise from the table, but Kath stopped her.

'Oh, surely you can sit for a few minutes? The cheese will wait.'

Annie's mouth gaped in surprise.

'Er . . . I will sit for a few minutes, thank you.'

'I've been thinking,' Kath piped up suddenly as she spread a handful of flour across the table, 'I thought it'd be nice if we all got together and had tea in the front parlour this afternoon.' She scooped a large lump of dough from the bowl to the side of her, threw it on the table and started to knead. She looked over at Annie. 'Well, what d'you think?'

'I . . . er . . . think that would be very nice.'

'Good. I've made some cakes. I thought the children would like them. You're invited too, Molly.'

'Me?'

'Yes, why not? We're all one big happy family now.' She turned the pastry over and started to roll again. 'I've got a small announcement to make and thought this afternoon's get together would be the ideal time.'

'Oh!' Annie uttered.

Kath grinned. 'You'll have to wait, Annie, like the rest of them. But I think you'll be surprised by what I have to say.' She turned to Molly. 'If you'll be good enough to light the fire in the parlour, and bring in plenty of logs so we'll be nice and warm for our tea party?' She picked up the pastry and laid it over a plate.

'I'd better get on with my jobs then,' Annie said.

Kath looked up. 'Yes, okay, Annie. Dinner will be at the usual time and the tea party ... well, let's say about four o'clock. That's plenty of time for us all to finish and get tidied up.'

'Right. I'll see you dinnertime,' Annie said slowly. She looked over at Molly, raised her eyebrows and headed out of the door.

'Do I have to go, Mam?' Georgie moaned loudly. 'I'd sooner stay and play with Scrap. Tea parties are for older 'uns. I'll only be bored.'

'Yes, you do have to go,' Annie said firmly. 'And, Georgie Higgins, you're to be on yer best behaviour, is that understood? I want no nonsense from you. And when you're offered some cake, don't take the biggest piece.'

'Eh! Why not?'

''Cos it's not good manners, that's why not. Now pull yer socks up and let's get going.'

He stared at his mother. 'You look nice, Mam.'

Annie finished tying her boot laces and looked over in surprise at her son. 'Do I? Thank you very much,' she said warmly, smoothing her hands over her blue dress. The fresh country air and manual exercise had given her the kind of shapely curves any woman would have been proud of, but Annie was unaware of her attractive appearance as she rushed over and gave her son a big kiss on his cheek.

'Ah, Mam.' Georgie grimaced, wiping his cheek with his hand.

'Oh, I see. Too big for kisses, are we?'

'Well, I am nearly seven.'

'Yes, but as you said, not quite. So give us another.'

She made to grab him, but Georgie was too quick for her and disappeared through the trap-door and down the ladder.

As they walked hand in hand out of the barn, Annie's

attention was caught by a movement in the farmyard. She strained her eyes and recognised her friend Matty closing the large wooden gate behind her.

'Matty!' Annie exclaimed warmly as she lifted her skirts and ran across the yard to meet her. 'What on earth are you doing here?'

'Fine greeting, I must say.'

'I'm sorry, Matty. It's lovely to see you, but a bit of a surprise. You're the last person I expected to see.'

'It's a surprise to me too. I never thought I'd walk up this yard again.'

'Well, why are you?' Annie asked, perplexed.

'I've been invited.'

'Invited! Who by?'

'Kath.'

Annie stared at Matty in bewilderment. 'But I don't understand . . .'

'Me neither,' Matty interrupted. 'But I had a note. It was a peace offering. Kath wants us to be friends.'

Annie's mouth dropped open. 'No, Matty. You must be mistaken?'

'No. I know I ain't that good a reader but there was no mistaking what it said. It's a pity I screwed it up, you could have read it for yourself.'

'Oh, Matty, it's not that I'm doubting what you're saying, it's just that I can't take it in.'

'It took me a while, I can tell you.'

'Well, maybe I'm all wrong about her then.'

'What d'you mean?'

'Well, since my grandmother died, Kath has changed out of all recognition. It's hard to believe she's the same person. But despite myself, I can't help but feel it's all a cover up for something.' Annie grimaced and shook her head. 'It would be nice to think she's changed. Writing you that letter must have taken some guts after the way she's treated you. Maybe I am wrong about her.'

'Maybe,' Matty said, shrugging her shoulders. 'But you

know as well as I do, Annie – people don't change. The time to make things right between us was when your grandmother died. She could have asked me to the funeral. I was hurt when she never, nor Archie neither. I desperately wanted to come. It cut me dreadfully to think me old friend was being buried and I wasn't there to pay me last respects. This invite came out of the blue and knocked the stuffing out of me, I can tell yer. I'm only here 'cos of me curiosity. Nothing else.' She scratched her chin. 'Anyway, we'll soon find out one way or the other.'

'Hmm, we will,' Annie said thoughtfully.

Just then Georgie sauntered up to them and gave Matty a big cheeky grin. She leant over and ruffled his hair.

'Hello, lad. How a'you?'

Annie's eyes gazed proudly down at her son. Then she gasped in horror. Georgie stood at the side of her, his hair covered in straw, his shirt hanging out of his trousers and his socks round his ankles.

'Oh, my god, Georgie!' she shrieked. 'What have you done to yourself?'

He looked up at her sheepishly. 'Nothing.'

Annie grabbed him by the scruff of his neck. 'Excuse me for a moment, Matty.'

She laughed loudly as she watched Annie drag him across the yard and back up to the loft. She heard him give a loud wail, and presumed Annie had smacked him. Several moments later they reappeared, Georgie looking decidedly tidier than he had done a few moments before.

'Who'd have kids?' Annie moaned as she rejoined her friend.

'No need to tell me, gel. I've had three, remember?'

'Huh. Don't know how you managed. I've got enough on me hands with one.' She smiled ruefully. 'We'd better get up to the parlour before he has chance to do anything else.'

The fire burned brightly in the grate as all the guests in the parlour tucked into delicious sandwiches and cakes made specially for the occasion by Kath. The conversation was

211

stilted to begin with, but after the sherry was passed round, everyone began to relax and enjoy the proceedings.

Kath, sitting in a comfortable armchair by the fire, a pink velvet cushion in the small of her back, eyed her guests in turn.

Annie, Matty and Molly, sitting on the horsehair chaise longue, discussed village gossip. Archie, seated in the armchair opposite, gazed at her intently, eyes shining with love and devotion. Georgie, crouching by the fire, was inching as far away from Lucy as possible while she plied him with sandwiches and cake as she had been told.

Kath leant over and refilled her glass with sherry, smiling inwardly to see the small gathering and to think of how she had made it come about. It was getting near the time for her announcement and her heart quickened. This was going to be a very pleasurable experience.

Archie took a sip of sherry and placed his glass down on the hearth. He inched himself forward on to the edge of his chair and clasped his hands together, smiling broadly at his wife.

'Well then, our Kath. What's this surprise you have for us? I think we're all ready to hear it now. I hope it's something good? Is it new plans for the farm? Is that it, Kath?'

Several pairs of eyes looked at her in expectation.

'Oh, Archie,' she scolded playfully. 'Yes, it is something to do with the farm.' She pouted and batted her eyelashes at him. 'You've spoiled my surprise now.'

'Oh, no, Kath,' he said worriedly. 'It was only a guess. We still don't know what it is, do we?'

'No, that's true,' she said coldly. 'You've really no idea, have you?'

The change in her tone made them all stare quizzically at her. Annie turned her head and looked quickly at Matty, cold fear stealing over her.

Kath motioned to Lucy and Georgie. 'You two go and play outside while we grown ups talk, and, Molly, go and start cleaning up the kitchen.'

For once, both children rose and hurried out of the room followed by Molly. Kath waited until the door had closed behind them. She raised her head, smiled at each of them in turn and took a deep breath.

'I'm glad you all came here today, it makes what I have to say so much easier . . .'

'Easier!' Matty said sharply. 'What are you up to, Kath Burbage? I don't like the sound of all this . . .'

'Do you mind?' Kath interrupted. 'Remember, you're a guest in my house and I would ask you keep your silence until I've finished what I have to say.'

Matty rose awkwardly out of her seat.

'I ain't staying to hear this . . .'

'Oh, I'd advise you very strongly to stay, Matty. After all, this concerns you as much as anyone.'

'Eh!' She slid back down in her seat, face covered in confusion.

'Now, can I continue?' Kath looked at them in turn and inhaled deeply. She put her hand behind the cushion and pulled out a long brown envelope which she placed carefully across her knees.

'This week, I achieved my dream. The one I've been planning for since I married Archie.' She smiled slyly and watched as the puzzled looks appeared on their faces. 'My dear husband here,' she inclined her head towards Archie, 'signed over the farm to me. It's all mine now.'

'No, I didn't,' he said, bewildered. 'I didn't sign anything over to you.'

'Oh, but you did, my dear. Remember?'

A picture formed in his mind. The blazing fire, him warm and relaxed with his pipe after an appetising meal. Kath with her arm round his shoulders telling him not to bother to read the forms, just to sign where she had indicated. The visit to the solicitor's . . .

'Oh, my god!' he uttered, his hand shooting to his mouth. 'You . . . you can't do this, Kath!'

'I can and have,' she said triumphantly. 'It's all in here.'

She picked up the envelope and waved it in the air. 'It's all legal. You signed the documents and Annie and Reggie witnessed your signature.'

'That was a dirty trick, Kath!' Annie shouted. She turned towards her uncle, her eyes ablaze in fury. 'Uncle Archie, you can't let her do this to you.'

'Well, that'll teach you to sign things without checking first,' Kath said smugly. 'The farm's mine and there's nothing anyone can do about it.'

'We knew it,' Matty said sharply. 'We knew you were up to something, Kath Burbage, but this . . . well, I can't believe anyone could sink to this level.'

'And what level's that?' Kath asked sarcastically. 'You mean sink so low as to steal my husband's farm from under his nose?' She laughed. 'This place would have been nothing without me. I'm only taking what's mine.'

Annie, sitting with her fists clenched tightly, looked over at Archie slumped in his chair, face registering complete and utter bewilderment.

'Uncle Archie, what are you going to do? Are you going to sit there and say nothing and let Kath get away with this . . . this . . .'

'Clever plan,' she cut in. ''Cos it was clever. To be honest, I never realised it would be so easy. You all really fell for the act I put on, and none of you realised I was laughing behind your backs. Well, I don't have to pretend any more, thank God. If anyone suffered it was me, being so nice and friendly to people I detest. You can do what you like – contest it, take me to court.' She shook her head. 'But you won't stand a chance. Your mother left no will, Archie. Or if she did, then it doesn't exist now. The farm passed automatically to you and was yours to do whatever you liked with. You very kindly turned it over to your loving wife because you'd had enough of farming and your marriage and wanted out. It's all written in black and white in the documents which you signed and Annie and Reggie witnessed.'

She rose serenely from her chair and stood with her back

to the fire. She looked over at Matty. 'I'm glad you came to see his downfall. You've always hankered after him. Well, now he's all yours – and I hope he's more of a man with you than he ever was with me!' She turned to Annie and narrowed her eyes. 'Don't think for a moment I fell for your pitiful act. You might have taken Archie in, but not me. I knew all the time you were after your share of the farm.'

Annie leapt up, outraged. 'How dare you?' she hissed. 'What you say isn't true and you know it!'

'Isn't it?' Kath replied nonchalantly. 'Well, I happen to think otherwise.' She bent down to pick up the brown envelope from the chair, straightened herself and eyed them each in turn. 'Oh, when I think of all the years I've waited for this moment. And it was all worth it, believe me.' She walked slowly towards the door, turned and smiled sweetly. 'Please feel free to finish your drinks and have something more to eat or it'll only go to waste and that would be a shame. Then I'd be obliged if you'd remove yourselves from my premises. Thank you.' She turned and walked out of the door, closing it gently behind her.

The room fell silent. Annie and Matty stared at each other, their mouths wide open in stunned disbelief. Annie looked across at her uncle and took several steps towards him.

'You can't just sit there and do nothing,' she snapped. 'Uncle Archie, for goodness' sake, get after her and sort it out.'

He raised his eyes slowly to meet hers. He shrugged. 'But what can I do?' he whispered pathetically.

'Do?' Annie repeated, running her hand over the top of her head. 'Well, you'll have to do something. You can't just sit there and let her get away with this.' She knelt down and placed her hands on his knees. 'You do realise what's she's done? She's taken your farm off you. You've no home, Uncle Archie, no livelihood.'

'Yes, I know.'

'But this farm has been in your family for generations. You and my mother were born here, and your father and grandfather before that. Surely you're going to put up a fight?' She turned to Matty in desperation. 'Matty, you tell him, please? He doesn't seem to realise what's happened.'

'Archie . . .' she began.

'It's only a joke,' he said softly. 'It's Kath's idea of a bit of fun. You'll see. She'll come back in a minute and tell us so.'

'Oh, no,' Annie groaned. She raised herself and sat down next to Matty. 'He can't take it in.' She shook her head. 'What are we going to do?'

Matty breathed deeply. 'Archie, now you listen to me! This is no joke. This is very serious, and you have to go after Kath and demand to see those documents. If you won't, me and Annie will.'

Archie raised his head and looked at them both. 'You're wrong, you know. Kath wouldn't do this to me. She wouldn't, really she wouldn't.'

'Okay, Archie. Put our minds at rest. Go after her and ask to see those documents. Then we'll all know.'

'Okay, yes, I will,' he said, raising himself slowly and walking towards the door. 'You'll see I'm right, though.'

He opened the door and departed, leaving the two women staring after him.

Annie turned to face her friend. 'Oh, Matty, I never expected this.'

'Me neither, gel. I always knew Kath were cunning, but this! I wouldn't have believed it if I hadn't heard it with me own ears.' She picked up her half empty glass of sherry and drank the remains. 'Good drop of sherry that.'

'Matty!'

'Sorry,' she said, sighing deeply. 'Well, there's one thing for certain. Until we sort this lot out, you'll all have to come and stay with me.'

'Don't be daft. How on earth are you going to put up another three? You're overcrowded as it is. 'Specially since your son got married and his wife moved in.'

'We'll manage.' She looked up at Annie and narrowed her eyes. 'I don't understand.'

'Understand what?'

'About the will. I know for a fact yer grandmother made one. So where is it?'

Annie stared at her thoughtfully. 'Matty, you don't think Kath's destroyed it, do you?'

'She could have,' she said, nodding her head. 'But I don't think so somehow.'

'Don't you?'

'No. I firmly believe your grandmother hid it somewhere. But where, that's the worry?'

An idea suddenly came to Annie's mind. 'Matty, there's something I haven't told you. Well, not just you.'

'Oh! What?'

'Well, you remember when my grandmother died? We – me and Molly that is – told Uncle Archie and Kath that we found her in bed.'

'So?'

'Well, we never, Matty. We found her in the barn. She'd been trying to climb up the ladder into the room me and Georgie live in.'

'Oh!'

'Yes, the ladder had broken and she'd fallen down. I know it was wrong to lie about it, Matty, but it seemed the only thing to do at the time.' Annie sighed deeply. 'We covered up the facts because Archie would have been upset knowing he should have repaired the ladder, and also because Molly had been left in charge and you know what Kath's reaction would have been. She'd have sacked her.'

'I see.' Matty frowned. 'But why are you telling me all this?'

'Don't you see, Matty? My grandmother was trying to get into the loft for a reason.'

'Oh! The will. Yes, that'd make sense.'

'I know. But for the life of me I can't think where she would have hidden it. I searched that room high and low for me mother's hidey-hole, and found nothing.'

Matty exhaled deeply. 'Well, it must be in the house

somewhere, but under the circumstances we can't very well go poking about. At least not 'til we find out what Archie has to say.' Matty clumsily eased herself up off the chaise longue. 'I think we should go and pack up your stuff and wait for Archie in your room.'

'You don't think . . .'

'No, I don't,' Matty cut in sharply. 'Kath's done what she says she has. I've no doubts on that score. We'll need to get Archie back to my house as quickly as possible. We can discuss matters at more length then. I don't feel easy in this house, Annie. The sooner we get away from here, the better.'

After leaving Annie and Matty in the parlour, Archie slowly made his way up the stairs and across the broad landing. He stood outside the bedroom door and hesitated. Sounds coming from within confirmed the presence of his wife. He slowly placed his hand on the door knob and let himself quietly into the room.

Kath heard him and turned her head nonchalantly. 'Oh, it's you,' she said tonelessly.

Archie stared over at her as she continued to throw clothing into a large brown trunk.

'What are you doing, Kath?'

She sniffed loudly, turned and placed her hands on her hips. 'What does it look like, you soft ha'porth?'

'You're packing?' he said, bewildered.

She gave a loud belly laugh. 'How did you guess?'

He moved slowly towards her. 'You didn't mean all that in the parlour, Kath? It was just a joke, wasn't it?'

'Joke! D'you honestly think I'd go to all that trouble for a joke?' She narrowed her eyes. 'The farm's mine, Archie. You'd better believe it. These clothes are yours, ready to take with you. Where you go is no concern of mine and to be honest, I ain't interested, just as long as you leave the farm and take that trollop of a niece and her son with you.'

'Kath, please.' Archie reached out and tried to take her in his arms.

She recoiled, staring up at him in disgust. 'Don't you ever

218

touch me again, you hear? I loathe you, Archie Burbage! The thought of you near me makes my skin crawl. I only married you to get away from my mother and the hovel we lived in. Sharing your bed sickened me to me stomach. I deserve this farm for what I suffered all these years.'

Archie gasped at her words. Before he could stop himself he had swung back his arm and slapped her across the face.

Kath's hand flew to her smarting cheek. 'That's it, hit a woman! That's all you're capable of . . .'

'Stop it, Kath!' he cried in anguish. 'I'm sorry, I didn't mean to hit you. Please, please, forgive me.'

'Forgive you?' Kath shook her head. 'You really are a pathetic creature. I've taken your farm away and you want me to forgive you? You're a poor excuse for a man, Archie Burbage, and the sooner I'm rid of you the better.'

He started to tremble as the impact of her words slowly sank in.

'I'd . . . I'd like to see those documents.'

'You can see what you like, it won't make any difference.' She opened a drawer in her dressing table and threw the brown envelope towards him. 'I trust you can understand them?' she said sarcastically. She watched in silence as his eyes scanned the contents. 'See, I told you,' she said triumphantly. 'It's all legal. Now get out. Go to your precious Matty. See how long she puts up with you. You've always hankered after her. Well, now you've got what you always wanted.'

Archie threw the papers down on the bed. 'That's not true. It's you I always loved. What have I done to deserve this treatment?'

'What have you done?' Kath repeated sharply as she made a grab for the envelope. 'I'll tell you what you've bloody done! Nothing. It's been like living with a puppet all these years. I've pulled the strings and you've done exactly as I've said. Not once have you ever stood up to me. It's been boring, Archie, dull and boring. I might as well have been married to me grandfather for all the excitement I've had with you.'

'You don't meant that, Kath,' he said disbelievingly. 'Surely it ain't been that bad? You know yourself, life on a farm's hard work. There ain't much excitement in our kind of life, you get too tired, but you knew all this when we got married. Anyway, how are you going to manage this by yourself?'

'I won't be by myself.'

'Eh! What d'you mean?'

Kath turned and faced him. 'John Matthews is moving in.' She watched with pleasure the look of astonishment on her husband's face. 'I've loved that man for years, but his farm wouldn't support the kind of life we wanted so we waited. And believe me it's been worth it! We're going to put the two farms together. We'll have the biggest spread for miles around and the respect from all those heathens round here to go with it. When this comes out, they'll all sit up and take notice of Kathleen Burbage.' She threw back her head. 'What do you think of that, eh?'

Archie froze, his eyes staring at Kath unblinkingly. It took a few moments for her words to register. 'John Matthews?' he uttered.

'That's what I said, John Matthews.'

'I don't understand. He's coming up here? But what about our Lucy, what's she going to make of all this?'

'You really are the limit, Archie,' Kath laughed. 'Couldn't you see what was going on right under your nose?' She walked round to where he was sitting and bent down, pushing her face into his. 'We've been carrying on for years. Lucy ain't yours – she's mine and John's. You ain't capable of making babies, Archie Burbage. Your mother knew the truth, but couldn't prove it.' She looked at him and smirked. 'I've been telling you for years that she's mine, but you never took the hint. Why, the child looks nothing like you. I've only been waiting for your mother to die so I could get the farm.' She sighed deeply. 'God, she fairly took her time. I began to think she'd live for ever. As soon as we can, we're getting married.'

'Married! But you can't, Kath, you're married to me.'

'Not for much longer, I ain't. I've already seen about a divorce. I don't care how much I have to lie to get one, I won't stay married to you a moment longer than necessary.'

Archie's body sagged. He rose, pushing Kath aside as he rushed towards the door, her laughter ringing in his ears.

Annie finally found him crouched in the hole in the hedge, near the farm gate. She knelt before him and eyed him. She knew instinctively that this was not the time for conversation. Standing up, she gently took his arm and guided him towards the dray that already held their belongings. She made him climb up to join Matty and Georgie, and after a tearful goodbye from Molly, the three drove in silence to Matty's house.

Chapter Fourteen

Four days later, Archie still had not spoken of his ordeal. Annie and Matty had tried their hardest, using every conceivable way they knew to coax him into discussing the situation and then hopefully make some sort of plan of action. But to no avail. Archie remained silent on the subject that was causing him so much grief.

Her uncle's state of mind was causing Annie great distress and she had hardly slept over the last four days. She knew something would have to happen soon. If it didn't, all hope of salvaging anything would be gone.

She cornered Matty in the kitchen. 'There must be something we haven't tried? It's as if he's died, Matty. We need some sort of shock to bring him back to reality.'

'I know.' She sighed. 'But we've tried everything we can think of.'

'I just wish we knew what happened between him and Kath. I have a terrible feeling that she said something else. Something so terrible it's sent him over the edge.'

Just then Georgie sauntered into the tiny scullery, his face the picture of misery as he walked right past them and sat on the floor at Archie's feet. Annie wrung her hands together and followed her son. She looked at him anxiously.

'What's the matter, Georgie?'

'Nothing,' he sighed. 'I just miss the farm and Scrap. I'm worried in case he's missing me.' His voice trembled and he swallowed hard to get rid of the lump in his throat. 'I want to go back, Mam. Why can't we go back? I miss it all so badly, even Lucy.'

'So do I, lad.'

Annie's head jerked up at the sound of Archie's whispered words. She watched transfixed as he raised his hand and ruffled Georgie's hair. Suddenly a tear rolled down his cheek, then another and another, until his choking sobs summoned Matty and she came rushing through to stand beside Annie.

The two women looked at each other then back at Archie.

'That's it, Archie. Let it all out,' Matty said. She looked at Annie and smiled wanly. 'Thank God,' she whispered.

Finally, Archie's agonising sobs lessened and he looked across at the two women through watering eyes.

'What am I going to do?' he pleaded. 'Please, help me. Please.'

Annie motioned to Georgie to leave the room. She waited while he responded, then took a deep breath.

'Uncle Archie,' she said softly, leaning forward and clasping her hands together. 'You must tell us what happened in the bedroom. What was it Kath said to you?'

He gasped. 'I can't. I don't want to think about it. Please don't ask me to tell you.'

'You'll have to, else we'll never get this mess sorted out.'

Archie's shoulders sagged. He stared for several minutes into the fire. Annie's heart raced anxiously, wondering if her probing had sent him into a relapse again. Finally, much to her relief, he raised his head and relived his nightmare.

Both women listened intently, disbelief at the rest of Kath's deviousness showing on their faces.

Matty walked over and swung the big black kettle over the fire. 'I don't know about you, Annie, but I need a stiff drink after that. And as the pub's shut, we'll have to make do with tea.'

Annie nodded in agreement.

'What a terrible mess,' she sighed. She looked over at her uncle, sitting drained of all emotion in the chair opposite. 'Matty is positive my grandmother made a will. Have you any idea where she would have hidden it?'

He slowly shook his head.

Annie looked anxiously over at Matty, then turned back to face her uncle. 'I have something to tell you.' She took a deep breath and proceeded to tell Archie the actual events of the morning she and Molly had found her grandmother.

'So you see, Uncle Archie, we think she was attempting to climb the ladder into the loft, but had a heart attack or something before she could do it. It must have been for a reason and we think it was to get her will. Are you sure you have no idea where it could be?'

Archie shook his head again.

Matty walked over and handed them both mugs of tea. She stood before Archie and placed her hands on her hips.

'There's only one thing for it.'

'Oh, what's that?' Annie asked.

'Archie will have to make a visit to the big house and speak to the squire, see what he can make of all this.'

'Oh, do you think he can help?'

'We don't know 'til we try, do we? Archie, what d'you say?'

He shrugged his shoulders pathetically. 'I can't see what he can do and I don't think it's fair to drag him into all this.'

'Well, what other ideas can you come up with?'

He looked at her blankly.

'I thought so. Right, you go up tomorrow. Tell him the whole tale and see what he can advise. And in the meantime, rack yer brains as to where that will could be. 'Cos, by God, I know it's somewhere. Okay, Archie?'

He nodded his head. 'Yes, all right.' He sniffed loudly, pulled out a large handkerchief and noisily blew his nose. 'I'll take Georgie with me for company, if you like?'

Annie smiled. 'I bet he'd love to go. Ask him when he comes in.'

Matty leant over and whispered in Annie's ear, 'That's the way to treat yer uncle. You have to be firm and tell him what to do. It's the only way he knows.' She straightened and rubbed her hands together. 'Right, I'd better start getting the dinner. My three hungry sons and daughter-in-law will be home from work soon, and you, Archie, could do with some food inside you. You ain't eaten properly for days.' She walked through to the scullery and Annie followed.

'As long as I live, Matty, I don't think I shall ever come across a woman so evil. Fancy letting Archie believe that Lucy was his all these years! That's despicable, Matty. I don't know how she can live with herself.'

Matty placed the potato she had peeled into a large black iron pan.

'She's no conscience, Annie. That woman has never lost a night's sleep in her life.' She waved the potato knife in the air. 'By God, I hope I live to see the day she has her downfall. I'll never rest in me grave if I don't.'

Annie inhaled deeply. 'Me neither, Matty. Me neither.'

Chapter Fifteen

It was a bitterly cold December morning. The icy wind roared mercilessly, seeping through gaps in windows, doors and clothing. Village residents hurried about their tasks, eager to complete them and get indoors as quickly as possible in order to warm their chilblained hands and frozen toes. Archie, with Georgie perched by his side, covered by a thick woollen blanket, drove the dray slowly back to the farm. This journey was one he didn't want to make, but one he had been forced in to by Matty and Annie.

Each clip-clop of old Neddy's hooves on the hardened mud road jangled his already fraught nerves and by the time they reached the farm outskirts, the tension that was building inside him had reached fever pitch. He desperately wanted this part of the operation over with as quickly as possible so he could get away and breathe more easily.

Concentrating on nothing but the task in hand, he unbridled the horse and let it through the farm gate, parking the cart securely for Reggie to dispose of at his leisure. Turning his back to the farmyard, Archie grasped Georgie's hand and tried to smile.

'Come on, lad,' he said, trying his best to sound enthusiastic. 'We've a fair walk ahead of us, but with a bit of luck we can make it before noon.'

'Can't we just say hello to Scrap?' Georgie pleaded.

Archie froze. 'No!' he exclaimed. 'Not today, lad.'

Just then a shout reached their ears and they both turned to see Molly racing towards them, her skirts billowing behind her in the raging wind.

'Oh, Mister Burbage,' she panted. 'Have you come back? Oh, please say you have. It's awful here without you all. I don't know how much longer I can bear it.' She looked up into her master's face and was shocked at how ill and drawn he looked.

Archie shook his head. 'Sorry, gel. We've just brought the horse and cart back. We have to hurry and be on our way. Tell Reggie to get old Neddy in . . .'

'Oh, Master Burbage,' she said, shaking her head. 'Reggie's gone.'

'Gone?'

'Yes. I don't know where to. He said he wouldn't stay and take orders from either of them, and wouldn't come back 'til a true Burbage was in charge again.'

Archie rubbed his hand over his jaw and exhaled loudly. 'Oh! Well, that's up to Reggie. I'm sure a man like him won't be outta work for long. Now we must be off . . .'

Molly's face fell at his words and tears stung the back of her eyes. She quickly knelt down and hugged Georgie to her.

'Oh, it's so good to see yer,' she whispered. 'A'yer behaving yourself?'

Georgie nodded. 'How's Scrap?' he asked forlornly.

'Miserable. The poor creature's been kicked out of the house and just sits in the barn all day, waiting for yer to come back.'

Archie took a deep breath. 'We really have to go, Molly,' he said, looking anxiously across the yard.

'Oh, can't yer come up to the house? They've gone out. They won't be back for a while. I could mash you a cuppa and get you something to eat.'

'No, Molly. But thanks for the offer.' He patted the girl's arm and they both hurried away, leaving her staring sadly after them.

The walk to the big house took longer than Archie had anticipated and it was with relief that they finally entered the gates and made their way past the coaching house. The gravel drive was lined with trees and shrubs and in spring, summer and autumn the blaze of colour was a sight to see. Winter had stripped everything bare, the force of the wind swayed the branches dangerously, but for all this the walk was still majestic.

Rounding the bend, the big red mansion house loomed before them. Georgie stared in wonder, overawed by its size and the many windows that winked at him as the December sunlight broke through a gap in the thick clouds. He gripped his uncle's hand tighter. Archie remained silent, trying hard to prepare himself for his audience with Sir James.

Just then, he appeared from around the side of the house. He was dressed in his shooting clothes, carried a hunting gun over his shoulder and had two retrievers dancing at his feet. He paused for a moment and frowned at the sight of visitors walking hesitantly towards him. He sighed deeply and went over to greet them, the dogs bounding playfully behind him.

'Burbage,' he addressed Archie, hand outstretched in greeting. 'Good to see you. I'm sorry I did not get to your mother's funeral. I was called away on important business. But I trust you got my apology?'

'Oh, yes, sir,' Archie said, taking off his cap and clasping it between his hands.

'Good.' He lowered his eyes and acknowledged Georgie. 'Come to have a look round, have you?'

'Er . . . well, no,' Archie said, stumbling over his words. 'I'd like a word, sir. If it's convenient?'

James Richmond smiled. 'Yes, of course. Come into the house. But first, let's see to the young lad.'

Right on cue a maid appeared on the front steps. Sir James beckoned her over.

'Agnes, take the young fellow here to Cummings. Tell him to take care of him and show him the stables and get him something to eat. Bring him back in about an hour.'

The maid bobbed a curtsey, took hold of Georgie's hand and led him away.

'Right. Let us go into the library, we won't be disturbed there.'

Archie followed the squire into the house and through the large entrance hall. Paintings of ancestors adorned the walls, and ornate gilt chairs and highly polished tables lined the walls. As he walked across the wooden floor, the noise from his hobnailed boots echoed around the high walls. He felt small and insignificant and for a moment panic rose up in him. He wondered what on earth he was doing there, and what he was going to say.

On entering the library the dogs immediately settled themselves in front of the fireplace. Archie, as invited, sat on the edge of a deep red leather chair, politely refusing the drink he was offered.

Sir James Richmond, a tall distinguished man of forty-five, sat down behind his enormous, highly polished mahogany desk. A fire burned brightly in the grate and the room felt warm and comfortable. His handsome face stared steadily at the man seated before him and a slight frown formed on his brow. It was obvious that Archibald Burbage was deeply worried about something and needed his help. Maybe the rumours spreading round were correct for once?

'What's the problem, Burbage? How can I assist you?' His voice, though firm, was full of concern and cut through the silence that had prevailed since Archie had declined the drink.

'Well, sir,' he stuttered, 'I don't really like to bother you with this.'

'No need to apologise, man. I'll help if I can, you know that. So out with it.'

Archie nervously poured out his story and Sir James listened intently, stroking his chin now and again in astonishment.

When Archie had finished Sir James rose. He perched on the edge of his desk and eyed Archie thoughtfully. How was it possible, he thought, that this man could have signed away his whole life without realising it? He took a breath.

'It's a bad business indeed,' he said, shaking his head. 'She's a clever woman, your wife, she'd be a real asset to some unscrupulous business people.' He slid off the desk, walked over to the fireplace and stood with his back towards it. 'If it's any consolation, I had an ancestor once who betrayed her husband. Said his loyalties lay with Cromwell when everyone who knew him was in no doubt he was for the King. He was executed, and all because she wanted to marry someone else.' He ran his fingers through thick, greying hair. 'Still, this is not solving your problem. But what can be done about it? Seems to me she's tied you up good and proper.' He paused thoughtfully. 'The Women's Property Act that came into force some years back has made everything so difficult.'

'What d'you mean, sir?' Archie asked, bewildered.

'Well, it's much easier now for women to inherit property in their own right. Before the act, they had a devil of a job, it usually going to the next male heir regardless of how many times removed he was from the deceased.' He shook his head. 'To get your property back is going to be difficult. These new laws have changed everything.'

'Oh!'

'Don't look so downcast. All's not lost yet. Let me just think about it for a few moments.'

Sir James paced up and down before the desk. Archie watched mutely. Finally, the squire stopped walking and turned to face him.

'Unless you're prepared for a long court battle, Burbage, the only answer I have is that you have to find your mother's will. There might be something in it that can overturn what your wife has done. I'm not promising, mind. If everything has been left to you, as I trust it should have been, then you have no grounds against her, and I'm afraid to say your wife would know that. No, your only hope is to find that will and hope that your mother had the foresight to have put some sort of clause in against anything like this happening.'

231

Archie lowered his head. 'My mother wouldn't think to do anything like that, sir. She was a simple farmer's wife with no head for business. A bit like me, I'm afraid.'

'I wouldn't underestimate your mother, Burbage. On the occasions we met, I was impressed by her.'

'Were you?'

'Yes, and so was my father. He always spoke very highly of your parents. They suffered like most when we had the outbreak of brucellosis and potato blight in the middle of the last century, but they didn't go under and sell up like a lot of farmers did. They marshalled their resources and fought back. That takes hard work and planning, Burbage. So don't write them off as poor country folk.' He paused for a moment. 'There's been Burbages farming that land for nearly as long as Richmonds have lived here. It'd be a shame to see it pass to others. Especially in this manner.'

'Yes, sir, I agree,' Archie uttered apologetically. 'My parents weren't ones for much talk. I knew they never had an easy time of things but I never realised they'd suffered so much.'

'Well, I only know because my father was so passionate about farming and always drummed into me never to take the land or the people for granted. We may have acres of land and property, but we have to work as hard as you to maintain and keep it.'

'Yes, sir,' Archie muttered. 'I'll remember that.'

Sir James strode round the desk and placed his hands firmly on Archie's shoulders.

'You haven't done so badly, Burbage. You're a good farmer, one of the best round here.' He tutted loudly. 'To be honest, I'm pretty dismayed by all this. But I can only repeat my advice. You must find that will. It's the only hope you've got.' He walked towards the fireplace and turned to face Archie. 'Matthews no longer owns his farm, hasn't done for over a year. So amalgamating the two is out of the question.'

Archie raised his head, his face filled with puzzlement. 'I never knew that.'

'No. It was kept very quiet. He'd got himself into trouble and needed money badly. He approached me and I bought the land, keeping him on for the time being as tenant as he begged me to do.' He breathed deeply. 'To be honest, the land's going to waste. I'm on the verge of evicting him.'

'Oh! Does he know this?'

'I should imagine so,' James answered flatly. 'The man's no fool yet has made no effort as far as the farm's concerned. Anyway, I've given him enough time and I've a couple in mind just right to take over the tenancy. They'll look after the land, and if they want they can buy it at a reasonable price. I'll give them that opportunity, it's only fair.'

Archie frowned. 'Oh, dear. I wonder what Kath will make of all this?'

Sir James's eyes opened wide. 'I wouldn't have thought that that was any of your concern, Burbage. Getting your land and property back is your main problem, not your wife's welfare.'

Archie sighed deeply. 'Yes, sir. You're right, it is.' He rose. 'Thank you for your time. I know you're a busy man and I do appreciate it.'

'Any time. I'm always here.'

Sir James stretched out his hand and shook Archie's firmly. 'I hope it all works out for you. If not, I'm sure I can find you work round here.'

'I appreciate that, sir.' Archie turned and headed for the door. 'I'll collect young Georgie. And, once again, thank you.'

'Cummings can take you back in the buggy.'

Archie stepped back in surprise. 'Oh, there's no need for that, sir. We can walk.'

'It's no trouble. Cummings has to go out anyway.'

Archie graciously accepted the offer, turned and left the room, leaving Sir James Richmond staring thoughtfully after him.

Georgie, filled with excitement at the prospect of being driven home in the squire's buggy, chattered non-stop all the journey. Archie never heard one word of his adventures in the stables, his mind filled with his own problems. The talk with Sir James had made him see matters in a new light. He now realised that what Kath had done was not only against him but against his parents and all the preceding Burbages. All their hard work and sacrifice would be in vain if he let Kath get away with this. His heart sank. The trouble was he still loved her, despite all she had done, and it was going to be very hard for him to act against her. But he had to. If not for himself, then for his ancestors. And now of course there was Annie and young Georgie to consider. What would happen to them if he sat back and did nothing? They couldn't all stay at Matty's forever.

Later that night Matty's back room was bursting at the seams. Archie, Annie, Matty, her three sons and daughter-in-law were all gathered round the table discussing Archie's problem. Pot after pot of tea had been mashed and drunk and finally Georgie had been sent across to the Cherry Tree Inn for a jug of beer. Voices had been raised and heads shaken in disagreement.

Matty turned to Annie. 'Looks like Archie's talk with the squire was worth it.'

'Yes,' Annie agreed. 'His attitude's changed. He seems to want to get the farm back.' She smiled warmly and turned back to join in the debate.

Bernard, Matty's youngest son, took his mother aside.

'Why are you getting involved in this business, Mam? That's the man that ditched you, ain't it?'

Matty glared angrily at her youngest son, all eighteen years and six foot of him. 'Archie's an old friend of mine, and it's nothing to do with you what happened in the past or what I do now. Now make yourself useful and put some plates and mugs on the table. And if you can't say anything useful, keep your gob shut!'

'All right, Mam! I was only thinking a'you,' Bernard said defensively. He eased his long body off the chair and collected the plates and mugs from the kitchen. On his return he looked over at Annie who was listening intently to his sister-in-law. She had her head tilted to one side. Tendrils of dark hair had escaped from their pins and her long dark eyelashes fluttered up and down as she spoke. He watched as she closed her eyes for a moment in weariness, her lashes resting on creamy smooth skin. He sighed deeply. My, she was a pretty woman, he thought longingly. Heaps above the other girls he knew in the village. Pity she was so much older than him, she would have made the perfect wife. He put the crockery on the table and addressed the gathering.

'Why don't we just break in?' he announced. 'We'll soon find that damned will. If there is one, that is.'

Matty looked at him in disgust. 'I've told you before, our Bernard, if you've nothing useful to add to this discussion, keep your mouth shut.'

'Why can't we break in, Mam? What's to stop us?' Graham, Matty's eldest, asked.

'My god!' she groaned loudly. 'I've raised a bunch of thieves and cut-throats. You can't just break in. It ain't Archie's farm any more, and Kath could get the bobbies on to us and have us charged, yer daft sod.'

With Matty's outburst the room lapsed into silence. Discussions were halted for a time whilst sandwiches, beer and more tea prevailed. Matty finally pushed her plate away from her, placed her elbows on the table and rested her chin in her hands. She looked across at Annie.

'Are you sure you checked every nook and cranny in that loft? Is there anywhere you might have missed?'

Annie raised her head. 'I looked everywhere, Matty. In all the drawers. Under the bed. I tapped the walls. I even looked under the wood stove just in case. No, I can assure you, I looked everywhere.' She gave a wry laugh. 'The only thing I didn't do was prise up the floorboards.'

'Well, that's it,' Archie sighed, defeated. 'If Annie's

checked the loft, then I'm beat. I can't think of anywhere else it might be.'

Complete silence filled the room as they all looked at each other in turn.

Matty groaned. 'Maybe the hidey-hole never existed. If there had've been one, then the loft is where it would be. She was always in that loft. Either there or sitting in the hole in the hedge,' she added.

'Oh!' Annie exclaimed loudly as a memory flooded to mind. 'That's it. I think I know where it might be.'

'You do!' Several voices rang out in unison.

'Yes. I think the hidey-hole is under a stone in the hedge.' Annie related her story. 'I've never given that night another thought since. To be honest I'd forgotten all about it until you mentioned my mother used to sit in there. But I bet that's where it is!'

'Well, there's only one way to find out,' Bernard said excitedly.

All eyes were upon him.

'I suggest we go up there tonight and examine it,' he said, rubbing his hands together in glee. 'Me and you could go, Archie. If we wait until about twelve o'clock, they'll all be asleep.'

Several voices sounded in agreement.

'Oh, I don't know . . .' Archie said hesitantly. 'What if we're caught?'

'God, man. D'you want your bloody farm back or not?'

'Yes, 'course I do.'

'Well then!'

Annie sat bolt upright in her chair. 'Uncle Archie, would you mind if I went with you instead of Bernard?'

Archie looked at her in surprise. 'Why, gel, it's not really a woman's place . . .'

'I know that. But if this does turn out to be what we're looking for . . .' she said hesitantly. 'Well, it was my mother's secret place and I want to be the one to open it. There might be something she left that was personal.'

Archie's mouth set grimly. 'I don't know.'

'Please, Uncle Archie,' she pleaded.

'Okay,' he agreed slowly. 'Although I still ain't convinced . . .'

'Good,' Annie cut in. 'I won't let you down, I promise.'

A plan of action was formulated and when there was nothing else to discuss, the rest of the family retired to bed leaving Matty, Annie and Archie sitting around the remains of the fire, waiting for the hour when they would set out on their mission.

The night was freezing cold and inky black as they made their way up the rutted track towards the farm.

Archie suddenly stopped and groaned. 'Damn!' he exclaimed. 'I forgot to bring a lamp. We'll need one to see what we're doing.'

'There's one in the barn,' Annie ventured.

Archie stared at her blankly.

'I'll get it if you don't want to go into the farm, Uncle Archie.' She placed her hand on his arm. 'It's all right, I understand.'

'No, no,' he replied quickly. 'You'll fall yer length in that yard. It's dangerous in the dark. You can stay by the gate . . .'

'We'll both go,' she cut in. 'We're in this together, remember.'

The farmyard was deathly quiet as Archie pushed open the gate just enough to squeeze through. It creaked loudly and they both held their breath. Annie's heart thumped loudly in her chest. That noise alone, she felt, was enough to wake anybody. Archie stood by the gate, his hand clutching the top of the wooden post as he stared across the yard at the house. The curtains were closed and all was in darkness. He wondered if John was up there now with Kath. His heart lurched and his stomach churned as a sickening sensation reared up in him. Damn the man, he thought angrily.

A soft padding sound reached their ears and they froze in

horror. Suddenly, Archie's shoulders relaxed and he squatted down to greet Scrap who was trotting towards them, wagging his tail in delight at his master's presence.

'Hello there, boy,' Archie whispered, patting the dog's head.

Annie wiped the back of her hand over her forehead. 'Oh, what a fright. I could have done without that.'

'Me too.'

Archie motioned to Scrap to keep quiet, grabbed hold of his collar and, treading as softly as possible, guided them over the yard. It was a relief to them both when they arrived at the barn undetected.

'There should be a lamp around somewhere,' he whispered as he let go of Scrap's collar and straightened himself up. He found the lamp hanging on a wooden post, unhooked it and shook it to see if there was paraffin in it. There was.

'Better wait 'til we get back behind the hedge before I light it,' he said softly, making to walk towards the barn door.

Annie caught his arm. 'I just want to take a look in my old room first.'

'Why? For God's sake, gel, let's just get out of here and get on with what we came to do!'

Before he could stop her, she had begun to climb the ladder. Shrugging his shoulders, he followed her.

Inside the loft, Annie drew the curtains over the tiny window as Archie lit the lamp. The room lit up in a soft glow and, as Annie gazed around the room that she had made so homely, a rage of anger swept over her. Someone had been in and thrown everything around. All the bedclothes were piled on the floor, the peg rug she had so painstakingly made had been thrown over a chair and the straw mattress was slumped against the far wall.

'It's just as I thought,' she said through clenched teeth. 'Kath's been in here looking for the hidey-hole. I know she has. Why else would this place be in such a mess?'

Archie moved quickly towards her. 'Never mind that, gel,' he whispered anxiously. 'Let's get out of here before we're caught.'

Annie sniffed loudly and nodded in agreement. She waited while he blew out the lamp then followed him out, inching slowly down the ladder in the darkness.

They said their goodbyes to Scrap and silently stole down the yard.

Archie sighed with relief as he pulled the gate closed behind them, threw over the metal hook and joined Annie who was standing in front of the hole in the hedge.

'It's there, Uncle Archie,' she whispered, pointing with her finger. 'Under that stone.'

He fumbled in the darkness to re-light the lamp. The hole was illuminated in ghostly light and Annie jumped as a rabbit, sheltering from the cold wind, scurried away across the field. She bent down, steadied herself and heaved the stone aside, revealing a hole big enough to get a large hand inside. Straightening up, she turned to Archie and grinned in triumph.

'This has to be it,' she said, trying to keep her voice as low as possible.

He moved over and shone the light down into the hole.

'Can you see anything?' she asked hesitantly.

'I might if you get your head outta the way,' came the disgruntled reply.

Annie quickly moved aside.

'I still can't see anything,' he grumbled. 'Only mud. I think you've been mistaken, Annie. There's nothing in here.'

'Let me have a look,' she said quietly.

She knelt down and peered inside, grimacing as a nest of wood lice swarmed around, showing displeasure at being disturbed. She sat back on her haunches.

'You're right, Uncle Archie. There's nothing here!' she exclaimed. 'Oh, it's all been a waste of time.'

'Never mind, me duck. At least we tried.'

She rose and brushed down her skirt, her whole face bathed in disappointment and hopelessness. She looked out across the dark fields, shivering as the cold wind rustled through the trees and grass. Wrapping her arms around her body, she turned her eyes back to the hole. She knelt down again and stared into it.

'It could be buried under the mud. If it's been there years, stuff would have fallen on top, wouldn't it?'

Archie nodded. 'It might, I suppose.'

Annie raised herself. 'You'll have to poke around, Uncle Archie. I can't put my hand in there, not with all those creepy crawlies.'

He laughed softly. 'A few insects never hurt anyone, yer daft ha'porth. Here, hold the lamp.'

He passed it to her and knelt down. Placing his hand inside the hole, he began to claw at the hard mud with his fingers. Annie peered around, feeling uneasiness steal over her. The icy wind rustled through the branches of the hedge and she felt unseen eyes upon them. She shuddered as she turned her attention back to her uncle, wishing he would hurry so they could get back to the safe, warm confines of Matty's homely kitchen.

He pulled out his hand. 'It's no good, Annie, the ground's too hard.'

She let out a soft cry of anguish and looked around frantically.

'We must find something to dig with.'

'It's pitch black, Annie. How we gonna find a spade or whatever in the dark? And I ain't going up to the barn again, that's for sure.'

'We'll use something else.' Her eyes scanned the surrounding earth. She quickly bent down. 'Here, try this,' she said, handing Archie a flat piece of slate.

He examined it. 'Might do the trick.' He bent down and began to scrape away the frozen mud.

The minutes passed slowly by as bit by bit the stubborn earth began to crumble away. Suddenly, he felt the slate hit something hard. He scraped harder until enough of the hard object was revealed, allowing him to grasp it and pull it from its hiding place.

Annie swung the lamp round, letting the light fall full

upon his hand. They both stared at a bulky, mud-clogged sacking bag, tied around the top with a thin piece of brown leather.

'You open it, Annie,' he said, offering her the bag.

She sat back, placed the lamp on the stone and gingerly untied the leather strap. She tipped the bag up and they both stared in awe as the contents scattered out on to her skirt.

'Oh, my god,' she gasped. 'It's sovereigns, Uncle Archie, and there's hundreds of them.'

'Put 'em back,' he uttered, bewildered. 'And let's get out of here – quick!'

Annie gathered up the gold coins as quickly as possible. She looked up at him.

'But what about the will? We ain't found that yet.'

Archie breathed deeply. 'There's no will in that hole, Annie, and if there was, it would have rotted with age by now.'

Annie sat back and uttered a small cry of anguish.

'We came to find the will. We can't go back without it. And, anyway, I don't think this place is my mother's hidey-hole after all. It's a hiding place all right, but not my mother's,' she said with conviction. 'If it had've been, there'd be something of hers inside, wouldn't there? Even if it was something little.'

Archie nodded in agreement. 'Yes, there would.'

'I think somebody's hidden these sovereigns and for some reason never came back for them. What do you think?'

He shrugged his shoulders. 'I can't see why anyone would hide a fortune like that and just leave them. It doesn't make sense.'

'No, it doesn't.'

They both lapsed into silence, the dark night enveloping them as they sat, each with their own thoughts.

Annie slowly raised her head. 'Uncle Archie, my grandmother was trying to get into the loft when she died. Surely that must mean something?'

'Yes,' he agreed. 'But what?'

She ran her hand backwards and forwards over her brow. Suddenly her eyes opened wide. She grasped her uncle's arm.

'We've been looking in the wrong place, Uncle Archie. The hidey-hole isn't inside the room, it's outside.'

Archie stared at her. 'Eh? I don't understand?'

'Come on,' she said, jumping up. 'There ain't time to explain.'

Blowing out the lamp, he reluctantly followed her once more as they stole silently across the rutted yard and into the barn where he relit the lamp and shone it up to where Annie was pointing.

'There's a hole in that rafter just as it meets the trap-door,' she whispered. 'It's been made on purpose and a piece of wood fits over it like a cover. Georgie knocked it out once. I just thought it was loose, but now I'm not so sure. Go and look, Uncle Archie. I can't, I'm too nervous.'

Without a word, Archie climbed the ladder whilst Annie held the lamp. He ran his fingers over the beam until he felt a knot in the wood. He stuck his finger in the hole and pulled off the cover.

'Yer right, Annie. There's a hole here big enough to get me hand inside.'

He groped around.

'Is there anything?'

'Just a minute, Annie,' he snapped.

He pulled out his hand which held a yellowing envelope, the red seal of authority shining in the lamplight.

'It's addressed to me,' he said.

'It's the will then, Uncle Archie. It must be.'

He slipped the envelope into his pocket.

'Just check to see if there's anything else.'

Archie nodded and once more put his hand inside the hole.

'There is something,' he said slowly.

He pulled out his hand and, supporting himself on the beam, leant over and handed Annie a tortoiseshell hair comb, a piece of yellowing lace and the dried, faded remains of a long dead rose. The rose disintegrated, falling on to the straw-covered floor. Annie looked at it for a moment then turned her attention back to the comb and lace. She held them tenderly and clasped them to her chest. Archie replaced the wooden cover, climbed down the ladder and joined her.

'These were my mother's, Uncle Archie. At this moment I feel close to her.' She felt tears prick the back of her eyes and sniffed softly. 'Oh, Uncle Archie, why did she have to die?'

His shoulders sagged and he placed his arm tentatively around her shoulders. 'We all have to die sometime,' he whispered, trying to comfort her. He took a deep breath. 'Let's get out of here, Annie. I don't know where Scrap has got to but he could start barking and wake them up, then we'll be done for.'

Annie placed her treasures tenderly in her coat pocket and waited whilst Archie blew out the lamp and replaced it on the hook. They deftly crossed the yard and went back down the track towards Matty's house.

It was about two-thirty in the morning when they finally let themselves into the tiny kitchen. Annie walked through into the living room and smiled at the sight of Matty, fast asleep in the chair by the dying embers of the fire. Her head had slipped to one side and her mouth gaped open. She tiptoed over and gently placed her hand on the older woman's arm. Matty jumped and opened her eyes, staring at Annie in confusion.

'Oh, I must have dozed off,' she said, yawning loudly. 'Couldn't keep awake any longer.' She eased herself up. 'How did you get on then?' she asked.

'We think we've found the will, Matty.'

'Oh, thank goodness for that,' she said with relief. 'I've sat here worried sick in case it was all a wild goose chase.'

Annie picked up the poker to rake the fire. 'We found something else as well,' she said cagily.

'What?'

Annie laid down the poker and walked over to the table. She wrenched the heavy bag from her pocket and emptied out the contents. They jingled and rolled over the cloth and Matty rose as hurriedly as her stiff joints would allow to join her friend. She gazed down in amazement.

'Where did you find these?' she asked.

'Under the stone in the hedge. But that wasn't my mother's hidey-hole, Matty. That was somewhere else.'

She proceeded to relate the events of the night to the older woman.

Matty's hand went to her mouth. 'I was right then.'

'It looks like it. I've a feeling that these are the proceeds from that quarry robbery you told me about.' She looked at Matty, eyes wide in alarm. 'It was my father, Thomas McIntyre. Who else would have chosen the farm.' She clasped her hands together. 'The money must have been hidden there all this time. But why? Why take all this money then just leave it? It doesn't make sense.'

Just then Archie joined them.

'Oh, you've shown Matty our haul then?'

'Yes.'

Matty turned to face Archie. 'What about the envelope? Have you opened it yet?'

'I was just about to.'

'Well, get to it, lad. I want to know what's inside it. I'll make some tea in the meanwhile.'

Matty busied herself whilst Archie sat in the chair she had just vacated. Annie sat opposite, clasping her hands together in anticipation as she watched him carefully break the red wax seal and gingerly pull out the contents.

'Is it the will, Uncle Archie?'

'Yes, it is.'

'Thank God for that!' Matty gasped, placing her hand on her chest. 'What's it say then, Archie? Can we fix Kath or not?'

He paused for a minute, trying to digest his mother's wishes. He bowed his head and exhaled loudly. 'It seems she's left the farm to you, Matty,' he uttered.

'To me?' she said in astonishment. 'What in God's name

for! Here, let me have a look.' She snatched the paper out of Archie's hand and scanned her eyes quickly over the words. 'This makes no bloody sense to me,' she said, shaking her head rapidly. 'I can't understand a word of this legal stuff.' She thrust the yellowing paper towards Annie. 'Here, you have a go.'

She accepted the sheets and studied them hard. 'Well,' she said, raising her head. 'That's what it says, Matty. "I hereby bequeath the farm . . ."'

'Yes, I read that myself,' Matty cut in. 'But why?'

Archie fingered the envelope, slipping his hands inside the opening. 'Oh, just a minute.' He pulled out another piece of paper and opened it. 'It's a letter from my mother.'

'Come on then. What's it say?' pestered Matty, sitting down on a chair by the table.

Archie sat in silence as he read it. Finally he raised his head and held the letter out towards Annie. 'You read it. This is all too much for me.'

Once again, she accepted the proffered piece of paper.

'Read it out loud so Matty can hear,' he said softly.

Annie gulped hard and cleared her throat.

'"My dear Archie, I am getting Mr Grimble to write this for me. Never was any good at writing, so I'm putting me trust in him. He said he will word it as I speak, so you will know it does come from me.

'"My wishes will come as a bit of a shock to you. But, son, I know what Kath's up to. I overheard her talking to John Matthews in the barn. It was late one night a few years after your wedding. It was disgusting, son. They were lovers and had been for ages. I could tell by the way they were speaking that they were making plans for the farm when I died. I was upset and shocked more than I can tell you, and knew I had to do something about it. I had to put a stop to her somehow.

'"I did try to warn you, but you took no notice. You're too kind and soft-hearted, that's your trouble. Over the years I thought she'd grow to love you and forget John Matthews. It didn't take me long to realise that that was wishful thinking

245

on my part. Anyway, I'm getting old, son, me time's about up and I'm beginning to forget things and want to get my house in order before it's too late. If I'd been a younger woman, I'd have stood up to her and sorted her out. But I haven't been well now for a while and I'm getting worried and want to know that you're taken care of when I'm gone.

"'I went to see the old squire for his advice. He was very good and put me in touch with Mr Grimble. He advised me to leave the farm to Matty, on the understanding that it's yours to live and work for the rest of your life, then it's to pass to Matty. Dear Matty. You should have married her. She would have made a good farmer's wife. I've kept in touch with her and I know she can be trusted to carry out me wishes. If Kath dies or you come to your senses and get rid of her, then the farm is automatically to go back into your name.

"'I still hope, with all my heart, that our dear Mary Ann will come home. If she does, she's to get her share. I know you will see her right. Try and find her, Archie. It broke my heart when she went. I've always felt in my bones that Kath had something to do with that, but I could never get to the bottom of it. I want our Mary Ann to know that we still love and care for her, whatever she has done. It can't be that bad that she has to abandon her family.

"'I have to tell you, son. Please forgive me, but you have to know. Lucy is not your child. I knew when Kath was pregnant that the baby was not yours. When you were four, we nearly lost you. You had a really bad do of mumps and the doctor said it were unlikely that you would have children. When Lucy was born she had brown eyes. Yours and Kath's are blue. Kath stuck me out on it, but you were so delighted with the baby I could not say anything. So I've done all this to make sure you get your rights and I hope you understand.

"'Your loving mother.'"

Archie choked back a cry of anguish and wiped a tear from his eye.

Matty looked thoughtful. 'Well,' she said, 'I did tell you

she'd got something up her sleeve. And, you know, I always had a feeling about young Lucy. If the old lady was here now I'd give her a big hug. This is just what we need to get yer farm back. What d'you say, Archie?'

He sniffed loudly. 'There ain't much I can say, is there? I'm just upset that me mother knew all along what Kath was about, and didn't tell me.'

'Come on, Archie. She said in her letter that she'd often tried to tell you. Anyway, what would you've done? I'll tell yer. Nothing. You'd still have let Kath carry on the way she did. You'd still have buried your head, pretending nothing was wrong.'

'Oh, Matty,' Annie interrupted. 'You're being a bit hard on him.'

'She's right, Annie love,' Archie muttered, easing himself up. 'I'm going to bed. All this is too much for me to take in. I'll see you in the morning.'

Annie and Matty watched in silence as Archie, his whole body sagging in despair, stumbled through the door that led up the narrow stairs towards the two small bedrooms, one of which he shared with Matty's two younger sons and Georgie.

Matty turned to Annie. 'You're very quiet, gel? What's up. Ain't yer pleased about all this?'

'Oh, yes,' she said softly. 'I'm glad Kath will get her comeuppance. She doesn't deserve the farm.' She shook her head sadly. 'It's my uncle I feel sorry for. All he asks for is a quiet life. He ain't equipped to handle this sort of situation.'

'You're right, gel. He's not. I've known Archie Burbage nearly all me life, and he's always shied away from trouble. We'll have to go with him when he confronts Kath, to make sure she doesn't get one over him again.'

Annie nodded. 'If she's any sense, she'll not make a fuss. I'm sure she could be prosecuted for what she's done.'

'Well, I don't know about that, me not understanding legal stuff. But one thing's for certain – that farm's mine and I can't wait to see her face when she finds out! I've waited many years to see her downfall.' Matty sighed deeply. 'It's

247

funny though, Annie. I don't feel so happy about it as I thought I would.'

'That's because you're not a malicious person, Matty.'

She struggled to rise. 'Let's have another cuppa. Then I must get to bed.' She swung the black kettle over the embers. 'It's been some night, me duck, ain't it?'

'Yes,' Annie sighed wearily.

'And tomorrow's gonna be worse. We've to get Archie to face her and that Matthews.'

Several minutes later, Annie accepted the hot mug of tea that was offered her. She took a sip and placed the mug on the hearth.

'Matty?' she said hesitantly.

'Yes, me duck?' Matty said slowly, raising eyes which were bloodshot with fatigue.

'Those sovereigns . . . what we going to do about them?'

'Do! What d'you mean?'

'Well, shouldn't we hand them over to the bobbies?'

'Phew!' Matty exhaled loudly. 'That we do not. You found 'em fair and square. They're yours.'

'Oh, Matty. No, they ain't. They're from the robberies . . .'

'Robberies!' Matty placed her mug down and folded her arms under her bosom. 'Now you listen to me, gel. Those . . . robberies, for want of a better word, happened over twenty-odd years ago. People have forgotten about them and what was taken, and to be honest I never heard any mention of sovereigns.' She leant forward. 'Anyone could have buried them there. We get lots of strangers hanging about.'

'I don't think so somehow,' Annie said softly. She paused, deep in thought. 'I think that Thomas McIntyre must have entrusted my mother with those sovereigns. She hid them, and he was to come back for them later.'

'We don't know that, Annie. Thomas McIntyre could have put the money there himself.'

'No,' Annie said coldly. 'He asked her to hide it for him. That's not to say, though, that she knew where it came from. His conversation with you in the yard all makes sense now.'

'Ah, but we don't know for sure he was involved in the robberies. It was only assumed 'cos he had red hair. There could be all sorts of explanations for why that bag was hidden there, and it might have nothing to do with Thomas McIntyre or your mother. To be honest, Annie, I'm too tired to discuss all the possibilities now. Just take my advice. That money is like a blessing. It'll give you and Georgie a new start in life. Think, Annie, you could do all sorts of things with it.'

'I could,' she agreed forlornly. 'But it wouldn't be right.'

'Oh, Annie!' Matty exclaimed. 'Are you going to give up the chance of a new life because it might not be right? I thought you had more sense in yer than that. Okay, say we hand over the money to the authorities tomorrow. What then? You go back to the farm, or better still to Leicester and the workhouse, and in the meantime the money stays where it is because the rightful owners can't be found after all this time. Then there's the other matter.'

'What other matter?'

'Think of the scandal. If anyone in the village got wind of this, yer family's good name would be dragged through the mud. Is that what you want?'

Annie lowered her head. 'No.'

'Well, then. Take the money and use it wisely. I'd try and keep quiet about it, but if anyone should find out, just say it was your inheritance from yer grandmother's will.'

'Oh, Matty.' Annie's eyes sparkled. 'There's lots I could do with it.'

'I bet there is,' she agreed. 'And it's better in your pocket than some rich bugger's who doesn't really need it.'

'You're right, Matty. I'll take it. I know it's probably dishonest of me but I'll do it.' She clasped her hands together. 'We can split it between the three of us.'

'That we won't,' Matty said tartly. 'That money is nothing to do with me.'

'Oh, but you've been so good to me,' Annie said as she rose to take her friend's hands. 'I'd feel better if we evened it out.'

249

'No, gel,' Matty said firmly. 'I appreciate your intentions. But let me put it this way. I've lived and worked in this village all me life. I get on well with me neighbours and if I suddenly came into money, there'd be lots of talk. People wouldn't understand, and I wouldn't be one of them any more. I know I ain't had the happiest of lives, but I know me friends and me place.' She grimaced. 'What would I do with it anyway? Give it me sons? Then *they'd* ask questions. No, it's better this way. Please understand, Annie.'

She went back to her seat. 'Yes, I do understand. I suppose if my Charlie had suddenly come home with a pocketful of sovereigns the talk in the courtyard would have been rife and then we'd have been frozen out for being above the rest of them. Uncle Archie might need the money when he gets the farm back. I can help him then. I suppose Kath will leave and move in with Matthews?'

'Let's leave the whys and wherefores 'til tomorrow, gel. Now's not the time to start assuming things.'

'No, I suppose you're right.'

Matty looked at her. 'Is there something troubling you?'

She slowly nodded. 'I was just wondering about Thomas McIntyre.'

'What about him, me duck?'

'I was just wondering what really happened to him?'

Matty sighed. 'I don't think we'll ever find out. I think you've got to forget about him, me duck. Whatever he did or whatever he was will remain a mystery. Just count yourself lucky you had a proper father, and I'm not talking about Thomas McIntyre! I'm talking about the man who brought you up. He's the one who loved and cared for you, taught you to read and write, made you the person you are today. That were your father, Annie, not Thomas McIntyre. You had a better start then most people in life, even though you were left without a mother, so count yourself lucky.'

'Oh, Matty.' Annie sniffed. 'You're so right. What would I do without you?' She kissed Matty affectionately on the cheek. 'There's just one other thing.'

'What now?'

'Do you think that you and Archie will get together?'

Matty sighed and shook her head. 'My dear, you're just a romantic at heart.' She smiled wryly and shook her head. 'He'll take Kath back, you'll see.'

Annie's eyes opened wide in amazement. 'Never, Matty! He'll never do that, not after what she's done.'

'He will. For all Archie's faults, he's very loyal. Kath'll play on his sympathies when this all comes out and he'll feel sorry for her.'

'But what about John Matthews?'

'Once that rotter knows that Kath hasn't got the farm, he'll be off. Anyway, Matthews has a reputation as far as the women are concerned. It wouldn't surprise me if he had another stashed away somewhere. It's rumoured he's got one over Desford way.'

'Oh, Matty, I couldn't stay at the farm if Kath was still there. Not after all this.'

'No, neither could I. But why not wait and see what happens tomorrow before you make any rash decisions?'

'I thought living in a town was bad enough, but the carryings on in village life beat a town's scandals any day.'

'Don't they just?' Matty agreed. She yawned loudly. 'I really must get some sleep, Annie, and it's nearly time to get up!'

She nodded and hugged her friend tightly. 'Regardless of what happens, you'll be glad to get this house back to yourself.'

'I've enjoyed your company, Annie. It's just a pity about the circumstances.'

Matty struggled over and pulled the curtain back across the recess, revealing the hidden bed that they shared. Slowly, she pulled off her dress, laid it over the back of a chair and turned to face Annie. A warm smile spread across her lined face at the sight that greeted her. Annie, exhausted from her night's adventures, was cuddled in the armchair sound asleep. Picking up a thick woollen blanket, Matty covered the younger woman up before she herself climbed gratefully into bed.

Persuading Archie to face Kath proved a major operation the following day. 'She might be out.' 'I'm tired. Let's go tomorrow.' Excuse after excuse at the thought of the impending confrontation. It frightened the wits out of him. Finally, with Matty and Annie bullying him, he relented, knowing deep inside himself that the sooner he got this over with the better. It was agreed that the two women would go with him.

'Alf from the blacksmith's yard will take us in the cart.' Matty said. 'He owes me a favour.'

'I'd sooner walk,' Archie said. 'It'll give me time to get me thoughts in order.'

Matty grimaced. 'He's a bloody selfish sod sometimes,' she moaned to Annie. 'But I suppose the exercise will do me leg good. Get your coat, gel, before he comes out with another excuse.'

Georgie having been deposited with the family next-door, and with the threat of snow falling from the heavily laden skies, the three set off. They walked in silence, Matty nor Annie wanting to give Archie any excuse to change his mind. His steps slowed to a near halt as they approached the farm gate. He stopped and turned to Matty, his face ashen and drawn. She pushed him on the shoulder.

'No time to dally, man.'

He slowly nodded and pushed open the large wooden gate. They reached the kitchen door and he knocked hesitantly, holding his breath. Muffled voices could be heard and the sound of footsteps. Archie quickly turned and eyed the two women standing at the back of him. They both looked at him reassuringly. He grimaced as the door opened and Molly stood before them, her mouth gaping in surprise.

'Who is it?' Kath's voice bellowed from inside.

'It's . . . It's the master.'

'The master!'

Before Molly could say another word the door was yanked further open and Kath stood glaring at them. Molly, sensing a confrontation, raised her skirts and fled over the yard and into the barn.

'What d'you want?' Kath demanded. 'You took everything with you the other day . . .'

'We need to talk,' Matty said, pushing Archie aside.

Kath laughed. 'We've nothing to talk about. Now get off my land before I have you thrown off.' She placed her hands on her hips and glared at them mockingly.

Matty, suddenly tired and fed up with the whole situation, pushed her aside and strode into the kitchen, a startled Kath staring open-mouthed after her. John Matthews, seated at the table with the remains of a meal in front of him, shifted awkwardly in his chair. Matty eyed him haughtily before she turned to face Kath.

'I said we need to talk, and talk we will,' she said, motioning Annie and Archie to join her.

Kath's face reddened in anger. She turned to face Archie. 'What's the meaning of this?' she screamed. 'Can't you get it through your thick head that this farm is mine and you have no right just to walk in here unannounced.'

Archie lowered his head. 'Sit down, Kath,' he said softly.

'Don't you tell me to sit down in me own kitchen.' She turned to John. 'Don't just sit there, do something!'

He shrugged his shoulders.

Annie nudged Archie. 'Come on, Uncle Archie. Tell her.'

'Tell me what?'

'Kath,' Archie began, clearing his throat. 'We've found me mother's will.'

'What?' Kath gasped, her mouth gaping open. 'You can't have. She didn't make a will. You're lying.'

'We did, Kath,' Annie said coldly.

Kath leapt forward and grabbed her by the shoulders. 'What's this got to do with you, you little upstart?' she shouted, shaking her violently.

Annie thrust her away and she fell heavily against the table. Kath eyed her warily and wiped the back of her hand over her mouth. 'Anyway, it doesn't make any difference, the farm's mine. Archie signed it over and there ain't nothing you can do.'

''Fraid there is,' Matty said smugly. 'The old lady left the farm to me. So you see,' she said, stepping forward and wagging her finger in Kath's direction, 'it wasn't Archie's farm to sign over to you in the first place.' She paused and raised her head triumphantly. 'Kath Burbage, all your planning and scheming was for nothing.'

Kath shrank back in shock. She looked over at John who was staring blankly at her. She slumped down on a chair, bewilderment and confusion covering her face. She narrowed her eyes. 'I don't believe you. You're bluffing.'

Matty motioned to Archie. 'Show her the will. Then she might believe us.'

He stepped forward and placed the yellowing envelope in front of her. She made a grab for it and quickly scanned the contents. Her body sagged.

'Oh, John!' she cried. 'It's all been for nothing. All the years of putting up with him and his mother has all been a waste of time.' She let out a loud wail of anguish. 'No! No! It can't be true.' Tears gushed down her face and she held her head in her hands, rocking backwards and forwards in despair. Finally, she raised her head, stood up and groped her way round the table towards him. 'We'll have to go to your place,' she whispered defeatedly.

He lowered his eyes and ran his tongue over his teeth. 'We can't do that, gel.'

'Why not?'

'Because the farm ain't mine no more.'

'Ain't yours? What do you mean? I don't understand.'

John Matthews stood up and walked round the back of his chair. 'Just what I said, Kath. The farm ain't mine. I sold it to the squire a couple of years back. I'm only the tenant.'

254

'What?' she gasped in disbelief. 'You sold it, you swine, and you never told me! And all this time I've been sitting here waiting for the old lady to die so we could put our plan in operation and join the two farms together.'

He shrugged his shoulders. 'I needed the money, Kath. I'd n'ote else to sell.'

'Money!' She ran forward and grabbed hold of John's arms, looking into his eyes. 'Is that all? I'd have got you the money somehow.'

'Not as much as I needed.'

'Oh, John. All I ever wanted was to be married to you and have the biggest farm hereabouts so I could hold me head up,' she sobbed. 'We'll still have to live at your place for the time being while we sort something out.'

John sniffed loudly and wiped the back of his hand under his nose. 'We can't.'

Kath looked at him questioningly. 'Can't?'

He directed his gaze away from her. 'I ain't the tenant no more. I've had notice to quit.' He looked at her mockingly. 'So, my sweet, I'm just like you. Homeless.'

'You bastard!' she screeched. She threw back her arm and made to strike him. He put out his hand and stopped her, gripping her wrist tightly.

'Now, now, Kath. You've had your fun and I've had mine. But unlike you, I have other irons in the fire.'

She drew back in horror, rubbing her arm where he had held her in his iron grip. 'What d'you mean?' she whispered.

'Mildred Aldwinckle, that's who I mean. She's just ripe and ready for the taking. Got her dangling on a string I have, and her father owns land. It'll all come to her soon and I'll be set up for life. Can't say she'll be as much fun as you, though.' He sauntered over to the back door and grabbed his coat off the hook. 'Now, if you don't mind, I'll leave you folks to it. I'll send someone up for my things later.' With that he walked through the door and disappeared down the yard.

Archie stared after him then turned and looked at his wife. He walked over and placed his arm around her shoulders.

'You're better off without him, Kath,' he said softly. He raised his head and looked across at Annie. 'Make her a cuppa tea, will yer, please?'

Annie's mouth fell open. 'You want me to make Kath a cup of tea?'

Archie stared at her in bewilderment. 'Annie, can't you see she's had a hell of a shock? Where's your compassion?'

Annie's face hardened. 'I'm sorry, Uncle Archie, but at this moment in time I ain't got none!'

'Neither have I,' Matty agreed.

Annie headed for the door. 'Excuse me, I need some air. I'll be outside if you should want me.'

'Me too,' Matty said.

Both women hurried out of the back door.

Archie stared after them for a moment, then tentatively turned back to face his wife.

'Sit down, Kath. I'll make you a cuppa.'

'Cuppa! I don't want a bloody cuppa,' she spat. She looked up into her husband's face and narrowed her eyes. 'You amaze me, you do. I nearly succeeded in taking everything off you and you want to make me a cuppa tea.' She flounced around the table, stopped and turned back to face him. 'Why don't you hit me or shout at me or something?'

He looked at her aghast. 'Oh, Kath, I couldn't do that. Anyway, I don't believe this was all your doing. I think Matthews egged you on. I'm right, Kath, ain't I? You never really planned all this on yer own. Matthews helped yer?'

Kath stared at him suspiciously. Suddenly, she burst into floods of tears. Archie rushed over to her, placing his arms around her, and hugged her tightly.

'There, there, Kath. It's all right. Everything's gonna be all right,' he soothed.

She pulled away from him and sank down on a chair. 'You're right, Archie. It was him,' she sobbed. 'It was all his idea. It started years ago. I was having a bad time with ... with yer mother. She never liked me. She made life as difficult as she could. She was the mistress in the household and I couldn't have a say in anything, not even what we had for dinner. You never saw that side of yer mother, Archie. Not like I did.'

He pulled out a chair and sat down besides her, his face wreathed in anguish.

'John was just someone to talk to,' she continued, nervously twisting her handkerchief around her fingers. 'He understood how I felt.'

'You could have talked to me,' Archie whispered.

'Oh, no, I couldn't,' she said, shaking her head and sniffing loudly. 'You wouldn't have heard one word against your mother.' She raised her head and stared at him through watering eyes. 'Lucy was an accident, Archie. I swear she was. John took advantage of me when I was feeling low. Up 'til then I thought he was a good friend. Anyway, he knew the child was his and threatened to tell you if I didn't do what he said.'

'He what!'

'Honest, Archie. He was vile and I had to go along with him because I couldn't bear the thought of hurting you.'

'Oh, Kath, Kath,' Archie moaned sorrowfully. He grabbed hold of her hand and squeezed it tight.

'I'm so ashamed, Archie. But please believe me, it was him who put me up to all the horrible things I've done. I'm so sorry.' Tears gushed down her cheeks again.

'Don't, Kath. Don't upset yourself.' He took a deep breath. 'Look, we'll start again. You can forget Matthews. Now that things have come to light, he won't dare bother you again. What d'you say, Kath?'

'Oh, yes, Archie. But can you ever forgive me?'

'Of course I can. I know you were under the influence of a bad man, Kath. It's not your fault. You were misled by his good looks and charm. Even I thought he was a fine person. Look how wrong I was.' Archie sighed deeply and rubbed his hand over his chin. 'Most of this has been my fault. I've never made an effort to be sociable. I will in future. We'll entertain and I'll take you out visiting. I promise I'll make the effort.

Life's not been easy for you, I can see that now. Will you give me another chance, Kath? Please.'

She eyed him from under wet lashes. 'Yes, Archie, I will. But what about Lucy?'

Archie grimaced. 'What d'you mean?'

'Well, she's not yours, is she?'

'Oh, Kath. I've brought that child up from the day she was born. It won't make no difference to me. I promise you it won't. After all, none of this is the child's fault.'

'No, it's not.'

'Does she know?' he asked hesitantly.

'Know? Oh, about John. No, she doesn't,' Kath said hurriedly.

'Well, then. Nothing will change. She'll think I'm her father like she's always done, and I must try a bit harder to spend more time with her.'

'Oh, Archie,' Kath whispered lovingly. 'And I promise I'll be a good and dutiful wife, you see if I don't.'

He sighed deeply in relief. 'Well, that's settled then. Now, come on, dry those eyes and I'll make you that cuppa. Then I'll go and see Matty and Annie and explain what's happened.'

Kath started to shake. 'Oh, they won't like it, Archie. They'll try to tell you I'm lying . . .'

'No, they won't, Kath. Calm down. They'll be pleased for us, you'll see. Before you know it, things round here will be back to normal. But a lot happier this time.'

She jumped up and threw her arms around him. 'Oh, Archie, thank you. You're a good man and I don't deserve you.'

He blushed beetroot red. 'Ah, Kath. Don't be daft. You're me wife. I'm duty bound to stand by you.'

She smacked him playfully on the arm and fluttered her eyelashes at him. 'I'll make the tea while you go and tell Annie and Matty the news.'

He hugged his wife tightly. He felt new life flood through him now that his nightmare was over. Never, ever did he want to go through that pain and anguish again as long as he lived. He pulled away from Kath, raised his head and walked smartly towards the back door. He was now the master of the farm again and had his wife and family around him. What more could a man wish for? He stopped and turned to give her a reassuring smile.

'I won't be long.'

'Take your time,' Kath answered. 'You must be hungry. I'll start preparing your dinner.'

She watched as her husband departed, then stood for a moment staring at the closed back door. A steel hard glint shone in her eyes and a sly smile played on her thin lips.

Meanwhile, Annie, Matty and Molly sat on wooden stools in the large barn, waiting nervously to hear what had transpired after they left the kitchen.

'Oh, I hate this hanging around,' Annie sighed. 'Especially in this weather. I'm freezing.'

'Well, we could go back into the kitchen,' Matty said mockingly.

'Not on your nelly!' laughed Annie. 'I'd sooner die of cold out here than hear Kath's lies.'

'You're right about the lies. She'll have Archie so convinced he won't know whether he's sitting on his arse or his head!'

'Oh, Matty,' Annie scolded.

'It's true. She tells that many lies, she believes them herself.'

'Well, let's hope he's learned his lesson this time and ain't so gullible.'

'Archie? Never. He's too soft, Annie. He'd sooner believe what she has to say. It's easier for him that way.'

'Well, I don't think I can work for her any longer,' Molly interrupted. 'I'm praying he kicks her out. She treats Scrap better than she treats me, and I've had enough.'

'Well, you'd better pray hard, gel, 'cos any minute now Archie will come in here and tell us everything's back to normal.'

'Oh, no,' Molly groaned. 'Well, there's nothing for it. I'll have to get a job in one of the factories. I'll turn socks, I'll even sweep the floors. Anything will be better than working for her.'

Annie sighed. 'Let's stop this. Until my uncle informs us, anything could be happening and we're just going round in circles making guesses.'

'Yer right, Annie. I'm the one to blame,' Matty said solemnly. 'I still say I'll be proved right, though.'

The three lapsed into silence for several moments.

Molly raised her head and eyed Annie thoughtfully. 'If Matty's right, will you and Georgie be moving back up here?'

Annie stared blankly at her for several seconds, then exhaled loudly. 'Oh, I don't think so,' she said, shaking her head. 'I couldn't, not after all this.'

'Well, what will you do?'

Annie looked at Matty, then back to Molly. 'I don't know. I suppose the only thing for me to do would be to go back home.'

'Home! You mean to Leicester?'

Annie nodded her head.

Molly's mouth gaped. 'Oh, no,' she cried in anguish. 'You can't, Annie. I'd miss you both. Anyway, you can't go back, you've nowhere to go. Only the workhouse.'

Annie bit her bottom lip and lowered her head. 'Well, things have changed slightly. I've managed to save a bit and . . . er . . . my uncle has given me some money. It should have gone to my mother by rights.'

'Oh! Oh, well. That puts a different light on things. Oh, but Annie, I will miss yer. You and Georgie are the only friends I've got.' Molly's face puckered and a tear rolled down her cheek.

Annie smiled warmly. 'I'll miss you too, but you can always come and visit once we get settled.'

Molly's face lit up. 'Can I? Oh, thanks.' She suddenly gasped for breath as a thought struck her. 'Let me come with yer, Annie? Please? I could be a help. You know what a good worker I am and I've always longed to go to Leicester.' She clasped her hands together. 'Please take me with you?'

'Oh, Molly. It ain't settled we're going yet, and what about yer mother?'

'Oh, me mam won't mind. Once I explain she'll be glad for me. Honest she will. I can't stay with Kath, Annie. It'd be the death of me. And I can't bear the thought of being stuck in a factory all day. I'd die, honest I would.'

Matty laughed. 'You ain't got much choice, Annie.'

She tutted. 'I can see that.' She paused for a moment. 'All right,' she relented. 'If I do go back, and providing that your mother agrees, then you can come. But the first sign of any nonsense and I'll send you right back, understand?'

Molly let out a shriek of delight. 'Oh, Annie. Thank you. Thank you. I won't let you down, I promise.'

'Someone's happy.'

Three heads jerked up to see Archie approaching them. He rubbed his hands together and smiled at them warmly.

'Everything's back to normal. I've sorted things out with Kath and from now on life round here will be a lot happier.'

Matty dug Annie in the ribs with her elbow.

'So,' she gulped, 'you've made it up and you're having her back?'

'Yes, I am, Annie. She is me wife, after all.'

'Yes, but . . . What about all that's happened?'

He grimaced. 'Kath's not had an easy life, Annie. She was completely taken in by John Matthews. We all make mistakes and Kath realises what she's done and wants us all to try again. I'm willing, Annie. I married her for better or worse. We've had the worse times, the better ones are from now on. Now, come on, be happy for me.'

Annie breathed deeply. 'I am,' she said slowly. 'Very happy.'

'Good. I knew you would be. I told Kath as much. Now, why don't you go and collect your and Georgie's things? The sooner you both get settled back in here, the better I shall like it.'

'But will Kath?' Matty muttered under her breath.

Archie turned to her. 'I can't thank you enough for all you've done.' He placed his hand in his pocket and pulled out a sovereign. 'I want you to have this, in payment for having us all to stay. If it's not enough . . .'

She shoved his hand away. 'Don't you dare insult me, Archie Burbage.'

'I never meant to . . .'

'No. I know you never,' Matty snapped. 'But you listen to me. I think you're a bloody fool. That woman has hoodwinked you good and proper and she'll see you in hell, you mark my words.'

'Matty . . .' Annie started.

'Don't Matty me!' she cried angrily. 'Someone has to say it. Well, all right, I wish you well, but don't say I didn't warn you. And just remember – the farm is in my name. I'll be keeping me eyes on her and just you let her make one false move . . .' She turned to face Annie. 'I'm getting out of here before I say anything else. You know you've a bed at my house if you want one.'

She nodded and watched Matty storm out of the barn.

'Just a minute, Matty,' Archie shouted. 'I'll get the dray out and drive you back.'

She turned on her heel. 'You needn't bother. I bloody walked up here, I can bloody well walk back.' She turned and disappeared out of the door.

Annie made to run after her.

'What's going on?' Archie cried. 'I thought you'd all be happy for me.'

Annie stopped and turned back. She tightened her lips and her shoulders sagged.

'Oh, Uncle Archie,' she groaned. 'Matty's upset. Well, we're all upset. These last few days have been dreadful and Matty's entitled to say what she thinks.' She walked over and placed her hand on his arm. 'But as long as you feel you're doing the right thing, that's okay. It's you who has to forgive Kath not us.'

'And I have, Annie. She was taken in by that Matthews feller, it's not her fault.'

'If that's what you choose to think,' Annie groaned softly. She looked at him standing before her, shuffling his feet awkwardly, and her mind screamed. What a fool! What a bloody fool he is. But she could see there would be no moving him. Kath had him where she wanted him and nothing Annie or anyone said would make any difference.

'Look, everything's sorted out,' he said cheerfully. 'You and Georgie can move into one of the bedrooms, you'll be really comfy . . .'

'No.'

'No?'

'I'm not staying, Uncle Archie. I'm taking Georgie back to Leicester.' She smiled over at Molly, listening intently to the carryings on. 'And Molly is coming with us.'

Archie's face fell. 'No, Annie. Please change your mind. Your home's here with us,' he pleaded. 'I can't bear the thought of losing you both now. Is it something I've done?'

'Uncle Archie, my decision is nothing to do with you. I'm a town girl at heart and I need to go back.' She grabbed hold of his arm and pulled him out of Molly's hearing. 'The money we found . . .'

'What about it, Annie?'

'I'm going to use my part of it to start a new life for me and Georgie. I know it's not honest of me, I should hand it over to the bobbies, but Matty and I had a chat and she made me see reason.'

Archie nodded. 'Whatever Matty said, she's right. That money has been hidden that long it's been forgotten about. You keep it all, Annie. You deserve a new start and I'm sure you'll do well.'

She smiled and sighed in relief. 'Thanks, Uncle Archie. But I feel strongly you should have a share.'

'I've enough already for my needs, and the more Kath has the more she spends. Let's face it, neither she nor Lucy is lacking for anything.'

'No, I grant you that. You provide well for them. Anyway, if I stayed here for even a short while it might make things difficult for you both. You and Kath need time to yourselves. Having me around will only annoy her and bring back memories.'

Archie looked at her thoughtfully. 'Yes, you could be right.' He placed his hands on her shoulders. 'Promise me, if things don't work out, you'll come back?'

Annie smiled up at him. 'I promise.' She reached up and kissed his weatherbeaten cheek. 'I love you, Uncle Archie. You gave me a home when I needed one and I'll never forget your kindness or what you've done for both of us.'

'Oh, Annie.' He sniffed loudly. 'You remind me so much of yer mother.'

'Do I?'

'Oh, yes. I shall miss you as much as I miss her.'

She gulped back the lump that had formed in her throat.

'I shall write, Uncle Archie, and visit when the time's right.'

'You must do that, gel. I'm no writer, but I'm sure I can put some sort of note together.'

'I'll look forward to it. Now, you'd better get back to Kath. She'll wonder what's happening.'

'You're going now?' he gasped forlornly. 'Won't you stay and have something to eat first?'

'No, but thanks for the offer. I'll just make a few arrangements with Molly, then if I hurry I'll catch up with Matty and spend the night with her. I'll catch the carrier cart into Leicester in the morning.'

'If yer sure?'

'I'm sure.'

Annie hugged her arms tightly round herself as she watched him make his way out of the barn and back to his wife. She took an extra deep breath, turned and smiled wanly at Molly.

With arrangements made for the morning, Annie lowered her head as she walked down the yard and through the gate.

As she pulled the cumbersome wooden gate closed she looked across the yard for the last time. Memories flooded back. Their arrival, bedraggled and worn out, and the first encounter with her beloved uncle. The arguments with Kath and her subsequent revelations. John Matthews. She shivered violently. She didn't want to think of John Matthews.

Had all these things, that had changed her so much, happened in such a short space of time? It was fate that had brought her to this farm and now fate was sending her back to her beloved town, a not much older but far wiser person. For the first time she felt able to cope with anything that life had to throw at her.

She raised her head, shot the iron hook across the top of the wooden post, turned and gathered her skirts, to run down the track to catch up with her friend.

Seated on the back of the dray, with their meagre possessions around them, Annie, Georgie and Molly waited for their journey to begin. Tearful goodbyes had been said to Matty and her family, and unbeknown to Matty, Annie had placed ten sovereigns on top of the mantelpiece, knowing her friend would find them easily.

The snow that had been threatening the day before began to fall. Molly chuckled.

'It's gonna be a white Christmas, Annie.'

She smiled and raised her eyes heavenwards. 'Yes, it looks like it.'

She clutched Georgie to her and pulled the blanket further up around their legs as the cart started to roll forward. She looked down at him and smiled warmly.

'We're going home, son,' she whispered. 'We're going home.'

Chapter Sixteen

Annie's eyes travelled slowly around the poorly furnished but comfortable living room of the small redbrick terraced house in Forest Road. She sighed deeply and closed her eyes momentarily. The journey back to Leicester, although uneventful, had exhausted all three of them. They had sat huddled together, growing colder and colder, the swirling snow falling heavily as the day wore on. They arrived back in High Street just as the market was at its busiest and Annie felt sudden excitement well up in her as they alighted from the dray, collected the loaded brown bag and set it down on the cobbles. She stood for a moment savouring the atmosphere that had long been denied her.

Her eyes lit up. Wrapping her arms around her, she hugged herself. This was where she belonged. These were her people. It suddenly hit her just how much she had missed it all. She watched in fascination as people scurried around, intent on getting their shopping and hurrying home out of the biting wind. The countryside had been a nice enough place. It had also been peaceful and much slower paced, but nothing could match the hustle and bustle of her town.

She caught Molly's expression out of the corner of her eye. The girl's face was wreathed in wonderment as she surveyed the activities going on around her. She turned to Annie and smiled broadly. She returned the smile, heaved up the brown bag, grabbed Georgie's hand and led them through the thronging crowds towards their destination.

Forest Road was situated off the main Humberstone Road,

not far from the horseshoe-shaped courtyard she had had to leave. As they plodded down the long row of shabby back to back terraced houses a lurking fear nagged at Annie's mind. What if Martha wasn't at home? Or, even worse, would not be able to offer them a bed? It was getting late and finding somewhere else to stay would be difficult. But she didn't want to have to find lodgings. Selfish though it seemed, after what she had been through over the last few months she felt a desperate need to be with her family.

Annie's fears were unfounded. Martha was thrilled at their unexpected arrival. She opened the door and gasped in delight at the sight of the three bedraggled people facing her.

'Oh, Annie, Annie! You've come back. Oh, oh!' she screeched in excitement as she threw her arms around her sister-in-law and hugged her tightly. 'You have come back to stop, ain't yer?'

Annie nodded. 'If you can manage us, we have.'

'You should know better than that. We'll manage if I have to sleep in the coal hole.' She gazed at Annie lovingly. 'And just when I thought Christmas was going to be so miserable. Oh, you've answered me prayers.' She quickly bent down to hug Georgie. 'I couldn't even be bothered to make a pudding, but I'll make one now, and a cake, you see if I don't!'

Annie laughed loudly as Martha herded them through to the fire and plied them with hot tea and bowls of warming home-made soup. Georgie helped her to fill the copper that stood next to the brick fireplace in the kitchen, so hot water would be ready for a much needed wash down. The next few hours were spent in reminiscing and sorting out the sleeping arrangements, which would be tight. The house had only two small bedrooms.

It was Martha's decision to move her mother into the front room. Annie felt guilty as this room was usually kept for visitors and held the only decent pieces of furniture. But Martha was adamant and said the move would have to have been carried out eventually as her mother found climbing the stairs increasingly difficult.

All the arrangements accomplished, Georgie and Molly retired gratefully to bed leaving the two women to chat in peace. Annie smiled contentedly and leant back in her chair.

'It's really grand to be back, Martha.'

'It's good to have you back. I've missed you something rotten these past few months.' Martha wiped her coal-covered hands on a cloth and pulled the two worn leather armchairs closer to the fire. 'Come and sit over here, me duck. It'll be warmer for yer.'

Annie rose, settled herself gratefully in the comfortable chair and stretched her feet out on to the hearth, wriggling her toes as the warmth seeped through them. She yawned loudly. 'Oh, I ain't felt so relaxed for ages. I could sit here for ever and let the world go by.'

Martha tutted. 'Yes, so could I,' she said. 'But I've got things to do and so have you, gel.'

'Yes, I know,' Annie nodded in agreement. 'But it's a lovely thought all the same.'

After washing her hands, Martha sat down opposite Annie, rested her elbows on her knees, placed her chin in her hands and studied her sister-in-law intently. 'Is it really all true about your uncle and his conniving wife? I'm having trouble taking it all in.'

'It certainly is. You don't think I'd lie to you, do yer?'

'No, Annie, 'course not,' Martha said apologetically. She sucked in her breath then exhaled loudly. 'You've surely been through it these past few months. I think I'd have done away with myself . . .'

'No, you wouldn't. It's surprising what we women can put up with when we have to. Anyway, I had Matty to turn to, so I wasn't completely on my own.'

'I know, but all the same . . .'

'Martha,' Annie said sternly, 'I want to forget all about that now. I'm home and that's what counts.' She lowered her head. 'What I've told you about John Matthews is between you and me. The only other person who knows is Matty and I want it kept that way, please.'

'Come on, Annie.' Martha's head jerked up. 'You wouldn't have told me if you thought I was going to spout it to all and sundry.'

'No, I'm sorry,' she said quickly. 'It's just very personal, that's all, and to be honest I promised meself I wouldn't tell anyone.' She felt tears sting the back of her eyes. 'It's degrading having to admit you've been completely fooled by a man, then having him take what he wants from yer and toss yer aside like you're nothing.' She sniffed loudly. 'It still hurts, Martha. Even after all this time.'

'Oh, Annie. What can I say?' Martha said remorsefully.

'Nothing. Just promise me you won't tell anyone?'

'Your secret's safe with me,' Martha said. She took a deep breath and frowned fiercely. 'Bert'd kill John Matthews if he ever found out.'

'He's never going to find out, though, is he?' she said sharply.

'No, Annie, rest assured. I promise.' Martha paused for a moment, sensing her distress. She clasped her hands together. 'Oh, I wish I had some rich relatives to give me money,' she said jovially, changing the subject. 'Bet you thought your boat had come in?'

Annie blushed, ashamed at the lie she had told.

'Well, as I said, my grandmother left it to my mother and Archie thought it only proper that I should have it.' She paused and looked Martha straight in the eyes. 'I intend to think very carefully about how to use it though, I ain't going to waste it. I'll never get another chance like this.'

'No, yer right there, gel. You need to think long and hard.'

'Yes, I thought of nothing else on the journey home. I want to use it to make a future for me and Georgie.' She frowned. 'But I ain't sure how yet.'

Martha paused thoughtfully. 'I suppose there's lots of things to consider. What about going back into sewing again?'

'Oh, no. I'm never gonna sew for other people again. I want

something different, Martha. Something ... Oh, I don't know ... a change. Yes, that's it. A complete change from whatever I've done before.'

Martha bent forward and patted her sister-in-law's knee. 'I'll say one thing, Annie, you're a changed person. You're not the Annie who left here all those months ago.'

She smiled wanly. 'I don't think anyone would be the same after what I've been through.' She took a deep breath. 'In a way I'm glad I met Kath. As much as I disliked her, she taught me a lot. She showed me that if you want something badly, you've got to go out and get it. I don't mean like she did, by conniving and lying and using people, but by working for it and not letting anything stand in your way. D'you know what I mean, Martha?'

She nodded slowly. 'I think I do.'

Annie sat up in her chair and set her mouth grimly. 'There's no way Georgie is ever going to get into the position that I faced. Whatever I do, I'm going to make sure my son wants for nothing.'

Martha looked at her admiringly. 'I've no doubt whatever you decide you'll make a success of it, and me and Bert will help.'

'Thanks, Martha.'

'In the meantime, you can all stay here for as long as you like, while you sort yourselves out.'

'It's very good of you. But hadn't you better square things with Bert first? I mean, there's Molly as well now.'

'Bert won't mind, you should know that. And, anyway, it'll be company for me. Mother's not what she was. Her mind wanders. I can't hold much of a conversation with her, and she can't even mash a cuppa without scalding herself.'

'I'm sorry, Martha,' Annie said softly, remembering her own grandmother.

'Oh, that's all right, Annie. I'm getting used to it now and there ain't much we can do about it. The doctor says it's old age. Well, she is nearly sixty and she's had a good innings.'

Martha sighed and wrung her hands. 'It's ironic. It's like having the child I never had. But it's sad when it's yer mother.'

'Yes, it is. But be assured, while I'm here, I'll help as much as I can.'

'Thanks. You could take her to the lavvy now and again. If she goes on her own, she gets lost. We found her the other night wandering down the road in her underwear. Blue with cold she was. 'Course, the poor old sod never remembered a thing about it and for a few days afterwards she was back to her normal self, then her mind goes again. I hope you can put up with all this?'

'I think so. Nothing could be worse than Kath's moods and wondering what she was planning next, believe me.'

'No, I suppose not,' Martha agreed. She picked up the poker and raked the fire. 'Our Geoigie looks well on his stay up at the farm. Fairly filled out he has, and you ain't told me much about this Molly yet. She seems a nice gel, but she's got her head in the clouds a bit, ain't she?'

Annie smiled. 'Yes. She's a smashing girl, but she's got a lot to learn. She wants a job in one of the big stores.'

'Yeah. She told me while we were sorting the beds out. But after being bossed about by Kath for so long, I can't see her taking much stick from those floor walkers, can you? Right sergeant majors they are – walk around as though they own the place. I went into Marshall's and Snelgrove one day, just to have a look round to see what I couldn't afford.'

Annie eyed her keenly. 'Go on, you never did!'

Martha laughed. 'I did. I had a right mood on me and I thought, If Marshall's and Snelgrove is good enough for that posh lot, then it's good enough for me! So I marched in there and had a good nosey round.'

'Oh, what was it like?' Annie asked in awe. 'It's something I've always wanted to do but never had the nerve.'

'It was all right. But I felt right outta place. The staff look down their noses at yer and they talk that funny you can't understand what they're saying. To be honest, I couldn't get out quick enough. Give me Straw's corner shop any day. At least you know where you stand with him.'

Annie laughed loudly and shook her head. 'Well, if Molly does get a job, she's gonna have her work cut out just trying not to drop her aitches.'

'Besta luck to her, that's what I say. But she needn't bother trying it on when she's here.'

'Oh, she wouldn't do that, Martha. Not our Molly. She's too down to earth.'

'Good. Never forget yer place, that's what I say.'

Annie looked up at the clock on the mantelpiece as it struck ten o'clock. 'Bert's late. You said he was working. Is he doing a foreigner or something?'

Martha stared at Annie for a moment. 'Er . . . no. Just some overtime.' She stopped abruptly and quickly changed the subject. 'Did I tell you about Elsie?'

'Elsie?' Annie said, frowning. 'No. What about her?'

'Her husband's left her.'

'You're joking?' Annie said aghast, her eyebrows shooting up in surprise. 'Left her? Poor old Elsie. Blimey, I know her and Billy weren't that close, lots a' couples ain't, but it never crossed me mind that he'd ever leave her.'

'Well, he did, and you'll never guess who with?'

Annie's face went blank. 'I've no idea. Who?'

'Maggie Henshaw.'

'Maggie Henshaw! I don't believe it.'

'True as I'm sitting here. 'Parently it were all planned from the start, right down to her doing a flit and then him joining her later. Two of them kids of hers are his. Seems they've been carrying on for ages. Well, years, I suppose.' She nonchalantly shrugged her shoulders. 'I mean they must have been, mustn't they?'

Annie nodded. 'I can't believe it. Poor Elsie.' She paused for a moment. 'I must go and see her. She might be slovenly but she's been a good friend to me over the years, 'specially when my Charlie died. I'll go and see if there's anything I can do.' She yawned loudly. 'Gosh, I'm tired. I'll have to think about going to bed soon.' She yawned again. 'Come on, tell me about Bert, Martha? You've been ever so cagey about him. What's going on?'

Martha stared at Annie in stunned silence. She had been dreading this moment. She jumped up out of her chair and swung the kettle across the fire.

'Fancy another cuppa?'

Annie leant forward, intrigued. 'No, I don't fancy another cuppa, and why are you avoiding my question?' She tilted her head to one side. 'Have I asked something I shouldn't? Is Bert doing something wrong?'

'Oh, no, Annie,' Martha gasped. 'It's nothing like that.' She paused and bit her bottom lip. 'It's just that, well . . .' She took a deep breath. 'Bert's got a new job. He's had it for a while. It's a really good job, Annie, and he's doing ever so well . . .'

'Martha that's great,' she cut in. 'Why've you been afraid to tell me such good news?'

Martha's shoulders sagged. 'It's difficult, Annie. You see, well . . .' She paused for breath and slowly raised her eyes. 'Bert's working for Joe Saunt.'

'Joe Saunt?' she said questioningly.

'Yes. The bloke who gave Charlie the job the day he . . . he died.'

'Oh.' Annie slumped forward and clasped her hands together. 'You mean, Bert has Charlie's job?'

'Yes,' Martha whispered. 'Look, me duck, if Bert hadn't accepted that job, someone else would have jumped at it. He had no choice. You know good jobs don't come up very often and Bert hated working in the factory. He agonised over his decision, Annie, believe me. He never slept properly for weeks. But we all know Charlie would have wanted him to take it.'

Her shoulders sagged. 'Yes,' she said, sighing deeply. 'You're right, Martha. He would have. But I still don't understand how Bert came to fix things up. Did he go and ask for the job?'

'Oh, no, Annie. It was nothing like that. A couple of days after the funeral, Bert suddenly realised that Joe would not know what had happened to Charlie. Probably think he'd not bothered to turn up. Bert didn't want his brother's memory to be spoiled like that so he went round to see Joe and explain. Bert and I discussed it first, whether he should go and see Joe. You were very ill at the time and we didn't think it necessary to bother you with it.'

'I see,' Annie said sharply. 'And what happened then?'

Martha scratched her head nervously. 'Joe's a lovely man, Annie. He was really sorry about what happened.'

'Yes, I appreciate that. Sorry enough to offer Bert Charlie's job, is that it?'

'For God's sake, Annie. It weren't as cold-blooded as that. Joe really needed a good man and Bert fitted the bill.' Martha's face clouded over. 'Let's face it, Charlie couldn't do it, could he?' she blurted.

'No, he couldn't.' Annie stared at Martha, eyes ablaze. ''Cos he was dead, and it were your husband's fault!' She stopped abruptly. 'Oh, God!' she uttered, then burst into floods of tears, her body shaking uncontrollably.

Martha grabbed hold of her. 'Forgive us, Annie. I never dreamed you'd take it like this. If we'd known you'd be so upset, Bert would never have taken that job.'

Annie raised tearful eyes. 'It's me who should be apologising, Martha. I never should have said that. I really don't begrudge Bert the job. Your telling me just brought back Charlie's death. Him getting that job was to be the start of our new life.' She held her head in her hands as the tears began to fall again.

Martha knelt before her. 'I was dreading telling you,' she whispered. 'Bert felt that he was stepping into his dead brother's shoes, but he had to take the job, Annie.'

'It's all right, really it is. Charlie always said you had to take what chances you got. And you're right, he'd have wanted his own brother to have it more than anyone else. It's just all come as a bit of a shock. I'm so sorry for what I said.'

Martha sighed in relief. 'Are we still friends then, Annie?'

''Course we are, you daft ha'porth. It's just me being stupid.' She straightened her back. 'I'm going to bed now, love. You don't mind, do you? I just want to go to sleep and start a new day tomorrow. Will you give Bert my love?'

'Yes, me duck, 'course I will. Sleep well.'

Although exhausted, Annie took an age to fall asleep. She cuddled into Georgie, finding his warm body a comfort. It felt good to be back in Leicester and she felt more secure than she had done for months. She suddenly tensed as a niggling worry shot through her. What did she do now? What lay in store for her and Georgie? She relaxed slightly. The money she had hidden in the big brown bag would be their salvation. Her only problem was how to use it.

But regardless of any of this, Christmas was only days away and a couple of sovereigns out of the bag would not be missed. The holiday was going to be good this year. They would have goose with all the trimmings, apples, oranges, and the ingredients for a pudding. There was money for a present each. She smiled in the darkness as she listened to the gentle breathing of Georgie and across the small room, Molly asleep on the shake down. Yes, she would make sure that this was the best Christmas ever for all of them. That past, it would be time to concentrate on planning for their future.

She rose the next morning feeling refreshed and raring to go. She clutched her thick calico nightdress around her as she padded over the cold floorboards and peeked through the curtains. She was momentarily taken aback as she gazed out into the dismal snow-covered street. The muddy yard, fields and trees she had expected to see were not there. Of course, she was back in Leicester. Smiling to herself, she dropped the curtain, tentatively poked the ice on top of the water in the jug and quickly washed and dressed. Then she gently woke Molly and Georgie.

'Come on, you two, time to rise and shine. We've a lot to do today.'

Georgie yawned loudly. 'Do I have to get up, Mam?'

'You do,' she answered sternly. 'If you don't get up, you won't be able to come Christmas shopping.'

He was suddenly wide awake. 'Christmas shopping?' he said excitedly.

'Yes, and if you behave yourself, you can get a little something for Arthur and take it round to him. Molly, you can get something for your mother and we'll make up a food hamper and send it to her by the carrier cart.'

Georgie and Molly both leapt out of bed and began to dress.

Martha's face was a picture of bewilderment and delight as later that morning Annie placed two sovereigns in her hand and told her to get what she wanted to make their Christmas special.

'I could buy up the shop with this, Annie. Are you sure?'

'More sure than I've ever been. This is gonna be the best Christmas ever. I'll help you with all the preparations and I'll get Georgie and Molly to make some paper trimmings. We're gonna have the lot, Martha. Mince pies, roast spuds, stuffing . . . you name it, we'll have it.'

'Oh, Annie!' Martha gasped as she donned her coat and grabbed her shopping bag. 'I'm off before you change yer mind and they sell out at the market.'

Christmas was far better than even Annie could have hoped. The atmosphere in the little terraced house was electric as they all sat around the fire on Christmas morning, opening their presents and breathing in the delicious smells that wafted in from the kitchen. Even Jean, Martha's mother, was a delight and on her best behaviour all day. The celebrations came to a close with the singing of Christmas carols and thick slices of cold Christmas pudding.

'It's been grand, just grand, Annie,' Martha whispered as the two women took the dirty dishes through to the kitchen. 'I've never seen our table so full of food, and the look on those kids' faces when they opened their presents! Oh, Annie, I'll never forget this day. Never. Even our Bert seems back to his old self.'

Annie smiled warmly. 'Yes, it has been grand, and that's the way I wanted it. In a few days Old Father Time will herald the arrival of nineteen hundred and five and who knows what that'll bring? But whatever, at least we can look back and have our memories, even if we've nothing else.'

'Oh, we can that, Annie.' Martha sighed deeply. 'I don't know how to thank yer.'

'No need. You're me family and you've done more than enough for me over the years.' She placed her hands in the small of her back. 'Oh, I don't know about you but I'm just about ready for bed.'

Martha nodded in agreement and, arm in arm, the two women walked back into the small living room for one more carol before bed.

Chapter Seventeen

Annie slid the envelope across the desk at the smiling woman who faced her. Neither the woman nor the room had changed since the last time she had sat in this chair, but she had and was very conscious of that fact.

She watched intently as the envelope was opened and the contents revealed.

'Paid with interest?' Gilda raised her eyebrows. 'There's no need for that, Annie.'

She sipped the sherry she had been given and tried not to shudder as the strong liquid hit the back of her throat. 'I said I'd pay you back, and if I'm honest I owe you much more than money. If it wasn't for you I wouldn't have gone to find my mother's family. And if you hadn't have found me that night, I dread to think what would have become of me.'

'It's all fate, Annie. I was meant to meet you that night. Anyway, I never had any doubts about you. I'm a good judge of character, you have to be in my profession. I am surprised though at how quick you've paid me back. I didn't expect to see you quite so soon.' Gilda shook her head and sighed deeply. 'You've certainly been to hell and back, gel, since we last met.' She sat back in her large leather-covered chair, clasped her hands together and rested them under her chin, gazing thoughtfully at the young woman facing her. 'I'd love to meet that auntie of yours,' she said coldly. 'I've met some rotten people in my time but she'd beat the backside off any of them.'

'Yes, I'm sure she would.' Annie smiled. 'But that's all in the past now, Gilda. I'm only looking to the future and I feel better now that I've paid you back. The money you gave me was a comfort 'cos there was many a time I thought I'd have to use it.' She paused for a moment. 'It all seems such a long time ago, like something I've dreamed, part of a nightmare.'

'We all have nightmares, Annie. Some more real than others. The main thing is you've come through. And if you want my honest opinion, you've blossomed. You're now an independent woman and I think you could tackle anything that came your way.'

Annie nodded. 'Yes, I could, Gilda. Even I've got to admit that I ain't the cowering little girl who sat here all those months ago.'

Gilda frowned deeply. 'Oh, I don't know about cowering little girl, Annie. Your world had just about caved in and you had nowhere to turn. Don't demean yourself like that.'

Annie turned pink with pleasure and rose from her chair. 'Well, I'd better be going before you chuck me out. You've a business to run and gels to see too,' she said, smiling broadly.

Gilda laughed. 'Cheeky beggar! But you're right. They need me, you don't. Now get out. Go on, be off with yer.' She laughed loudly as she rose, glided around her desk and hugged the younger woman warmly. 'Take care of yourself and that lad of yours. And if you ever need me . . .'

'I know, Gilda. Thank you.'

They stared at each other for a second, each with a tear in their eye. Annie leant forward and kissed Gilda on the cheek then turned and left.

Annie kicked the door shut with her foot and put her shopping bag on top of the table. She looked fondly over at her brother-in-law sitting by the fire, reading the newspaper, his long legs stretched out over the hearth. He lowered the paper as she entered, peering over the top at her, and smiled warmly, nodding his head in the direction of Martha's mother asleep in the chair opposite.

'Hello, Bert,' said Annie softly. 'Martha's just on her way in. We had a smashing trip up the town.' She surveyed the contents of her shopping bag. 'You don't get much for your money these days, do you? I'm gonna have to get a job soon. Nearly all me savings from me farm wages have gone.'

'There's always yer nest egg.'

'Oh no, Bert,' she said, fiercely shaking her head. 'I ain't touching no more of that. I've already dipped in far more than I should have.' She peeled off her coat and hung it up on the hook on the back door.

He raised his eyebrows. 'Well, a'you thought any more on what you're going to do with it, then?'

'I've thought plenty, but nothing definite comes to mind.' She sighed deeply as Martha entered.

'What a'you two chattering about?'

'I was just telling Bert that I'll have to get a job soon.'

Martha put down her bags and walked over to stand in front of her mother. Her face saddened at the sight that greeted her. Her mother's head had rolled to one side and her mouth gaped open, showing bare gums and a trickle of saliva running down her chin.

This grotesque apparition wasn't her mother. This wasn't the woman who had fought with her dad on a Friday for his pay and fed the family on one pot of stew for a week.

Martha's head jerked up as she realised she was being spoken to. She swung round. 'What! I'm sorry, what did you say?'

'I said, I'll have to get a job soon. I've been back nearly three weeks now and I've done nothing about it but talk.'

'Oh, yes, that's right,' Martha said absent-mindedly. She walked over to the table and started to empty the contents of her shopping bag.

'Well, me and Bert had a good talk after you went to bed last night. Didn't we, Bert?'

He nodded and folded up his newspaper. 'Yes, and I told Martha that I could contact a few of my old oppos in the factory where I worked. I don't hold out much hope, there's talk of lay offs, but with your background as a seamstress, there might be something. You never know 'til you try.'

'That's the trouble, Bert. I can't see meself stuck in one of those airless places all day, scratting for a few miserly coppers a week. Just the thought of it fills me with dread.' Annie sighed forlornly. 'But I suppose if needs must. I really had high hopes of doing something for meself. But what? That's the question. I don't want to run a tea shop or have a lodging house or go back to dressmaking . . .'

Martha sniffed. 'You should count yourself lucky you've got a choice. I remember when you did dressmaking for a living. It wasn't beneath you then.'

'Come on, gel,' Bert cut in. 'I don't think Annie meant it like that.' He stood up and walked over to Martha, placing his hand tenderly on her arm. 'What's troubling yer, love?'

She shrugged her shoulders. 'Oh, nothing. I'm sorry. I'll make a cuppa. You always think better with a cuppa in your hand.'

'I'll make it, Martha. You sit down with Bert and rest your feet. You must be tired after all the traipsing we've done today.'

Annie stared worriedly at her for a moment. It was unusual for her sister-in-law to be so edgy. There was obviously something on her mind. She swung the kettle across the fire and headed for the kitchen.

Several minutes later, Annie handed Martha and Bert steaming mugs of tea which were accepted gratefully. She sat down on a chair at the table.

'I wonder how Molly's getting on?' she said lightly.

'She should be back soon, then you'll know,' Martha answered tartly. 'If you ask me, she was damned lucky to get the interview, a girl like her with no experience.'

'Why do you say that?' Bert looked at his wife anxiously. 'She's a good-looking gel, only needs training. Any shop'd be lucky to get her, if you ask me.'

'Yeah, I'm sorry, I'm just tired from being dragged around the town. I really hope she gets on all right.' Martha took a sip of her tea. 'By God Annie, I'll say one thing for you, you make a lovely cuppa.'

The women looked at each other and smiled warmly.

'What's the matter, Martha?' Annie asked after a moment. 'You're really touchy just lately.'

Martha grimaced and looked over at her mother. 'I think it's her.' She lowered her eyes and wiped away a tear. 'She's really worrying me, Annie. Look at her. She doesn't even look like me mother, not the mother I knew anyway, and if she gets any worse I might have to have her put away. The thought frightens the life out of me. How can you have yer own mother committed? It doesn't bear thinking about.'

'Oh, Martha. You poor dear. Look, you need a break. Why don't you and Bert have an afternoon out next Saturday? Me and Georgie will keep an eye on Jean. I know it's cold, but there must be something you could do?'

Martha's face lit up. 'Would you really? That'd be grand, Annie, wouldn't it, Bert? I quite fancy going to the music hall.'

'If Annie's sure she can manage, I'll say!'

'Think no more about it. That's settled then. You two just decide where you're going to go.'

Annie emptied her cup and gazed thoughtfully at her brother-in-law. 'I've been thinking, Bert, I've got to be realistic. D'you think you could ask about to see if there's any work going that might suit me? I'm not fussy, really I'm not. But if I don't get something soon I'll have to start dipping again into me nest egg. And before I know it it'll be gone, and that won't do.'

'Yeah, sure. Although I can't promise much.' He scratched his head. 'I ain't heard of much recently.' He paused for a moment and then laughed. 'The Black Swan tavern on Belgrave Road is looking for a barmaid. I know that for a fact, 'cos the last one got the push. Something to do with finding her round the back with a customer.'

Annie raised her eyebrow and looked keenly at Bert. 'Are they?'

'You're not thinking of doing that, Annie Higgins?' Martha said sharply.

'Why not? D'you think barmaiding is beneath me or something? It can't be any worse than milking cows.'

'Be serious, Annie,' Bert laughed. 'I was only joking when I suggested being a barmaid. The Black Swan ain't a fitting place for you to work. No, leave it with me, I'll start making enquiries in the morning.'

Annie pondered for a moment then looked at them both, her eyes twinkling. 'I quite fancy being a barmaid. I'd like to give it a try anyway. It'd give me a breathing space, while I decide what to do with me inheritance.'

'Bert, she's serious!' Martha cried. 'Do something. Tell her it's only sluts and prostitutes that work behind bars.'

Annie raised her head sharply as a picture of Gilda came to mind. 'And what would you know about prostitutes? They might be decent people for all you know, just trying to earn a living.'

'Annie!' Martha gasped. 'How can you say such a thing?'

'I can,' she said coldly. 'Anyway, I'll find out meself what it's like when I go down tomorrow.'

'Leave her, Martha. Let her find out the hard way,' Bert said sternly.

'Bert, you can't let her go ahead with this.'

'For God's sake, you two! I'm only going to enquire about it. Anyway, I've seen the Black Swan from the outside and it doesn't look that bad a place.'

'Yes, but it's what goes on inside that's the problem,' Martha retorted. 'I've heard all sorts of tales.'

'And are they all true?'

'Er . . .' Martha lowered her head. 'I don't know,' she said sheepishly. 'I'm only going on what I've heard.'

'Well, don't pass judgement then. I'll let you know how I've got on after I've been to see the landlord.' Annie leant across the table, her eyes twinkling mischievously. 'I wonder how long it takes to learn to be a slut?'

Martha and Bert looked at her in surprise, then burst into laughter.

'You really are the limit, Annie,' Bert said affectionately.

'If our Charlie were here, he'd tan yer hide.'

'Well, he's not, Bert, and I'm sure that under the circumstances he'd wish me the best. He'd know I was doing it out of need.'

'Yes, he would. That goes without saying.'

The three turned in surprise as the door burst open and Molly flung herself into the room, excitement written all over her.

'I got it!' she exclaimed. 'I'm gonna be working in the corset department. Only as a runabout to the assistants, but it's a start.' She proceeded to strut around the table. 'Mrs Syndicombe, she's the head buyer for the lingery department, who interviewed me . . .'

'Lingery?' queried Martha.

'Yeah, you know, posh underwear. Anyway, Mrs Syndicombe reckons you get nowhere in life without a good corset. You'll have to get one, Annie. When I've done me training, I'll measure you up. I might be able to get you discount, although I'll have to check into that.'

'You cheeky young devil!' Annie said, jumping up and hugging Molly tightly.

'You can't breathe in them things. They pull you outside in with all them bones and metal bits,' Martha said dryly. 'Never fancied one meself. Too much like hard work trying to get into them.' She smiled warmly. 'Oh, but I'm glad for you, Molly. When do you start?'

'Next Monday, eight o'clock sharp. And they said I've got to go to evening classes for . . . what is it called? Oh, yes, evolution lessons, to learn to talk proper to the clients.'

'Evolution lessons, eh?' Annie said, looking most impressed. 'My, we are going up in the world.'

Molly clasped her hands together, her eyes sparkling. 'Oh, it's a wonderful place. The floors are covered in thick carpet and I'll have to serve tea and biscuits to all the posh lady clients. I'll be working with another gel about my age. I think me and her will get on well together. She said she'll help all she can. Weren't that nice of her, Annie?'

'Yes, it was.'

'And there's loads of other departments. The store sells everything. There's even a beauty parlour where you can go and get done up. Mind you, it's pricey, I'll never be able to afford it. Oh, ain't it exciting? I can't wait to start me evening classes and learn to talk posh. My mother will have a fit when I visit her. She won't be able to understand me.'

Annie giggled. 'Well, come back down to earth. You can act fancy after you're started your job. Did you see Georgie on your way home?'

'Yes, he's playing marbles outside in the gutter with Arthur and some other kids.'

'Good.' Annie smiled. 'It's been an eventful day one way or another. I'm going to see about a job meself tomorrow.'

'Oh!' Molly exclaimed.

'Yes, it's for a barmaid.'

'A what? Annie, you're never thinking . . .'

'That's enough from you, young lady. I've had enough on the subject from these two.' She turned to face Martha. 'Come on, let's get the tea. Your mother will wake up in a minute and she'll be starving.'

Annie rose promptly the next morning. She had an errand to do before she went to see about the job and wasn't looking forward to it. She was going to visit Elsie and that meant returning to her old haunts which would rake up painful memories. The prospect frightened her. Despite all this, Elsie was her friend so she would have to steel herself and put her own feelings to the back of her mind.

She dressed carefully in a dark blue skirt and white blouse she had picked up on the second-hand stall at the market, and after seeing Georgie off to school, set off.

As she hurried down the street, she was glad she had pushed vanity aside and put on two pairs of thick woollen drawers for the icy January wind was whipping straight through her and she hoped she reached her destination before she froze to death. The new year had certainly come in with a vengeance as high winds, snow and hard frosts had transformed the little market town into a scene that could have been mistaken for the wastelands of Siberia. Standpipes had frozen up, trams had stopped running, and wood and coal were getting hard to come by. Pneumonia and influenza were rife. People were taking to their beds in droves and very lucky if they ever rose again. Anyone who hadn't caught something by now was fortunate.

Annie arrived at her destination and stamped her numb, booted feet on the hard ground. The courtyard had not changed. The old rusty pump still sat in the middle, icicles hanging from a leaking joint. Dirty children, their feet covered in old pieces of sacking tied up with string, slid over frozen puddles while their mothers tried unsuccessfully to fill their buckets with discoloured, polluted water. As much as she tried Annie could not avert her eyes from her old cottage. She stood and stared, saddened by the sight that met her. Hanging at the tiny windows were dirty net curtains full of moth holes and yellowing from lack of care. A large mangey mongrel dog sat shivering by the door and howled as it spotted her. In the months since she had lived there the cottage had fallen into further disrepair and a lump stuck in her throat at the sight of it.

She turned abruptly on her heel and headed for Elsie's door. Before she reached it she could hear the screams and shouts coming from within. She knocked hesitantly and waited.

The door slowly opened and a violent smell of damp, grease and urine enveloped her. She recoiled, gasping for breath, as Elsie's fat body stood framed in the doorway. She stared impassively at Annie and folded her arms.

'Oh, it's you,' she grunted. 'I'd heard you were back. Never expected to see you round here, though. What d'you want?'

'I've come to see you, Elsie.'

'Oh! What for?'

Annie stared at her old neighbour for a moment, surprised by her attitude.

'I came to see how you were and bring you a few things. But if this is how you are, I'll go.' She turned and made to walk away.

'Hang on,' Elsie shouted. 'Being's you've bothered to come, you'd better come in.'

She wobbled back into the filthy room and Annie followed. Clearing a space on the cluttered table she put down her basket. She looked fondly at Elsie and smiled warmly.

'How are you?'

'What's it bloody look like?' she said nastily. 'I s'pose you heard that Billy left me for that tart Maggie Henshaw, and I s'pose like the rest of 'em you knew all about it?'

'No, I didn't, Elsie! I knew nothing about it 'til our Martha told me yesterday.'

'Oh!' Elsie lowered her head in shame. 'I'm sorry then, Annie. I've been harsh on yer for no just reason. Only I've been the laughing stock round here since Billy went. Seems everyone knew about it but me. And I was very hurt when you left without a word.'

Annie smiled wanly. 'I'm sorry about that. I should have left a note but there wasn't much time.'

'Ah, that's all right, gel. Martha explained. And to be truthful I was jealous. I'd love to just up and off, but I can't, can I?'

'No,' Annie agreed. She exhaled loudly. 'How are you managing, Elsie?'

'Managing? That's a joke. I scrape by on what the kids bring home, and that ain't much. If we're lucky and the butcher's in a good mood we have a pot of stew made with scrag ends but most of the time it's spuds and bread and lard. The kids are good. They always come home with a few bits of coal and wood.' She gave a bellowing laugh. 'Last week our Herbert followed the coal cart right over King Richard's Road way and picked up all the dropped lumps. Had a good bagful, he did, and what with the wood we'd already scrounged, we'll manage a good fire for a couple of weeks. After that, who knows?' She paused and eyed Annie's basket keenly. 'You said you'd brought me a few things?'

Annie smiled. 'Yes, but it's not much,' she said, pushing the basket forward.

Elsie delved in and pulled out the contents.

'Oh, Annie, Annie!' she breathed excitedly as she stared at the sugar, butter, eggs and other foodstuffs. She picked up a blue paper wrapper and held it lovingly in her hands. 'Tea!' she exclaimed. 'I ain't had a decent cuppa for weeks. And what's this?' she said, pulling out another parcel.

'Stewing meat.'

'Stewing meat!' she gasped. 'Oh, what can I say?' Her eyes brimmed with tears. 'I can't thank you enough.'

Annie put her hand in her pocket and pulled out a sovereign. 'I want you to have this.'

Elsie accepted the sovereign and stared at it in disbelief. 'Where d'you get this from?'

'My inheritance from me grandmother.'

'Oh, and you want me to have it?'

'Yes, if it'll help you.'

'Help? Annie, it'll pay off the arrears. I'm on the verge of being kicked out. You don't know what this money means to me.'

'I can imagine, believe me.' She rubbed her hands together. 'Well, am I gonna get a cuppa or what?'

"Course, Annie, 'course.' Elsie threw the kettle across the fire and grabbed two grubby mugs from the table, putting in a drop of milk and two heaped spoons of sugar. Annie watched, her fingers itching to grab a sweeping brush and cloth and give the room a good going over.

'How's the baby?' she asked, remembering that Elsie's latest arrival had not yet been mentioned.

'Strapping,' she replied, grimacing fiercely. 'Would you believe it? After all me troubles, I gives birth to a bouncing six-pound baby girl.'

Annie rose and walked over to the makeshift cot stuck on a

pile of wooden boxes in the corner of the room. She peered in. 'Oh, Elsie, she's lovely,' she whispered.

Elsie grinned. 'Yeah, she's not bad. Got my looks.'

'What have you called her?' asked Annie, running her finger down the side of the baby's face.

'Annie.'

She straightened up and looked over at Elsie. 'Annie?' she repeated.

'Yes, after you. You've always treated me equal, Annie, and I've valued your friendship over the years. Others laugh at me but not you. If my Annie turns out like you, I'll be well pleased.'

'Oh, Elsie.' Annie felt humbled at the compliment this woman had just paid her. 'I'm honoured, really I am.' She walked back and sat down. 'Does Billy send you any money for the kids?'

Elsie threw back her head and guffawed. 'Billy? Send me money! I ain't seen that bloke since the day he scuttled outta here. To be honest she's welcome to him. I wouldn't have him back for love nor money.' Her eyes narrowed. 'I hope he beats her up like he used to me. But the fact is, he was my man and she'd no right to make a play for him. If I ever see her she'll regret what she's done, I'll make sure of that.' She stopped abruptly and eyed Annie. 'Anyway, enough of me. What a'you gonna do with yerself? I don't know how much yer granny left yer but I don't suppose it'll last forever?'

'No, it won't. That's why I'm off to see about a job.'

'Oh?' Elsie looked at her with interest. 'Doing what?'

'Barmaiding. And before you say anything, it can't be as bad as mucking out the cows.'

Elsie raised her eyebrows. 'I wasn't going to say anything. I think it's a good idea. You might enjoy it.'

Annie smiled. 'D'you think so?'

'Yeah, you just might,' said Elsie, filling the mugs with tea. 'I wish I could go out to work. It drives me mad in here all day. Besta luck to you, that's what I say. At least you ain't sitting on yer arse, Annie.'

'Thanks, Elsie. I'll let you know how I get on.' She drained her mug. 'I'd better go and see about that job before someone else snaps it up. I'll come again next week. If you need anything, I'm staying at our Martha's for the time being.'

'Thanks, Annie. It's been great seeing you, and thanks for all the stuff. I hope you get that job.'

'So do I.' She stood up and put on her long black coat. 'Well, here we go again, facing the elements. I've never known it so cold.'

'Me neither. It's cold enough to freeze a monkey's . . .'

'Elsie!' Annie cut in sharply.

She shrugged her fleshy shoulders. 'Well, it is, ain't it? I was only going to speak the truth.'

The corner of Annie's mouth twitched. 'Tarra, Elsie.'

'Tarra, me duck.'

After leaving Elsie's cottage, Annie hurried through the biting wind up the Humberstone Road, down into Charles Street and along Belgrave Road. She hesitated outside the Black Swan, her heart thumping noisily in her chest as she willed herself to enter. She could hear the strains of conversation and a piano being pounded. Someone was attempting to sing a popular music hall song, but from where she stood outside on the cobbled pavement it didn't sound very promising.

Her resolve of the day before started to desert her. Behind those black-painted doors lay a world totally alien to her. She was beginning to doubt whether she wanted to be a part of it. Just as she was about to leave a group of people approached, and before she knew it she had been caught up with them and herded through the doors.

Inside, the group dispersed and she was left standing on the threshold. She blinked rapidly and gave a quick gasp for breath as the smell of stale beer and tobacco fumes hit her. She coughed discreetly and quickly took in her surroundings. The place was smaller than she had imagined. A long

291

wooden counter ran along the far end of the room and behind it she could see a shelf that housed various assorted bottles. The long mirror at the back of the bar made the room look twice as big as it actually was.

She watched in fascination as a man wearing the largest white apron she had ever seen began to pull at one of the three black handles that sat on top of the bar. He pulled long and hard until it would go no further, then slapped a tankardful of foaming ale in front of a customer. Annie nodded to herself in satisfaction. So that was how a pint of beer was poured. By the fireplace at the far end of the room sat a small rotund man, emitting volumes of smoke from a large clay pipe. Several others sat around tables, playing table skittles and dominoes. She turned back towards the bar and took a deep breath as she saw the man in the white apron staring at her.

'Can I help yer, missus?' he shouted.

Annie froze for a moment. She quickly regained her composure and walked slowly towards the counter.

'Yes, please. I'd like to see the boss.'

The barman stared blankly at her for a second. 'Oh,' he laughed. 'You mean the governor, or landlord as he's rightly known? He's in the room at the back.'

The barman nodded his head in the direction of a door and Annie made her way towards it.

'Just go through. He was there the last time I saw him.'

She thanked him and found herself walking down a long dark corridor. The sound of clanking bottles assured her she was heading in the right direction. Just before she reached the back yard she came upon a small room and saw a large, elderly man sitting on an upturned crate, gulping at a bottle of beer. His eyes alighted on her as he drank long and deep. He took the bottle from his lips and wiped them with the back of his hand.

'D'you want me?'

'Are you the landlord?'

'What of it?'

Annie breathed deeply and raised her head. 'I heard you were looking for a barmaid.'

'So?' The landlord took another gulp of beer.

'I'd like the job.'

'Oh, you would, would yer? Done this kind of work before?' he said tonelessly.

'No sir, I haven't,' she replied. 'But I'm quick to learn and I'd like you to give me a try.'

He set down his bottle on the stone slab and looked up at her with interest. 'It's hard work, gel.'

'I'm not afraid of hard work.'

'What kinda thing yer done before?'

'I was a seamstress and just recently I worked on a farm.'

'On a farm, eh?' he laughed sarcastically. 'Milking cows is a far cry from pulling pints.' He inched himself off the crate and stood up, facing her. 'I don't think this life's for you, me duck. I need someone with experience. Why not try round the factories? Yer might find something more suitable.'

Annie's shoulders sagged. She suddenly wanted this job more than anything. 'If I'd wanted work in a factory, I wouldn't be here. And as for experience, how am I supposed to get it if you won't give me a try?' She took a step forward. 'Look, I'm honest and reliable, and milking cows ain't so far removed from pulling pints. You still have to get the liquid into the container.'

The landlord threw back his head and laughed. 'Well, I never thought on it like that before.' He placed his hands on his hips. 'A'yer strong enough to carry crates up from the cellar?'

'I shovelled cow and pig muck and wheeled it over the yard.'

The landlord's eyes twinkled in amusement. 'What did yer say yer name was?'

'Annie Higgins.'

He held out his hand. 'Wilfred Biddles. Welcome to the Black Swan.'

Annie smiled broadly and accepted the proffered hand.

'Come on through. I'll introduce you to the rest of the staff.'

She followed Wilfred as he walked down the corridor. He pointed to the door on the right. 'That's the parlour and through here is the tap room. It's gets a bit rough sometimes. Think you can handle it?'

Annie shrugged her shoulders. 'There's only one way to find out.'

Wilfred laughed. 'I like you, Annie Higgins. I think me and you are going to get on well together.'

For the next half an hour he showed Annie what would be expected of her. Pulling a pint and getting the right head on top was more difficult than she had imagined, but Wilfred assured her that she would soon get the hang of it. She was surprised to learn that all the 'shorts' were poured in different measures, and the last job at night was to empty the spittoons, sweep the floor thoroughly and cover it with fresh sawdust.

'Well, Annie Higgins, think you'll cope?'

'Yes, I think so.'

'Right, I think we'll put you on the day shift for a start. That's six till six. Report to Sid.' He inclined his head towards the middle-aged, pleasant-faced barman who had addressed her when she first arrived. 'He'll show you the cellar work first.'

'Oh, I thought the job was for a barmaid!' she said in dismay.

'Oh, me duck, you can't work on the bar without knowing how to look after the cellar. What if no one's around and a barrel needs changing? The regulars won't wait. They'll want their ale.'

'Oh, I see.'

'Still interested?'

'Oh, yes,' she agreed quickly.

'Good. Then report to Sid in the morning. And I hope you ain't squeamish 'cos there's plenty of rats down the cellar.'

He turned and left her staring after him in horror.

'Don't mind him,' Sid piped up. 'Biddy the cat and Horace

the potman keep the rats down. You'll enjoy it here, we're a good crowd.'

She raised her head and smiled. 'I'll see you in the morning then.'

'Yeah, look forward to it.'

Annie left the pub, deeply worried that she had done the wrong thing.

Her first day was gruelling. Being female was of no consequence. She was expected to pitch in and tackle the work the same as everyone else. She learnt how to roll heavy wooden barrels across the cellar floor, how to stack them in rotation so the contents settled, then to connect them ready for pulling. Pipes had to be cleaned regularly, shelves kept stocked, floors swept and covered with sawdust, and all other manner of jobs.

By the lunch break, Annie's head was reeling with all the things she had to remember. She sat on an upturned beer crate in the yard and gazed down at her potted meat cob. The last thing she felt like was eating. She was physically and mentally exhausted. Farm work was easy compared to this. She looked across at Sid sitting by her munching his cheese and onion sandwiches.

'Where's Wilfred?' she asked.

'Oh, him. You won't see him 'til much later. He had a good skinful last night, so he'll be nursing an 'angover. Drinks like a ruddy fish. He's in the right trade, all right, and doesn't have to pay for it neither.'

Annie looked at him in surprise. 'Drinks, does he? He didn't appear to be drunk when I met him yesterday. He seems such a nice man.'

'He's a decent bloke all right, and good to his staff, not like some of the governors I know. He thinks no one knows about his drinking.' Sid finished the last of his sandwich and took a large gulp of ginger beer. 'He lost his wife through drink.'

'Did he?'

'Yeah. It's quite a funny story really.'

'Oh?' Annie looked keenly at him.

'He used to own a greengrocery business and his wife couldn't understand why it took all day for him to make his deliveries, so she decided one day to do it herself. She took the 'orse and cart out . . .' Sid started to laugh '. . . and the 'orse stopped at every pub on the round. 'Parently, Wilfred's missus was furious and there was a hell of a stink. She kicked him out and he came here to work for his uncle. When his uncle died, Wilfred was left the place. 'Course, it was ideal for him. He could drink when he liked and there weren't anyone to stop him. He drinks all his profits.' Sid paused for a moment and ran his hand through his thinning grey hair. 'It's a shame really, he could have done a lot with this place. There's rooms upstairs that's never seen daylight for years.'

'Rooms?'

'Yes, at least six, and that's apart from his rooms. He could have let them out for a start, there's people crying out for lodgings. He could make a tidy sum just doing that.'

'Yes, he could. What a waste.'

Sid jumped off the crate and eyed Annie. 'Eh, come on, gel. The draycart with the deliveries will be here soon and we ain't got this cellar properly sorted out yet.'

Later that day the pub was packed to overflowing. Annie finished lining a shelf with bottles and straightened her aching back. She looked out across the room and spotted an old man tap dancing by the piano. She smiled and nudged Sid who was pouring a pint.

'Who's that?' she asked.

Sid looked across the bar and shook his head. 'That's old Willy. Goes round all the pubs. See, people are putting money in his hat. That's how he pays for his drink.'

Sid suddenly stopped what he was doing and ducked under the trap door in the counter. Over the other side, he leant on top of the counter and addressed Annie.

'Here we go!'

'Here we go, what?' she asked in bewilderment.

'There's a bloke sat in Bill Bagshaw's chair. He's one of our regulars and if I don't move him there'll be hell to pay when Bill comes in. He'll stand for no one sitting in his seat, no matter who they are. Hold the fort for me, I won't be a tick.'

Annie shook her head in amusement and watched as Sid moved the customer to another seat. There's far more to this pub lark than I realised, she thought. I just hope I can master it all.

Annie carefully carried through the enamel basin full of warm water and set it down next to the comfortable armchair by the fire. She sat down, lifted her skirt above her knees, peeled off her woollen stockings and placed her feet tentatively in the bowl.

'Ah,' she sighed in contentment as she relaxed against the back of the chair and closed her eyes.

She had the whole house to herself for a while; Martha and her mother were at a neighbour's having a natter, Bert and Molly were still at work and Georgie was round at Arthur's house. She intended to enjoy her few stolen moments of solitude to their fullest.

She had been at the tavern for over a month and was really enjoying the work. She had learnt most of the aspects of the job by now and tackled all the tasks set her with relish. She felt at ease with the rest of the staff and the customers, who all loved her happy disposition, although woe betide any who tried any nonsense. Annie stood for none, as they had all quickly learned.

Wilfred Biddles had chosen well and knew it. He was even teaching her to do the books, something he had never done with a member of staff before. She was learning quickly, was adept at adding a column of figures and at this present moment in time was even helping him with the biannual stock take.

Martha and Bert had stopped chiding her over her chosen profession and looked forward every evening to hearing the latest escapades down at the Black Swán.

The only drawback to the job was her feet. They ached

considerably and to come home, find the house empty and be able to soak them with no interruptions, was sheer bliss.

So relaxed was she that night that she did not hear the door open and someone enter.

'Hello.' It was a soft manly voice that spoke.

Annie's eyes opened wide in surprise and for the slightest fraction of a second she saw a vision of Charlie. Her body froze. She blinked and the moment was gone. She stared at the tall, handsome man standing before her, his eyes twinkling in amusement at the predicament he had caught her in. He took off his cap and walked towards her, hand outstretched in greeting.

'You must be Annie?' he said, giving her a warm smile. 'Sorry to disturb you. I've been knocking on the door for ages . . .'

'What can I do for you?' she snapped abruptly, eyes darkening at this stranger's nerve, walking into the house unannounced. He obviously knew who she was but she hadn't a clue about him. She quickly raised herself up and threw down her skirt which fell with a splash into the water. She felt the sodden material cling around her legs and grimaced with distaste.

'I was looking for Bert,' he said hesitantly.

'Well, he's out. And I'd be obliged if next time you don't just barge in unannounced.'

The man took a sharp intake of breath and raised his head. 'I do apologise,' he said coldly. 'Only Bert and Martha have always told me just to walk in if I am ever in the area.'

'Oh, I see,' she replied slowly. 'Well, they never told me that.' She frowned. 'Who are you?'

'I'm Joe Saunt, Bert's boss.'

'Oh!' Annie gasped. So this was the man that Charlie, Bert and Martha had rated so highly. Her eyes quickly travelled over him. A strange sensation ran through her as it struck her that this man did have a certain look of Charlie about him. Was it his height, which must have been over six foot, or his hair, a stray strand of which had fallen across his

broad forehead? He pushed it back with one long firm hand.
No, it was none of these things, he didn't look like her
Charlie at all, she was imagining it. But he did have a
presence about him which unnerved her. She felt his eyes
scrutinising her, strong white teeth showing beneath his
wide smile. She felt the hairs rise on the back of her neck.
She raised her hand nervously. 'Er . . . Bert's either still at
work or he's nipped into the pub for a quick one before his
dinner.' She looked down, embarrassed. 'Look, I'm sorry for
being so sharp just now . . .'

'That's all right,' he interrupted. 'It's understandable in
the circumstances. It was my fault. I must have given you a
shock?'

Annie smiled and her eyes softened. 'Well, you did rather.'

Joe's shoulders relaxed and he returned her smile. 'I think
we'd better start again.' He held out his hand. 'Pleased to
meet you, Annie. May I call you Annie? Only Bert's told me
so much about you I feel I know you very well.'

'Has he?' Annie said laughingly as she accepted the
proffered hand. 'All good, I hope?'

'Oh, yes. Bert's very proud of his sister-in-law.' He paused
for a moment, his bright green eyes locking into hers. What
an attractive woman, he thought, as he took in the heart-
shaped creamy olive-skinned face, the long dark lashes
fringing those striking deep blue eyes. And not having had
the opportunity to view many women's legs, he thought hers
were marvellous, shapely and slender – even if her feet were
stuck in a basin of water!

The sketchy descriptions he had gleaned from Bert as his
employee had chattered about Annie had never conjured up
this vision of loveliness, with not a trace of the tragedy he
had been told she had suffered showing on that pretty face.
No, they certainly hadn't. He shuddered as a strange
sensation travelled through him, quickly straightened his
back and averted his eyes towards the blazing fire. 'I know
it's a bit late, but I was sorry about your husband. He seemed
a fine man.'

'He was,' Annie said softly.

She studied Joe for a moment and could not help but notice his uncared-for appearance. His trousers, just a little too short for his long muscular legs, were coming down at the hem, his shirt collar was grubby and his jacket needed a good press. She felt it was a shame that a man in his position should look so shabby. Bert, as one of his workers, was far better turned out and that was down to Martha. She knew Joe was married, Bert had mentioned that fact. Then why was it he looked like this? Joe interrupted her thoughts.

'When you see Bert, could you ask him to pop back to the factory? One of the machines has broken down and I need him to look at it.'

'Yes, 'course I will. As soon as he comes home.'

'Thanks.' He forced his eyes back to hers. 'I'll be off then.' He turned and headed for the door. 'Nice to have met you,' he mumbled as he departed, leaving her staring after him.

It was several moments before she looked down at her soaking wet skirt and groaned as she lifted the sodden material out of the bowl of now cold water. So much for peace and quiet, she grumbled inwardly. She raised her eyes and looked at the clock ticking merrily away on the mantelpiece. The family would all be home soon. Her few moments of solitude were gone.

Later that evening they all sat around the table eating their supper. Bert had arrived not long after Joe had departed. Annie had given him the message and he had gone straight out again. Martha had put his dinner in the oven, complaining that it would all be dried up by the time he got home.

'So you finally met Joe today?' she said as she took a large mouthful of bread. She frowned fiercely at her mother spilling gravy all down her front. 'Look at her. Babies make less mess than her!'

'She can't help it.'

Martha ignored Annie's remark. 'What d'you think of him then?'

'Who?'

'Joe.'

'Oh, he seems like a nice man, though what he thought of me I don't know. I was soaking me feet in a bowl of water when he came in.'

'Joe wouldn't take no notice of that, Annie. He probably thought it was quite funny. He's got a good sense of humour.' She picked up a plate of bread and butter and handed a slice to Georgie. 'That's the third piece you've had, lad. You hungry or something?'

He nodded and looked across at his mother. 'Can I go out, Mam? The lads are waiting for me. We're playing marbles.'

Annie frowned. 'It's a bit dark.'

Georgie groaned, his face puckering in dismay. 'We're only on the front.'

'All right, but not for long.'

She laughed as he scraped back his chair, grabbed another piece of bread and ran out of the door.

'I don't know where he puts it all,' she said, turning to Molly. 'What are you doing tonight?'

'Me? Oh, I'm dog tired. I'll help you with the pots then I'm going up.'

'But it's only seven o'clock,' Martha said, aghast. 'You young things ain't got no stamina.'

'Well, I weren't exactly gonna go to sleep,' Molly said slowly. 'I've got to practise walking with some books on me head. It's for me deportment and I didn't want you all laughing at me.'

'Oh, I see. Well, in that case you get off upstairs. Me and Annie will do the pots. Okay, Annie?'

'Yes, go on.'

Molly smiled at them and hurriedly left the room in case they changed their minds.

Annie pushed her plate away. She rested her elbows on the table and placed her chin in her hands.

'He seemed really nice,' she said, staring into space. 'He's a very good-looking bloke and had a lovely smile. I thought he'd be older somehow. Judging by his looks he can't be much more than thirty.

'Who?'

'Joe.'

'Oh, it's him you're talking about. He's thirty-two and I agree with you, he is an attractive man,' Martha said, smiling warmly. 'He's good to Bert and it's nice to see my husband so happy in his work at long last. I think he'd work for nothing for Joe. Got a lot of respect for that man, has our Bert.'

'Yes, I can tell by the way he talks about him. Has he any family, Martha?'

She narrowed her eyes questioningly. 'Yes, two girls. Why?'

'Just asking.'

The conversation stopped for a moment as Martha poured another mug of tea for them both.

'He's not happy, though.'

'Isn't he?'

'No. For one thing he's got problems with his business. The shoe trade's going through a bad time at the moment, so Bert tells me. Joe's got a lot of competition. He's getting by, but I think business could be a lot better. He's been out and about trying to drum up as much trade as he can. Bert reckons things will pick up. I hope so. I'd hate him to be laid off.'

'D'you think there's a chance of that?'

'If Joe's wife carries on spending money like it was water, yes, I do.'

'Oh. What's she like then?'

Martha frowned.' ''Course you wouldn't know Millicent Saunt, or Milly Scroggins as she was before she pushed Joe into marrying her.'

Annie's eyes lit with interest. 'What d'you mean?'

Martha folded her arms. 'I knew Milly Scroggins years ago when we were scruffy kids playing in the fields up by Green Lane Road. Right little madam she was. 'Course, I didn't know she'd married Joe 'til Bert mentioned it. She always said she'd marry a businessman, though God knows how she managed it. She's pretty enough, I'll say that, but she's nothing else going for her. She's no brains at all in that head of hers.'

'Martha,' Annie cried. 'It's unlike you to be so unkind.'

'Unkind!' she exclaimed. 'I'm not being unkind, I'm being truthful. I'm sure if Joe hadn't been so blinded by a pretty face, he'd have done much better for himself.'

'Is she that bad?'

'Yeah. And full of her own importance. You should have seen her face when she found out I was Bert's wife. Nearly dropped dead, I can tell yer, 'cos she can't parade round showing her airs and graces with me. I know her background.'

'I seem to have heard all this before. Kath's origins were something like this.'

'Oh, she's a tartar, but she ain't nasty and spiteful like you've said Kath is. Milly's just a lazy madam that likes to spend money and parade around like royalty, acting above her station. That's all.'

'I wonder how a nice bloke like Joe got tangled up with her?'

Martha shrugged her shoulders. 'Don't ask me. Bit like your Archie, I suppose. Love's blind, Annie. Men don't see what's under their noses.'

She nodded in agreement. 'Yes, you're right. Seems a shame though. You'd think she'd want to look after him a bit better, wouldn't you?'

'The likes of you and me would. But some women ain't bothered, Annie. They get that ring on their finger and that's that.'

Annie sighed deeply. 'D'you think he loves her?'

'Must do. He stays with her.' Martha paused thoughtfully. 'I expect there's lots of women throwing themselves at Joe Saunt. He'd be some catch all right, wife or no wife.' She stopped abruptly and eyed Annie with interest. 'I hope you ain't getting ideas along on that line, Annie Higgins? Joe's the loyal type. He wouldn't look at another woman.'

'Martha,' Annie retorted sharply, 'how could you think such a thing? Why, I only met the man for the first time today. After what I've been through, I'll never look at another man, believe me.'

Martha smiled sarcastically. 'Well, for someone who ain't interested in men, you're asking a lot of questions about a certain one.'

'It's only out of interest in Bert's boss, that's all.'

'Is it?' Martha said casually. She suddenly jumped up and raced around the table. 'Mother! For God's sake! Annie, get a cloth,' she shrieked as her mother tipped a cup of tea all over the table. It spread over the cloth and dripped on to the floor.

The conversation about Joe Saunt was brought to an abrupt end.

Annie finished polishing the counter, stood back and smiled in satisfaction. She raised her eyes as she felt a presence on the other side of the bar. She quickly recognised the tall, fair-haired figure and an unexpected tingle of excitement shot through her.

'Hello, Mr Saunt,' she said, trying to sound casual. 'And what brings you to the Black Swan?'

'Oh,' Joe stuttered. 'I just happened to be passing this way, and . . . er . . . as it's my lunchtime, I thought I'd have a quick bite to eat. You do food, do you?'

'Oh, yes. Not much choice, I'm afraid, you've come in a bit late. But I'm sure we can rustle up something.'

'Good, anything will do.'

'What will you have to drink? Light or dark ale or something else?' Annie tried to smile, alarmed by the fact that she was beginning to blush.

'Light, please. Just a half as it's only lunchtime.' He turned and gazed around at the half-filled room. 'Not a bad place.' He turned back to her. 'I've never been in here before.'

'Oh, then now you have, you'll have to come more often,' Annie said before she could check herself.

Joe smiled. 'I will. Do you work here most days?'

'Yes, most,' she said softly, placing his glass on the bar. 'If you'll excuse me I'll go and see what's in the kitchen.'

She turned and fled through to the back.

Joe made his way over to a vacant table by the window and sat down on the wooden bench. He slowly sipped at his drink and gazed thoughtfully into the fire. He shouldn't have come in, he knew that, but he just had to see her again. It was three weeks since he had first clapped eyes on her and he couldn't get her out of his mind. He had never felt like this before; no woman had made his body ache the way she had, and certainly not after just the few minutes he had spent in her presence. It wasn't just her pretty face, it was her whole personality he felt drawn to and if truth be known these alien feelings frightened him.

He looked expectantly across the room to see if she was coming back. She wasn't and he lowered his head. Him being here was wrong. He had lied to her. He had come out of his way to pass the pub and this wasn't the first time. He had walked up and down the street on several occasions, this being the first he had dared to venture in.

Just what kind of magic did she possess that fascinated him to such a degree he could hardly sleep? He didn't have the answer. All he knew was that he must not come back after today. He would also have to avoid the house in case she was there. His feelings for her were such that he couldn't concentrate properly on anything he was doing and his business was suffering enough without this. People were beginning to notice and ask questions. He would have to put a stop to this nonsense before it got out of hand. And it was nonsense. He was a married man with children.

He raised his head as she approached and watched silently as she placed a plate of sandwiches on the table.

'Just bread and cheese.'

He smiled. 'That's fine, thank you.'

'If you come early next time, you might be lucky and get something hot.'

305

'I will,' he said casually. 'I often pass this way. It'll be nice to get something warm for me dinner for a change.'

Annie returned his smile and hesitated before turning back to the bar and the rest of her customers. Joe stared thoughtfully after her. Coming into the tavern for his lunch surely could do no harm? He could pass the time of day with her and she need never be aware of his true feelings. It was a public place after all. What did it matter that it was streets away from his factory? It would do him good to get away now and again. Yes, no harm could come of that.

After this first visit, Joe became a regular at the lunchtime session. As much as he tried he could not keep away. Annie looked forward to his visits and found her eyes travelling towards the door when his usual time for arriving came around.

Despite being uprooted twice in a short space of time, Georgie settled down well again at school and he and Arthur were soon back to being the best of friends. Annie was pleased. Arthur was a good influence upon her son. He came from one of the poorest families around but they were honest, hard-working people and Arthur's loyalty to Georgie was having a steadying effect and helping him overcome the upheaval he had been through.

Molly was beginning to grow into a fine woman. The last few months had taught her many of the facts of life and she had fallen in love. Annie was quite perplexed. On being introduced she had taken an instant dislike to the lad. His name was Ernest and he was a second assistant in the carpet department. He was cocksure, his hair all greased back, and he smoked and drank profusely. He always seemed to have plenty of money in his pocket, though, which worried her as his wages couldn't be much.

Annie kept quiet about her feelings regarding Ernest and hoped Molly would in time see sense. Martha agreed. There was no point in causing trouble. Molly was a bright girl and surely in time would see Ernest for what he was. She was enjoying her job immensely and her elocution lessons were progressing well. She would often repeat to them the words and phrases she had to practise, raising quite a few smiles in the process as her pronunciation of some of the words was well off the mark. She had been asked to model corsets and lingerie for potential customers and for at least a week became quite unbearable with pride.

Annie began to think of moving. They had been with Bert and Martha for nearly four months and she felt in danger of outstaying her welcome. The money she paid to Martha for lodgings, little as it was, was very welcome and she felt that Martha, over the months, had grown to rely on it. But they needed their own place and Annie started to make enquiries about houses to rent in the same area. This way she could still be close to Martha and Bert but close her own front door at night.

A mild afternoon in April found Annie gratefully returning home to Martha's. The tavern had not been very busy, but Annie still felt tired and in desperate need of a mug of hot tea. She stopped abruptly in the hall as she heard her name being called.

'That you, Annie? Thank God!' Martha shouted as she ran to meet her. 'It's Mam, Annie. She's gone. And it looks as though Georgie's with her.'

'What!' she cried. 'I don't understand, Martha. What do you mean, gone?'

'I left them. Only for a minute, Annie, honest, just while I popped into Ada's next-door. When I came back, the front door was wide open and there was no sign of them.'

'What time was this?' Annie asked, her chest tightening in alarm.

'Just after four.'

'Oh, well, Georgie is most likely round at Arthur's.'

'No, he's not. Arthur's had to go and help his dad collect slack from the slag heaps.' Martha caught hold of her arm.

307

'Georgie was upset, Annie. Something had happened at school. To be honest I was only half listening. You know what kids are like, they're always moaning about something.' She wrung her hands together in despair. 'I know they've gone 'cos their coats are missing. So has Mam's old shopping bag, the one she takes everywhere with her. I've been up the park and checked all the streets, but no sign. What are we gonna do?'

Annie started to shake. If anything happened to Georgie she would not forgive herself. She pulled Martha through into the living room.

'Look, let's try to be calm. What time is Bert due home?'

Martha shrugged her shoulders. 'Any time really. All depends on what Joe has lined up for him.'

'Right. You go and tell Bert what's happened. I'll go and have another look up the park and other places they might be. I'll check all the neighbours as well. Someone might have seen them.' She gasped for breath, the concern she felt showing upon her face. 'We have to find them before it gets dark.' She looked across at the clock on the mantelpiece. 'It's just coming up to six o'clock. We've about two good hours of daylight left.' She felt tears sting the back of her eyes as the control she had managed to keep gave way. 'Oh, Martha, I hope they're all right. I couldn't bear it if anything happened to Georgie or your mother.'

Martha looked at Annie, her face betraying the horror of the situation. The thought of her mother in charge of a seven-year-old boy was frightening. She could not get to the end of the street without becoming lost. Sheer panic rose in her chest.

'I'll go and get Bert and anyone else who'll help us look.'

At eleven o'clock that night Annie dragged herself down Forest Road towards home. Her voice was sore from frantically shouting Georgie's name and her legs ached from the distance she had walked. Please be here, please God, please say they're safe, she whispered as she closed the front door behind her. She heard the low mumble of voices and her

308

heart lifted, only to sink again as she opened the kitchen door and saw three hopeful faces turn to look at her. The expressions on their faces told her everything. Georgie and Jean had not been found.

Martha moved towards her and placed her arm round her shoulders, gently guiding her towards a chair.

'Come and sit down, love. We'll find them, don't worry. They've got to be somewhere. It's just we ain't looked in the right place, that's all.'

'Don't worry?' Annie erupted. 'I'm bloody frantic. The whole neighbourhood's been out searching. We've looked everywhere, there's nowhere else left.' Tears raced down her face and she started to shake. 'Georgie shouldn't be out this time of night,' she cried. 'Anything could have happened to him. He's only little and your mother ain't got the sense she was born with.' She clutched Martha's arm. 'I'm sorry, I shouldn't have said that. She's your mother and you must be just as worried as I am.'

Martha smiled wanly. 'It's all right. You're upset, it's only natural to be angry.' She shook her head sadly. 'It's all my fault, I should never have left them.' She bit her bottom lip and stared over at Bert and Joe, seated at the table nursing mugs of hot tea. 'Joe thinks we should tell the police . . .'

'Joe?' Annie uttered. Up until that moment she had not been fully aware of his presence. Her head jerked up and she stared at him for a second, suddenly feeling comforted by his nearness.

'It's good of you to be here,' she whispered.

'It's the least I can do. I have children of my own, Annie. I understand how you must be feeling.'

The mention of his family sent a cold shiver through her. It was a reminder that he was a married man and was only here out of concern for the missing members of Bert's family. She raised her head.

'Do you really think we ought to get the police?' she said tearfully.

'Yes, I do. Especially in the circumstances.'

'What do you mean, circumstances?' Annie cried. 'Is there something you know that I don't?'

'No. No. I just meant, well, Georgie is only seven and he's with an old lady who . . . well, you know. She hasn't got all her faculties. That's all I meant.'

'Oh, yes, I see.' Annie's shoulders sagged. 'Yes, get the police, we have to do something. I can't stand this not knowing.'

'I'll go,' said Bert, jumping up from his chair. 'And try not to worry, they can't have gone far.'

'I'll go with you,' Joe volunteered.

The two women watched in silence as the men departed.

Annie sank down on a chair by the fire and accepted the mug of hot tea that Martha handed to her.

'Oh, I feel so helpless,' she groaned. 'It's really dark and cold now, Martha, they could freeze to death out there.' Pictures of the pair rose up in her mind and her voice rose hysterically. 'What about the river? Say they've gone by the river or the canal and fallen in? Oh, Martha! The trams! I know what they can do. Look what happened to my Charlie, and he was an adult. Georgie wouldn't stand a chance with all that traffic. I shouldn't have gone to work, Martha. I should be at home looking after him . . .'

'Stop it, Annie, stop it! It's no good thinking like that. I'm as worried as you are but it's no good imagining things. Your Georgie's more sensible than you give him credit for.'

'How can you say that, Martha? He's only seven. What if a man approaches him . . .'

'I said, stop it!' Martha shouted. 'Let's see what the bobbies have to say. We've done all we can for the time being.'

Annie stared at Martha and took a deep breath in a vain attempt to calm the hysteria that filled her. She slowly nodded. 'Yes, you're right. He's a good lad, Martha, he wouldn't do anything stupid. I just hope to God they've gone for a walk and got lost.' She took a sip of tea and ran her fingers through her dishevelled hair. 'If he comes home safe, Martha, I'll never shout or smack him again.'

Martha managed a watery smile. 'And I promise never to get cross with my mother.'

They lapsed into silence, each with their own thoughts. Suddenly Annie frowned and looked over at Martha. 'Where's Molly?' she asked, concerned.

Martha stared blankly for a moment. 'Oh, she's out. I forgot to mention it what with all that's going on. She must have come home from work while we were out looking for Georgie. She left a note.' She frowned. ''Course, the poor gel won't know what's happened, will she?'

'No, she won't. But it's after eleven and she should have been home by now,' Annie said, raising her voice, anger replacing worry. 'I'm not standing for her being out this late at night. She's in for it when she comes home.'

'Calm down, Annie. I agree she is late, but see what her explanation is when she comes in.'

'Martha, we've enough without worrying about her. I've no idea where she is, though I suppose she's with that Ernest.'

'More than likely. But she is sixteen, Annie.'

'Sixteen or not, she's no right to be out this late. I promised her mother I'd look after her.'

Martha laid her hand on Annie's arm. 'You're just upset 'cos of Georgie, me duck. Calm down, she'll be home soon.'

'She'd better. I don't like her out with Ernest. It worries me.'

'Well, try not to think about it. Why not go to bed and get some sleep?'

'Sleep! You must be joking. I'll not rest again until my son is safe at home.'

Annie rubbed her eyes as she accustomed herself to the dark room. Whilst sitting in the chair she had dozed off into a fitful sleep. She rose stiffly and checked the kettle for water, afterwards swinging it across the remains of the fire. After the police had been informed, Joe returned home and she had persuaded Martha and Bert to go to bed, promising to wake them if there was any news.

311

The clock showed the time to be two-thirty in the morning and Annie shivered, a feeling of impending doom settling upon her. Her son and Martha's mother had now been missing for over ten hours. Something terrible must have happened to them or why else were they not at home, tucked safely in their beds? And to add to her worries, Molly still had not returned.

Physical and mental exhaustion were taking their toll. Her eyes felt gritty, her skin taut and dry, and her hands shook as she tried to make herself a cup of tea.

A sound reached her ears and she strained to hear where it was coming from. As she walked hesitantly towards the back door the sound grew louder. She sprang upon the door and wrenched it open. Huddled on the doorstep was Molly, tears of despair cascading down her cheeks. Annie stood for a moment in shock, trying to sort out her muddled thoughts.

She bent down, took hold of Molly's arm and helped her up. 'What on earth has happened to you?' she cried, taking in the ripped, mud-stained skirt. The girl's cheek was badly cut and caked with congealed blood, her chin had a large bruise which was turning black, and her hair, usually so neat and tidy, was hanging loose from its pins. Thoughts raced through Annie's head as she supported her dishevelled, shaking charge through to the living room. She sat her down in the chair by the fire and looked hard at her.

'Molly, I need to know what happened. Has Ernest . . . has he . . .'

Molly shook uncontrollably as tears welled up in her eyes again. 'What, Annie . . . has he what?' she asked, bewildered.

Annie knelt before her and took hold of her hands. 'You know, Molly. Has he . . . did he . . . take advantage of you?'

Molly looked at her blankly, large brown eyes staring wildly until it suddenly struck her what Annie was getting at. 'Oh, no. It's nothing like that.'

Annie's body sagged in relief as she slipped back and sat on the edge of the chair opposite. 'Oh, Molly, thank God. I thought the worst. But tell me, please. What happened?'

Molly sniffed loudly. 'Oh, Annie. It was awful, awful. I'd arranged to meet Ernest tonight.' Her eyes opened wide in alarm. 'I left a note, Annie, honest I did.'

'I know,' she interrupted. 'Just get on with it, please, Molly.'

She sniffed loudly and wiped her hand under her nose. 'We'd arranged to meet outside the store, only when I arrived, he wasn't there. I waited for ages and then got fed up so I started to walk around a bit. I was mad, Annie. I thought he'd stood me up. Anyway, I found meself round the back of the store, the bit where they bring in all the goods, and I heard voices. I was frightened but wondered what was going on, so I crept up behind a wall and peeped round.'

'And?'

'It was Ernest and this other fella – they were loading stuff on to a cart.'

'What kind of stuff?' Annie asked, frowning deeply.

'Rolls of lino, boxes and other things. It was dark, Annie, I couldn't see properly.'

'Stealing them, you mean?'

Molly nodded her head. 'Yes.' She paused for a moment as a sob caught in the back of her throat. She breathed deeply and composed herself. 'I must have made a noise because the next thing I knew, Ernest was dragging me out from behind the wall and threatening me. He was angry, Annie, I've never seen anyone so mad. The other bloke started to shout at him. Ernest told him to shut up, said that he would deal with me. He held me that tightly, Annie, I couldn't feel me arm. Look.' She pulled up her sleeve and showed Annie the large bruise above her wrist.

Annie shuddered and exhaled deeply. 'The bastard.'

Molly gave an unexpected laugh. 'I don't know what possessed me, Annie, but I suddenly blurted that I was going for the bobbies.'

'Oh, Molly, you never?'

She nodded. 'Well, they were stealing, Annie, and it's wrong.'

Annie clasped her hands together. 'Is that when he did this to you?'

'Yes. He punched me in the face and I fell over. When I tried to get up and run away, he grabbed my skirt and it ripped.' She raised her head. 'But it's all right, Annie. I got him back,' she said smugly.

'How?'

'Well, I managed to get up before he hit me again and I kneed him in his whatsits.'

Annie clasped her hand to her mouth. 'You did?'

'Yes,' Molly said, a smile of satisfaction spreading across her face. 'And it bloody well hurt him, I can tell yer. He fell on the ground moaning and that's when I ran home. The other bloke was too busy trying to get away with the cart to bother about me.'

'Oh, Molly.' Annie's shoulders sagged. 'What am I gonna do with you?'

Her face fell. 'You ain't gonna send me home are yer?'

Annie smiled and shook her head. 'No, 'course not. I'd never do that, you're like part of the family now. But you didn't half give me a fright. I've been worried to death about you.' She frowned and looked severely at Molly. 'I hope this has taught you a lesson?'

'Oh, it has, Annie. It has.' Her eyes misted over. 'I thought he loved me,' she said sadly. 'If he had, he wouldn't have done this to me, would he?'

Annie sighed. 'No, my love. I'm sorry to say he wouldn't.'

Molly hesitantly raised her eyes. 'Are you mad with me? I daren't come home for fear of what you'd say. I've been traipsing the streets for ages. I thought I'd wait until you'd gone to bed, so you wouldn't find out.'

'Oh, Molly, I'm not mad. I'm just glad to have you back home safely. When I first saw you, I thought ... I thought ...'

'No, Annie,' Molly cut in. 'Nothing like that happened, honest.'

'Well, thank God.' She walked around the table and placed

314

her hands on the back of a chair. 'Something has to be done about Ernest. We can't leave it like this.'

Molly's head jerked up. 'No!' she cried hysterically. 'He'll kill me. Please don't do anything. Please.'

Annie ran her hand over her forehead. 'Okay,' she said, trying to keep her voice light. 'Just forget what happened if you can. Although you ain't gonna be able to go to work in this state. Mrs Syndicombe will have a fit.' She paused. 'Let's get you cleaned up, and then you must go to bed. We'll sort something out in the morning.'

Molly rose and rushed to Annie, hugging her tightly. 'Thanks, Annie. I'm ever so sorry about all this, really I am.'

Annie smiled as she pulled away from the embrace. 'It's not your fault.'

She walked into the kitchen, filled a bowl with clean water, added some salt and proceeded to clean Molly's wounds. That done, she sat back and eyed the girl thoroughly.

'Now go to bed and try to get some sleep. It's very late.'

Molly's eyes alighted on the clock and she frowned. 'Why are you still up at this time?'

Annie hesitated. 'Oh, I couldn't sleep,' she said, not wanting to burden the girl any further tonight. 'Now go to bed,' she repeated. 'And try to forget about Ernest.'

'I'll try, Annie,' she whispered slowly. 'But it's gonna be hard, 'cos I still love him.'

'You think you do. But mark my words, you'll soon meet someone else, and before you know it you'll be in love again.'

Molly managed a smile, awkwardly stood up and kissed Annie warmly on the cheek. 'Night, night,' she whispered.

Annie watched her go, then froze as she heard a gentle tapping sound coming from the back door.

She went over and opened it, finding Joe standing on the step. He looked searchingly into her ashen face.

'I couldn't sleep, Annie. Any news?'

She shook her head, standing aside to allow him to enter. He walked through to the living room and stood in front of the fire, pulling off his cap and playing with it between his fingers.

'It's good of you to come,' she said slowly, feeling an immense sense of comfort well up inside her.

'It's the least I can do.'

Suddenly, Annie burst into tears. Joe rushed forward, placing his arms tightly round her. She rested her head against his shoulder and sobbed, her body moulding into his as she let go of all her pent up emotions.

He gasped at the nearness of her.

'Oh, Joe, I can't stand this any more,' she choked. She suddenly realised the intimate situation they were in and pulled away. She placed her hand over her mouth and raised her eyes towards his. 'I'm sorry,' she said, face reddening in embarrassment.

'Sorry for what?' he said softly.

'For . . .'

Joe placed his arms around her again. 'It's all right,' he said quickly. 'You needed a shoulder to cry on and it just happened to be mine.' He pulled slightly back from her and looked into her red-rimmed eyes. 'Annie, I'm always here if you should ever need me.'

'Oh, Joe . . .' She stopped abruptly, pulled away and walked across the room, standing against the window. She turned to him and smiled wanly.

'Thanks. It's always nice to have a friend to turn to,' she said flatly.

She walked back towards the fire and placed several lumps of coal on to the embers. He stood and watched her, his mind in a turmoil.

That finished, she swung across the kettle and sank down in the armchair.

'I need to ask your advice.'

'Oh?' he said, frowning slightly. He sat down in the chair opposite.

Annie proceeded to tell him about Molly's escapade.

He sat back and listened intently, his face portraying none of the anger he felt towards the man who had harmed such an innocent, lovely young girl. He knew without a doubt that

316

Molly had not warranted Ernest's treatment of her and vowed silently that he would suffer. When Annie had finished, he nodded slowly.

'Leave it with me. I'll deal with it.'

'Will you? Oh, but Joe, Molly mustn't be associated. There could be some backlash.'

'Don't worry,' he said reassuringly. 'I said I'll deal with it. Trust me.'

Just then the front door banged loudly. Annie jumped but was unable to move, frozen in fear of the unknown.

'Oh! It might be the bobbies,' she gasped.

Joe jumped up and ran to the door. Several moments later he returned.

'They've been found.'

'Oh, thank God!' Annie cried, her shoulders sagging in relief.

'Georgie is down at the station, asleep in one of the cells, but Martha's mother . . .'

'What's wrong with her?'

'She's in hospital, Annie. She's in a bad way.'

She clasped her hands together. 'I'll get Martha and Bert up.'

'Yes, do that, and they want you to go down and collect Georgie. The constable is waiting at the door. I'll come with you.'

'Will you? Oh, I'd appreciate that. But what about your family? Shouldn't you get back to them? They'll be wondering where you are.'

'Oh, I don't think so,' he replied.

'No, 'course, they'll all be asleep.' She rushed over to the door. 'I'll go and get Martha and Bert and then we can be off. I can't wait to see Georgie,' she said, running out of the room and up the stairs.

On the way to the station the policeman explained that the pair had been found huddled together in a ditch on the Uppingham Road. Georgie's cries had alerted a passerby and the police had been informed. Georgie was exhausted but

317

fine, no worse for his night under the stars. Jean was another matter. She was suffering from hypothermia and a broken hip. From Georgie's rambling explanations it seemed the pair had left home, both feeling unwanted. Annie froze. What had she done to make her son feel like that? She felt remorseful and saddened but determined never to let this happen again.

She sat on the wooden bench in the cold forbidding cell and hugged her son tightly whilst Joe looked on.

'Oh, Mam,' he wailed. 'I thought I'd never see yer again.'

'What happened?' she asked softly, still holding him tight in her arms, afraid to let him go. She raised her eyes and smiled warmly up at Joe.

'I had an argument with Arfur. He had to help his dad and I wanted to play marbles.'

'Is that all? Is that what this was about? Oh, Georgie, Georgie, you don't know what you've put us through.'

He bit his bottom lip and choked back a sob. 'Well, I got that new set that Uncle Bert bought me and I wanted to play with them and didn't have anybody to play with.'

Annie sighed deeply. This was all her fault. If she had been at home instead of at work then none of this would have happened.

Georgie raised his eyes to his mother's. 'I was upset and Auntie Jean said we should run away. She said nobody wanted her either. She said we'd find somewhere we could live together and she'd look after me.'

'Oh, Georgie,' Annie groaned. 'Promise me you'll never run away again. Nothing's so bad it can't be sorted out. Promise me, please?'

'I promise, Mam, honest I do.' He sniffed loudly. 'Auntie Jean's poorly, Mam, ain't she? Is it my fault?'

'No, no, 'course it's not.' She hugged him again and he rested his head on her shoulder. 'Auntie Jean's always running away. You being with her this time probably saved her life.'

'Oh.'

'I think we should get the lad home,' Joe said, ruffling his hair.

She looked up. 'Yes, you're right.' Annie looked down again at Georgie and her eyes softened. 'I think the best place for you is bed, young man.'

After thanking the police, they left the station and headed for home. Joe saw them to the door and then departed for his own home.

Annie sat in the chair with a mug of tea between her hands, desperately tired but her mind too preoccupied to sleep. Georgie was tucked safely into bed and she had stood and watched him for several moments, his angelic face showing none of the trauma he had experienced as he soundly slept. Words could not have expressed her feeling of thankfulness at having him lying there. Nothing like this must ever happen again. She knew if anything had happened to her son it would have finished her. It was up to her to prevent any recurrence of this escapade.

She loved the tavern but the long hours spent there were partly to blame for this dreadful happening. It would be a wrench but she would have to find some other means of employment. Her son was everything to her and whatever she did in the future would have to fit in with his needs. At least the terrible events had brought this home to her and for that, at least, she was thankful.

She realised it might take a while to find something suitable, so in the meantime decided to ask Wilfred Biddle to re-jig her hours at the tavern to coincide with Georgie's schooling. That way she could work and be at home when he needed her. It would mean less pay, but no price was worth her son's welfare.

Martha returned from the hospital with a stricken face.

'She'll never come home, Annie. Her mind's completely gone. She didn't even recognise me, her own daughter, and they reckon Hillcrest Hospital is the best place for her. Everyone knows that once you go in there it's only a matter of time before the end.' Tears of anguish rushed down her face. 'Oh, how I've wished to get rid of her and now I feel so guilty. Of late, I've begrudged everything I've had to do for her and I feel so terrible and selfish. I pleaded with the doctors to let her come home. I'd look after her. But they wouldn't let me. Said she were a danger to herself. I've heard such dreadful things about that place. They strap 'em to the beds, and give 'em stuff to shut 'em up when they can't handle 'em, and they're hardly fed. Oh, Annie, Annie! It don't bear thinking about, my mother stuck in there.'

She rushed over and pulled the distraught woman towards her. 'There, there, love. I'm sure they're only doing what's best. You couldn't possibly watch her twenty-four hours a day and she was bad enough before this happened. You can visit her, Martha, as much as you like, and I'll come with you. It's for the best, lovie, I'm sure it is.'

'Yes, I know, I know,' Martha sobbed. 'But she's my mother, Annie. Surely she should end what's left of her life with me, not in that stinking hole?'

She broke away from Annie, rushed from the room and up the stairs where she threw herself on the bed, crying bitterly for the cruel way in which life had treated her mother.

Joe came into the pub one lunchtime several days later. He found a spot at the end of the bar out of earshot of everyone else in the room and beckoned Annie over.

'That little problem you told me about . . .'

'Oh?'

'It's sorted.'

'Is it? And what about Molly?'

'Her name was never mentioned. But the lad will be behind bars for a long time,' he said gravely.

'How did you manage it?'

'Least you know the better.'

'Yes, you're probably right. Luckily, I managed to convince Mrs Syndicombe that Molly had fallen down the stairs. She's no fool. I just hope she believed me.'

'I'm sure she did. How is Molly?'

'Bearing up. She's looking a lot better than she did. Anyway, I can't thank you enough.'

'My pleasure. I told you, any time.'

Annie smiled warmly. 'Can I get you anything?'

Joe hesitated for a moment. 'Yes, please. I'll have a bottle of light ale, then I must be off. Work is beginning to pick up, I'm glad to say, and we'll be working flat out for the foreseeable future.'

'Oh, Joe, I am pleased,' she said sincerely as she picked up a bottle of ale, unscrewed the top and started to pour it out.

He sighed. 'Yes, so am I. I would have hated to have laid off any of the workers, especially Bert, and it was getting close to that. I've managed to get several big orders, with a promise of some more.' He accepted the glass of ale and took a gulp. 'I can see us having to move to new premises in the near future. And between you and me, I'm thinking of promoting Bert to Works Manager.'

'Oh, Joe, that's wonderful news.'

'Yes. He's worth several men to me. But don't mention it, I've to see how things go first.'

'I won't,' Annie said, feeling proud that he had taken her into his confidence.

He finished his drink, said his goodbyes and left.

Annie stared after him. She hated to admit it, but her feelings for him were growing stronger every time they met. But she knew that he just looked upon her as a friend. After all, he was a married man and as Martha had so firmly pointed out, very loyal and not the type to mess around. Not that she wanted him to. Marriage was a solemn promise made between two people and those vows should be honoured regardless. She suddenly felt very guilty about her feelings towards him. He belonged to another woman and she had no right to hanker after him.

She sighed deeply and began to empty a crate of bottles, stacking them neatly upon the shelves.

Chapter Eighteen

'You're not serious, Annie?' Martha gasped as she looked across at her sister-in-law in disbelief.

Annie smiled. 'Very serious.' She placed her elbows on the table and rested her chin in her hands. 'I've given this a lot of thought, Martha. This is just the thing I've been looking for. I'm good at this kinda work and I love it. Between Wilfred and all the other staff, I've learned all I need to know to run it successfully. I've lots of ideas. That place could make a packet with the right person in charge.' She breathed deeply and raised her head. 'I'm sure I'll make a good go of it, Martha.'

'Oh, I've no doubts you will. But owning a tavern? Well, I never thought the Higgins family would ever own anything.'

Annie laughed. 'There's a first time for everything. Just think on it, Martha, my very own business.'

'Phew! Don't bear thinking about. I don't know what Bert's gonna make of all this, he's only just got used to the idea of you working there. I think he thought you'd get fed up and leave. Still, I wish you luck. And I suppose if you need a hand any time . . .'

'Martha!' Annie interrupted. 'You work behind a bar?'

'Why not? If it's good enough for you. I ain't got me mother to look after any more so I've got plenty of time on me hands.'

Annie leant over the table and placed her hand affectionately on her sister-in-law's arm. 'Thanks. I'll probably take you up on that offer.'

'I was afraid you might,' Martha laughed. She picked up the teapot and poured them both a cup of tea. 'I suppose we should be drinking something stronger to celebrate.'

'No. Tea's fine for me.' Annie grimaced. 'To be truthful, I don't really like that alcohol stuff.'

Martha gave a loud laugh. 'And you thinking of buying a tavern! I shouldn't let the regulars hear you admit that.'

'I won't. I want them to buy as much as they can.'

'Well, I'm sure Bert will do his bit.'

'You make it sound as though he's a drinker.'

'No. Not my Bert. As you know he does like a pint after work, but that's all, I'm glad to say. What I meant was, he'll change his drinking place to yours.'

'Good. I hope lots of men will.' Annie took a sip of her tea. 'Wilfred was really shocked when I made him the offer.'

'I bet he was.'

'I think he was more surprised that I had the money. But as he's not in a position to turn down my offer, he accepted. It's a shame really that he drank all the profits away. Apart from that he was a good landlord. Still, that's not my problem. My problem is persuading the brewery to sell me their ale.'

'Oh, d'you think they'll turn you down then?'

'I hope not. But breweries can be funny about who they sell to, and being's I'm a woman . . .'

'What's that got to do with it?'

'Plenty, Martha. Breweries are old fashioned. They're run by old men who live in the past. They think a woman's place is at home, looking after the kids.'

'Well, they're right really,' Martha said.

'How could you say such a thing? If lots of women never worked, many kids would starve.'

Martha reluctantly agreed. 'Yes, I suppose yer right.'

'I am!' Annie retorted. 'I need to work to keep my son and I see this tavern as the start of greater things.' She paused for a moment and looked at Martha tenderly. 'This will mean Georgie, Molly and myself will be able to move.'

'Move?' Martha frowned. 'Oh, no, Annie. Surely you can stay here? If you go, I shall miss you all.'

Annie smiled warmly. 'Yes, I know. It's been grand living

here. But it's nearly a year now, Martha, and we can't stay here for ever. If I hadn't have decided on the tavern, then I would have found a house for us all. You've made us so welcome and I can't thank you enough for that. But I need a place of me own, and really I need to be living on the premises. That's what decided me – the accommodation going with the job. I can work and be on hand for Georgie. I'll be there all the time for him.'

'Yes, I understand. This tavern sounds ideal,' Martha said forlornly.

'We'll still be here for a while yet. All the papers have to be drawn up and some alterations done first.'

'Alterations?'

'Yes. I want to decorate and put in a proper kitchen. I'm gonna cook food, Martha, good nourishing food, and also use the rest of the upstairs rooms for lodgers. I've worked it all out. I should just about have enough money.'

'My, you have given this a lot of thought.'

'Yes, I have. I am going to get the full potential out of the tavern and I mean to start as soon as possible.'

Martha sighed deeply and stared into space. This news had come as a shock to her. Fancy Annie owning a tavern. She grimaced. Women like Annie didn't work in drinking establishments, let alone own them. You were either brought up in the places and inherited them or you were rough and ready. Annie was neither of those things. Admittedly, she had been brought up in a shabby rundown area, but Annie somehow always seemed above all that. She had an air about her that said she really belonged in higher places. Not that Annie was superior. She was the type of person who instantly put you at your ease and could adapt to any situation. Oh, lord. Did she really understand what she was undertaking? Martha slowly raised her head.

'I'm pleased for you, Annie. Really I am,' she said, trying to keep her voice light.

'Thanks, Martha. I hoped you would be.'

'What about Joe? Have you told him?'

Annie frowned. 'I may have mentioned it, but that's all. Why?'

Martha raised her eyebrows. 'There's one thing I ain't, Annie Higgins, and that's daft. You're in love with the bloke. Don't look like that at me.' She stretched across the table and took Annie's hand. 'Oh, Annie love. Does he know?'

She shrugged her shoulders and shook her head. 'I've no idea, Martha. Sometimes I think he feels the same, but I know it's only wishful thinking on my part.' She raised her eyes to the ceiling. 'I've tried not to feel this way for him, Martha, but I can't help it. I'd do anything for him. I lie at night wishing his wife would leave him or . . .' She stopped abruptly. 'Martha, it's wrong what I feel, and I know it.'

'You have it that bad, eh? Well, love, we can't help our feelings. But you're gonna get hurt. If Joe ever left Milly, she'd see him in hell.'

Both women sat in silence for a moment.

'The way I feel about Joe is different from Charlie. I really loved Charlie and when he died I thought the end of the world had come. But this love for Joe . . . well, it's deeper somehow. I find it hard to describe but I can sense what he's thinking, and when I stand next to him I feel his presence so strongly. I just wish to God he wasn't married. Oh, I know that sounds wicked but I want him so desperately. I've tried and tried to shut him out, but it doesn't work. That's why I want this business, Martha. I can throw myself into it and try to forget him.'

She nodded in understanding. 'I don't see how you can forget him when he keeps coming to see yer.'

'I know. But how can I stop him? Anyway, I don't want him to stop. I'd sooner have him just as a friend than not at all.' Annie scraped back her chair and stood up. 'Oh, if only he wasn't married, Martha. We could be together. I'd make him happy, I know I would. He wants someone who cares for him, someone who'll look after him the way he deserves.' She walked over and stood in front of the fire, clasping her hands together. 'I'm a wicked woman, Martha. Go on, say it.'

She shook her head. 'You're not wicked, me duck. You're just in love. I can understand perfectly how you feel.'

'Can you?'

'Oh, yes, Annie. I am a woman after all.'

She managed a smile. 'I've got to get it through my head that he's a happily married man.'

'I've told you before, I don't think he is.'

'Yes, you did,' Annie said quickly, her eyes flashing in Martha's direction.

'I think it's his children that keep him tied to Milly. I think the love, if it ever was love, died a long time ago. Certainly in Joe's case. I can't speak for Milly.'

'Do you? Oh, Martha, that's sad.'

'Yes, I know, but it happens. I know lots of women stuck with husbands they'd sooner see the back of. Mind you, Annie, in Joe's case I'm only going on the odd word or two that he's said, and the fact that he never seems to want to go home. I've never heard him say a bad word against Milly, I'll say that for him.'

'No, neither have I.' She took a deep breath and bit her bottom lip. 'Maybe all this is in my imagination? Oh, Martha, what am I gonna do?'

'There's nothing you can do,' she said firmly. 'Not about Joe. He's too much of a man to walk out on his family.'

Annie frowned deeply. 'Well, that'll teach me to fall in love with a married man with morals, won't it?' She looked hesitantly at Martha. 'You won't tell Bert none of this, will you?'

'I don't have to, love, he already knows.'

'Knows? How?'

'Just by the way you are with each other. People ain't blind, Annie. Anyway, don't worry, Bert won't say a word. He's much too high a regard for the pair of you. I suggest you get busy with your plans and concentrate on making a go of it. That'll keep your mind occupied with other things.'

Annie breathed deeply. 'I intend to, Martha. Hard work is a good cure for all ailments. Me dad always used to say that.'

'And he was right. Now let's get the dinner on, else we'll have two hungry men and one young girl shouting blue murder.'

Several weeks later all the paperwork for the buying of the Black Swan was well underway. Things were progressing nicely. All Annie had to do now was overcome the one big obstacle that stood in her way, and that was persuading the brewers to give her a chance.

A warm morning in late May of 1905 saw her dressing carefully in a new tan ankle-length skirt and matching three-quarter jacket, made from pure wool. It was edged with thick black coils of braiding and her crisp white high-necked blouse enhanced the outfit to perfection. She had spent more than she intended but she wanted to look smart and the part. She smoothed her dark hair into a neat coil at the base of her neck, pinched her cheeks to add some colour and determinedly set off for her destination.

Her knees trembled as she sat in the waiting room of Brewster and Company, brewers to the nobility. She sat stiffly as her eyes darted around the formidable oak-panelled room, trying to quiet her churning stomach. She was dreading the interview with Mr Brewster Senior. The old man had insisted on seeing her in person. The brewery had gone into her background thoroughly, checking her finances to make sure she had funds and that they were legitimate, and also that she was of sound character. All that was left was to persuade them to sell her their ale.

A tall thin man eyed her haughtily through his pince nez as he sat behind a high wooden desk. He raised them further on to his nose as a bell sounded, slammed shut the large red ledger he was working on and entered an office behind him. He returned almost immediately and beckoned her over.

'Mr Brewster is ready for you now,' he said coldly.

He stood aside as she entered another oak-panelled room. This room was no cheerier than the one she had just left and she felt her heart sink as she saw a small bony old man sitting behind an enormous walnut desk. His thinning grey hair hung limply to his collar and his grey eyes watched her shrewdly. She heard the door shutting behind her and ventured forward.

The old man held out his hand and indicated a chair before his desk. He eyed her as she hesitantly sat down. His eyes returned to the papers in front of him and he leafed through them for several moments. He picked them up, shuffled them together and placed them to one side. All his movements were slow and methodical and Annie felt unnerved by his manner. He slowly raised his eyes.

'I'm afraid the answer is no, Mrs Higgins,' he said matter-of-factly.

'No!' she gasped. 'But I don't understand. Why?'

'I don't have to give you any explanation of my decision. My answer is final and that's that.'

'Oh, but I want a reason,' Annie heard herself say. 'I'm not standing for being dragged half across town just for you to have the pleasure of saying no.'

The old man smiled mockingly. 'Our decision was right.'

'What d'you mean?'

'I mean your attitude. I knew to take on a woman with no experience was a mistake, and let's face it, my dear, you don't come from a very good side of town and haven't exactly had an education. How do you propose to run a tavern when all you've done is . . .' he picked up the sheaf of papers and glanced over them, '. . . been a seamstress and worked on a farm? What kind of recommendation is that, eh? Your time working in the trade hasn't exactly been extensive, has it?'

Annie lowered her head, her anger subsiding. He was right. What qualifications did she have to run a business? She saw all her dreams quickly evaporating. But she would have one last try at winning him over.

'I can understand your reasons for saying no, Mr Brewster. But I have learned everything there is to know under Mr Biddles, and for your information it's my money that's being put into this business, not yours. Your company is not really risking anything. So if I do fail, what have you lost? Nothing, as far as I can see.'

'Oh, but our good name would be associated with your failure and that wouldn't do.'

'Yes, but what if I make a success?'

Mr Brewster shook his head firmly. 'Can't see that, I'm afraid. I have a good nose for this sort of thing and I can only see failure. Now if you'd been born into the trade, that would have been a different matter.' He rose stiffly. 'The only thing I can recommend is that you try brewing your own ale. If that succeeds we may give you a try at a later date.'

'Brew my own ale?' Annie said questioningly. 'How is that done?'

'See, my dear, there's so much you know nothing about. Many landlords still brew their own ale.' He folded his arms. 'I suggest you give up this whole idea and go back to sewing.' He rose, struggled around his desk and stood before her. 'Now if you don't mind, my dear, I have things to do.'

Annie slowly stood up. She eyed him for a moment, biting back the things she wanted to say to this bigoted little man. Graciously she thanked him for his time, turned and left the room.

She stumbled slowly down the steps of the building, tears of anger and frustration blinding her eyes. She felt a hand on her arm and blinked rapidly.

'Oh, Joe,' she sobbed. 'It's you. What on earth are you doing around here?'

'I just happened to be passing.'

She gave a watery smile. 'You always manage to be passing at the right moment.' She sniffed loudly, pulled out her handkerchief and blew into it. 'He turned me down, Joe. They won't sell me their ale. What am I going to do?'

He firmly hooked her arm into his. 'The first thing you're going to do is have a cup of coffee. I know a very nice coffee house on the High Street, and if you're a good girl I'll buy you a currant bun.'

'Oh, Joe. I couldn't eat anything. Really I couldn't.'

'You will, it'll make you feel better. Then we'll discuss what to do next. Come on.'

Without further ado he guided her through town towards the coffee house where he ordered freshly ground coffee and currant buns for them both. They ate in silence. Once finished, Joe sat back and smiled across at her.

'It's so unfair,' she blurted. 'I wanted this business so badly to give Georgie a secure future. It seemed the answer after he ran away. I vowed I'd find something that'd enable me to make a future but where I could be on hand for him. I know this is just what I'm looking for, and now my plans are all ruined because of that . . . that miserable old devil!' she cried as she pushed away her empty plate. 'I passed all their conditions but the old man said I was too young, with not enough experience, and if I went bankrupt his brewery would be involved and their name would be blackened.'

'I can see his point. But I also think he's being very unjust.' Joe shrugged his shoulders. 'But that's business, Annie. It's a harsh world and we all have to face setbacks.'

She looked at him with narrowed eyes. 'D'you mean I shouldn't give up?'

He smiled. 'You're getting the idea.'

'Try another brewery, you mean?'

'I always knew you were a bright woman. Brewster's are not the only brewers in town, are they? And if you're so determined to do something for that lad of yours . . .'

Annie beamed. 'Joe Saunt, what would I do without you?' She blushed and bowed her head. 'I'll go to see them all if necessary. I'm gonna get this tavern, and that's that. I'll show that Mr Brewster he's made a big mistake, not supplying me.'

Joe patted her arm. 'That's the spirit, gel. Does me good to see the smile back on your face. Come on, we'll have another cup before I have to get back to work.'

A week later Annie sat facing Mr Hoskins of J. Pen &

Company. Henry Hoskins was thirty-five years old. He had thick honey blond hair, a pleasant face and twinkling cornflower blue eyes. His mother had always said he'd have made a very pretty girl. Much to her relief, he'd turned into a handsome, very bright and charming young man.

He had escaped the chains of marriage, never finding a woman who had enchanted him enough to take the final step. As he sat with his hands clasped under his chin, listening intently to the young woman seated before him, his heart raced. For the first time in his life he was encountering a woman with brains as well as looks, and one who for her background was very articulate. He sat back and tried to detach himself. He needed to be clear on her business sense not just her looks and charm.

'I'm going to start by giving the place a good white wash all over, inside and out,' Annie continued, unaware of his scrutiny. 'The spittoons are going. I don't care what the old customers say, there'll be no room in my tavern for antiquated items like that. And there'll be no using of the slops to make up the ale neither. I'm going to put in some new tables and chairs and do food.'

Henry sat forward, his face wreathed in interest.

'Food?' he asked.

'Yes. Good, plain cooking. All freshly done, served on clean plates, and with a smile. I feel there's a real need for it. 'Specially at lunchtime for the workers who can't get home.' She grinned mischievously. 'And if they're eating, they'll be drinking, won't they?'

'I would certainly hope so.'

'And I'm going to do up the rooms upstairs and make them look nice and homely 'cos I'm gonna take in lodgers and I want them to feel comfortable. That'll be another sideline.' She stopped abruptly and looked expectantly at Henry, wondering if she had gone on about her ideas for far too long. 'Well, Mr Hoskins, what d'you think?'

'I think, Mrs Higgins, that J. Pen & Company would be delighted to do business with you.' He watched a broad smile break out on her face. 'And to show good faith, I'll give you your first two barrels of ale free.'

'Oh, Mr Hoskins, thank you,' she breathed delightedly. 'You've made the right decision. I won't let you down.'

'I hope not, young woman,' he said. 'I have to admit that I admire you. You seem to have everything planned, right down to the last detail. I like to see progress in the trade and I like your ideas very much. It might shake the other landlords up a bit. Yes, people like you are what's needed now. The trade has been allowed to stagnate for far too long.' He scratched his chin and frowned slightly. 'My uncle, unfortunately, is not so liberal-minded. He'll see this as a reckless gesture on my part.'

'Oh!' Annie's face fell. 'D'you think he might turn me down?'

'No, he can't. It might have been a different matter if I hadn't owned half the business. But it's me that's taking the gamble with you, and he'll see things my way eventually because you're going to be a success, Mrs Higgins. You promised me, didn't you?'

Annie's face lit up in delight. 'Yes, I am that. And as a gesture, the first drink you have on my premises will be on the house. After that you'll have to buy it like everyone else.'

'Thank you,' he laughed. 'I'll take you up on that.' He stood and offered her his hand. 'Right, I'll leave you for a moment while I sort out the paperwork with my assistant.'

An hour later, Annie sedately turned the corner of the street. She walked several yards down the cobbles then raised her arm in the air and shouted at the top of her voice.

'Whoopee!'

She lifted her skirt and skipped as fast as she could, dodging across the muddy road, narrowly missing a horse and cart, her face a picture of delight and merriment. Her plans were coming to fruition and she couldn't wait to get home and tell everyone the news, especially Joe. He would be so pleased for her, and it was only because of his advice that she had progressed this far.

She raced past two old ladies. They stopped and stared after her in disgust. They looked at each other and nodded in agreement.

'Drunk!'

Chapter Nineteen

Two hectic months later, Annie stood on the cobbles in Belgrave Road and looked across at the building facing her. A feeling of delight and excitement tinged with apprehension swept over her. She wrapped her arms around her body and hugged herself, squinting slightly as the early morning August sun rose over the roof of the Black Swan and shone down, casting a soft glow on the newly white washed walls. The once grimy windows that had been caked in the dust of years now sparkled. Annie felt proud that the hard toil they had all pitched in with over the last few weeks had achieved such astounding results, more than she had ever envisaged.

The badly neglected rooms upstairs had been thrown open, cleared of their cobwebs and ground in dirt and given a new lease of life. They had pretty sprigged curtains hanging at the windows, large beds covered with hand made patchwork quilts, oak wardrobes and tables. The cupboard at the top of the stairs held an enormous pile of freshly laundered linen. Everything was ready for their first occupants.

The once grimy cockroach-infested kitchen now gleamed and with its newly installed black-leaded range was ready to produce mouthwatering meals for the ever increasing numbers of hungry customers she prayed would patronise her establishment.

She smiled warmly. All their hard work had paid off. The old Black Swan had been positively transformed and under the new ownership of Mrs Annie Higgins would, she vowed to herself, become the best and most respected hostelry in

Leicester. And, if she wasn't being too optimistic, for miles around.

Annie nodded in satisfaction. Life was certainly getting better. Georgie had settled well after his adventure and she, regardless of what was in hand, made an effort to make more time for him, whether it be to hear his stumbling efforts to read, listen to his constant chatter or once, when his friends were otherwise occupied, play marbles in the gutter. She felt she had learned a hard lesson that night and one that she was never going to forget, regardless of her changing status in life.

Young Molly was blossoming into a lovely woman under her guidance, and ever since that dreadful night had taken to asking Annie's opinion on any number of matters relating to her everyday life. She had a lovely nature, was always ready and willing to help with any manner of chore, and her sense of humour and mimicry enchanted all who met her. She had become the perfect elder sister for Georgie, watching over him with a sisterly care. Annie blessed the day she had agreed to bring her with them.

She unfolded her arms, straightened her olive green linen dress and walked slowly across the road. She just had time to instruct the staff once more before the doors would be thrown open ready to receive their first customers.

Her only fear was that men, egged on by their wives or other believers in old-fashioned values, would give a landlady a wide berth. Her fears were unfounded. Before many weeks had passed the Black Swan's reputation for good food and ale served by happy, polite staff had grown to such an extent that she had had to employ another barman to cope.

All her rooms were fully booked for months ahead. Her lodgers, mainly working men away from their homes, found the comfort that Annie provided a haven after a hard day's work. They returned time after time, genuinely disheartened if she had nothing to offer them.

She knew she had succeeded when a gentlewoman approached her and enquired if she would consider letting her hold her daughter's wedding reception in the large parlour since it was impossible for it to be held in her own home. The arrangements were too far advanced to be cancelled and the poor woman had reached a stage of panic wondering what to do with her fifty guests. Annie was delighted to be of assistance. This gave her another idea and the *Leicester Mercury* was soon running advertisements: family parties catered for and entertained to the highest standards.

Annie kept having to pinch herself. The business was progressing far better than she had ever dared hope. But she worked long hours, her standards were high and she paid her staff well. These principles were obviously paying off. She was proud of the fact that all the people who had shown faith in her were being rewarded in the knowledge that their instincts had been correct. It was a comfort to know she had money in the bank. No longer would she have to make do and mend. She was very aware though that businesses could fail, and that she could very quickly return to the poverty she had once known. She worked even harder to make sure this never happened.

She looked forward with great enthusiasm to the future and what it would bring her. If she was successful then all would benefit, and that fact alone lent her renewed determination.

The results of the first stock take gave Annie grave concern. Something was wrong. She checked the columns over once more, frowned deeply and slammed shut the black ledger.

'I can't understand it, Joe. We've both gone over them and I'm at least ten pounds down. That's a lot of money.'

He ran his hand through his fair hair. 'Well, we could start again. Maybe we've missed something.'

Annie shook her head. 'We both know we've checked everything at least three times. You run your own business, Joe, you know instantly when something's amiss. There's one thing Wilfred Biddles taught me well and that's how to

337

do the books. He'd been in business all his life and they were like second nature to him.'

Joe nodded in agreement. 'Well, this can only mean one thing, Annie.'

'Oh, what's that?'

'It's got to be one of the staff.'

She shook her head fiercely. 'Oh, no, surely not? I can't believe that. They're all such nice people. They work hard and I pay them well. Why would they steal from me?'

'I don't know, Annie, but it must be one of them. There isn't any other explanation.'

She rubbed her hand across her forehead in exasperation. 'God, this is the last thing I need. I don't know how to handle this, Joe.' Her eyes opened wide in alarm. 'What if it's all of them? What do I do then?'

'It's not all of them, Annie.' He looked across the table at her and his eyes softened. 'You see, this is what happens. Someone gets itchy fingers and the suspicion falls on everyone. This is your business, Annie. You've worked damned hard to make a go of it. Do you really want to see it fail because someone is being dishonest?'

'No, I don't.'

'Well, sort it out. You're the only one who can do it. Because if you don't, whoever it is will get greedier and your profits will be non-existent shortly.'

Annie breathed deeply. 'You're right. Thanks, Joe. I do appreciate your help. I knew something was wrong but didn't quite know what.'

'I've told you, any time.' He rose and smiled warmly at her. 'I must be going, I'm afraid. If I don't hurry, I'll be late.'

'Oh, Joe, I'm so sorry. I've kept you from your family. I've been very inconsiderate.'

The corner of his mouth twitched. 'Oh, that's no problem. Millicent's arranged a musical evening, that's all, and I'm on strict instructions to attend.' He grimaced. 'We have the President of The Gentlewomen's Society attending.

338

Millicent is thrilled. I've been told it's quite an achievement to get this woman to one of your do's.'

'Oh, a musical evening, eh?' Annie said, looking impressed. 'What kind of music, Joe?'

He shrugged his shoulders. 'Oh, I don't know. Three severe-looking elderly ladies playing cellos, I think. It's not quite my idea of an evening's entertainment. I'll have a job keeping myself awake. But Millicent seems to think it will move us up in society circles. She's even arranged for a woman to come in and prepare some kind of fancy food.' He exhaled deeply. 'I suppose as long as it keeps Millicent happy . . .' He stopped abruptly and smiled at her. 'I'll see you soon, Annie, and you take care of yourself. I hope you get that business sorted out soon.'

'Yes, I will. The sooner the better, eh? I hope you enjoy your evening.'

Joe gave a laugh as he placed his cap on his head, turned and left the room.

He walked down the road, his steps slowing to a dawdle. He didn't want to go home, he had known that all the time he had been sitting in Annie's small sitting room helping her sort out her problems. He wanted to stay with her, to be allowed the privilege of taking off his shoes, stretching his long legs on to the hearth, sitting contently all night, listening to her merry chatter and infectious laugh.

Excuses for his visits were getting more and more trivial and he was sure she knew. But the look in her eyes when he arrived kept him going back, time after time. He felt wanted, needed and very welcome. Which was more than he felt in his own home. If 'home' was the word for the four walls he returned to every night. He was just the provider, the figurehead in a loveless marriage. His two daughters, once his pride and joy, were turning into replicas of Millicent: grabbing all they could, giving nothing in return. He was only there tonight to complete the picture so that she could hold her head up and play her part, convincing others what a happy, successful family they were.

It was all lies, but what could he do? They were his responsibility. ''Til death do us part' the vicar had said. The words were etched deeply into Joe's mind. They seemed so cold and final, but he had agreed to abide by them and his integrity would force him to do so.

He sighed deeply and quickened his pace. He might as well be home on time. If not, Millicent would be more unbearable than she normally was and that thought really wasn't worth dwelling on.

Annie stared blankly at the girl seated opposite her and watched the tears flood down her cheeks.

'Why, Gladys? I don't understand you. I pay all my staff much more than the going rate. You get to take home any leftover food and you work in nice surroundings, much better than any other tavern in town. So why steal from me?'

Gladys Harbuttle blew hard into her handkerchief and sniffed loudly.

'I'm sorry,' she blubbered.

'But you still haven't told me why?'

'It was Harry's idea. He said you wouldn't notice. He said women shouldn't be in business.'

'Oh, did he! And who's this Harry?'

'Me boyfriend,' she said, lowering her head in shame.

Annie inwardly groaned. Boyfriends were becoming the bane of her life.

'And what exactly were you both up to?' she said coldly.

Gladys bowed her head even more. 'I'd give him too much change and slip him a couple of bottles of gin every week, usually on a Saturday when everyone else was too busy to notice.'

'And what did he do with all this gin? Drink it?'

'Oh, no. He sold it.'

'So, he was not only drinking here practically free, he was selling my spirits also?'

Gladys nodded.

'And what did you get out of all this?'

'Eh?'

Annie leaned forward. 'Did you split the profits?'

'Oh, no. I never took a thing.'

Annie sighed deeply and leaned back in her chair.

'Let me get this straight. You not only took money out of the till, you took bottles out of the store cupboard – and you never received anything for your troubles?'

'No.'

'But why? Why do something like this for no gain on your part?'

Gladys stared at her blankly.

'Oh, I see. It was to keep Harry, is that it?'

Gladys nodded again.

Annie looked at the plump, unattractive girl and her heart went out to her. The Gladyses of the world didn't stand a chance in the love stakes and this girl was obviously very aware of it and was hanging on to the only person who had ever shown her any kind of attention.

Annie solemnly shook her head. 'You know what this means, don't you?'

'No?'

'I'll have to let you go. Not only have I lost my profits, I'm losing a good barmaid. I'm very disappointed in you. When I first came here you were so helpful and kind. It was through you I really got a feel for the place and settled down. I trusted you, Gladys, and you have let me down badly.'

'Oh, Annie,' Gladys sobbed. 'Please don't sack me. I wouldn't get another job like this, and with me mam and dad not working, we'd all starve.'

'But didn't you think on that while you were cheating me? No, I suppose not. It's been going on that long it's become natural to take whatever you wanted.' Annie paused thoughtfully for a moment. 'Go downstairs and wait in the yard. Tell Sid I want to see him.'

Gladys nodded and scuttled off.

'Well, Sid. What do I do about Gladys? Do I sack her or give her another chance?'

He shrugged his shoulders. 'Don't ask me. I've never been consulted on staff problems before. Mr Biddles took care of all that.'

'Well, *I'm* consulting you. You're my head barman, Sid, and to be honest, you of all people should have spotted what was going on.' She frowned at the now quailing Sidney Pickles. 'Right, I want everyone assembled at four o'clock in the parlour. No excuses. I want them all there. If there's customers to be served, then they'll have to wait.' This was against her usual ruling: Customers come before everything. But she had a problem, and the sooner it was sorted out the better.

'Yes, missus,' Sidney said, flicking his forelock.

At four o'clock sharp she stood facing all eight of her workforce, face set grimly as she addressed them.

'Because of one girl's actions you all came under suspicion. I will not have a situation like this again. I cannot run this business without the trust and loyalty of my staff. If anyone disagrees with this they can leave now. For those of you who wish to stay, woe betide if ever any of you let me down again. I'll have you out of the door before you know it.'

She paused for breath and eyed each of them in turn.

'Gladys has been foolish but I have decided to give her another chance, and I don't expect her to be punished any further by you.' She stopped speaking and watched Gladys's face light up in disbelief. 'But don't be fooled into thinking I'm an easy target. When I first came here I was one of you. I learned all the tricks there are to know so don't think for a moment I'm blind to anything that might go on. This has taught me a lesson, a very hard lesson, and I have learned well from it. Now please return to your work and I hope never to have to speak to any of you like this again.'

She breathed deeply as she watched them file out. She hoped she had handled the situation well and had impressed on all of them that she would stand no recurrences. She also hoped she had been fair and just. But only time would tell.

Chapter Twenty

Georgie thundered up the stairs and threw his satchel into the corner of the small living room.

'Mam, I'm home,' he shouted at the top of his voice.

Annie woke with a start from the snooze she was having after the lunchtime session. She rubbed her eyes and stretched herself.

'Hello, son. Had a good day?'

'All right.'

Annie swung her legs down from the sofa and looked fondly at her eight-and-a-half-year-old son. His red hair was darkening and losing some of its curl. He was growing and threatening to become as tall and handsome as his father.

'What did you do today then?' she asked with interest, rising and picking up his belongings.

'Not much.'

'Not much? That's what you always say. You must have done something?'

Georgie shrugged his shoulders. 'Me and Arfur are bestest in class at our times tables. I had to stand up and say them on me own today.'

'Well done,' Annie said in delight. She rushed over and gave him a tight hug. 'I'm really proud of you.'

Georgie struggled from her grasp. 'Ged off, Mam.'

'Oh, I see. Too big for a hug from your mother, are you?' Annie grabbed him again and gave him a big wet kiss on his cheek. 'Well, how do you like that then?'

'Mam!' Georgie retorted, disgusted. He pulled a face and

wiped his cheek with the back of his hand. 'Can I have something to eat?'

Annie released her grip. 'Yes, there's some bread and cheese in the larder. I'll make a sandwich for you.'

Several minutes later Georgie sat on a wooden stool in the tiny kitchen swinging his legs beneath the table, his mouth crammed with bread and cheese.

'I seen Auntie Kath on the way home from school.'

Annie looked at her son and frowned. 'What have I told you about speaking with your mouth full? I didn't understand a word you said.'

Georgie gulped hard. 'I said, I'd seen Auntie Kath today.'

Annie's head jerked up. 'Don't you mean someone who looked like Auntie Kath?'

Georgie took another bite of his bread. 'No, it were definitely Auntie Kath. She was standing over the road. When she seen me she walked off.' He scraped back the chair and stood up, ramming a piece of bread and cheese into his pocket. 'I'm off now, Mam. Can I take this sandwich for Arfur?'

Annie nodded absent-mindedly. She shook her head and shrugged her shoulders. He must have been mistaken, she thought, fear of the past rearing its ugly head. Now what on earth would Kath of all people be doing around here? No plausible reason came to mind. Georgie was definitely seeing things. She rose, cleared the table and went to freshen herself before the evening shift came on, giving no more thought to the conversation.

Next morning Sid popped his head around the kitchen door as Annie was helping the cook prepare vegetables.

'There's a woman to see yer.'

She stopped what she was doing. 'What does she want? A job?'

'Didn't say.'

'What's her name?'

'Didn't say.'

344

Annie put down the potato she was peeling and wiped her hands on her apron.

'Did she say anything?'

'Just that she wanted to see yer. Asked for yer by name. I got the impression she knows yer.'

'Oh!' Annie fumed. She hadn't any appointments and wasn't expecting anyone. They were short staffed at the moment due to illness and she had no time for social visits. 'Ask her to wait in the parlour, I'll be through in a moment.'

Annie finished what she was doing, quickly checked her appearance and walked towards the parlour. She put a smile on her face and opened the door. She froze as she recognised the woman standing at the far side of the room. How could she ever forget that profile? Georgie had been right. She would know in future not to dismiss his seemingly idle chatter. The woman turned and smiled a greeting.

'Hello, Annie. Nice place you have. Seems you've done really well for yerself.'

She shut the door and took several steps into the room. 'Well, you'd already know that from the letters I sent my uncle.' She clasped her hands together and raised her head. 'What are you doing here, Kath?'

'I've come to ask your help, Annie. Like you did of me.'

Her face darkened. 'And why should you of all people need my help? If I remember rightly you were quite capable of managing things for yourself.'

Kath flinched at her tone. 'Look, we can't talk here. Can't we go somewhere more private?' she asked as she weaved her way through the tables already set up for a private function that was to be held later in the day. 'I only ask that you'll hear me out. Then, if you want me to, I'll go.'

Annie's mind raced. What on earth could Kath possibly want from her? It had never crossed her mind that they might meet again. All the evil that this woman had concocted! Annie wanted to throw her out and her instincts told her to do just that. But her better nature took over and she found herself leading Kath up the stairs and into her private living room.

They sat facing each other in silence until her aunt finally spoke.

'I treated you badly, Annie.'

'You admit that then?'

Kath nodded. 'Yes, and not just you. I've been a bad, selfish woman and it took you to make me realise it.'

'Me?'

'Yes,' she said slowly. 'After you left, neither Archie nor the farm seemed the same.'

'That's because of what you did. He probably couldn't forgive you.'

'I admit that, Annie, and I tried very hard to put things right. I tried to act the way you would, but I never seemed to get it right. Everything I did was wrong. Archie would look at me strangely. I suppose he was waiting for me to be cruel and nasty and couldn't get used to the idea that I'd changed. The folk in the village were worse. None of them would speak to me after it all got out.'

'I can understand that, Kath. Reputations are hard to live down and people have long memories.'

She sighed softly. 'I've left Archie. It was the best thing to do. Even he agreed in the end and seemed quite relieved.'

'Left him?'

Kath nodded. 'Yes, several weeks ago. I've been trying to make a go of things on my own. But I can't, Annie, and that's why I've come to you. It would never have worked out between us. He deserves better than me, and this way at least he has a chance.'

'And what is it you want from me?' Annie said coldly, already knowing the answer.

'I wondered if you would take us in? Just until I get meself straight.'

'Us being . . .'

'Me and Lucy.' She lowered her head. 'I've never seen John Matthews since the day he left the farm.'

Annie flinched at the mention of his name. It brought back painful memories, ones she would prefer to forget.

'I'll work hard, Annie,' Kath continued. 'I'll do anything you ask of me. I just want you to know that I'm not the old Kath that you knew. I want another start where no one knows me. That way maybe I can build a life for me and Lucy. Please, please give me a chance?' she said, raising her eyes pleadingly.

Annie sat back in her chair and sighed softly. Just what was she to do? She eyed Kath searchingly. Was it possible for anyone to undergo a complete personality change? She certainly seemed to have done so. The woman seated opposite her was softer. The old Kath would never have begged help from anyone. Annie put her hand to her chin, considering. If only she could spare the time to pay a visit to her uncle and Matty She would certainly know then whether Kath was telling the truth or not. But there was no way she could leave the tavern for the foreseeable future and letters took their time. Too much time. She had a decision to make now, one she would have preferred not to have faced.

She breathed deeply. She had taken a chance on Gladys and it had worked. Maybe it would with Kath. And, in any case, would she ever forgive herself if she found out later that Kath was genuine and she had turned her away? An idea began to form in her mind.

'I'll give you a chance. Just one chance, mind, and if you ever let me down . . .'

Kath's face lit up in relief. 'Oh, thank you, Annie. You won't regret this, I can assure you.'

'I hope not,' she said, taking a deep breath. She rose and stood with her back to the fireplace. 'There's a small building attached to the side of the tavern. I had thought of converting it into extra bedrooms, but with a little work we could make it into a shop.'

'Shop?' Kath repeated.

'Yes. You could make those delicious meat pies, bread and

347

cakes and we could sell them. You can keep half the profits and the room above will do for your living quarters. It only needs freshening up. It was all white washed and painted when I did the other alterations. I've just never got around to using it.'

'Oh, Annie,' Kath breathed. 'It sounds perfect. How can I ever thank you?'

'You can thank me, Kath, and you know how.'

'Yes, I do,' she said slowly. 'And it won't be long before you reap the benefit of my thanks.'

Annie looked at her for a moment, reading several meanings into those last words. She took a deep breath. She had said she would give the woman a chance and already she was doubting her.

'Come with me and I'll show you over the place,' she said, wishing she felt happier about the situation.

'Annie Higgins, you amaze me!' Martha stared at her sister-in-law in astonishment. 'You really mean you're letting her stay?'

Annie shrugged her shoulders. 'What else could I do?'

'You could have told her to clear off.'

'Martha!'

'Well, Annie, for God's sake. The woman's bad.'

Annie sighed. 'Well, I've agreed to have her now. But I can assure you, I'll be keeping me eyes on her. She won't be able to breathe without my knowledge.'

'You'll need eyes in the back of your head for that one.'

Annie grimaced and nodded.

'I just hope you don't live to regret this decision.'

'So do I, Martha.'

The time seemed to fly and before Annie realised, Kath had been with her for over two months. The shop had been set up and like the tavern was flourishing. Kath's reputation was spreading and people came from far afield to buy some of her pies and bread to take home for their dinner, and of course they would also pop into the tavern for a quick drink. Annie's idea had been a good one and she was pleased.

Kath was as good as her word. She was pleasant and sociable and not one nasty word or retort had passed her lips since the day she had arrived. She went about her work with a spring in her step, a smile on her face and a nice word for everyone, and even pitched in behind the bar whenever they were busy.

The biggest shock had been Lucy. The girl had undergone a transformation. She was a pleasure to have around. Her sunny disposition captured everyone, even Georgie, and the pair quickly became fast friends. She had even been introduced to Arthur and the rest of the gang and was readily included as a member, which was an honour indeed, especially for a girl.

Annie was glad she had taken them in. Her decision had been correct. She was just so thankful she hadn't followed her first instincts and gone the other way.

Chapter Twenty-One

Sid poked his head around the parlour door as Annie was putting the finishing touches to the tables for a special dinner she was preparing for that evening. She had a party of seventy people coming in and hoped it wouldn't be too much of a squash.

'There's a bloke to see yer. Looks quite smart and he's got a briefcase.'

Annie looked at Sid and narrowed her eyes. 'What's he want?'

'Didn't say.'

'What's his name? Didn't say,' echoed Annie. 'Oh, give me a minute to take off me apron then show him in. He'll have to see me in here, I ain't got time to go upstairs,' she said flatly.

Why can't people come at a decent time, not when I'm at my busiest? she thought crossly. She whipped off her apron and patted her hair, pushing a stray tendril back into place.

The door opened and a man entered. A wide smile crossed his face as he held out his hand in greeting.

'Good morning, Mrs Higgins. I'm Bernard Millington from Brewster's Brewery. I am their chief salesman.'

Annie accepted the proffered hand and shook it firmly. 'And what do Brewster's Brewery want from me?'

Her eyes quickly scanned the man. He was in his mid-forties, smartly dressed, cleanshaven and with a shock of thick greying hair, showing just the final traces of the bright auburn it had once been. He had an air of confidence about him, obviously gained over the years in his profession and by the calibre of people he met. His slate grey eyes never left her face as he put down his briefcase, entwined his hands and took a deep breath.

'I have a proposition for you, Mrs Higgins.'

'Oh! What kind of proposition? As you are no doubt aware, I don't do business with Brewster's.'

'This proposition isn't anything to do with Brewster's.' He stopped abruptly and looked around the room. 'Er . . . Is there anywhere we could speak more privately? I see you'll be expecting people in here shortly.'

Annie frowned. She really had no time to spare at the moment but was intrigued by this man and decided she might as well hear him out.

'Wait here. I'll get someone to take over for me, but I can't be long.'

She left the room in search of Kath and found her bustling around in the kitchen, lifting the lids on pans and sniffing and tasting the contents with a large metal ladle. 'Kath, can you take over for me in the parlour? You know what to do. I just have to see someone for a moment.'

She stopped what she was doing and turned to face Annie as she wiped her hands on her snow white apron. 'No problem. This meat for the batch of pies I'm making for tomorrow is just about done. Take as long as you like.'

'Thanks, Kath. Oh, and please don't forget to make up Elsie's food basket, and put plenty in. Georgie can take it round when he comes home from school.'

'Yes, I'll do that. But if you don't mind me saying, it must cost you a fortune to keep sending these baskets up.'

Annie smiled, knowing what Kath was thinking. 'It does. But Elsie wouldn't survive without them. She's my friend, whatever you might think of her, and I'll do whatever I can for as long as it takes.'

She left Kath to her tasks and showed Bernard Millington into her living room, motioning him to take a seat.

'Would you like a drink?'

'No, thank you. I don't while I'm talking business.'

Annie sat down opposite and waited.

'You've made a great success of this place, Mrs Higgins. It's unrecognisable from its origins with the Biddle family. That's one of the reasons I'm here.'

'Oh, I don't see . . .'

'I'll come straight to the point, Mrs Higgins. I know you're a busy woman.' He took a breath. 'I've worked for Brewster's all my life and now I've got a chance to do something to improve my lot. But I need a partner.'

'Partner? I'm not interested in any partnerships. I prefer to work on me own.' Annie made to rise.

'Please, hear me out. I think you'll be interested in what I have to say.'

'All right.' She relented. 'I'll listen, it's the least I can do.' She settled herself in her seat once more.

'As I was saying,' Bernard Millington began again, 'I've worked for Brewster's for a long time and have been a very loyal employee. But I feel it's time to do something for myself. I've come into a . . . well substantial amount of money.'

'Oh!'

'Yes. From an old great-aunt who lived up north.'

'Ah.' Annie smiled. 'That explains your accent.'

'What about my accent?' he asked.

'Well, it's not from around here, is it?'

'Yes, actually it is. I lived for a while with the aunt I've just mentioned and it's surprising how quickly you pick up accents and mannerisms. Obviously I haven't managed to lose them.' He sat back in his chair. 'To get back to the point of my visit, I've found out that the Imperial Hotel is coming on the market. I've done a lot of research and I'm satisfied that the place has great potential, over and above what it's doing now, and its position in the town couldn't be better.'

'The Imperial?' Annie said quizzically. 'That's on Humberstone Gate, isn't it?'

'Yes, it is. As I said, the ideal location.'

'I've never heard a thing about it coming up for sale. Are you sure?'

'Mrs Higgins, let me assure you I wouldn't be here if I wasn't absolutely positive of my facts. We supply the hotel with our ale and other products. I know the proprietor very well. He told me confidentially that he wants to retire. His family have owned the hotel since it was built and he wants to go and live in Lincolnshire with his only daughter. He doesn't want to make it general knowledge in case the other members of the family get wind.' He lowered his voice. 'There's a deep rift that's been going on for years. He wants the sale cut and dried so he can leave quietly and without their knowledge.'

'Oh, I see.'

'He obviously wants a good price but is willing to take any reasonable offer.' Bernard Millington inched forward, a look of excitement crossing his face. 'I've thought long and hard about this, Mrs Higgins, and if I can get the right person to come in with me, someone like yourself . . .' He gestured with his hands. 'You've done a marvellous job with this place and I've watched your progress with interest. I know for a fact old Brewster is kicking himself for not giving you a chance.' He waited and watched the look of pleasure spread across Annie's face. 'Just think what we could both do with the Imperial. Why, we'd have a gold mine on our hands.'

Annie stared thoughtfully into space. 'Mmm. It's a big place. I've never been inside, but it certainly looks extensive from the outside.'

'It is,' Bernard enthused. 'The Imperial has twenty bedrooms, a large function hall that's hardly used, two bars, and the biggest cellar you could imagine.'

'Does it need a lot of work doing to it?' Annie asked, thoughts running rife through her head. 'If so it'd cost, a big place like that.'

'Not much, unless we wanted to make big alterations. Knocking down any walls or adding to it. But we could do things like that later. There's nothing major that struck me. And, anyway, don't forget the costs would be split two ways.' Bernard stared at her expectantly. 'Think of the potential,

Mrs Higgins. Think what could be done with a place like that? The possibilities would be endless.'

'Yes, I know,' Annie said, frowning deeply. She paused and eyed him. 'How much does he want?'

'Only four thousand.'

'How much?' Annie gasped. 'I could buy a dozen taverns and a brewery for that kinda money.'

Bernard smiled. 'Hardly, Mrs Higgins. All right, I admit it's not cheap, but it's on a prime site. And anyway the price is between two of us, remember?' He frowned, sighed deeply, rose and picked up his briefcase. 'I can see I'm wasting your time. It's nice to have met you.'

She stared up at him. 'Just a minute. Give me time to think.'

He sat down again.

Annie sat quietly for several minutes. Finally she raised her eyes in Bernard's direction. 'I'll need an inspection of the place before I even think any more about it. Can you arrange one?'

'Yes, of course. I'll get in touch when I've fixed it up. But you'll have to keep quiet about all of this.'

'Oh, why?'

'As I said before, apart from not wanting his family to know, if word got round in the trade that he was selling other people might be interested and the price could shoot up out of our reach. There's a lot of people who'd be interested in the Imperial, believe me.'

'Yes, there would be. All right, I won't say a word.'

Bernard Millington shook her hand. 'I'll be in touch. No, please don't get up, I can see myself out.'

Annie sat back in her chair. She placed her hands behind her head and stared up at the ceiling. The Imperial. Even the name sounded majestic. If she could get her hands on a place like that and make a success of it as she had done with the Black Swan, she'd be made for life. Georgie and her future would be more than secure. The idea of a partnership didn't appeal to her in the slightest but she had been most impressed by Bernard Millington. He seemed so positive and obviously knew what he was talking about. But raising half the money she needed for her share wasn't going to be easy. Raising all of it would be nigh on impossible.

She checked her reflection in the mirror and wondered what Joe would make of all this. She smiled. The thought of him always sent a pleasurable thrill through her body. Should she risk breaking her promise to Bernard and ask Joe's advice before she went any further? She frowned. Joe might try to talk her out of it. Tell her to build this business a while before expanding. No, she decided firmly, I'll keep this matter to myself, at least for the time being. Besides, she hadn't seen much of Joe over the past few weeks. His business had suddenly boomed, he was working all hours and could do without her problems at the moment.

Bernard Millington has approached me because of my reputation and expertise, she thought proudly. That in itself tells me all I need to know. I'll do this by myself. Besides, places like the Imperial don't come up very often, if ever. I might never get another opportunity like this again.

A warm feeling rose in her. This proposition interested her, interested her greatly, and she couldn't wait to investigate further.

Eh, little Annie Higgins being a partner in the Imperial Hotel!

Now that she had given the idea more thought, the possibility interested her beyond belief.

Three days later, Bernard Millington met Annie at their appointed time outside the entrance to the Imperial Hotel.

He strode up to her and guided her out of earshot of the impressive commissionaire, elaborately dressed in a dark blue, heavily braided uniform.

'I'm sorry, Mrs Higgins,' he whispered. 'But our appointment with Daniel Shipton, the landlord, has had to be cancelled. His daughter's not too well and he's gone up to Lincoln to see her.'

356

Annie bit her lip in disappointment. 'Oh, and I was so looking forward to seeing the place. I've arranged to be covered for a couple of hours. I don't know when I'll manage again. Getting away from the Swan is going to be difficult over the next few weeks, I have so much on.'

Bernard pursed his lips. 'His absence needn't stop us. We can still look around.'

'Can we?'

'If you wish. Although we'd have to be discreet.' He eyed her keenly. 'But if you think about it, this could work in our favour. We could view the hotel unescorted and see exactly what we want, within reason. Besides, we have to make up our minds almost instantly. Any delays could cost us the place.'

'Yes.' She paused thoughtfully. 'All right,' she said, eyes twinkling. 'Discreet it is.'

She stood in the foyer of the Imperial Hotel and gazed around. She tried to calm the overwhelming feeling of excitement that enveloped her. She knew the instant she walked through the double entrance doors that the place had great potential.

The hotel was enormous compared with the Black Swan and she could easily visualise the magnificent functions she could organise and hold comfortably within these walls. The large foyer was dominated by a reception counter, serviced by smart uniformed staff. Through an archway, a room twice the size of her parlour housed high-backed armchairs and low tables where guests could sit and partake of refreshments and entertain their friends. Every spare corner housed aspidistra plants, protruding from elaborate jardinieres. Annie had no love of these plants and smiled to herself. If she moved in, they went.

Guided by Bernard Millington, they quickly surveyed as many rooms as possible. If questioned, they were to be visitors looking for guests. They managed to slip in unobserved to a bedroom and Annie looked around in awe. The

357

elaborate furnishings made her lodging rooms feel sparse and rather homely in comparison.

She grabbed hold of Bernard's arm. 'Are you certain that he's selling? Seems criminal somehow to sell a place like this, 'specially when it's been in the family for so long.'

'I'm certain. Anyway, I've already told you his reasons.'

Annie nodded slowly and they continued with their tour. The more she saw, the more enchanted she was. And the more too she realised that the asking price was a never to be repeated bargain. She'd be a fool to let this chance pass her by.

She breathed deeply and tried to hide her excitement. They sat down in the foyer and Bernard ordered coffee. It was served in tiny white china cups by a stiff waiter who bowed as he turned and left them. Bernard spooned several spoons of demerara sugar into his cup and stirred it slowly. He picked up his cup, took a sip of the delicious coffee, put it down and smiled across at her.

'Well, what do you think?'

Annie paused for a moment before she spoke. She didn't want to appear too keen. 'I think it's got possibilities,' she said slowly. 'The decorations are in excellent order and I have a few ideas on how we can bring in new customers.' She ran her tongue over her teeth. 'How much do you think he'd come down?'

'Down?' Bernard shook his head gravely. 'He won't, Mrs Higgins. I've already got him as low as he'll go. I haggled with him before I even approached you about our partnership. He knows as well as I do that the place is worth much more than he's prepared to take. The land alone, because of the location, is worth over a thousand. Then there's the building and the goodwill. But now that you've seen the place, even you have to admit it's a bargain?'

Annie smiled. 'Yes, it is.' She raised her eyes to meet his. 'I'm interested, Mr Millington. Very interested. It's a pity I couldn't have met Mr Shipton to discuss matters.'

'I agree. But in a way, I'm relieved. Because he doesn't know I'm thinking of taking a partner.'

'What difference would your having a partner make to him?'

'None, I suppose. It's just that I've never mentioned the fact before. You see, he's very jittery about the situation. As I've said before, if his family got to hear about it, it could jeopardise everything. Don't forget, I've known him a long time and over the years we've become good friends; he trusts me and I wouldn't like to do anything to break that trust.'

'That's very commendable of you, Mr Millington.'

'Thank you,' Bernard said, smiling broadly. He looked hard at her for a moment. 'Mrs Higgins, let me put your mind at rest on one matter I know is bothering you.' He bent forward. 'You can trust me. I know what I'm doing. It may seem all cloak and dagger to you but even you must have been in the trade long enough to know that the buying and selling of businesses like this goes on all the time. How often have you heard that pubs and taverns have changed hands and you knew nothing about it until the new owner had settled in? Whether it be for financial reasons or just to stop trade from dropping off.'

Annie sighed and relaxed. 'Yes, you're right. I bought my own place in similar circumstances. The creditors were after Wilfred Biddles and he needed money fast and was only too willing to accept mine. He could have got a better price if he'd have waited, but he hadn't the time.'

'Well, this is not quite the same, there are no creditors after Daniel Shipton, but he does want a quick sale. I personally think he's pulling the wool over his family's eyes, keeping them in the dark about the sale of this place, but how or why is really none of my business. I want this place, Mrs Higgins, and I want it in partnership with you. I'll leave you to run the place as you see fit. Because,' he paused slightly, 'I intend to be a sleeping partner.'

'You do?' Annie said, leaning forward.

'Yes. I wasn't going to say anything until I knew you were

interested, but I intend to retire to a cottage in the country. I, er . . . have a lady friend and we're going to settle down,' he said shyly. 'I see this place as an investment. I could live on my share of the profits quite comfortably. As you would be doing most of the work, it's only fair that your share would be greater than mine.'

Annie looked at him quizzically. 'But why not just invest your money? Why go to all this trouble if you're not going to be on hand?'

Bernard smiled. 'That's why I picked on you, Mrs Higgins. I know what you'll do with this place, and I know my money will give me a far higher return in the long run than any bank.'

'You trust me that much?'

'Yes. You have an excellent reputation in the trade. Landlords I have spoken to hold you in high esteem, even though you have taken custom away from them. They only wish they'd thought of your ideas first.'

'Do they? I never realised. I must be honest, I do have plenty and can't wait to get started on the Imperial.' She clasped her hands together. 'I still have to think about it seriously, though.'

Bernard nodded. 'Yes, that's understandable. I never expected a woman of your intelligence to jump into a venture such as this without careful consideration. Well, I've done all the convincing I can. It's your choice now. But I can only give you a couple of days before I need a firm commitment.'

'Oh, it's not the hotel, Mr Millington. Your powers of persuasion have convinced me I can't live without the place. I don't think I could ever sleep soundly again knowing it was in someone else's hands. No, it's the raising of the money that's my concern. I could be risking everything I've got. I have a son to consider. I could be putting his whole future in jeopardy.'

'Let me assure you, Mrs Higgins, buying this place poses no risk. I hope you'll pardon me for being presumptuous, but I've worked out that the maximum loan you would need would be paid off in a matter of ten years at the most, that's with trade as it stands now – and that is also presuming you need to borrow all of your stake. But, please,' he raised his hand and smiled at her sincerely, 'I want this to be your own free choice. As you say, you have a lot to consider. It's not the same for me. My stake was an inheritance. If I lost it, I would reluctantly return to my job, but I know that will never happen because I'm positive the hotel is a sound proposition.' He paused for a moment. 'Just one last word and I'll leave you to make your decision.' He took a breath. 'I'd hate you to turn this down and regret it later.'

Annie smiled. 'So would I. Please give me a week, Mr Millington. That's all I ask.'

He shook his head slowly. 'I'm afraid that's too long, Mrs Higgins. He's expecting my offer in the next day or so.'

'As soon as that? But I'll need a week . . .'

'He won't wait that long, Mrs Higgins. If the money is the problem, I know a good chap with a sound reputation and he won't fiddle you with high interest rates.'

Annie ran her hand over her brow. 'All right. Give me his name just in case and come to the tavern the day after tomorrow. I'll give you my answer then. Although I can't see what all the rush is for. This is a mighty big undertaking and I would have liked longer to think it through.'

'Sometimes we have to make snap decisions. That's what this game is all about.'

'Some game,' Annie said as she rose and Bernard followed.

They stopped outside the imposing entrance doors and firmly shook hands.

'Until Thursday afternoon,' he said. He touched his hat and left her to take one last look at the Imperial Hotel before she made her way home, her mind full to overflowing.

After the Black Swan had been locked up for the night, Annie sat by the fire deep in thought. It was well after midnight and all were in bed.

She lay back in her chair and closed her eyes. She wanted the Imperial Hotel. She wanted it more than anything and

361

couldn't believe her luck that Bernard Millington had come to her above everyone else. He seemed such a sincere man and she felt honoured by his high regard for her. She knew she wanted to make a great success of the place if only to repay his trust.

But raising the money required was going to prove a problem. She had thought long and hard over the matter and had to act quickly if she was going to proceed. She didn't want to sell the Black Swan; it would always be a reminder of her humble beginnings. Besides, she was very attached to the place and it would break her heart to have to part with it, despite her strong desire for the Imperial.

She much preferred, if possible, to raise a mortgage. That way she could keep the Swan. It was worth far in excess of the money she had paid, business couldn't be better, and she knew her bank manager would be only too willing to take a risk. But it would not raise all she needed. There would still be a shortfall.

Suddenly a picture of Joe came to mind. Would he be willing to make her a loan? She knew his business was doing better than ever, she also knew he had good business sense. Would he trust her enough with his money until she could pay it back with interest?

She opened her eyes and held her hands out towards the fire to warm them. She would ask him. No harm could come of that. If you didn't ask, you didn't get. Wasn't that the saying? She would ask him tomorrow when he came by for his lunch. If he declined then she would raise the shortfall by other means. She wanted that hotel.

Suddenly a sound startled her and her head jerked up. She saw Molly framed in the doorway.

'Oh, Annie. I'm sorry, I didn't realise you were still up.'

She smiled warmly. 'Come in. What's up, can't you sleep?'

'No,' said Molly, walking in and sitting on the rug by the hearth. She pulled her nightdress over her bare legs and sighed deeply.

The tone of her voice and her deep sigh made Annie eye

her charge. It suddenly registered with her that the young girl had been very quiet of late, and she became concerned.

'Is there anything troubling you, Molly? You've been very quiet these past few weeks? It's not anything to do with Kath, is it?'

'Oh, no. Kath's all right. I must admit I was very frightened when she first came here. Thought she'd soon be up to her old tricks. But no, she treats me all right. And Georgie – fair fusses round him, she does.'

Annie smiled, glad of what she was hearing. 'Well, what is it then?'

Molly grimaced and sighed deeply. 'It's me job, Annie, I hate it.'

'Hate it! But it was your dream to work in a posh store. Why do you hate it? What's gone wrong?'

Molly sniffed as tears stung her eyes. 'It's that Mrs Syndicombe – she treats me like muck. Molly do this. Molly get that,' she mimicked. 'And since I had that trouble with Ernest, she won't let me do any modelling. I still haven't served any customers either.'

'Oh, Molly. Surely it ain't that bad?'

'It is. Her and the three other assistants earn all the commission. All I ever get to do is clear up after everybody and serve the tea. And them floor walkers! All they do is look down their nose at me and make me feel awkward. I think it's 'cos I come from a village. They think I'm a country bumpkin. I tell you, Annie, I'm just miserable, only I didn't want to say in case you sent me home.'

Annie rose and rushed over to the young girl. 'Molly, me duck. Why didn't you tell me before? Are you really that unhappy?'

'I'm not lying, Annie. I hate the place. I dread going in every morning.' She sniffed loudly again. 'Can't I work here for you?' she asked.

Annie stared at her. 'It ain't really the life for you, is it? Your mother let you come because she thought you'd be working in a shop, not a tavern.'

'She won't mind, Annie. She don't care what I do so long as I'm happy. Anyway, I help you out when you're short. I know I ain't worked behind the bar, but that's only 'cos you won't let me. But I've helped with the setting up and waitressing.'

'All right, Molly,' Annie cut in. 'I don't like the thought of you being unhappy.' She paused for a moment whilst Molly stared at her expectantly. 'Look, I tell you what. I'll let you work here on one condition.'

'Anything, Annie!'

'That you write to your mother and ask her permission first.'

Molly's face beamed in delight. 'Oh, she'll let me, Annie. She trusts you. I'll write tomorrow. No, tonight. I'll do it tonight. And does that mean I don't have to go into that place ever again?'

Annie looked at her tenderly. 'Not if it makes you so unhappy.'

'Oh, Annie,' Molly said, clasping her hands in delight. 'I'm so relieved. I'll get up at the crack of dawn and give the place a good going over for you.'

'No need for that. But, yes, you can get up at a reasonable time, I'm sure I can find you plenty to do. I've a supper to arrange tomorrow for the Market Traders' Society.'

'Oh, that's sounds good. I'll do whatever you want.'

The next lunchtime, Annie sat facing Joe in her small living room.

'I'll lend you the money, Annie. But why all the secrecy?'

'I can't tell you what it's for, Joe, not at the moment. I promised you see. But you do trust me, don't you?'

He smiled. Truth be told, he would lie down and die for her. ''Course, I do,' he said quickly. 'I'm just concerned that it's not anything underhand.'

'Oh, Joe, as if I'd get involved in anything that wasn't sound. All I can say is that it's the chance of a lifetime and I'd be a fool not to go after it.'

'Well, it must be a good proposition if the bank has agreed

to give you the majority of the finance needed. Now if you'd have asked me six months ago, I'd have had to have said no. As it is, I can just about spare what you need.'

Annie nodded, ashamed at the white lie she had told him. She hadn't approached the bank, they would have taken too long and would want to know too many details. She had gone to a money lender on Bernard Millington's recommendation. His rates were high, but she was in no doubt that they would be paid back in full, and in less time than Bernard Millington had predicted if all went according to her plans. If it didn't . . . She shuddered. But it would, she had no reservations. She had worked out the finances down to the last detail.

'I'll tell you all about it as soon as I can.'

'All right, Annie. I'll see my bank and have the money for you at the end of the week.'

She sighed in relief. 'I can't thank you enough, Joe. Without your help I wouldn't be able to go ahead with this deal.'

Joe smiled thoughtfully as he rose, kissed her lightly on the cheek and headed for the door.

Chapter Twenty-Two

'Hello, Mrs Higgins. And how are you on this fine day?'

Annie looked up from the tankard of ale she was pulling to see Henry Hoskins weaving his way through the tables towards her. She smiled broadly, showing the delight she felt in seeing her friend. Over the two years they had been dealing together Annie had built a lasting trust and admiration for this attractive man. She had often turned to Henry for help and advice and he had always willingly given her his time and expertise.

'Hello, Henry. What a nice surprise.'

He took off his hat. 'I woke up this morning and thought, I'll go and see Annie, a visit is long overdue. How's things?'

'Fine, thank you. Would you like a drink?'

'Yes, please. A bottle of brown ale would go down nicely and I'd like to see your menu. I hope you'll join me?'

'Of course.' She looked over towards the fireplace. 'There's a table over there. I'll join you in a moment.' She finished serving her customer, poured them both a drink and went over to join him at the table.

'You shouldn't be serving customers,' he said jovially. 'You're the landlady, you have staff to do that sort of thing.' He gave a merry laugh. 'I bet you still go down the cellar and change the barrels.'

'And sweep the floor,' she said, her eyes twinkling. 'I like to keep my hand in, Henry. Besides, the personal touch goes a long way.'

'I'll say,' he quipped, looking round the packed room. 'I see I'm lucky to get a table today.'

'There'll always be a table here for you, Henry Hoskins.'

He smiled warmly. 'Yes, I know, and I appreciate it.'

Annie picked up her glass and drank deeply. 'Enough of the pleasantries. What really brings you here?'

'Could never fool you, could I, Annie?'

'No. You're too open. I can read your face at a hundred yards and you've something on yer mind. So out with it.'

'You know I own half the brewery?'

'Yes.'

'Well, the old man wants to retire and I'm debating whether to buy the other half of the business from him.'

'Are you? she said with interest. 'Why, I think that's a great idea. Although I'll miss yer uncle, I really like him.'

'And he you. He said giving you a go was the best thing I ever did.'

Annie smiled. 'Bless him.' She leaned back in her chair and placed her hands together. 'So, Mr Hoskins, you're about to become the full owner of the brewery, and may I add the best brewery in town. So what's your problem?'

'I need to drum up more trade, Annie. Admittedly, Hoskins' is doing very nicely, but not as nicely as it could do. I have to think of new ideas that will beat the competition. The likes of Everard's have the monopoly. It's breaking that monopoly that's the problem.'

'Yes, I see. And you've come to me for some ideas?'

Henry looked at her shamefaced. 'Yes, I'm afraid so.'

Annie narrowed her eyes. 'Well, for a start you could make sure your deliveries are on time.'

Henry gaped. 'What d'you mean?'

'Henry, the number of times I've had to borrow a barrel from another source when you've let me down! Sometimes I have to wait two days and it's not good enough.'

'Oh, well,' he said, huffing and puffing in self-defence. 'Breweries are never on time with their deliveries, everyone knows that.'

'Exactly. Why not make a firm promise that Hoskins' will deliver when they say they will? That in itself would have any landlord banging on your door. If you kept the promise, that is.

'If we ain't got any ale, Henry, we lose money. And no one likes to turn paying customers away.'

Henry rubbed his chin thoughtfully. 'Yes, I never thought on that problem seriously before.'

'Well, now's yer chance, 'cos I for one would be delighted to have my deliveries on time and regular. Save me a lot of trouble and I could plan my order so much better.'

'Yes . . .' He paused for a moment. 'Anything else you can think of?'

'Plenty. But first let's order our meal. I don't know about you but I've been up since five this morning, and I'm famished.'

Over home-made steak and kidney pudding, thick gravy, potatoes and fresh garden peas, followed by sticky treacle pudding and custard, Henry and Annie discussed ways and means of making improvements to the brewery.

'So what you're saying is,' Henry summed up as he pushed away his empty pudding plate, 'that I should offer incentives?'

'Yes. Give the landlords reasons to change to your brewery and make sure they stay with you. You could offer a free barrel every three months to the landlord who sells the most ale. A prize for the cleanest establishment, offer reductions in prices for bigger orders. The possibilities are endless.'

'I can see that. But it takes a mind like yours to come up with ideas like this.' Henry smiled in satisfaction, leaned back and clasped his hands together. 'Annie Higgins, you're a Godsend. You've given me so much to think about that I don't know where to begin.'

'Good, I'm glad about that. And the brewery won't suffer by giving these incentives. Your profits will soar because you'll have more orders on your books.' She paused and eyed him thoughtfully. 'Now that's out of the way, what's your other problem?'

'Other problem?'

'Come on, Henry. I've known you long enough. You could have thought of all these things just as well without me.'

'That's where you're wrong, Annie. You come into your own when it comes to things like this.'

'Okay.' She relented. 'I'm flattered. But I still insist it was all an excuse to cover the real reason for your visit.' Her face grew concerned. 'What's the matter, Henry? Are you in trouble of some sort?'

He laughed. 'No, of course not. How could an upright citizen like me be in trouble?' He lowered his eyes. 'But I do have something on my mind.'

'Oh?'

Henry took a deep breath. 'I wondered if you and Georgie would like to come to the Abbey Park Show tomorrow night?'

Annie grimaced. 'Oh, I can't, Henry. We're so busy at the moment.'

He leaned forward. 'Annie, the place will run itself without you for one night. Come on, it'll do you good to relax and enjoy yourself.'

She sighed deeply. 'All right, Henry. If you're sure there's not someone else you'd sooner take, I'd be delighted. Georgie has talked about nothing else since he saw it advertised on a bill board. I can't remember the last time I had an evening out. Thank you. It was nice of you to think of us.'

Henry's face lit up with pleasure. He'd wanted to ask Annie to go out with him since the first time they had met.

'Right,' he said eagerly. 'I'll pick you both up about six. Don't bother about anything to eat, we can get something from one of the stalls, and you'd better wrap up. It could turn cold later on.' He reddened with embarrassment like a young schoolboy asking for his first ever date.

Annie did not notice. 'We'll look forward to it.'

Henry made to rise, wanting to rush away in case she changed her mind, but Annie stopped him.

'Before you go, do you know anything about Bernard Millington?'

'Bernard Millington!' he exclaimed. 'The one who works for Brewster's, you mean?'

'Yes, that's the one.'

'What d'you want to know about him for?'

'Henry, I only asked a question. I don't want an inquisition.'

370

He shrugged his shoulders. 'He's a thoroughly decent man. He's worked for Brewster's for donkey's years. Knows the trade inside out. I nearly persuaded him once to come over to us, but his loyalty proved too much. Brewster is a lucky man and he knows it. Why?'

'Stop asking questions, Henry. I just heard his name mentioned and I was curious, that's all.'

'Has he been round here trying to get you to go with Brewster's?' Henry said, frowning fiercely. 'They turned you down, remember. But I wouldn't put it past old man Brewster to try and coax you over to them now that you've proved your worth.'

'No, no, they haven't. I'll never change my supplier from Hoskins', you know that, Henry. So will you stop this nonsense or I shan't ask you anything ever again.'

'All right, I didn't mean to pry.' He stood up and put on his coat and hat. 'I'd better let you get on. I'll just pay for the meal and I'll see you both tomorrow.'

'Your meal is on the house, no arguments, and we'll be ready waiting for you, six o'clock sharp.'

The next morning, Annie walked into the pie shop and gazed around admiringly. She made her way to the counter and smiled warmly at Kath who was rearranging her goods on the shelves.

'You've done wonders,' she said.

Kath returned the smile. 'Yes, it's coming along nicely. If trade carries on this way, I shall be sold out by twelve. To be honest, I'm thinking of doubling what I make. I know I can sell it.'

'You'll need someone to help if you do that.'

'Yes, and also with the preparations. I really prefer to do the cooking by myself, but if I'm to expand . . .'

'Yes. Well, I know the very person to help with the cooking.'

'Oh, who?'

'Molly.'

Kath nodded. 'Of course. I've already taught her all the

371

basics. She'll do fine.' She hesitated. 'That's provided she'll work with me?'

''Course she will. I'll talk to her.'

'What about the preparations? Do you know of anyone who'll come in and help with that?'

Annie paused thoughtfully. 'I might. I'll need to have a good talk with her first though. There are certain things she'll have to do before I'll allow her in my kitchen.'

Kath eyed her quizzically. 'How d'you mean?'

'Nothing. I'll just say that the person I have in mind is a good woman and needs the money. Anyway, leave it with me. I'll go and have a chat with her and see what I can do.' Annie paused for a moment. 'How are things with you?'

'Me? Fine. Why?'

'Just asking. You seem to have settled well and the shop speaks for itself. One of Kath Burbage's pies is a must for dinner round here,' she said laughingly. 'Can I just say that I'm glad I took you in, 'cos I nearly didn't, you know?'

'Yes, I can appreciate that,' Kath said, lowering her gaze. 'I was a gamble, there's no denying it.'

'Any regrets about leaving the farm?'

'Oh, no,' Kath replied, shaking her head fiercely. 'Best day's work I ever did. No, everything is progressing nicely. Far easier than I ever thought it would.'

'Oh?'

'Er . . . yes. I've a few shillings building up for me and Lucy. We'll be able to find our own lodgings soon.'

'Kath, you can both stay here for as long as you like. This arrangement has turned out far better than I'd hoped. Is the room above not comfortable enough for you both?'

'Oh, yes. But it's a bit small for me and Lucy.'

'Kath, how thoughtless of me. You've been used to better surroundings. I apologise. That room is quite a comedown for you, I see. It's served its purpose but it's no long-term solution. I'll help you look for lodgings when you're ready. No, better still, maybe we could find a small house for you to rent? That'd suit you both better. You'll be able to afford it with the way the shop is going and I'll help you furnish it.' Annie stopped as several customers came through the door.

'Ote left?' a shabbily dressed woman shouted. 'Only me old man'll go mad if you've sold out. 'E loves your pies. I can't make 'em like you do.'

'Yes, come in,' Annie addressed the woman, smiling broadly. She turned back to Kath. 'See, I told you, you're famous.' She made to walk away, stopped and turned back. 'Oh, by the way, would you be willing to keep an eye on the tavern tonight? Only I've been invited out to the Abbey Park Show. And I wondered if Lucy could come with us?'

Kath raised her eyebrows in surprise. 'Yeah, sure. But it's unusual for you to be going out. Is it with someone nice?'

Annie laughed. 'Yes, he is nice. But he's just a friend. I was going to say no but I thought it would do me good.'

'Oh, you should take what opportunities you get. You never know what's around the corner. Life can change overnight, we both know that.'

Annie eyed her quizzically for a second as Kath turned and proceeded to serve her customers. Then she walked out of the pie shop, donned her light summer coat and hat and headed down the street.

'So what d'you think, Elsie?'

She puffed out her cheeks. 'Well, I don't deny I'd jump at the chance to get outta this place for a few hours, and the money'd be a Godsend. But I take offence at yer telling me I've to wash proper before I'm allowed in the kitchen!'

'Come on, Elsie,' Annie said softly as she leaned on the rickety table. 'I'd be saying the same to anyone. You have to be very careful where food is concerned.'

Elsie sniffed loudly and folded her flabby arms under her vast bosom. 'Yeah, I s'pose.' She paused for a moment. 'I know I need to clean meself up a bit.' She lowered her head, ashamed. 'I sometimes don't wash for weeks. Don't seem no point somehow.'

'Well, there is now,' Annie said firmly. She delved into her purse and pulled out two half crowns. 'Go up to the market this afternoon and get yourself something to wear.'

'Oh, Annie, d'you mean it?'

She smiled. 'You just be at the tavern at six o'clock sharp. Now, you're sure that your Sophie will be all right with little Annie?'

'Oh, yes. Right mother hen she is, I've no problems on that score. Oh, I can't wait. It'll be great to have a purpose again, and I'll be able to buy the kids some shoes.' She eyed Annie questioningly. 'Er . . . this don't mean my food baskets stop, does it? Only . . .'

'No, Elsie. I wouldn't dream of it. And if there's any pies or bread left over . . .'

'Oh, good,' Elsie cut in, then looked at Annie in alarm. 'I wasn't being rude, only those baskets have been me saving. I wouldn't have managed without them.'

'I know, and it's my pleasure. Anyway, I'll see you tomorrow.'

'Washed and spruced up,' Elsie quipped.

Annie laughed as she rose, left the cluttered, dirty cottage and made her way back to the tavern, glad to have been able to do something positive for Elsie and her children.

Later that afternoon, Annie had just finished her tea when Kath poked her head around the door of the living room.

'There's a Bernard Millington to see you, Annie.'

She rose from the table. 'All right, Kath, send him up, please,' she said, picking up the dirty plates. She looked across at Georgie and Molly. 'You two make yourself scarce, please. I have some business to attend to.' As the two departed, she noticed Kath still hovering by the doorway.

'He seems a nice man, Annie. Is this the one who's escorting you all to the show tonight?'

Annie grinned. 'No, it's not. He's a business colleague. Now, please just send him up.'

'All right. Only asking.' She raised her head in the air. 'He's been here a couple of times, ain't he?'

'Kath . . .'

'All right. I'll send him up.'

Bernard Millington entered the room and took off his hat.

'Please sit down,' Annie said, motioning him to an armchair by the fireplace. 'Can I offer you any refreshment?'

Bernard smiled. 'No, thank you. I'd like to get down to business.'

Annie breathed deeply and sat down opposite him.

'My answer is yes.'

'Oh, good, good. You won't regret this venture, Mrs Higgins. It'll be the making of both of us.'

'It'll have to be, I can't afford to fail,' Annie said gravely. 'I've mortgaged myself to the hilt. If this doesn't work out, I'll be back where I started. With nothing.'

'Don't think like that. I'm sure if you weren't positive we wouldn't be sitting here now, planning our future.'

'No.' She smiled. 'We wouldn't. Right,' she said, clasping her hands together, 'I can have all the money together by Monday. Is that early enough?'

'That'll be fine.'

'What about your share?' Annie asked cagily. 'Will you bring that with you?'

He looked at her steadily. 'Daniel Shipton already has my share.'

'Has he?'

'Yes. I gave it to him this morning as a deposit and show of faith.' He extracted a long brown envelope from his briefcase. 'I have all the papers in here. Would you like to examine them first before you sign? We might as well iron out any problems now. Daniel Shipton has agreed them and is pleased with the way things are progressing.'

Annie took a deep breath. 'Yes, I would. I was just about to ask.'

He passed the envelope which she accepted and carefully pulled out the white papers, bound at the edges with thin white ribbon and written painstakingly in scripted blue ink.

'It's all in order, Mrs Higgins. But please take your time to examine them.'

She intended to as memories of her uncle handing her a

similar document flooded to mind. She carefully flicked over the pages of the deeds. When she arrived at the last page and the red seal of authority shone out at her where all the signatures went, she raised her head.

'It seems fine to me.'

'Are you sure? Because once you sign, then it's all legal.'

'I'm sure.'

'Good. Then we proceed?'

'We proceed,' she echoed. 'I'll get my quill and ink.'

Annie very carefully signed her name where indicated on the several pages and Bernard followed suit, signing with a flourish. He blotted the wet ink, folded up the documents and put them back into his case.

'That's it then,' Annie said.

'Yes. All that remains is for you to hand over your money and Daniel Shipton to do his bit,' he said, smiling as he put the document back into his briefcase.

Annie stared at him thoughtfully. 'Mr Millington,' she ventured, 'you had the documents drawn up and had paid over your share. What if I had declined your proposition for any reason?'

He raised his head. 'I had someone else lined up, just in case, and two sets of documents prepared.'

'You did?'

'Oh, yes. I had to cover every eventuality. Please don't be offended.'

'I'm not. I'd have done the same thing in your position. Will the other person be disappointed?'

'Very. But that's business.' He rose and shook her hand. 'We still have many things to discuss, but first let's deal with the legalities. Don't get up, I'll see myself out.'

Annie nodded and watched him depart, her mind racing as a great thrill surged through her body. She couldn't wait to tell everyone. Just a few more days, then she could break the news. And what a sensation it would cause.

Henry called promptly at six o'clock. He was dressed in a thick warm woollen coat and muffler. His eyes shone when he saw Annie.

'Georgie has been excited all day. I had a job to make him eat his dinner.' She paused. 'I hope you don't mind, Henry, but is it all right if Molly, Lucy and Arthur come along as well?'

'No, no. The more the merrier,' he answered. It didn't matter to him how many people came as long as Annie was amongst them. He rubbed his hands together. 'Are we all ready then?'

'I'll just give them a shout. They're all gathered in the living room.'

She tucked her arm inside Henry's as they strolled around the park, weaving their way through the thronging crowds. The night air was chilly and she found herself wishing she had put on a pair of thicker stockings. She laughed as she saw Arthur mesmerised by the jollities that were taking place around them. The travelling fair was in full swing and stalls selling all manner of goods and food were packed together. It reminded her of the Crowpie festival of Ratby, but on a much larger scale. She suddenly realised Henry was speaking to her.

'I'm sorry, Henry. What did you say?'

'I said, a band plays on a Sunday in the bandstand. It's really pleasant to come and listen.' He looked at her hesitantly. 'I could always bring you sometime?'

Annie smiled up at him. 'That would be lovely. I brought Georgie here one Sunday afternoon last summer. The flowers were beautiful.' She shivered as the night chill seeped through her. 'Shall we get the kids something to eat before the fireworks start?'

They made their way to a stall and joined the queue. A tall man was standing in front of them. As he turned his head slightly, Annie's heart leapt as she realised who it was.

'Joe.' She spoke his name softly and tapped him on the arm.

Any hopes that Henry had regarding Annie were quickly and cruelly dashed as he saw how the pair looked at each other. So this was the man whom she talked of so highly.

'Annie,' said Joe, eyes shining in delight. He suddenly caught sight of Henry and his eyes narrowed.

377

'Joe, this is Henry Hoskins,' she said as she quickly introduced them.

Joe held out his hand to Henry.

'Pleased to meet you. Annie talks very highly of you.'

Henry looked at Joe for a second as he returned the handshake.

'Sorry I can't say the same. Annie's never mentioned you to me.'

She was startled by Henry's blatant lie and noted in surprise the jealousy in his voice. She turned to face Joe, reddening in embarrassment.

'Are you here on your own?' she asked lightly.

Joe slowly turned to face her. 'No. Millicent and the girls are over there.' He motioned with his hand.

Annie turned and looked in the direction he had indicated. She saw a small, pretty woman in her early-thirties, standing with two young girls aged around twelve and fourteen. They were all very fashionably dressed and had a look of boredom on their faces. The girls waved at their father, motioning him to hurry with their food. Joe smiled at them and turned back to Annie.

'They didn't really want to come. I thought it would do them good. Only from the comments I've been getting, we might as well have stayed at home!'

'Oh, I'm sorry to hear that,' she said softly. 'We've had a wonderful time, haven't we, kids?'

A unanimous 'yes' rang out and Annie smiled.

'Maybe you should have come with us,' she said before she could stop herself. She clasped her hand to her mouth. 'Oh, I didn't mean . . .'

'I know what you meant, Annie, and I appreciate the offer,' he said. 'But I'm sure I'd only have got in your way. You seem to have enough company as it is without me tagging along.' He looked at Henry out of the corner of his eye.

'Yes, she does,' he said sharply before Annie could speak. He nodded in the direction of the food stall. 'It's your turn. You'd

378

better hurry else you'll miss it, and your family is waiting for you.'

Joe's eyes darkened. He made to speak but instead turned on his heel and faced the counter. Armed with his order, he bade goodnight to Annie, Henry and the children and walked away towards his family. Annie watched him disappear through the crowds. Meeting Joe with his family had cut her deeply. She had always known of their existence, but seeing them in the flesh was a different matter. She turned to Henry, eyes ablaze with anger.

'You didn't have to be so rude, Henry.'

His eyes opened wide in astonishment. 'Rude? I wasn't rude, Annie.'

'Yes, you were. Joe's a very good friend of mine.'

'I could see that,' he snapped.

'He's just a friend, Henry. Like you are.'

'Oh!' The last thing he wanted was to be classed as just a friend. He tried to smile. 'Well, he seemed to have a very nice family. We should have asked them to join us.'

Annie stepped back at his remark and lowered her head. 'Yes, maybe we should have.' She turned from him, gazing out across the crowds, pretending to be engrossed in their activities.

He stared at her. His few words had hurt her badly. She obviously liked this man far more than she was prepared to admit and the thought sickened him. He knew then that above all else he wanted Annie, wanted her badly. She was everything he had ever looked for in a woman and he would be proud to have her as his wife. He was prepared to wait. Friends can become much more, given time, he thought positively. I'm free and single. Joe Saunt is not.

He placed his hand tentatively on her arm. 'I apologise, Annie. I don't know what came over me.' He smiled warmly at her as she turned to face him. 'Please don't let this little matter spoil our evening.'

'No,' she said softly, and raised her eyes to his. 'It's me who should be apologising.' She turned her gaze to the children waiting patiently on the grass. 'Let's get them some food. The poor things must be starving. And we'd better hurry and get a good place for the firework display.'

'Good idea.' He turned to face the food stall owner and placed his order.

Apart from that incident, a wonderful evening was had by all and Henry smiled tenderly at Annie as he finally wished her goodnight on the doorstep of the tavern.

'Thanks for coming with me. I can't remember the last time I had such a good time.'

'Me neither,' she replied. 'Now I must get this lot to bed.'

'I'll see you soon then?'

'Yes, I'll need to speak to you shortly anyway.'

'Oh!'

'Some business I hope to put your way.'

'Oh, only business. I was hoping we could . . .'

'Henry, not now. Please, I'm very tired,' Annie said quickly, knowing what was coming.

'All right,' he said, trying to hide his disappointment. 'I'll see you soon then.' He turned and ran to hail a passing hansom cab.

Annie lay in bed that night unable to sleep. All she could see was a picture of Joe, her beloved Joe with his family. She felt desolate in spite of the new venture she was about to undertake. Her feelings for Joe rose far above her plans for the Imperial, blotting them out like an eclipse of the sun. If only he could be by her side, her life would be complete. But that would never be and the sooner she accepted it the better.

She turned over and snuggled down under the inviting covers, but it was well into the night before the blissful release of sleep could overtake her.

Chapter Twenty-Three

Annie sat by the fire, staring into the flames. It was several hours before Bernard Millington was due, but she was eagerly awaiting his arrival. Her whole future was in the bag at the side of her chair. She leaned over and absent-mindedly touched it. Two thousand pounds lay inside. A small fortune, which in a few hours she would hand over. She had thought when she had found the sacking bag of guineas that never again would she ever see so much money all at one time. How wrong could you be? Kath was right when she said you never knew what was around the corner.

Two years ago Annie never would have thought she'd be the owner of a thriving tavern. Two months ago she'd have laughed if anyone had said she would be on the verge of buying a hotel.

Life was strange. It held different things for different people. It all depended on what you were made of. If you sat back and let life pass you by, waiting for others to do something for you, then you would never amount to anything. She had learned that well over the last few years. But if you wanted to succeed and were ready to take any opportunity that arose, then it was all for the taking.

She breathed deeply at the sound of steady footsteps on the stairs. She had left instructions for Bernard to be shown straight up. This would be him, although he was far earlier than they had arranged. She rose and waited for the knock on the door.

A look of surprise appeared on her face as Joe entered.

'Just passing. I thought the kettle might be on,' he said, looking around to see if anyone else was in the room.

'Oh, Joe,' she said tenderly. 'You don't have to be just passing. You're welcome here any time, you know that.'

'Yes, and it's always a pleasure to sit by your fire.' He walked over to her and gently placed his hands on her shoulders, looking at her searchingly.

'You look very pleased with yourself. Are you going to tell me yet what's going on?'

'I can't, Joe. Not today. But tomorrow I'll be able to.'

'What difference does it make whether it's today or tomorrow?'

Annie looked at him for a moment. She clasped her hands together and sighed. 'Oh, all right. After all, you are helping me to finance the deal. Sit down.'

Joe did as he was told and looked at her expectantly.

'I'm going to buy the Imperial Hotel. I'm doing the deal in a couple of hours.'

She watched the look of surprise cross his face.

'The Imperial! You mean that big posh hotel on Humberstone Gate?'

'Yes.'

'But you'll never be able to afford that place, Annie. It'd cost a fortune.'

'It is. But not as much as you'd think. The owner wants to retire and his asking price is well below what he'd get if it went to auction. Anyway, I'm not doing it all by myself, I'm going into partnership.'

'Partnership! Who with?'

'A man called Bernard Millington. Henry Hoskins knows him very well.'

'Oh, him,' Joe said, frowning fiercely.

'Didn't you like Henry when you met him?'

'Eh? Oh, I've nothing against him,' Joe replied sullenly. 'Anyway, I've never heard anything about this hotel being for sale.'

'Well, you wouldn't,' Annie said sharply. 'You're in the shoe trade not the hotel business.'

'Point taken. What's it costing then?'

Annie lowered her gaze. 'Four thousand. But that's between two of us.'

'Four grand! My, God, Annie, you must have hocked everything to raise that kinda money. Does the price include all the furniture and whatnot?'

She frowned. 'I don't know. I presume so.'

'What d'you mean, you don't know? Didn't you discuss that with the owner?'

Annie bit her bottom lip. 'No.'

'Why not?'

'I haven't met him.'

'Annie,' Joe said crossly, 'how on earth can you buy a hotel without meeting the owner?'

'Bernard Millington is dealing with all that. You see . . .'

'Oh, I see. What do you know about this man?'

'Enough. He's a good man, Joe. Well respected in the trade and Henry knows him very well. If you want to come back later tonight you can meet him. Then you can make sure I'm not throwing away your money. Where are you going?' she said in confusion as Joe rose and headed for the door.

He turned sharply to face her. 'I ain't worried about my money, Annie. It's you I'm concerned about.'

She took several steps forward. 'Well, don't be. I know what I'm doing.'

'Do you?'

'Yes. Keep out of this, Joe. If anything should jeopardise my buying this hotel, then I'll never forgive you.'

'Then so be it,' he snapped.

'What do you mean?'

'Just what I said,' he said coldly. 'I can see nothing I say is gonna change your mind. And I wish you luck.' He turned abruptly, wrenched open the door and strode out, slamming it shut behind him.

Annie stood for a moment, staring at the closed door. She sank down in her chair, her shoulders sagging as tears rushed to her eyes.

'Damn you, Joe Saunt!' she murmured. 'Damn you, damn you, damn you!' She looked up sharply as Kath entered.

'Everything all right?' she asked hesitantly. 'Only I heard raised voices and saw Joe charging down the stairs.'

'Yes, fine,' Annie snapped, fighting back the tears. 'Please leave me, Kath. I'm expecting a visitor shortly and I want to be on me own to collect my thoughts.'

Kathy hurriedly left the room.

Bernard arrived precisely at six o'clock. He strode through the door and smiled broadly at Annie as he entered the living room and put down his briefcase.

'Everything all right?' he asked, rubbing his hands together.

Annie nodded and picked up the brown leather bag.

'Do you want to count it?'

'No. That won't be necessary. We have to trust each other if we're to have a successful business partnership.'

Annie watched as Bernard transferred the money to his own briefcase. Very shortly the hotel would be theirs and she could tell everyone the exciting news. The next few months were going to be busy, exceptionally busy, and she hoped she could cope.

Bernard finished his task, snapped shut his briefcase and smiled across at her.

'Well, all that remains is for me to write your receipt.'

Annie hesitated. It suddenly seemed distrustful of her to make him do this. But nevertheless she went over to the oak bureau that stood in the small recess by the side of the door and handed him a sheet of paper. She watched as he leant on the table and proceed to write, dipping his pen into the fresh bottle of ink she had also provided.

'I'll feel happier when we have the legal documents signed and sealed.'

Bernard looked up. 'So will I. But we've not long to wait.'
He straightened up. 'I'll be back around ten.'

'Ten. That seems a long time?' Annie queried.

'Well, I'm just playing safe. It could be before that, but you know how long these things can take.'

'Yes. Until ten then.'

Bernard shook her hand firmly, donned his hat, picked up his briefcase and headed for the door. He put his hand on the door handle and turned to face her. He opened his mouth to speak, then frowned as a loud commotion could be heard coming from outside the door.

It flew open so forcefully Bernard was thrust back into the room. Annie gasped, unable to comprehend what was going on. She stepped back against the table as Joe, Henry and a man she had never seen before burst into the room, followed closely by a screaming, distraught Kath. She had hold of Joe's jacket and was trying to pull him back. He turned and thrust her forcefully away. She fell against the door, slamming it shut.

'Don't listen to them, Annie,' she screeched furiously. 'I tried to stop them, I told them you were engaged, but they wouldn't listen to me.'

'What the hell's going on?' Annie demanded.

Joe gasped for breath. 'Ask him,' he said, pointing to Bernard who was standing by the bureau bewildered.

'Me?' he said in surprise. 'Whatever's going on is nothing to do with me. I'm just off to a business meeting. You'll have to excuse me or I'll be late.'

He made to leave but noticed his way was being blocked by Henry. He gulped hard, his eyes widening as he gripped his briefcase to his chest. He tried to make a dash for it but Joe leapt over, pinning him against the wall.

'You're going nowhere, mate,' he said savagely. He pulled Bernard into the centre of the room and pushed him down on to the chair. 'Tell her,' he demanded. 'Tell Annie what's going on.'

She turned to him, confused.

385

Bernard froze as he looked from one to the other. He shrugged his shoulders. 'I don't understand any of this,' he said. He made to rise. 'I have to go else I'll miss my appointment.'

He was pushed back again by Joe. 'I said, you're going nowhere.'

'Ask him his real name, Annie,' Henry said, grabbing her arm. 'Go on, ask him.'

'I know his name,' she said crossly. 'It's Bernard Millington.'

'No, it isn't, Mrs Higgins.'

Annie turned abruptly as the strange man spoke for the first time.

'I'm Bernard Millington.'

Her mouth dropped open. 'No, you can't be.' She turned back to face the man seated in the chair. 'Tell them, Mr Millington. Tell them they're making a mistake.'

The man she knew only as Bernard Millington started to shake uncontrollably. He clutched the briefcase even tighter as he raised his eyes and looked at the four people standing menacingly over him. His throat closed up in fright.

'See – he can't,' Joe cut in coldly. He pushed the other man forward. ''Cos this is the real Bernard Millington. This man is an impostor.'

Annie's legs buckled beneath her, the horror of the situation hitting her full force. Joe caught her and guided her to the armchair where he sat her down.

'I'm sorry, Annie. I had to do this. This man was taking you for all you'd got and I couldn't let him get away with it.'

She looked up at him blankly. 'No, no. It can't be so!'

'It is, Annie,' Henry said. 'I've known Bernard many years. I of all people can vouch for him.'

'But why? Why?' she cried, looking over at the impostor.

Joe straightened his back and folded his arms. 'You'd better tell us, 'cos you ain't leaving this room until you have.'

Bernard shrank back. He ran his fingers through his hair and rested his eyes upon the floor.

'It wasn't my idea. Honestly it wasn't. It was all hers.'

'Hers!' Annie gasped. 'Who are you talking about?'

The man gulped for breath and shifted awkwardly in his seat.

'Kath Burbage,' he blurted.

'Kath?' Annie screeched. 'Oh, no,' she groaned loudly, slumping back in her chair. 'I don't believe it. Why? Why?'

'Why don't we ask her?' Joe said, seizing Kath by the arm and thrusting her forward.

Annie jumped up. 'Kath . . .'

'Don't Kath me!' she spat, shaking herself free from Joe's grasp. She glared at Annie, eyes ablaze with fury. 'I nearly had you this time. If it hadn't have been for these interfering bastards, I'd have got you good and proper.'

Annie froze. 'But why?'

'Why?' Kath laughed sarcastically. 'You really don't understand, do you?'

She lunged forward and pushed Annie hard on the shoulder, knocking her back against the table. Both Joe and Henry leapt after her. Joe won. He grabbed her, gripping her arms tightly behind her back. Kath struggled against him, but to no avail.

'Your mother and grandmother had it in for me from the start,' she shouted furiously. ''Specially your grandmother. She made me life a misery, watching me like a hawk. It was easy getting rid of your mother, and I had only to wait for the old lady to die then the farm would have been mind. But you turned up. I always knew of your existence but I never thought for a moment you'd turn up like you did.' She glared at Annie. 'I had Archie in the palm of my hand 'til you started to interfere.'

'You had no rights to that farm, Kath,' Annie cried. 'It belonged to the Burbage family. What you tried to do to my uncle was despicable.'

'Oh, no, it wasn't. It was me that built it up. It wasn't even paying its way when I moved in. It was my ideas that made it successful. Anyway, you don't know what I had to put up with. The farm was payment for all my years of suffering.'

'Suffering!' Annie exploded. 'You don't know the meaning of the word. I'm only thankful I was there with Matty to put a stop to your game.'

The impostor, who had been listening to the proceedings, suddenly leapt out of his chair. 'Am I understanding this right, Kath? Is this woman related to Mary Ann Burbage?'

Annie turned abruptly to him. 'Yes, she was my mother.'

His eyes opened wide in alarm. 'Where did she hide them? I want to know, they're mine by rights,' he shouted.

Annie turned to Kath in bewilderment. 'Who is this man?' she demanded.

'Him?' Kath erupted. 'He's a nobody. A thieving traveller I met years ago. Only he ain't much good at thieving . . .'

'Kath!' the man cried.

'Shut up,' she shouted, breaking free and wagging her finger in his direction. 'This is all your fault. If you'd done what I said, they wouldn't have got on to you.'

Annie turned to face the impostor. 'I shouldn't decry him,' she said icily. 'He's a very clever actor. He had me convinced all right.' She eyed him. 'What's your real name?' she demanded.

The man threw back his head. 'You needn't think I'm telling you . . .'

'His name's Thomas McIntyre,' Kath said savagely. 'And he's as much involved in this . . .'

Annie clasped her hand to her mouth and stumbled backwards.

'But . . . this man's my father. You got my own father to plot against me!'

Kath looked at her blankly. 'Father! This man ain't yer father. What gave you that idea?'

'Matty said . . .'

'Oh, Matty,' Kath bellowed. 'What does she know? Your mother wanted everyone to think that, but she had no designs on Thomas McIntyre, whatsoever. Why, he's a gutless wonder, no good to man nor beast. It was John Matthews she was after. He's yer father.' She watched mockingly as a look of horror spread over Annie's face. 'She fell badly for him. Only he was mine, mine, and there was no way I was going to stand by and let anyone else have him. So I got me own back. I made her leave the farm, the dirty slut. Anyway, he weren't interested in her. Once he found out she was pregnant he upped and went to sea. Marriage and babies didn't figure in his plans. He'd had what he wanted, and she gave it willingly.'

Annie clutched the back of a chair so tightly her knuckles turned white. 'Did he know I was his daughter?'

''Course he did. But he ain't about to acknowledge the fact, if that's what yer thinking.'

'The bastard!' she screamed. 'I thought you were evil enough, Kath Burbage, but that man beats even you.'

'What d'you mean?'

Annie laughed hysterically. 'D'you mean to tell me you knew nothing of . . . of . . .'

Kath stared at her in confusion. 'I don't know what yer talking about. Anyway, I'm getting out of here. John is waiting for me. We're going to America together to start a new life.'

At her words, Thomas McIntyre lunged forward and grabbed hold of her shoulders, shaking her violently. 'You bitch, Kath! You told me you loved me. You said we were going to live together in luxury in the country where no one could find us. You've deceived me. You've still been seeing him all this time.' He let go of her and thrust her forcefully away.

She stumbled back, catching her leg against a chair. Toppling over, she fell heavily against the hearth. The sickening thud of her head hitting the cold hard stone echoed around the room and for several long moments they all stared at her motionless body, a stream of thick red blood gushing from behind one ear.

Deafening silence prevailed as each stood rooted to the

spot in stunned disbelief. Annie, the first to regain her faculties, rushed forward and bent over the woman who had spent most of her life planning and executing terrible deeds against her and her family, and who had caused them all so much grief and suffering. She gasped in fright as Kath's eyes unexpectedly opened.

'Kath, Kath,' she whispered. 'Don't move, we'll get a doctor.'

The small hard eyes bored into hers, filled with so much hatred and venom that Annie's blood ran cold. If she had ever had any doubts about this woman's feelings towards her, she had none now. Hatred oozed from Kath, filling the air with its poison.

Annie screamed as a hand shot out and gripped her by the wrist, sharp fingernails digging deep into her skin as she was pulled down to within inches of Kath's contorted face. Annie could feel the heat from the short sharp breaths that burst from the blue-lipped mouth of the dying woman, struggling desperately to speak.

'You . . . You bitch!' she rasped. 'I curse the day you and yer mother were born.'

Annie let out a cry of anguish as Joe leapt forward and prised Kath's finger's from her wrist, trickles of blood running down her arm where the nails had ripped open her flesh. He pulled the shocked and shaking woman against him protectively, his arms holding her so tight she had to fight for breath. They both turned and watched in horror as Kath's arm fell back and her head rolled to one side, mouth twitching into a mocking smile before she exhaled her last breath.

Chapter Twenty-Four

Annie paced backwards and forwards in front of the blazing fire. She stopped abruptly and faced the man seated in one of the armchairs.

'I can't take it all in, Joe,' she cried, closing her eyes to block out the horrors she had just faced. She opened her eyes again and ran her fingers through her dishevelled hair. 'I can't believe how stupid I was. Not only did I trust Kath after all that had gone before, but I was willing to risk everything I had without checking into it properly first. I was so set on getting that hotel I ignored all the warning signs. But I did see the documents, Joe, and they looked so authentic. We even signed them together.'

'Meaningless, I'm afraid, and probably drawn up by some unscrupulous, poorly paid clerk, more than likely from the same firm she used over the business with your uncle. There's plenty of corrupt people about if you have the right contacts. For a few pou   s someone would have readily done that job.' He looked haru at her. 'I hate to say this, but you should have had your own solicitor examine it. He'd have soon spotted that it was a fraud.'

'Yes, I should. But I didn't, did I?' she said miserably.

'No. But then, it's easy to see how you were taken in. McIntyre certainly knew his art and you didn't stand a chance against him, especially with Kath as his accomplice. It was a very clever fraud, planned right down to the last detail. When I think about it, the drawing up of those deeds was their only expenditure, plus probably a new suit and a briefcase for

McIntyre. Kath was being supported very nicely here while it took its time to come together.'

'Yes, and what an idiot I was. I gave her her own little business to run, with half the profits.'

Joe smiled warmly. 'That's your generous nature. But don't ever lose it, Annie. Not everyone would take advantage the way Kath did.'

She sighed deeply. 'Oh, Joe. I'm just so glad you saw through it all. What would have happened if you hadn't?'

'It was only the fact that you had never met the owner of the hotel that aroused my suspicions. Nothing else.'

'Well, I'm glad it did or I dread to think of the consequences.' She took a deep breath. 'It was greed, Joe, wasn't it? I was driven by greed.'

He nodded. 'Yes, but not in the way you're making out. You saw this as a means to secure your future. It's not the same greed that drove Kath.'

Annie lowered her head. 'No. But all the same . . .' She walked over to the other armchair and sat down. 'So many things have come to light tonight that I feel I'm in a dream, that I'll wake up and find it's all been a nightmare.'

Joe leaned forward and clasped his hands together. 'Did you not know before tonight who your real father was?'

Annie slowly shook her head. 'I thought I did. But John Matthews . . . Oh, Joe, the thought of him being my father!'

Joe studied her for a moment. 'Just what was it that man did to you, Annie?'

Her eyes opened wide in alarm. 'Eh? Oh, nothing, nothing. I don't wish to talk about it, Joe. That's one part of my life I want to block out forever. I'll just say that Kath's schemes are mild compared to what that man is capable of.' She shook her head fiercely. 'I just hope to God she was telling another of her lies when she said he was my father. But I'll never know, will I, 'cos she's dead. Thomas McIntyre has been charged with her murder and Matthews has disappeared, hopefully for ever. I can only say I hope he rots in hell, because that's all he deserves.'

Joe sat back, disturbed by her savage tone.

'Well, at least we stopped you from losing the tavern. That's one good thing that's come out of all this. Thankfully, the money you borrowed from the money lender can be returned and you'll only have interest to pay for the few days you have had it.'

'Yes, I suppose so.' She raised her head and smiled tenderly at him. 'It was all due to you. After what I said to you, whatever possessed you to check it all out? The way I treated you, you could have walked away and left me to it.'

'Could I?' He smiled thoughtfully. 'As I said before, Annie, the fact that you had never met the actual owner of the hotel didn't seem right to me.' He sighed deeply. 'McIntyre broke down completely at the police station. Kath had sought him out and put the proposition to him, promising love and happiness at the end. Now we know she had no such intentions towards the bloke at all. It was Matthews she was planning to run away with. I feel a little sorry for McIntyre, he was completely taken in by her lies. She wasn't taking Lucy either. She was planning to leave the child here.'

'Oh, Joe, that's terrible. How can any mother abandon her child?' Her face saddened. 'The poor little girl. She doesn't deserve a mother like that.' She stopped abruptly. 'If Kath was telling the truth, Lucy would be my half sister, wouldn't she?'

'It would appear so.'

Annie let the realisation sink in. 'Well, she can stay here. I'll look after her. She has no one else except an old witch of a grandmother, and I'd hate the thought of her being raised by that woman. Yes, she can stay here, I'll make sure she's all right.' She sighed deeply. 'What will happen to McIntyre?'

'He'll be hanged, Annie.'

She shuddered. The sovereigns had been his after all. He had confirmed that by his outburst just before Kath's demise. Her mother had been keeping them in a safe place for him. Should she tell Joe the truth about her inheritance? Annie glanced in his direction. What good would it do? She'd made her decision regarding the sovereigns a long time ago and no good would come of telling the truth now. She stood up again, her back to the fire, and Joe watched as a faint smile played on her lips.

'What are you thinking?'

Annie looked at him sharply. 'Oh, just about something that's been a family joke for years. I thought I knew the truth behind it once but realise I don't and most likely never will.'

'Oh?' He frowned. 'Come on then. You'll have to tell me or I won't sleep.'

Annie laughed. 'Our Georgie's hair colour.'

'What about it?'

'Well, it's red. Neither me nor Charlie, my mother nor anyone else related to us had that colour hair and we always wondered where he got it from. That's partly why I was convinced Thomas McIntyre was my father. He was that colour originally before he turned grey.'

'Oh, I see.' Joe looked at her fondly. 'Annie, you're a bright woman. You should've realised by now that Georgie's hair colour could be a throwback from generations ago.'

She stared at him for several seconds. 'Could it? Well, I never thought of that. You mean, it could come from a great, great something?'

'Or a great, great, great, great,' he said in amusement.

Annie laughed loudly. 'Oh, Joe. How stupid I've been. But I'm glad that's been answered at long last.' She looked at him tenderly. 'I'm glad about your money too. It must have been a terrible shock, knowing I nearly lost it all.'

'Money!' he exclaimed. 'That was the least of my concerns.'

'Oh!'

'My chief concern was you, Annie. Only you.'

'Me?'

Joe stood up and took her by the shoulders. 'Don't you know how I feel about you? I love you, Annie. I've loved you from the moment we met.'

Tears rushed to her eyes as she looked up at him. 'And I you, Joe. As much as I've tried not to.'

They fell into each other's arms. Joe bent his head and kissed her long and deep. He pulled back from her, searching her face, eyes full of love and concern. 'You don't know how long I've wanted to do that. But I have no right to feel this way, Annie.'

'Shush,' she soothed as she traced her finger along his lips. 'Kiss me again. Please, Joe.'

He willingly did as he was bidden. He kissed her cheeks, her neck and then her lips again and she responded eagerly, knowing that this was right. The two of them were destined for each other and at this moment in time nothing else mattered. He eased her down on to the rug by the fire, his overwhelming need and longing for her surging through him. She went willingly, giving herself to him as she had never done to any man before.

Their passion spent, Joe leant on one elbow and looked down at her.

'I'm sorry, Annie,' he whispered.

'Sorry? Why?'

'I took advantage of you. I shouldn't have.'

'Don't, Joe. Don't say things like that. We love each other. Making love was natural. I don't regret it, honest I don't. Do you?' she asked hesitantly.

'No, no. The best thing that happened to me was meeting you. You've made me come alive, Annie. You've made my life worth living.' He turned away from her. 'It's just that I had no right to make love to you. I'm not a free man, I've nothing to offer.'

'Oh, Joe. I don't want anything from you, only your love.' She grabbed hold of his arm. 'I've always known you were married, it's not as though that's a surprise. I'll never make demands, I promise.' She released her grip and took a breath. 'Do you love her, Joe?'

He got to his feet and started to dress. 'I don't know, Annie. I did when we got married. Now I feel obliged to look after her. It's not her fault that I've fallen in love with someone else.'

'Obliged? Is that all, Joe? You're going to spend the rest of your life with a woman because you feel obliged? What kind of marriage is that?' Annie said, desperately trying to control her emotions.

'I don't know. But it's one I'm stuck with.' He finished buttoning his trousers and turned to face her. 'I can't talk about this now. I must get home.'

'To her. Is that what you really want, Joe?'

'Don't, Annie. Not now,' he pleaded.

'But we can see each other, can't we?'

Joe bent down and gripped her shoulders.

'You don't understand. I love you, Annie. I want to be with you. Not sneaking round corners, pretending to others we're just friends. When I saw you with Henry, it nearly killed me. I wanted to grab you away from him and shout to the world you were mine. I was jealous, Annie. Something I've never felt before. I can't bear the thought that it will happen every time I see you with someone else. You're a beautiful woman. I can't expect you to sit around and wait for me.'

'But I will, Joe. I'll wait for ever if necessary.'

He closed his eyes in pain. 'I can't face all this at the moment. It's too much.' He opened his eyes, straightened up and grabbed his coat. 'I have to go.'

'Go! Not yet, Joe, please . . .'

But Annie's words were lost as he turned and rushed from the room.

She fell back, grabbing her discarded dress to cover her nakedness. Tears of frustration and desolation gushed down her face as her world collapsed around her. Finally she sat up and wiped her tear-stained face. Joe would come by as usual for his lunch tomorrow. She would see him then. They would both have had time to calm down and would be able to see things more clearly.

She managed a smile as she stood up and collected her clothes. It wouldn't do for anyone to come in unannounced, even at this late hour, and catch her like this.

Chapter Twenty-Five

A whole week had gone by and Annie had not heard one word from Joe. The days had dragged. The story of how she had nearly lost the tavern and how she had been taken in so easily by unscrupulous people was hard to live down, but somehow she managed. She was not managing to cope so easily with the non-appearance of the man she loved.

Finally, in desperation, she ventured near his factory. All appeared normal as she stood outside hoping to catch a glimpse of him. But to no avail. He didn't seem to be on the premises.

She walked the streets wondering what to do. She had to speak to him. She couldn't stand the thought that they had made love so passionately, so free from inhibitions, only for him to abandon her.

She found herself in Forest Road, by the little house where they had first met. She stood by the door and hesitated before she finally let herself in to see Bert and beg him to tell her any news he might have.

Bert stared up at her sympathetically. He loved his sister-in-law. He also knew that she loved Joe Saunt and that what he had to tell her would break her heart.

He stared at her for an age before he finally spoke.

'He's gone, Annie love.'

She froze in horror. 'Gone!' she exclaimed. 'What d'you mean, gone?'

'He's moved to Northampton. He's put me in charge of the business here and he's starting another. His family is following as soon as arrangements can be made.'

'Why?'

Bert's face softened as he looked up at her. 'He told me, Annie. He told me how much he loves you and how he can't bear the thought of not being with you. He thought it best to go away and let you get on with your life.'

'My life?' she uttered, collapsing on to a chair. 'My life's nothing without him.'

Bert put his hand on her arm. 'You'll get over him, Annie. You're young, you have everything going for you. You'll soon find someone else.'

'Someone else? There'll never be anyone else, Bert. I loved your brother dearly and he was my life, but Joe . . . The feelings I have for him are different. It's much more than the young love me and Charlie shared. I managed to get over Charlie. It took time, but I managed it. But not this. I'll never get over this.'

She rushed from the room, leaving Bert staring unhappily after her.

Annie walked slowly down the street towards the Black Swan Tavern. She felt neither the bitter cold nor the snow that lashed against her face. Her body felt numb. All she could think of was Joe and wondering how she would survive without him. She felt weary, tired of life. The tavern and the rest of her existence no longer held any purpose for her.

She stood with her back against the cold wall, staring across the street at the tavern. People were coming and going but she felt no part of the scene. She felt desperately isolated, as though no one else in the world was suffering the pain she was. An overwhelming desire to turn and run away rose up in her; she could not face going in, could not put on her usual happy smile and pretend nothing was wrong. She jumped as a hand touched her arm.

'Mam,' a small voice said. 'What a'yer standing out here for?'

She looked down to see Georgie's puzzled face staring up at her.

'You're soaked, Mam. I've been looking out for yer for ages. You'd better come in. It's bedlam in there.'

'Bedlam?' she repeated tonelessly.

'Yeah. Molly's burnt the spuds and there's people waiting for their dinners. The potman's drunk, Sid's chucked him out, and there's a man been waiting ages to see you about a "do" he wants you to arrange.' Georgie pulled at her coat. 'Come on, Mam. We need you to sort it out.'

She absent-mindedly ruffled his red, curly hair. 'All right. You go along. I'll be over in a moment.'

She watched him skip and run across the road to disappear inside the black-painted doors over which her name was written.

So this was what was meant by 'life goes on'.

She pulled away from the wall, straightened her clothes and walked across the road after her son.

Chapter Twenty-Six

Annie carried the bowl of water through to the tiny living room and set it down in front of the empty fireplace. Sixteen long, gruelling months had passed since the night Joe had walked out on her and they had been the hardest she had ever had to endure. Her feelings for him had not lessened, if anything they were stronger, but she knew they were futile. She longed for a man who was inaccessible, one who had chosen his family above her. And that was right, family should come first. But that did not deaden the gnawing ache that filled her every waking moment.

She went about her tasks as though in a vague dream, instructing her staff and dealing with clients with her usual expertise, but her zest and sparkle had died, the light and life behind her vivid blue eyes had faded. If anyone had noticed the change in her, they were too polite and respectful to say so. Life stretched endlessly before her with an empty void that only Joe could fill.

She had resigned herself to a life without love. If she couldn't have Joe, then no one else would do. Henry had long since given up and was courting a lovely woman ideally suited to him. There was even talk of marriage. She was pleased for him. He was a good man and deserved to be happy, which was something she could never have been able to guarantee. Joe would always come between her and any man who tried to gain her affections. As much as they tried, they would never match him and she would always be comparing them, which wouldn't be fair.

She sat down in the armchair. She had had a very busy

day and was revelling in her few stolen moments of solitude. The July sun streamed through the window and bathed her in its hot rays. She closed her eyes.

The tavern was flourishing beyond all expectations and her bank balance was healthy. The pie shop was now under Molly's charge. The girl had finally found her niche and was revelling in it. Elsie had settled in well and had lost a little weight with all the running around she was doing, and Annie could see the beginnings of romance blossoming between her and Sid. It was a funny situation. The pair were complete opposites but against all the odds seemed attracted to one another. Annie was pleased. Elsie deserved some happiness and that brood of hers a strong hand, which she felt sure Sid could give.

Poor Lucy had been distraught by her mother's death. The true nature of events had been kept from her and Annie hoped it would stay that way. After discussions with Archie it was felt that the girl would be best staying in Leicester under Annie's care, and after an initially traumatic period while she came to terms with her loss, the child was beginning to thrive.

Georgie had been a tower of strength and taken her under his wing – Lucy was now an accepted member of the 'gang', a prestigious honour indeed for a girl and considering what had gone before.

Kath had lied about Archie. They hadn't agreed on a separation. She had packed her bags late one night and disappeared with Lucy, leaving him confused and bewildered. He was now running the farm with the aid of Reggie and a woman from the village, and Annie could only hope that things would eventually turn out well for him and Matty. Hopefully, she wasn't being too romantic. Life sometimes held a happy ending.

Yes, apart from her own despair, things were shaping nicely and her hard work was going to pay good dividends in the long term. But what would become of her? Was she doomed to spend the rest of her life on her own? The thought frightened her. She had a lot of love to offer but doubted very much whether she would ever have anyone to give it to.

There was a tap on the door. She groaned. She wasn't in the mood for visitors. Besides, the bowl of inviting water sitting just to the side of her chair beckoned and she wanted to be on her own, something she had taken to more and more since that fateful night, often sitting well into the small hours after everyone was in bed, alone with her thoughts.

Before she had time to answer the door slowly opened and a tall figure hesitantly entered. She gasped as she saw who was walking towards her. Her chest tightened and her whole body momentarily froze. She leapt from her chair.

'Joe!'

He advanced slowly towards her. He took off his cap, placed it on the table and stared at her.

'Were you just passing?' she asked hesitantly. 'Do you want some tea or a drink? Maybe something to eat? I could rustle something up. How long are you staying . . .'

'Annie, Annie. Slow down.' He came towards her and placed his hands on her arms. 'I came here on purpose. I'm not just passing.' He lowered his gaze. 'To be honest, I've been pacing up and down outside the tavern all afternoon, willing myself to come in.'

'Have you? Why?' she asked, bewildered.

He raised his eyes and stared at her. 'Because I didn't know what to expect. I thought you might shut the door in my face.'

'Oh, Joe,' she said, aghast. 'I'd never do that to you. Never.'

He smiled. 'I wasn't to know that, not after . . . well, I wasn't to know after the way I treated you.' It was then he spied the bowl of water. He laughed. 'Annie Higgins, the first time I saw you, you were soaking your feet in a bowl of water. I hope I haven't interrupted you again?'

Annie looked down at the bowl and smiled briefly. She raised her eyes to meet his. She needed to ask a question and felt frightened that the answer might not be what she wanted to hear.

'Why did you come, Joe?' she said finally, breaking away from his grasp and sitting down in her chair.

'To see you.'

'Oh!'

He strode towards her, knelt by her chair and grabbed her hands. 'I had to, Annie. I couldn't live a lie any more. You filled my every thought and I couldn't bear being away from you any longer.'

She gripped his hands tightly and felt a warm rush of love race over her. 'Oh, Joe, I've longed for this moment. But I never thought it would happen. I've missed you so much.'

'Annie, Annie,' he uttered, sighing in relief. 'I prayed you'd say that. I'd lie awake at night and picture you, and then worry that you'd met someone else. I couldn't bear that.'

'Did you? Oh, Joe, I did the same. My life's been hell since you walked out without a word. I don't know how I've got through these last few months.'

'I'm sorry about that, Annie, but I couldn't see you again. I knew if I did I'd never be able to leave and at the time that seemed the only answer. I had to give my marriage a chance and the only way I could do that was to get away from you and Leicester.' He sighed deeply. 'But it was pointless. Whatever me and Millicent had between us died long before I met you, but I wouldn't admit it to myself. It took my love for you to realise what a sham my marriage had been for years.'

'What about Millicent?' she said softly.

'She knows, Annie. She's known for a long time that things weren't right, and she confronted me.'

'Oh!'

'Yes. It wasn't pleasant and things were said that I'd prefer to forget.' He lowered his head in shame. 'I've hurt her, Annie. I've destroyed her life and she's going to make me pay for it.'

'How?'

He raised himself and sat down in the chair opposite, wringing his hands.

'She wants everything in exchange for a divorce. The house and the businesses here and in Northampton. Though what she'll do with them, I don't know. She's no business sense.'

'Joe, you can't give up your life's work,' Annie said, distressed.

'I can and I have.'

'But that's not fair. It's your hard work that's given Millicent and your daughters the good life . . .'

'I know, I know,' he cut in. 'But there's nothing I can do. She wants everything or no divorce, and I can't live with her, Annie. I can't. I want to be with you.' He stopped abruptly and eyed her cautiously. 'That's if you'll still have me?'

Annie raised her head sharply. 'Joe Saunt, I'd have you under any circumstances. I'm just sorry that so many people have had to suffer for us to be together.'

He frowned. 'Suffer? Oh, Annie, Millicent isn't suffering. She's only hurting for the way I've dashed her hopes of being accepted into society. She doesn't give a damn for me and hasn't done for a long time. It's only money and position that she worries about.'

Annie bit her lip, her face clouding over. 'Joe, that's an awful thing to say. I can't believe she's that callous.'

'Take my word for it.' He stood up and paced the room. 'Annie, this is coming out all wrong. Millicent's a good woman in her own way. I don't wish to make her sound all bad. It's just that we weren't really suited. Her ideas were totally different from mine. All I ever wanted was enough money to live comfortably, a nice home and a loving wife to come back to each night. For us to sit by the fire and enjoy each other's company. Millicent didn't want that. She wanted a big house, servants and the high life. I didn't fit in and most times felt like an intruder in my own home. Even the girls hardly took any notice of me, and I tried, believe me I did.'

'I believe you,' she said sadly. 'You've always had an air of being unloved.' She smiled broadly. 'I'll change that, Joe. You'll always know how I feel about you. Be assured on that.'

He turned to smile warmly at her. 'I've only one concern and that's for Bert. He's managed the business in Canal Street exceptionally well and I'd trust him with my life, but how he's going to take the news about Millicent?'

'Don't worry about Bert. I can always find him a job. Besides,' she looked at him through her lashes, 'I was going to ask him and Martha to be the managers of my next tavern, when I buy it.'

Joe looked at her and his face creased into a smile. 'Annie Higgins, you never fail to amaze me. We'll make a grand team, you and I. And I'll do my level best to be a good father to Georgie and Lucy and Molly, 'cos they matter too, and maybe in the future when things have settled down we could invite my daughters over for a visit?'

'Oh, Joe, that'd be grand. Like one big family.'

He smiled at her. 'I knew from the moment we met that we were destined to be together.'

'So did I,' she replied happily.

Everything was going to work out for them. A few problems lay ahead for them both, but she knew without a doubt that in the end it would be all right. Whatever lay in store they would face and solve together. The empty void that had filled her disintegrated. In its place was her Joe. The one person who could make her life complete. She shook herself as she realised he was speaking.

'I've not much money, Annie, and it'll take me a while to get on my feet again.'

She raised her hand to stop his flow. 'The tavern and pie shop will support all of us for the time being. It was through your help and guidance I made a success of this place so you needn't feel guilty about joining me here. If it hadn't have been for you, I'd have lost the lot.' She gazed at him lovingly. 'You really have been in it from the beginning and deserve recognition. That is, of course, assuming you'll join me?'

'I'd be honoured,' he said with conviction. 'And by the time we're finished we'll be a force to be reckoned with in the trade. I don't know much about it, but I'm quick to learn.'

Annie laughed loudly. 'Nor did I. In fact I knew nothing, and look where I am now. A thriving tavern, plans to buy another, a smashing son, two lovely charges, and . . . you.'

'Yes, you've me, Annie. I'll never leave you again.' He took her in his arms and kissed her deeply. She responded readily, lost in the closeness of him. He pulled back and gazed at her. 'I'll need to rent one of your rooms until we can be married. And for me that can't come quick enough.'

'Me neither,' she said happily. 'But as for a room, you'll do no such thing. We belong together, Joe Saunt, and I don't mean to spend another minute away from you. I've waited long enough for this.'

He stared at her quizzically. 'But won't there be talk?'

'Let 'em,' she said. 'Martha once told me that only sluts work in taverns. Well, I'm about to prove her right, ain't I? Besides, we'll be married before anyone realises what's going on.'

He nodded.

She looked up at him, eyes full of emotion. 'Lock the door, Joe.'

'What?'

'I said, lock the door.'

He did so and walked slowly back to her. She stood up to join him and in the process her feet caught the side of the basin and she stumbled, falling upon the carpet. She lay there shaking with uncontrollable laughter.

Joe stood over her, his eyes filled with love and happiness. He couldn't believe that this woman, the one whose face had filled his every thought since the day he had met her, loved and wanted him as much as he did her. He felt honoured and humbled and suddenly unworthy of her.

Annie looked up into his eyes and held her arms wide in welcome. He smiled, sighed softly and fell down upon the carpet to join her.